To chris,
with love,
Xmas 2006.

Mary & John.

My brother's final book.

A COLD UNHURRIED HAND

Also by Michael David Anthony
The Becket Factor
Dark Provenance
Midnight Come

A COLD UNHURRIED HAND

HAND

MICHAEL DAVID ANTHONY

McHoo / The Rattlebone Chest

www.michaeldavidanthony.com
email: mda@mc-hoo.com

ISBN: 0 9553696 0 6
ISBN: 978 0 9553696 0 5
Published by McHoo, Tudor Lodge,
Troed-yr-Harn, Talgarth, Brecon, Wales
Printed and distributed by Diggory Press, Liskeard, Cornwall

for
Flt. Lt. Matthew Gibb,
51 Squadron, 4 Group, RAF Bomber Command
navigator in a Halifax Mk 3
shot down by flak over Bochum, Germany
during the night of 13th May 1943
on the 30th and final op of his tour
and who also survived Stalag Luft III

PROLOGUE

THE GRAVEYARD WATCH
RAF Frampton Wissey, Cambridgeshire, England
March, 1944

A thrush began singing.

Five rapid trilled notes, a pause, and again the repeated strain. As if some northern Pan, having plucked a reed from one of the sluggish fenland ditches and fashioned a pipe, had blown upon it to summon life, through the pre-dawn silence there came an answering twitter from across the drained marshland beside the aerodrome. Another call followed, and yet another, and then all at once, in a mounting cacophony of joy, it was as if all the birds of north Cambridgeshire were vying with each other to herald the first pale glimmerings of another dreary, drizzling-wet March day.

'You, girl! Stop fiddling with that blasted blind, will you? This night's not over just yet, confound your eyes!'

The vehemence of this unexpected outburst had a similar enlivening effect on the occupants of the dimly blue-lit operations room as the thrush's song had on his feathered colleagues in the dripping bushes and trees outside. The pasty-faced clerks and telephone operators, most of them female and very young, who sat slumped at the various tables and desks, at once straightened in their seats, while the unfortunate ginger-haired Waaf who had dared to raise the blackout blind to peep beneath it, dropped it instantly as if a charge of electricity had passed through the tarred fabric, her face flushing bright pink as she did so.

Except for the elderly honey-coloured labrador bitch who had lifted her head from his knee and was now gazing up at him in eager expectation, the originator of this savage outburst sat quite alone in the front row of the half dozen or so mostly empty lines of chairs that took up about a third of the room. Face almost hidden between the turned-up collar of his battered leather flying-jacket and with the gold-braided peak of his service cap pulled down low over his eyes, Group Captain 'Buster' Chesterton did not move. He sat leaning back, arms crossed, his chin sunk on his breast, a pair of white kid gloves clutched in one hand, his fleece-lined flying-boots stuck out at an angle before him as if still controlling the rudder-bar of one of the various Farmans, Sopwiths or other types of the frail and draughty wood-and-canvas machines he'd fought in over France almost three decades before. At that moment his entire posture was suggestive of a grey-haired, bushy-moustached Bonaparte drowsily supervising operations from outside the imperial tent at Austerlitz, Borodino or Waterloo.

But instead of Houssaye's kaleidoscope of vivid hues – scarlets, greens, blues and reds – and the flash of sabre glimpsed through billowing cannon smoke, the wall in front of him prosaically presented to his gaze a huge illuminated map depicting eastern England as far north as Berwick, and stretching across the North Sea to take in the whole of Holland, Denmark and Germany. Over this, two lengths of red ribbon were pinned, both stretching bar-straight towards the Continent from two separate points on the English coast. One, the more southern, represented the route of the main bomber force, running directly from Cromer to Essen, then doglegging north-westwards up into Friesland and back to the original point of departure. The second, northerly ribbon, showed the course of the 'spoof' or diversionary raid, this extending from Mablethorpe directly to Hanover, then heading seventy miles south-west before the final turn homeward across the relatively undefended skies of northern Holland.

Beside the map, occupying the other half of the wall, was a huge blackboard, divided horizontally and vertically by painted white lines. Chalked neatly into the rectangles of this grid were the take-off and return times of all but one of RAF Frampton Wissey's three-flight squadron of thirty Avro Lancaster Mk 2's, along with captain's name, aircraft number and identification call-sign. The twenty-nine aircraft on the board had been the station's contribution to the full force of six hundred and eighty-three heavily-laden bombers that had begun lumbering airborne an hour or so after dusk the evening before.

8

Having delivered his broadside, Chesterton remained Napoleonically slumped for a few moments more before raising his head a second time to look past the still blushing Waaf at the grey light seeping from beneath the loosened blind. Scowling, he glanced at his watch, his every movement intently watched by the dog, now fully awake and thumping her tail. Light was time, and time the enemy: each infinitesimal increase in the elevation of the still invisible sun was greedily sucking away more of what little could possibly remain of the sixteen hundred gallons of high-octane fuel pumped into the tanks of K-Kitty and H-Harry the previous afternoon, the only two aircraft on the indicator board lacking either a landing-time or the word *'diverted'*.

Still staring at the window, watching the light remorselessly increasing, Chesterton became aware of a muffled choking behind him. Frowning, he tried to ignore the sound. Finally, he jerked his head around to find it emanated from one of a pair of Waaf spectators who had slipped in not long before to sit at the back, like latecomers to a film. The girl in question was leaning forward, shoulders convulsing, attempting in vain to stifle her sobbing by screwing a tiny sodden handkerchief into her mouth, while her companion sat head-bowed at her side, face almost hidden by the turned-up collar of the greatcoat she was wearing.

'Sergeant, kindly clear this room of unauthorized personnel!'

The NCO addressed, a gaunt, whippet-faced woman of forty or so who until then had been sitting silently knitting in front of the two coloured telephones on her desk immediately laid aside her needles and, rising from her seat, bustled up the short aisle. Gloves tightly clenched, the station commander now contemplated the toes of his boots as the urgent whispering behind him ceased and the double doors at the back hissed open and closed as the intruders were hustled outside. Lifting his gaze as the Waaf sergeant re-passed him, he glanced again at his watch, and then leaned round to address the lean, bespectacled figure that had come to sit behind him at his right shoulder in the manner of an *aide-de-camp*.

'How long now, Alan?'

The younger man leaned forward confidently. 'Maximum time, twenty-eight minutes for K-Kitty, sir,' he said, articulating the words clearly for the benefit of his hearer, who, like the majority of those who had spent years flying open-cockpit aircraft, suffered from slight deafness. 'Thirty-six minutes for H-Harry.'

9

Chesterton nodded. Both the request for information and the answer given had been mere formalities. Everyone present knew exactly the time left to both overdue machines. 'Right,' he grunted, pulling himself to his feet, 'in that case, Alan, it's time you and I went out for a breath of fresh air.'

Preceded by the panting, tail-wagging labrador, and closely followed by his lanky companion, the station commander headed for the exit doors, leaving behind the silent telephones, the two blank spaces on the indicator board and the dozen or so mainly female witnesses to his night-long ordeal of presiding over Frampton Wissey's air operations. Despite the very latest forms of radio communication and the assistance of a whole host of technical experts of every sort, he knew very well that he had, in fact, less control over or ability to influence these events, once launched, than the meanest and blindest of the Olympian gods.

In contrast to their very public departure from the operations room, the station commander and his adjutant entered the adjoining section of the prefabricated building unnoticed. This was a hall bolted together from curved sections of corrugated iron and variously utilized as a general lecture theatre and camp cinema in addition to its officially designated purpose as aircrew briefing room. Apart from a few humorous cartoon sketches of the 'Pilot Officer Prune' type stressing the dangers of fast taxiing and the necessity for all aircraft to adhere strictly to ground control instructions, its only decorations were a series of stark black-and-white air recognition posters. These were all boldly labelled THIS IS YOUR ENEMY, and depicted three-directional silhouettes of various single- and twin-engined German fighters, some of the latter equipped with fearful arrays of airborne radar antennae protruding from the nose like the mandibles of some grotesque insect.

The previous afternoon the seats in front of the stage had been filled with over two hundred young men crammed in like schoolboys, noting down headings, heights, wind-speeds, marker flares, target times, known or likely concentrations of searchlights and anti-aircraft guns – the whole assembly vibrant with suppressed tension, and liable to burst into brittle, overloud laughter at the weakest joke or humorous aside from any of the succession of speakers addressing them. Now, however, some fourteen hours later, with the stage curtains closed and most of the folding chairs tidily stacked against the sloping metal walls, the dimly lit interior had the desolate air of some shabby provincial theatre after the final performance of a show that had failed.

In place of the rows of closely packed seats, trestle-tables had been erected and placed in pairs around the hall in the manner of church jumble-sale stalls. At one of these were seated six of the seven members of the crew of D-Dog, the last of the station's Lancasters to have landed. Still dressed in flying suits and with their parachutes, leather helmets and gauntlets, 'Mae West' flotation waistcoats and fur-lined Irvin jackets left heaped untidily on the polished linoleum-covered floor behind them, they slouched forward in their chairs, elbows on table, alternately dragging on cigarettes and sipping from mugs of tea heavily laced with rum. Facing them across the table was a red-haired, somewhat sour-looking female intelligence officer in her mid- or late twenties making detailed notes of the responses to her questions. A little apart from the crew stood a group of grave-faced spectators, comprising Wing Commander 'Jumper' Birdie, the recently appointed New Zealand squadron commander, two of his flight leaders and a pair of grizzle-haired American colonels visiting from one of the USAAF bomber bases nearby. The only other people present were the station padre and a white-jacketed mess orderly, who were conversing in low tones beside the tea trolley, occasionally glancing with looks of concern towards the dispirited-looking flyers and their unsmiling interrogator.

The station commander made to pass on, but then, changing his mind, turned instead towards the group at the table. Noticing his approach, the Waaf officer immediately rose to attention. As she did so, the seated men glanced round and then also began stumbling wearily to their feet.

'No, no, stay as you were.' Chesterton waved them back down. For a few seconds he stood surveying the row of haggard, heavy-eyed faces ranged in front of him, while his dog, as if sharing her master's concern, went from one to the next, nuzzling, pressing and rubbing her head against each of the flyers in turn. 'You ran into a spot of bother, I hear,' said Chesterton with a sympathetic smile.

'You could say that, yeah. That wouldn't be far off the mark.' The speaker was Pat Kelly, captain of D-Dog, a wiry, sandy-haired Australian in his mid-twenties. 'Having a Junkers 88 or whatever it was, jump us when we were a good ten minutes clear of the Dutch coast counts as a spot of bother, I reckon.' Pausing, he inhaled deeply on a cigarette, all the while looking coldly up at the station

11

commander. 'Especially,' he continued in the same mirthless, flat-vowelled drawl, 'with the bastard getting right under us and slamming a dozen cannon shells up our arse, and blasting away half of Pete Ellis's right leg in the process!'

Chesterton frowned, not at the information, which, anyway, he already knew, but at the lack of the customary 'sir', as well as the resentful bitterness of the speaker's tone. Saying nothing, however, he merely nodded. Wild-spirited and antipathetic to RAF discipline like many of those he habitually referred to as colonial aircrew, Flight Lieutenant Kelly was, nevertheless, an experienced and respected pilot – indeed, one of Frampton Wissey's seeming immortals, a second tour man who, against all statistical odds, had survived almost the full fifty operational missions stipulated for all bomber aircrew. Just one more sortie into enemy territory, and he and his two unwounded compatriots among the crew would be on board ship, returning home with the official thanks of the British Government and, in Kelly's case, with a richly deserved Distinguished Flying Cross and bar. Apart from that, it was as abundantly clear to the station commander as to everyone else present that he and his crew had been severely shaken by the chance attack that had severely wounded their navigator and come within a hair's breadth of killing them all.

'Yes, a bit of damned bad luck,' grunted Chesterton, nodding. 'Still,' he continued, managing a smile, 'at least you're all back alive, that's the main thing. Flying Officer Ellis will be well looked after in our hospital at Ely, on that you can depend. Now finish your interrogation here, then cut along and grab yourselves some breakfast. You'll all feel a damn sight better once you have some hot grub inside you.'

Not even the reference to the awaiting feast of sausages, bacon, tomatoes and two real eggs – a grateful nation's traditional and highly prized gift to all returning operational crews – seemed to stir the slightest interest among the dispirited youngsters. Concerned at their lack of response, and somewhat puzzled by their, it had to be said, *worried* expressions, Chesterton gazed at them a further moment before turning to address the Waaf intelligence officer who had remained respectfully standing behind the table.

'It's Mrs Taylor, isn't it? You're one of our new girls?'

'Yes, sir. I was transferred from Holme-on-Spalding-Moor just a few days ago.'

'So I heard. Well, I hope you'll be happy here in the East

Anglian wilds after the flesh-pots of sunny Yorkshire – eh, Barlow?'

Chesterton glanced round at the only Englishman in D-Dog's crew, a chubby, prematurely balding Mancunian flight engineer. Flight Sergeant Barlow's answering smile was brief and mechanical, however, and not a hint of his customary good humour showed in his eyes. Dropping his gaze, he stared without expression down at the open cigarette packet in front of him, a mere husk of the laughing, jovial man who had filed out of the briefing room just twelve hours before.

Disconcerted by another failure to breathe some cheerfulness into the demoralized crew, Chesterton stood frowning down at the bowed figures, searching for something else he could say that might lighten their mood. Defeated, he turned back to the Waaf. 'Right, Mrs Taylor, please carry on then.'

'Thank you, sir.'

With a nod towards the watching officers and a murmured greeting to the padre as he passed, Chesterton walked away, his face resuming the grim expression he was wearing when he left the operations room. Equally sombre, his bespectacled adjutant followed close at his elbow. The labrador, however, having turned her attention from the flyers themselves to their discarded flying-jackets and parachutes, and clearly unaffected by the men's mood or the funereal atmosphere about her, continued her eager sniffing and burrowing among the items heaped on the floor.

Halfway down the hall, Chesterton stopped suddenly, sensing that his dog had failed to take up her habitual position by his heels. Glancing around with a glare he located her still nosing around in the flying jackets. Something sweet in there, he snorted to himself, and gave an impatient whistle. Reluctantly the labrador raised her head and looked guiltily towards him. For a moment she appeared to hesitate, then with one last quick sniff at the clothing, bounded heavily after her retreating master. 'Damn the dog,' muttered Chesterton as she raced past him and his companion, heading straight for the further door, paws skidding on the polished linoleum, tail wagging excitedly in renewed anticipation of the open air.

A telephone rang and was answered immediately.

'Control Tower – yes?'

There was the briefest silence as the young Waaf clerk listened. Replacing the receiver, she looked round to meet the expectant gaze of the man sitting beside her at the long desk in front of the control room windows. 'Ops, sir – just to say the CO is on his way over.'

The slight heaviness of the girl's tone – indeed, the very shortness of the call – answered the duty air traffic controller's question even before he asked it. Nevertheless, having been the drinking and boon companion of the skipper of H-Harry for three months, and being himself still young, hardly into his mid-twenties, he could not prevent himself from asking with a studied drawl, 'No news on either of those two overdue kites, I take it?'

'No, sir.'

With a nod, Flying Officer Brewer, late of Fighter Command ('Fluff' to his brother officers, invariably and irreverently 'Quasi' or 'Quasimodo' to the rest of the station), glanced down to where, lit by the hooded lamps of the landing-board in front of him, the two remaining tagged tokens dangled from the otherwise empty row of hooks. He leaned back in his swivel-chair and stared up though the large, rain-spattered windows at the steadily lightening overcast sky, his melancholy expression completely at odds with his huge, blond, handlebar moustache.

With the crackling sound of one of 15 Squadron's late-returning Stirlings calling up Mildenhall Control coming over the r/t loudspeaker on the wall behind, Brewer remained staring out into the semi-darkness for a full half minute before awkwardly pulling himself to his feet. He turned down the collar of his greatcoat and straightened his cap. Dragging his 'gammy' leg (a result of bailing out of his blazing Hurricane fighter at a mere two hundred feet over Ashford in Kent one Saturday afternoon in late August 1940 to land on a tarmacadam schoolyard with such force as not only to smash leg and hip, but also to so dislocate and compact the vertebrae of his backbone as to leave him semi-crippled for the remainder of his life) he proceeded to limp lop-shoulderedly over to the glass-panelled sliding door and stepped out onto the balcony that encircled the upper storey of the control tower. He followed it round to the top of the flight of wooden steps, and then stood in the drizzle, looking towards the hotchpotch of buildings that bordered the south side of the airfield, comprising the Naafi and operations block, the main administration building, the hangars of B and C flights, the camouflaged water tower, the meteorological and photographic section huts, the redbrick officers' mess – everything needed, in fact,

14

for a miniature town of well over fifteen hundred inhabitants, complete with its own butchery, bakery, sick quarters, mortuary, stores, workshops, chaplaincy, barber's shop, armouries, pigeon-loft – piggeries even, where the slops from the various canteens and messes fattened a score of healthy porkers, each with its own identification number and a crude set of RAF roundels painted on its chubby pink flank.

In the pre-dawn dimness, Brewer at last made out the familiar shape of the CO's grey Humber saloon turning onto the airfield's oval perimeter track to begin the half-mile drive through the rain over to the tower where he stood looking down. Like some insignificant intruder passing through a peacefully browsing herd of gigantic herbivores, the car beetled along the taxiway between the huge four-engined bombers parked in front of B Flight hangars. Once clear of these rather dinosaurian Lancasters, the car swung past the wing tip of one of a pair of much smaller Mosquito aircraft belonging to the station's special combined photo-reconnaissance and meteorological unit. Now the car was splashing its way through the puddles along the concrete strip leading to where the hunched, vulture-like shape of the duty controller stood following its progress from his solitary eyrie.

"Morning, Fluff,' grunted Chesterton, returning Brewer's salute as he mounted the outside steps a few minutes later, followed by his silent companion. 'Still no sign of either of our missing sheep, I take it?'

'Afraid not, sir.'

As Brewer moved back inside the control room, the two visitors remained on the balcony outside, both turning to gaze away through the rain as if lining a ship's side to pay respect to the canvas-shrouded body of an unfortunate messmate or fellow passenger about to be committed to the deep. For the only female occupant of the control tower, the sight evoked no such maritime associations, however. Having spent a childhood in the depths of the Gloucestershire countryside as the eldest daughter of a railway signalman, Aircraftwoman Janet Forrester's only experience of sea travel had been a forty-minute trip on an Isle of Wight paddle-steamer (whose rusting remains had lain now almost four years on the bomb- and wreck-strewn seabed immediately north of the Dunkirk beaches). The sight of Brewer hunched in front of the large windows reminded her of her father at work before the row of vertical levers in his signal-box, whilst the two figures outside on the balcony

15

brought to mind nothing so much as passengers disconsolately awaiting a long-delayed train – an arrival which, from their expressions and general demeanour, clearly neither had the slightest expectation of ever witnessing.

She glanced up at the clock. Little time now remained before the word '*missing*' would be chalked into the two empty spaces on the operations board. Then, for the second time in four days, the Bedford half-tonner of the station police would begin grinding round the scattered sleeping-quarters in the early morning quiet like some latter-day death-cart, its driver and mate quickly and efficiently gathering together and whisking from sight all the potentially demoralizing evidence of the vanished flyers' all too brief sojourn at the camp. Again she looked from the controller's twisted back to the watchers on the veranda outside, first at the podgy features of the station commander, ruddy and mottled after years of open cockpit flying, then at those of his unlikely acolyte, the gangling, bespectacled, ever so slightly balding Flight Lieutenant Alan Blanding – 'Trott' Blanding as he was almost universally known, RAF Frampton Wissey's comparatively new and none too popular station adjutant.

Studying Blanding's lean face in the dimness, she found herself thinking that he seemed even more unnaturally pale, strained and unhealthy-looking than usual. Then she saw his head rise slightly. He seemed to stiffen. He turned to peer intently away towards the now already pale-flushed eastern horizon. Next moment he was bending to murmur urgently to the man at his side.

'Sir, I think they may have heard something.'

'What?' At the Waaf's words, Brewer spun round, glancing out at the figures on the balcony. Raising a pair of binoculars, he swung them back and forth in the direction towards which both men were intently gazing. A moment later, moving with remarkable speed for one so crippled, he scuttled through the door and out onto the balcony, his binoculars again sweeping the faintly glowing skyline.

'Yes! I've got her!' Brewer's glasses steadied. 'A heavy aircraft – four-engined job – boomed tail.' He paused. 'Looks like rotary Hercules motors.' Excitement grew in his voice. 'Yes, rotary engines, all right! Could be a stray Halifax from 4 Group – either that, or one of our own Lancs with its radio knocked out.'

Even within the control tower, Janet Forrester could now faintly hear the low drone of aero engines. Peering through the rain-speckled windows, she at last made out the distant machine, a black

16

dot crawling over the pinkish-yellowish light of the overcast dawn. Beyond the open door, the controller's commentary continued. 'One prop looks feathered – starboard outer. No, damn it!' Brewer's voice rose a full octave. 'Both the starboard engines are feathered and the crate's losing height!' Lowering the binoculars, he swung back to the doorway, calling out urgently, 'Ring for emergency landing. Sick-bay to be alerted; blood wagons and all crash vehicles to stand by.'

Before the phone could be raised, Brewer was back through the door, removing the thick-barrelled Verey-pistol from its hook. By the time his message had been relayed and the telephone receiver replaced on its rest, he was already back out on the balcony, thrusting a dumpy, fat cartridge into the flare-gun breech. With the fire-tenders and ambulances beginning to bump out across the grass towards the edge of the main runway, those in the control tower remained, eyes glued on the approaching bomber. Still an indistinct blur through the rain, it passed two miles northwards on its downwind leg, then began a hesitant, lurching turn to port. As it did so, briefly fuselage, wings and boomed tailplane were starkly silhouetted against the clouds like a dark, double-barred Cross of Lorraine.

'A Lanc, by golly!' exclaimed Chesterton triumphantly, thumping a gloved fist on the balcony railing. 'It looks as if at least one of our strays is back!'

'Yes, sir, but, Holy Christ, do you see the state of her?' cried Brewer, following every movement of the descending aircraft through his binoculars. 'She's been knocked all to pieces. There's a damn great hole in her starboard trailing edge and one section of the tail boom seems to be missing. From the look of things, I'd say she'll be bloody lucky to make the field!'

Nothing more was said. With the breeze carrying most of the sound away from the tower, the plane's two remaining engines remained a low resonant drone in the distance. Through the fine rain, the watchers saw the undercarriage unfold beneath the aircraft's black-painted belly, and then the crippled machine began an agonisingly slow turn towards the main runway.

Despite her eight months in the Women's Auxiliary Air Force, Janet Forrester's knowledge of the principles preventing the Lancaster's thirty tons of metal, petrol and human cargo from plunging earthwards was limited to the shaky little diagram a semi-inebriated Norwegian pilot had once drawn for her on a cigarette packet one Saturday night in the overcrowded back parlour of the Red

17

Lion down in the nearby village. She could nevertheless tell from the almost visible tension of the watchers outside and from the drifting, unsteady motion of the approaching machine that its condition was perilous. The watching men knew the pilot was having to struggle hard with the control yoke to keep his Lancaster's nose pointed towards the mile-long strip of rubber-streaked concrete stretching out ahead through the now suddenly increasing rain.

Crabbing sideways, one wing dragging low like a wounded gamebird, the aircraft grew steadily larger and more distinct. Dreading what the next moments might bring, Janet Forester gripped hard at her pencil. She gazed through the blurred glass towards the approaching aircraft, remembering the occasion just a few weeks before when a visiting worn-out old Wimpey on a navigational exercise from one of the operational training units or OTU's as they were known, had suddenly lost power whilst attempting to land in a hailstorm, stalling and cartwheeling down to explode in flames among the approach lights.

There was a sharp crack from the pistol held up at the end of Brewer's upstretched arm; a moment later a bright green flare drifted past the control tower. As if heartened by this sign, the Lancaster straightened. For what seemed seconds, it appeared to hang as if motionless above and beyond the perimeter fence, fine spray hazing white the leading-edges of its wings, a strip of fabric whirling loose in the slipstream – and then all at once the bomber was safely over the wire, its wheels skimming just a few feet above the runway. With a momentarily whiff of grey smoke and squeal of rubber, tyres bit the wet concrete and then the plane was firmly down, hurtling along the runway, a dark, blurred shape seen through the cloud of vapour thrown up in its wake. Just for an instant as it tore past, the mid-upper gunner was clearly silhouetted waving up from his Perspex-domed turret at the small cluster of figures above him on the control-tower balcony, fingers raised in what might or might not have been a victory sign.

'K-Kitty,' murmured Brewer, disappointment thick in his voice as he glimpsed the large, red identification letters stencilled along the aircraft's side. Thinking of the man with whom he'd gone halves with on the rare little supercharged K-type MG only just the week before, the duty controller continued to watch with his companions as the Lancaster slowed and came to a brief halt before proceeding to taxi on down the remaining short length of runway. As the now redundant fire engines and ambulances headed back to their original positions beside the control tower, the aircraft paused once more as it reached the intersection of runway and taxiway. Braking round on its starboard wheel, it began its laborious crawl round the perimeter track, its progress almost completely masked now from the spectators on the balcony by the slight hump of the airfield – that vital item of topography, allowing the drainage of the five hundred acres of first-rate arable land requisitioned by Government Compulsory Purchase Order in 1935 for the construction of a bomber station.

'That's it then,' murmured Chesterton, glancing at his watch some fifteen minutes later as the distant propellers finally kicked to a halt. 'Time's well up for H-Harry. There's no point in us hanging around here anymore.'

With the rain having stopped at last and the faint cries of newly awake sheep in the surrounding fields sounding infinitely plaintive in the damp silence, the station commander and Flight Lieutenant Blanding descended the control tower steps. Instead, however, of going straight to his car in which his dog was now loudly whining and barking by turns, Chesterton paused to gaze towards where the recently landed K-Kitty stood on one of the circular pans of hard-standing adjacent to the A Flight hangars.

Already an armourer, a tiny figure in the distance, was under the aircraft's belly, peering up into the opened bomb-bay to ensure that the racks were safely bare apart from the dangling rows of fuse-rings that showed that their lethal cargo had been released fully armed (if not, the sortie would be logged as a 'washout' and not counted against the aircrew's score). The remaining groundcrew were standing beside the fuselage, greeting the pale-faced beings now beginning to emerge from the rear hatch, each as if tribally marked with a white circle around mouth and nose from the pressure of the tight-fitting rubber oxygen masks worn throughout the long flight. Each man was clumsy with weariness and the heavy encumberment of multi-layered clothing and tight-buckled parachute harness, each man still half-deaf, numb and stiff after the hours of roaring engines, constant vibration and freezing cold.

As Chesterton and Blanding watched, the seven flyers clambered unsteadily out to take the offered cigarettes from the groundcrew, then turned to gaze wonderingly up at the gaping holes

19

in the wings, tail-unit and fuselage of the machine that had brought them safely home.

'I wonder what they're feeling?'

Surprised at the question, Blanding looked round at the CO. 'Simple relief I should imagine, sir – just happy to be back in one piece.'

Chesterton shook his head. 'No, I wasn't meaning the aircrew, Alan,' he said, drawing a short-stemmed pipe from his greatcoat pocket. 'I was thinking of the poor bloody groundcrew.' As he began packing the bowl, he continued to gaze towards the distant throng of men now already dividing into two groups – one, the slightly smaller, remaining with the aircraft, the other beginning to move towards the arriving collection truck. 'It must be damned hard,' he murmured, 'getting to know the men who fly the machines they look after, seeing them off at nightfall, welcoming them back hours later - going on doing so until the crew either finish their tour or, more likely, simply fail to return one morning.' Pausing, he lit his pipe, his face hazing in bluish smoke as he did so. 'Hard I mean,' he resumed between sucks, 'having to watch others go out month after month, yet never having a chance of experiencing what the boys in the air go though.'

'I suppose so, sir,' agreed Blanding, glancing at the speaker. During his time at Frampton Wissey, he had never heard his normally taciturn superior express himself so feelingly – not at least since his official car had been 'liberated' by a group of Canadian aircrew celebrating a belated transfer to the recently constituted all-Canadian 6 Group. The usually sombre grey saloon was discovered next day, festooned with balloons and streamers, and crudely painted overall in red, white and blue.

'Yes, deuced hard!' grunted Chesterton, shifting his gaze from the distant figures left beside K-Kitty to a similar-sized cluster of men in front of B Flight hangars. They were obviously H-Harry's groundcrew, and stood now, a forlorn knot of figures, still searching the horizon for sight of the missing aircraft, unable even now to turn their backs on the men they'd waved off the evening before.

Glancing again at his face, Blanding felt a sudden affectionate sympathy for the older man. By Air Ministry decree, it was strictly forbidden for bombers to carry unauthorized passengers during operations, no matter how senior in rank, and it was obviously torture for a veteran like Chesterton to remain on the ground. Having stood before the massed ranks of aircrew in the briefing room to wish them

20

best of luck, he'd invariably join the spectators at the take-off point, remaining in stiff salute as each of the heavily-loaded Lancasters in turn ran up its engines before thundering away into the night. Finally, next morning, like a prison governor attending the scaffold, he'd climb the control tower steps at first light, wearing flying jacket and boots in solidarity with his 'boys' – there to wait until the last of the stragglers had returned, standing what was universally known as 'the graveyard watch'.

'Right,' said Chesterton, beginning to walk on, 'now that the rain seems to have finally stopped, I'll take Sasha for a trot round the airfield. She and I could both do with the exercise. You take my car back and get the station unsealed.'

'Very good, sir.'

Releasing the pent-up dog from the vehicle, Chesterton turned back to the adjutant. 'Look, Alan,' he said, 'why not get off camp for a few hours? Go over and spend the morning in that cottage of yours. You look as if you could do with the break.'

Surprised by this unexpected concern, Blanding shook his head. 'Thank you, but honestly, sir, I'm quite all right.'

Making no answer, Chesterton looked down to meet the gaze of the impatient labrador which squatted before him in quivering anticipation. 'Well,' he sighed as if addressing the animal, 'let's just hope that the rumours are true and this has been the last op for a while. Unless there's a let-up soon, what with these recent losses we've had and the strain we've all been under these last months, they'll be more of us going to pieces.' He paused to suck thoughtfully on his pipe. 'Still,' he said, withdrawing it from his mouth and bending to rap the bowl on the heel of one boot, 'in the meantime, I'll try to see what I can do about getting someone to take a little of the weight off your shoulders.'

'Really, sir, no! I'm perfectly all right.'

With a non-committal grunt, Chesterton leaned into the car and, to the labrador's excited relief, drew out a dog lead. Swinging it in his hand, he walked a step or two out onto the grass, but then paused and turned to look back. 'You were a schoolmaster before the war, Alan. Where's it from, that line, *They also serve who only stand and wait?*'

Blanding stared at the questioner in surprise. 'John Milton, sir,' he answered awkwardly, a faint touch of colour rising in his cheeks. 'It's from his sonnet *On His Blindness*.'

21

'Ah yes! Of course – how ruddy stupid of me!' Turning away, Chesterton gazed out across the fens towards where the tower of Ely Cathedral could now just be made out, breaking the western horizon. He suddenly gave a short laugh. 'Well,' he said, looking back round at Blanding with a smile, 'all I can say is that your friend Johnny Milton should have joined the Royal Air Force – then he'd know all about having to stand around merely waiting! Standing idly by is what most of us are condemned to, I'm afraid.' His smile fading, he paused as if about to add something further, but then said brusquely, 'All right, Alan, off you go then and have the camp unsealed. When that's done, make sure you get off to bed and grab yourself an hour or two of good shuteye.'

So saying, he turned and began walking away, swinging the dog lead in his hand, with the elderly labrador waddling close behind him, sniffing the sopping wet grass at his heels.

CHAPTER ONE

Having removed tie and shoes, Alan Blanding took off his tunic and trousers and hung them over the back of a chair with customary care. He then sat on the narrow camp bed and fastidiously cleaned his owlish-round spectacles before placing them on the bedside locker next to a well-thumbed copy of Boethius's *Consolation of Philosophy*. Pulling his greatcoat over his shoulders, he lay back on the pillow and closed his eyes, inwardly praying that the rumours were correct and that the previous night's raid indeed marked the end of a gruelling five-month-long bombing campaign – one carried out in the coldest winter within living memory, in which winds, blowing direct from the Urals, had brought a series of blizzards sweeping in across the North Sea to transform the flat East Anglian landscape into a horizonless Siberia. In a matter of days, both RAF Bomber Command and the American 8th Army Air Force were due to pass under the overall control of General Eisenhower's SHAEF headquarters in preparation for Operation Pointblank, the so-called 'softening-up' of enemy coastal defences and transport communications prior to the impending invasion. With that, the now shortening nights and the start of the main lunar passage, it was confidently predicted by almost everyone on the base that no further sorties would be ordered until the exhausted and nerve-strained aircrews had been thoroughly rested and their squadron re-equipped with the higher and faster-flying Merlin-powered version of the world-renowned Lancaster.

Although officially living 'off station', Blanding usually slept the greater part of the week in this box-like cell at the back of the main administration block, a tiny, airless ex-storeroom overlooking the central camp road, but conveniently adjoining his office. He lay now in the stuffy semidarkness, head aching abominably, one nostril clotted with dried blood from the heavy nosebleed he'd suffered

23

during the course of the night. Having spent the best part of the last thirty hours on his feet, he felt absolutely exhausted. Yet for all that he didn't drop off to sleep immediately. Instead, he found himself trying to remember what he had done with the keys of the office safe after locking away the personal effects of the crew of the missing H-Harry ready for forwarding to the RAF Central Depository at Colnebrooke. For a full minute longer he struggled in vain to overcome what he recognized as a mere neurotic anxiety bred of fatigue. Finally giving in, he sat up and, leaning over to the chair, groped in the dimness for his uniform tunic.

Feeling the weight of the keys in the right-hand pocket, he snuggled down under the greatcoat again. Still unable to sleep, however, after a few moments he rolled over onto his back to lie gazing up at the ceiling. Group Captain Chesterton's oblique reference to his purely administrative, non-operational role had stirred those nagging doubts and guilts buried deep in his psyche, demons laid there thirty years before when he was still his teens. Along with hundreds of other public schoolboys attending the OTC training camp at Rugely in the summer of 1914, he had been summoned from a stiflingly hot bell tent one morning to hear an elderly reserve colonel proclaim that the German army had crossed the Belgium frontier and that, consequentially, the British Empire was mobilizing for war. In the four years that followed, as the great guns echoed over the Channel and the armies surged and fell along the Western Front, and while scores of the likes of 'Buster' Chesterton were fried alive, spinning parachuteless down in flames from the deadly swirling dances among the gaily-painted Fokkers and Albatrosses, he had continued to cram his Euclid, Latin and Greek, plodding his way through Horace, Virgil, Livy and Cicero while the fighting continued and the ever-growing list of school casualties was regularly read out in chapel. At last, after nearly four years, his own time came to be called to the distant slaughter. But then, just as suddenly as they had summoned him to hear the original war proclamation, bugles were sounding the final 'stand down', stranding him, a gawky eighteen-year-old junior subaltern of the Somerset Light Infantry, his feet literally a few yards short of the gangplank of the Calais transport.

Like the wall of a condemned cell suddenly falling, the armistice of November 1918 exposed a complete lifetime stretching ahead. Dazed and disorientated, Blanding had stepped forth into that life with an enormous feeling of thankfulness and relief, yet at the same time burdened by a vague but persistent sense of unworthiness at not having been chosen – of having being left, as it were, forever outside that dark hill into which the seemingly endless column ahead had disappeared. Still stunned by the unexpected reprieve, he had gone up to Oxford the following year to sit among the emotionally-scarred survivors of Gallipoli, Passchendaele and the Somme, an outsider from both their unspoken comradeship and the horrors that many still screamed and gibbered at in their sleep. Without sense of direction or any ambition he could name, he later returned to his old school as a classics and history master, remaining there for nearly two decades, a shy, earnest, hard-working bachelor, growing slightly old-maidish and faddish with the passing years despite an extraordinary dedication to rock-climbing and a growing if minor reputation as a mountaineer.

So things seemed to be set for ever until a chance meeting in the first month of the present war with a fellow ex-student from Balliol – one like himself, excluded from among those who had 'been out' in the first. Apparently, the man had spent the intervening years in the aeronautical industry, first as a designer and then going on to found a small aircraft company of his own, and who was thus able to pass on the name of a useful contact in the Air Ministry. So it was that, in early middle age, Blanding found himself back in uniform once more, but for a second time condemned to remain as it were at the safe end of the gangplank, forced again to endure the horrors and terrors of battle from the position of an onlooker.

With the memory of K-Kitty teetering across the fens towards the airfield still vividly in his mind, Blanding remained staring upwards at the ceiling. What, he wondered, had prompted the CO's odd reference to Milton's sonnet after the crippled bomber had landed? Had he discerned something in his recent behaviour that had caused him to refer to the emotional difficulties of enduring the passive role imposed on them both? Could it have had anything to do with the recent acrimonious row between himself and Barry Gilbert, the bumptious ex-seaside hotel manager employed as station accommodation officer, over some silly matter regarding hut numbering? Perhaps Chesterton thought he was beginning to go the same way as his previous adjutant, and had that been the reason why he'd spoken of finding him an assistant?

Blanding remained miserably gazing upwards for a few seconds longer. Recollecting, however, the amount of paperwork to be got through that morning, he rolled once more onto his side and, burying his head beneath the greatcoat, determinedly closed his eyes. A few moments later he finally drifted off into sleep, the image before him of the similarly excluded station commander wandering away across the wet grass, head bowed, hands clasped behind his back, the elderly labrador waddling at the heels of those ridiculously ungainly old flying-boots.

Then, all at once, the telephone began ringing in the adjoining room.

As if struggling upwards through treacle-like liquid, Blanding re-emerged into full consciousness. He lay a few moments, eyes closed, praying that the continuous ringing would cease and allow him to sink back into the blessed deep well of sleep. Loud and insistent, the sound persisted, however. Finally, with a groan, he half-rolled from the bed and in his stockinged feet staggered, groggy and yawning, out through the connecting door. Crossing the slippery linoleum to the telephone on the desk, he raised the receiver.

'Adjutant's office – yes?'

'Is that you, Mr Blanding, sir?'

'Evans?' Blanding's initial surprise at hearing the Welshman's voice changed almost instantly to profound irritation. It had been, after all, none other than Sergeant Evans of the station police who'd solicitously urged him to get a good sleep after handing over the more valuable personal effects of the missing crew. Now it seemed that the confounded man had dragged him from bed with some idiotic minor inquiry. 'Damn it, Sergeant! What the hell's the matter now?' he exploded, his anger increased by his sense of the ridiculous figure he made, standing shivering there on the bare floor in shirt-tails and socks. 'Whatever it is, couldn't it have bloody well waited?'

'Sorry, sir, but the CO has just been on the phone here to the orderly room. He insisted I should call you. He wants you and Mr Dawson to meet him over at the A Flight sheds.'

'Now you mean?'

Blanding blinked short-sightedly up at the clock. More than an hour had passed since he'd parted from Chesterton. By now, the latter should have been back with his wife and twin daughters in Wellesley Avenue, safely asleep in the largest and grandest of the pre-war houses provided for married permanent camp officers. Frowning, he turned back to the mouthpiece. 'Look, what's this all about, Sergeant? Any idea?'

'I'm afraid not, sir. The CO just said he wants you and Mr Dawson to get over to the sheds as fast as you can. He says for you to use his car as you have the key.'

Obviously, thought Blanding, this had to be some disciplinary matter if he and the station warrant officer were being called for. But what it could possibly be at this hour, he couldn't imagine. 'All right,' he said resignedly, 'ring the sergeants' mess and have Mr Dawson called then. Tell him I shall pick him up from the front entrance in exactly five minutes' time.'

The waiting figure's appearance gave not the slightest indication of a man newly roused from sleep, nor indeed one who had risen and dressed at lightening speed. As Blanding drove up, Warrant Officer Dawson was as immaculate as if he had been laid out fully clothed all night, freshly shaved, his hair brushed and gleaming like some sort of martial zombie, ready at a moment to spring to attention at a superior's call.

''Morning, sir.'

Dawson saluted smartly as the car drew to a stop beside him and Blanding leaned over to wind down the window.

'Jump in, Mr Dawson. The CO is awaiting us at the A Flight sheds.'

Having barked assent, the NCO carefully eased his bulky frame into the car to sit perched bolt upright beside the driver as if anxious to avoid all but the most necessary contact with the upholstery. Woodenly facing ahead, he neither commented on nor questioned the cause of this early morning summons as Blanding swung the heavy saloon out onto the airfield and began heading round the perimeter track.

Whatever his poker-faced passenger might or might not be feeling, Blanding felt highly keyed up. As he had thrown on his uniform and rushed off to collect the Humber, he had striven in vain to think what the CO could have possibly come across. Despite the occasional irascible outburst, Chesterton was neither martinet nor fool. Indeed, in many ways he was a more than averagely thoughtful man. The cause of this abrupt summons could, therefore, he thought, be no routine matter: the discovery of the odd can of illegally siphoned-off petrol, some vulgar or politically-inspired graffiti scrawled on some wall, or evidence of more petty pilfering from the station coal stocks. With an odd sense of dread, and yet at the same time with a keen anticipation, Blanding drove round the aerodrome towards where a number of A Flight bombers stood on circular concrete aprons either side of the rain-puddled taxiway, their wheels, engines, cockpit canopies and gun-turrets shrouded by brown waterproof covers.

'I see some buggers have been bloody lucky!'

Dawson had turned in his seat and was gazing with what seemed jaundiced satisfaction at the smashed tail-boom and the lacerated fuselage of the lately-returned K-Kitty, and then turned to look at those of the almost equally damaged-looking D-Dog parked on the adjacent apron. Although he'd served in the Royal Air Force since its inception, and before that in the Royal Flying Corps, the senior warrant officer's concerns related entirely to the smooth running and discipline of the station. The aircraft and the crews of the various squadrons which rotated through the camp – indeed, the very airfield itself – were quite peripheral to his life of duty rosters, equipment inspections and defaulter parades. In his mind, the dark, squatting Lancasters were little more than extensions of what he saw as the scruffy and grossly over-promoted ex-civilians who generally flew them now that the regular crews of pre-war days were either dead, prisoners-of-war or else transferred to administrative or instructional duties. Not that Dawson wasn't, of course, aware of the risks the crews ran over 'Happy Valley', 'Chopburg' or 'The Big City', as the Ruhr, Hamburg and Berlin were known. Neither was he unsympathetic to their high risk of dying unpleasantly (in the past, both in India and Iraq in the 1920's as well as over in France during the previous war, he'd dragged too many bodies from still-blazing crashed aircraft with the aid of long iron hooks not to know just how unpleasant those deaths could be). For all that, however, he could not help resenting their relatively cosseted existence, given extra allowances of milk, fruit juice and eggs and excused all but the most essential ground duties. Nor could he, as an ex-regular soldier, escape the feeling that the risky, individualistic nature of flying itself was somehow at odds, even prejudicial, to the blancoing of belts, burnishing of boots, the correct folding of blankets and all those other routines on which, as a boy entrant into the Royal Horse Artillery, he'd cut his martial teeth, and on which he profoundly believed that the security and well-being of nations and empires ultimately depended.

As the Humber turned off the perimeter track towards a pair

of huge, grassed-over hangars, there emerged from the nearer the burly figure of the station commander, accompanied by a sergeant-fitter in forage cap and sleeveless leather jerkin. Passing the labrador's lead to his companion, the CO strode forward to meet the car. 'Stay where you are, both of you. I'll use the back seat,' he called out, clambering in and slamming the door closed behind him. 'OK, Alan,' he instructed, 'drive back onto the taxiway and follow it on round until I tell you to stop.'

The brusque tone of the order, the lack of apology or explanation, confirmed the seriousness of the occasion. Glancing up at the driving mirror as he accelerated away, Blanding noticed the strained grimness in Chesterton's face – an expression he had so often seen during the wait for overdue aircraft. There was something in the CO's hard, angry look which reminded him of a fortnight previously when together the two of them had watched that old OTU Wellington with its trainee crew and outworn engines lose power on its final approach to stall and crash in a ball of flame twenty yards short of the main runway. Lowering his eyes from the mirror, Blanding looked across at Dawson. Now, however, in close proximity to his commanding officer, the NCO was sitting even more rigidly upright and staring ahead through the windscreen with an absolute blankness of expression.

'Stop here.'

Wondering what Chesterton could have possibly discovered in this remote corner of the airfield, Blanding drew the car up on the grass verge some ten yards or so from the end of the main runway.

'Right, switch off the engine and both of you come with me.'

Despite their ecstatic joy at greeting the first faint greying of the dawn, the majority of the birds in the hedgerows and trees had long since fallen quiet. The few brief tweetings and twitterings that broke the stillness, along with the intermittent bleats of the distant sheep, served only to emphasize the dreariness of the flat fenland landscape. The three thuds of their car doors slamming shut sounded dully in the damp silence but still started a hare that bounded away through a cloud of spray in the direction of the sand-covered gun-butts at the far end of the airfield.

Saying nothing and without meeting the eyes of either man, Chesterton turned and headed across the strip of wet grass that separated the taxiway from the ten-foot high boundary fence. In a forlorn attempt to keep his shoes dry, Blanding followed closely in his wake, endeavouring to tread in the footprints left by the other's flying-boots and feeling absurdly like the page in the Christmas carol as he did so. Behind trudged Warrant Officer Dawson, impassively grave.

'I take it, Mr Dawson,' called Chesterton, halting a few yards short of the wire-mesh barrier and turning to look past Blanding towards the man behind, 'that you had no knowledge of this hole in the fence? My dog drew my attention to it by running off and disappearing through that gap here.' The speaker pointed at the nearest of the metal stakes supporting the fence. Following the direction of his forefinger, Blanding saw for the first time that by one of the stakes the wire mesh had been cut upwards from the ground to almost two-thirds of the stake's height and then peeled back, leaving a narrow triangular gap. Glancing down, he also noticed a muddy track curving past him towards the improvised opening – a trodden way, deeply imprinted by a multiplicity of footprints, themselves woven through and overlaid by countless bicycle-tyre marks.

'No, sir – no knowledge of it at all.'

Blanding glanced round at the NCO's face, its blank obstinacy of expression perfectly matching the barked-out reply. Clearly, Dawson's answer had been nothing more than the formalized lie that Chesterton had as good as invited. Nothing in any of this was unexpected. As station warrant officer, Dawson couldn't officially know of any damage done to Air Ministry property, although all three men were perfectly well aware that, even in wartime, almost every aerodrome in Britain had its illegal exits and entrances that authority was normally content to wink at. Airfields were large places after all, needing bicycles or motor transport to transverse, and for those forced to work in their often freezing windy vastnesses, it was too great a temptation not to cut half an hour off the journey to the local village or pub by a judicious few snips with a bolt-cropper or wire-cutter. What was surprising, therefore, was not the gap itself or Dawson's response, but why Chesterton had not simply chosen to call his dog to heel and walked quickly past it with averted eyes. Even more amazing was why such an understandable and comparatively harmless breach of discipline should have warranted dragging Dawson and himself from their respective beds before even the sounding of reveille and the official commencement of the day.

Chesterton had turned back to the fence and stood now with knotted fists, gazing in apparent suppressed fury at the damaged wire. Puzzled, Blanding waited, looking out across the freshly-furrowed dark ploughland beyond, towards where the nearby village of Frampton Wissey nestled in a shallow fold of ground, its grey-slate roofs and stumpy, circular church tower emerging through the slight haze of ground-mist that hung over the winding, sluggish river from which both the little fenland community and the nearby RAF station took half of their name.

'I couldn't understand it!' burst out Chesterton suddenly, still staring at the cut wire. 'One moment Sasha was quietly sniffling along the edge of the peri-track; next thing she was high-tailing it straight for that gap. Before I could stop her, she was through it and out into the field, barking her confounded head off. Then she wouldn't return to heel when I called her back.' He broke off and looked back at Blanding with evident distress. 'Alan,' he said, his tone softening, 'I was hoping to have the MO here, but apparently he decided he ought to go off in the ambulance with young Ellis. In his place, I want you to squeeze through and see for yourself what the dog found.' Grimacing, he looked away. 'You can't miss it – it's lying just a few yards on the left, close up against the outside of the wire.'

Blanding glanced at Dawson, and for a moment their eyes met. Saying nothing, however, he approached the fence, and, with the NCO holding the loose mesh back for him, he carefully dipped through the gap. Once safely clear of the sharp ends of the cut wire, he straightened with difficulty, the soles of his shoes slipping on the greasy mud underfoot. Then turning, he looked along the heavily trodden narrow path that ran between the outside of the fence and the ploughed soil. Immediately he did so, he gave an involuntary gasp and stood momentarily paralysed, staring in horrified disbelief at the object which he'd been roused from sleep to see.

About ten feet away from him, the young woman lay on her left side in a parody of sleep, her lower arm stretched languorously over the black fenland soil, the hand open with the palm turned upwards towards the onlooker. The pink-mittened hand of the other arm rested across the upturned cheekbone and forehead as if sheltering her eyes from the pale watery sunlight now beginning at last to pierce the thinning blanket of cloud overhead. The whole attitude and appearance of the skirtless, half-naked form – the blond halo of curls about the half-hidden face, the dishevelled WAAF tunic with its pair of broad white chevrons on the sleeves and the torn-open blouse beneath, the bare legs drawn up into an almost foetal position

31

with rain-drops clinging like tears to the pale marble-like flesh, the obviously home-knitted mitten on the right hand – created an impression mockingly reminiscent of the vulnerability and sweetness of a slumbering child.

That he was looking at a corpse, Blanding had not the slightest doubt. About the body, there was not just a complete absence of movement but a total relaxation, so that it appeared to be moulded into the contours of the ground like a sodden rag-doll. Swallowing hard, he struggled for a second or two to master himself before taking a few careful steps forward. Halting a few feet from the outstretched hand, he bent and peered down at the inert form, noticing now that the curly blond hair over the girl's forehead was dark with congealed blood.

He straightened and looked back at the two men behind the fence. Chesterton stood looking away towards the village, face in profile, his head protruding vulture-like from the fleece-lined collar of his flying jacket. Dawson, on the other hand, was pressed against the wire, straining up on his toes to see whatever it was that was nestling hidden in the uncut grass fringing the field-side of the barrier.

'Step through if you would, Mr Dawson,' Blanding called out. 'I think you should see this for yourself.'

All the warrant officer's former impassivity had disappeared. As he stooped and eased himself carefully through the gap in the fence, there was a grim, hard set to his face – an expression that instantly transformed to a grimace of horror when he saw what lay sprawled on the muddy ground. 'Holy Christ!' Momentarily, Dawson stood as if transfixed; then he began stumbling past the adjutant towards the recumbent form.

'One moment, Mr Dawson,' said Blanding, reaching out to check the NCO's progress with a firm grip on his sleeve. 'This is obviously murder. We must be careful not to disturb the body or trample the ground around it any more than we need.'

Through the thick cloth of the greatcoat, Blanding could feel Dawson's body quivering. In the silence, he heard the man's breath coming in short rapid pants. 'Christ's sake! Whoever did this, God damn the evil bloody bastard to hell!'

Blanding's initial numbed horror was fast disappearing, and the vehemence of the warrant officer's curses, flat in the dank emptiness, mirrored his own sense of impotent rage. For a moment or two longer, the two men stood side by side, looking over at the girl's body until Dawson, having calmed himself, said quietly, 'Sir, I think I should check that she's dead. Make absolutely certain. Don't worry though, I'll be careful where I place my feet.'

'Go on then.'

The warrant officer approached the body indirectly, in an arc over the untrodden ploughland on their right. Blanding again glanced round at Chesterton. The station commander was now looking towards them both through the wire, distress evident in his face. Turning back, Blanding watched as Dawson, reaching the body, squatted down and leaned over to touch the outstretched wrist. As soon as his fingers met the inert flesh, the NCO winced and quickly withdrew his hand. Looking back at the adjutant with distress in his eyes, he shook his head. 'Ice-cold,' he called out. 'The poor kid's been dead for a fair while, I'd say.'

With the same care that he had used to step in Chesterton's footprints when crossing the grass, Blanding now trod in Dawson's tracks across the clayey soil, taking the same curving trajectory towards the body. Reaching the crouching man, he squatted beside him.

'Do you know who she is?'

Not replying, Dawson leaned over the corpse and carefully raised and drew back the matted curls from the blood-caked forehead, exposing a deep, ugly gash across the top of the left temple. He then bent and lowered his head to study what could be seen of the victim's face. Looking down at the large, thick fingers gently holding back the girl's hair and, at the same time, seeing the expression on Dawson's broad features as the warrant officer bent his head and peered beneath the mitten-clad hand at the half-hidden face, Blanding vaguely remembered that, like the station commander himself, Dawson had two daughters of his own, and he had a sudden vision of the person beside him as a younger man rising at night to comfort a sick or frightened child.

'Holy Christ!' Dawson glanced up at the adjutant and grimaced, then averted his face and stared away across the furrowed field, swallowing hard. Reluctantly, Blanding bent to examine the half-concealed features beneath the sheltering hand. Doing so, he saw what had shocked the other. What ordinarily would have been the face of a pretty young woman in her late teens or early twenties was a surreal mask, a composite put together from two different people: the closed eyes of the dreamless sleeper set against the snarl-like grimace

33

of the tightly clenched mouth, whose bloodless lips drawn back from the teeth gave an expression of indescribable horror or fear.

Shaken, Blanding raised his head to meet Dawson's look. 'Do you recognize her?' he asked again.

The NCO nodded. 'It's Summerfield, sir – Corporal June Summerfield. She worked in the wireless section.'

Frowning, Blanding glanced down again at the girl's body. Of the hundreds of skilled and semi-skilled personnel on the camp, cooks, butchers, bakers, batmen, telephonists, armourers, aircraft handlers, airframe fitters, parachute packers and the rest of the numerous service trades and occupations, he still knew comparatively few, forced as he was to spend the majority of his time at his desk. In any case, he was far from being a sociable or gregarious man, and generally kept very much to himself. Nevertheless, he was almost certain that he had recently come across Corporal Summerfield's name before, though in what connection he could not remember.

'Bloody hell, sir! Look at all that!'

Gently pulling aside the ripped-open blouse, Dawson had exposed enough of the girl's upper torso for Blanding to see what looked like heavy bruising as well as oily thumb and finger marks across the chest between the top of the white brassiere and the lower part of the neck. 'Whoever the vile bastard was,' murmured the warrant officer, 'he gave the kid a right hammering – and then had the cold-blooded gall to fucking well close her eyes when he'd finished!' He peered closer. 'Yes,' he added bitterly, 'and look at them thick smudge marks on her skin! There won't be any fingerprints to be had from them, you can bet your life – the murdering bastard was almost certainly wearing gloves!'

Releasing the collar, Dawson reached down and wordlessly plucked the tail of the torn blouse, drawing it up enough to expose just an inch or so of blue woollen issue knickers – the so-called 'passion-killers' that were such a joke throughout the air force. Pulling the blouse back into position, he sat back on his haunches and glanced at the adjutant with a significant frown. Blanding nodded. Getting to his feet, he carefully surveyed the wet soil about them, noticing as he did so the Labrador's paw marks amongst the weaving bicycle tracks and the numerous footprints outside of the fence. 'I see no sign of her skirt, stockings and shoes,' he said after a few moments, 'nor of her greatcoat, service cap or the second mitten.'

'If you ask me, sir, I reckon she was dragged here. There's

plenty of footprints all round her, but there's nothing to show any sign of a struggle.'

Blanding once more scanned the heavily trodden, ridden-over track along the edge of the ploughland before turning to look down again at the corpse. 'No, Mr Dawson,' he said, shaking his head, 'whatever did happen, she wasn't dragged here. There are no marks in the soil suggesting it. Anyway, just take a look at those bare feet and ankles. As you see, they're completely clean.'

'I reckon you're right, sir,' replied Dawson slowly. 'Then she must have been carried here and dumped.'

'Yes, I agree, but carried from where? That's the question.'

The warrant officer, still squatting at Blanding's side, seemed not to hear. Instead, he was leaned forward once more and began closely examining the marks on the girl's chest. Gently rubbing an index finger across the discoloured flesh, he raised it to his nose and sniffed, and then held the tip up towards Blanding's face. 'That's Castrol grease, that is. Whatever devil did this, he either works with or has been close to machinery of some sort.' Lowering his head, he bent and sniffed at the girl's dishevelled tunic. Frowning, he once more looked up at the adjutant, bewilderment in his eyes. 'You take a whiff, sir – that cloth stinks just as if the poor lass had been doused in kerosene.'

Squatting down beside the body again, Blanding bent and smelt the Waaf's tunic. Dawson was right: from the rain-sodden material came the unmistakable odour of paraffin oil. 'Good God!' he murmured, shaking his head. 'Where the hell has she been? In some sort of garage or outhouse?'

'Over there, sir – I'd stake my life on it!'

Dawson had stood up and was pointing across the bare ploughland towards the far end of the field where, beside a five-bar gate leading out into the lane beyond, stood a small, open-sided farm building, crudely roofed over with sheets of rusty corrugated iron. Within could be made out an upended two-wheeled cart and various pieces of agricultural machinery. 'A lot of the farmers hereabouts use kerosene-fuelled tractors,' he said. 'I'd bet a pound to a penny, that foul bastard was hiding inside that barn, waiting to spring out when the poor kid came past, and that's where the attack took place. If you like, sir, I could go over and have a quick shufti round inside. It wouldn't take me more than a few minutes.'

Blanding shook his head. 'No, Mr Dawson, I think we should

35

leave all that sort of thing to the civilian police. The less walking around disturbing things the better. The important thing now is for both of us to get back to the CO and make our report.'

'One of our own girls I take it, gentlemen?'

Face grim and haggard, Chesterton had been anxiously awaiting the two men's return at the other side of the fence. He'd refrained, however, from asking his question until, having held back the wire to allow them both to pass through the narrow gap unscathed, they again stood once again before him on Air Ministry property.

'I'm afraid so, sir,' answered Blanding. 'According to Mr Dawson, she's Corporal June Summerfield. She apparently worked in the wireless section.'

'Summerfield?' Chesterton looked down at the grass at his feet. 'Yes,' he said quietly, nodding his head. 'I think I can place her: a fresh-faced, pleasant girl who played in the badminton team; didn't she also have a small part in one of our Christmas reviews?' Pausing, he looked up as the sun now emerged from behind a dissolving haze of cloud. 'Lovely smile, I remember.'

'That's her, sir,' burst out Dawson, nodding emphatically. 'Very popular she was – a real poppet you might say.' He broke off, but then almost instantly resumed, 'It's a right bloody shame, that's what it is! A rotten, bloody sacrilege, if you'll pardon the expression, sir! If I could lay my hands on the sod who did it, I'd happily wring his dirty little neck myself!'

'Quite,' murmured Chesterton, turning away to look back across the airfield towards the camp, from where at that moment there faintly echoed the notes of a bugle sounding reveille. It was obvious to Blanding that to have come across the girl's beaten, half-naked body whilst brooding over the loss of yet another of the station's aircraft and crew had been an emotionally shattering experience for the CO. Although between them, the twenty-nine Lancasters unleashed from Frampton Wissey the evening before had possibly pulverised with high explosive or consumed in blazing phosphorus scores of the likes of June Summerfield along with the old and the very young, those sufferings and deaths were to Chesterton merely a regrettable but inevitable consequence of the harsh so-called 'area bombing' policy he helped implement – something that happened mercifully invisible to those flying twenty thousand feet or more above the flashing, pulsating heart of the target, and, in his mind, not a thing either to be questioned or, if possible, brooded upon. This death, however – the apparent cold-blooded murder of one of the young Waaf operators from the wireless section – he clearly saw as something altogether different: a personal act, undertaken for motives of perverted self-gratification, the whole thing a monstrous insult, a betrayal of the very ideals he profoundly believed the aircrews were nightly fighting and dying to preserve. For someone like him, thought Blanding, glancing at his troubled face, the discovery of the girl's half-stripped body lying curled up on the muddy soil outside the boundary fence was the equivalent to St George glancing round in the midst of combating the dragon to find the maidenly form he was defending had changed to a grinning ape, grotesquely mocking and mimicking his efforts – an occurrence so utterly unexpected and profoundly shocking that even now, forty-five minutes or so after he'd followed the barking dog through the gap in the fence, the station commander obviously remained sickened and stunned by what he had stumbled upon.

'I take it,' resumed Chesterton at last, speaking with difficulty, his gaze fixed on a nearby windsock, 'that the poor girl was interfered with?'

Blanding glanced at Dawson, then cleared his throat. 'There seems no doubt, sir, that Summerfield was the victim of a sexual attack. However, as her underclothes are still in place, it looks as if she died putting up a struggle.'

Chesterton looked round sharply. 'Putting up a struggle, you say?'

'So it would seem, sir.'

A look of something like relief crossed the older man's face. In the phrase Blanding had used, there was something that Chesterton was able at last to cling to and understand. '*Dying putting up a struggle*' was, after all, what he had known and witnessed many times since when, as an eighteen-year-old novice pilot, only a few months out of school and with barely fifteen hours flying time recorded in his flight log book, crossing the lines near Arras on his first patrol in the spring of 1915, he'd been pounced on by a pair of Fokker E-2's equipped with the terrifying new synchronised machine guns able to fire for the first time through the spinning propeller. In his old-fashioned, essentially Edwardian mind, the notion of a young woman fighting for her honour in a dark, deserted field became equated with the desperate dive for home he'd made that now long ago April morning – the wind shrieking through the bracing wires of the rickety old B.E.2c and his corporal observer kneeling up in the front cockpit, blazing back past his head with the Lewis gun until a well-aimed burst from one of the Fokkers had finally sent the machine drifting down to crash-land close behind the British lines, its engine riddled and useless, and with its gunner lolling dead over the brains-spattered drum of his now empty weapon.

'Well, Mr Dawson,' he said more briskly, 'if you wouldn't mind remaining here for the moment, the adjutant and I will go and report the matter to the proper authorities. We'll then arrange for a guard to be placed on the body and for you to be relieved.'

Leaving Dawson besides the fence, Blanding accompanied the CO back to the car. As they drove in silence round the perimeter track, he tried to remember what the sight of the young woman lying in the mud had reminded him of. Suddenly the answer came. As a small boy, he had once gone searching for birds' nests in the overgrown graveyard of his father's Dorset church. Beating a path through the thick undergrowth behind the old bier-house, he'd stumbled upon a white marble angel toppled from its plinth – one hand of the lichen-stained effigy sheltering the turned-away face just like the dead girl's in a typical Victorian attitude of stylized grief, the other hand stretched up towards him, palm open, as if attempting to ward off some evil too hideous to contemplate.

CHAPTER TWO

The two hundred and fifteen foot high tower of Ely Cathedral appeared on the hazy horizon like a beckoning finger. Spotting it, the pilot of the descending photo-reconnaissance Mosquito – one of the pair that had taken off less than an hour after the landing of K-Kitty – immediately dipped a wing and turned towards it, grateful for this prominent beacon in the otherwise virtually featureless landscape. Down below the early morning whine and rattle of electric milk floats and clip-clop of roundsmen's horses was momentarily drowned by the deep-throated snarl of Rolls-Royce Merlins as the Mosquito banked and swept low across the barely stirring fenland capital to set final course for RAF Frampton Wissey. Ten minutes later it was skimming over the north-eastern perimeter fence, undercarriage lowered and flaps fully down to make a perfect three-point landing.

In less than half the distance taken by the crippled Lancaster a few hours earlier, the twin-engined aircraft braked to a stop. Taxiing on to the junction of runway and peri-track, it paused to rotate on its starboard wheel before commencing its slow journey round the edge of the airfield to where photographic technicians were waiting to remove the high-altitude camera from its housing beneath the nose. Within ten yards of turning off the runway, however, the small aeroplane again squealed to a halt, port wingtip directly opposite and pointing towards the nearer end of a line of head-bent figures moving across the rutted ploughland beyond the perimeter fence, the misty grey-blue greatcoats and snowy white cross-straps, belts and cap-bands of the station police contrasting with the plain darker blue uniforms and helmets of their civilian counterparts.

Bellowing and trembling like some enchained beast, the Mosquito stood, engines thundering, a few yards short of the unusual collection of vehicles drawn up on the taxiway verge, its unauthorized pause almost hidden from those in the control tower by the pronounced curvature of the airfield. Through the perspex canopy, the snouted oxygen masks and leather-helmeted heads of its two-man

39

crew could be dimly made out as they peered towards the row of searching men in the field beyond the boundary fence and a small knot of nearer figures standing together just the other side of the wire. These latter were grouped around something which, even from the height of the cockpit, was concealed by the ragged fringe of grass at the base of the fence and the set of grey canvas screens erected immediately behind it.

Just over an hour earlier, the two young airmen had been looking down upon Essen, viewing with cool professional detachment the still-burning city over thirty thousand feet below them – where, more than eight hours after the final wave of bombers had passed over, the blackened, hardly recognizable bodies of men, women and infants were still being dug out of smouldering ruins. Here, however, a mere ten yards from the nearest of the bending, slow-moving searchers, both craned their heads to watch, eager as schoolboys to know what was happening. There seemed no obvious explanation for this unprecedented activity, however. Soon again growing acutely conscious of the ache in his buttocks from sitting on what increasingly felt like a concrete-filled parachute pack, and also remembering the waiting technicians and the motorcycle despatch rider impatient to rush the photographic evidence of the night's operations over to Bomber Command headquarters at High Wycombe in time for Air Marshal Harris's daily mid-morning conference, the pilot reluctantly released his brakes. Carefully steering the Mosquito past the pair of black Wolseley police cars, the three blue RAF Bedford trucks and the white civilian ambulance, he eased the twin throttle levers a fraction more forward, his thoughts, like those of his equally ravenous navigator, turning once more to the welcoming prospect of breakfast.

A mile from the taxiing aircraft, Alan Blanding was already breakfasting in the officer's mess, a large, elegant pre-war building, high-porticoed and adorned with Corinthian columns and marble front steps. Having finished a bowl of stewed prunes, he sat now, feeling slightly light-headed from lack of sleep, staring glassily down at the plate being laid before him. On its gleaming white surface was a slice of fried bread and two distinctly cindery chipolatas, all three objects half submerged in a bright red splodge of tinned tomatoes.

'Thank you, Jenkins – very nice.'

'Thank you, sir.'

40

Apparently impervious to irony, the silvery-haired steward gravely inclined his head. Withdrawing to join his spotty-faced young companion beside the hot-trolley, he immediately resumed a whispered conversation, interspersing his remarks with significant glances towards the adjutant, who remained head-bent, apparently gloomily contemplating his meagre and distinctly unappetizing dish.

It was still comparatively early, and the spacious, oak-panelled dining room was two-thirds empty. Most aircrew members of the mess were still asleep after the night's operation, either comfortably ensconced in a centrally-heated bedroom upstairs or, in the case of the vast majority, huddled like their NCO comrades under a mound of greatcoats and flying-jackets in one or other of the dozens of condensation-damp, corrugated-iron Nissen huts that had mushroomed in clumps around the aerodrome since the beginning of the war. Blanding had thus been able to get through the first part of the meal without the necessity of speaking to or even acknowledging the existence of any of his fellow breakfasters – apart, that is, from nodding towards 'Fluff' Brewer when he'd first arrived. This had been difficult to avoid as the air traffic controller, just come off duty, sat directly facing the door, an issue of *Motor Sport* propped ostentatiously open before him as a sign that he wished to be left alone, yet at the same time balefully glancing up whenever anyone entered as if in the vain hope of seeing the MG's joint owner arriving to join him for breakfast as usual.

Since sitting down, however, Blanding had gradually grown conscious of the unusual degree of attention he was receiving, not only from the two mess stewards, but also from the small groups of mainly administrative and technical officers dotted about the room. From the whisperings and head-turnings, it was clear that Corporal Summerfield's death was being discussed, and that everyone present, with the possible exception of Brewer, was aware that he had been one of the very first to view the body. Partly from the awe that notion inspired, partly owing to his comparatively advanced age (being at least ten years older than the majority present), and also because of his reputation as a somewhat faddish and testy martinet, no one was inclined to approach him with questions. Therefore, like the grieving Brewer, he was left alone to eat his breakfast in peace. However, for all the superficial similarity of their isolation, there was a world of difference in the way that he and the crippled ex-fighter pilot were being regarded.

41

Brewer, in fact, was hardly glanced at or mentioned at all. Over the four and half years of war, and especially since the start of the latest bombing campaign back in October, Frampton Wissey's tally of missing aircraft had grown steadily, and the non-return of H-Harry was only the latest of the scores of losses the station had suffered during that period. During the winter almost everyone present had witnessed at first hand the cost being paid almost nightly by the crews of Bomber Command: shrivelled, mummy-like corpses removed from burnt-out wreckage; mangled bodies and parts of bodies extracted from shell-torn fuselages; blood and gobbets of flesh sometimes having to be scraped or hosed out of shattered gun turrets. This the members of the mess wearily accepted as the inevitable result of the vast, impersonal process of modern warfare, just as they accepted the unending kaleidoscope of new faces that came and then vanished again as quickly and completely as Bede's sparrow flying into the mead-hall and out again. Nevertheless, living though they did cheek by jowl with violent death in some of its most violent and hideous forms, they preferred to avert their eyes from it wherever possible, leaving aircrew losses as a rarely if ever mentioned subject of conversation. The death whose cold breath Blanding had felt stroke across his cheek was something altogether different, however: a young woman, one of their own Waafs, set upon and killed in an apparent frenzy of lust or rage. To everyone present, just as for the station commander earlier, what had happened to Corporal Summerfield was an absolute outrage – a betrayal of all that was being fought and died for, the more monstrous and unacceptable in that it had apparently taken place sometime during the night, when others of her comrades were actually airborne, risking their lives over a dark and dangerous continent. Thus, with similar expressions of shocked disbelief changing rapidly to that of indignant fury, each new arrival at breakfast received the news, then turned to look across with awed curiosity at the man who had personally witnessed the unthinkable.

In an effort to blank out their barely concealed scrutiny, Blanding bent to the first of his chipolatas, turning his eyes as he did so to the copy of the *Daily Telegraph* lying beside his plate. Depressingly, it appeared that the Allies were still bogged down in Italy, frustrated alike by the stubborn German resistance at Monte Cassino and the continuing inability of General Lucas's forces to break out from the narrow Anzio beachhead. Equally bleak or even bleaker was the news that the Japanese were still advancing through Burma towards the northern borders of India. Forking the slice of sodden fried-bread into his mouth, Blanding turned over a page to see if General Zhukov's Red Army was doing any better on the Eastern Front or the Americans in the Pacific after their recent landings in the Marshall Isles.

'Hello, Trott! Mind if I join you?'

Dismayed by the intrusion, Blanding looked up to find Squadron Leader Palmer, Frampton Wissey's senior technical officer, standing over him, a heaped bowl of cornflakes in hand.

'Not at all, Peter – only too delighted.'

'Jolly good.'

Taking the seat opposite, the newcomer immediately set about wolfing down great spoonfuls of cereal. Blanding relaxed: Palmer was a likeable man, a tall, willowy bachelor of about his own age, a regular peacetime officer, whose mop of prematurely white hair perversely surmounted a face radiant with health and still amazingly youthful, and the nearest thing to a friend he had on the camp. Now, with a shaft of light from the window falling on his glowing cheeks, he appeared more boyishly young than ever, creating the impression that, in his zeal for his work and desire to keep abreast of the ever increasing sophistication and complexity of the aircraft and electronic equipment he was responsible for, he supped of the very elixir of life.

'I take it,' said Blanding, meeting the other's look with a smile and presuming on their friendship to defy convention and indulge in a little 'shop talk' within the sanctity of the mess, 'that you've just cycled back from having a look over those two damaged kites from last night's op. In what sort of state are they?'

The engineer shrugged. 'K-Kitty should be all right after a bit of patching up. Poor old D-Dog though is definitely off the road for the foreseeable future – it's either scrapping for her, or else being dismantled and carted off to a maintenance unit for complete rebuilding.'

'Really?' Wondering if Palmer had heard the news of the Waaf's death, but glad all the same to be talking of ordinary, everyday matters, Blanding pursued the subject. 'From what I could see when I drove past them both earlier, I'd have thought it was the other way round.'

Finishing his cornflakes, Palmer pushed away his bowl and then waved towards the two stewards. 'No,' he said, turning back to

43

the table, 'Kitty's damage is basically cosmetic: a couple of replacement engines and a new tail unit, and we'll soon have her back in the air. It's a completely different matter with Dog, I'm afraid: not only has her belly been ripped open by cannon-fire, but it looks as if the main spar has been badly over-stressed.' He gave a short laugh. 'God knows what sort of aerobatics Pat Kelly put the poor crate through last night! Whatever they were, from the look of things, I'd say he must have come within a whisker of shedding a wing!'

'At least he brought his crew back alive.'

'Oh, yes,' agreed Palmer, nodding, 'Don't get me wrong, old boy. Like most of the Aussie pilots, Kelly's damned good at his job, however bolshie and bloody-minded he can be on the ground. It was just rotten bad luck, getting spotted by a stray nightfighter when he was well out over the sea on his way home.'

'Have you heard how his navigator is?' asked Blanding as the steward placed an identical dish to his own in front of Palmer.

'Young Ellis?' The engineer shook his head as he bent to his plate. 'No,' he resumed, clearing his mouth, 'but talk is that he's pretty bad. Apparently, there's a good chance they may have to amputate the leg.' For a while the two men ate in silence while around them the noise level in the room steadily rose as a succession of latecomers entered. Finally, wiping his mouth with a napkin, Palmer leaned back in his chair. 'When I was over at the A flight sheds just now, I saw the civilian police and some of our own lads out combing the field beyond the perimeter fence. I imagine they're looking for the missing clothes and whatever was used to strike down the girl with.'

'I suppose so,' answered Blanding noncommittally. As he'd expected, the details of the CO's discovery were obviously already common currency around the hangars and workshops. Soon, he thought, the news of what had happened to the Waaf would be all over the camp and, by midday, be the gossip of every taproom, bar and village shop in the area.

'I hear it was poor old Buster himself who first found the body. Knowing him, the discovery must have hit the old boy pretty hard?'

'He was upset certainly when I was called out to the scene.'

'I can imagine,' murmured Palmer grimly, pouring himself a cup of coffee. 'And Buster won't be the only one, not by a long chalk,' he continued. 'Poppy was a damned popular girl.'

'Poppy?'

'Poppy Summerfield – that's how she was always known.' Palmer grimaced. 'God knows,' he continued, stirring his drink, 'it would have been bad enough if it had happened to any of our Waafs, but for it to happen to someone like Poppy seems somehow doubly vile.'

'You knew her?'

'A little – I met her around the flight sheds quite a few times.' The engineer sipped his coffee. 'She was chummy with a good few of the boys, both ground staff and aircrew.'

'Chummy?'

Palmer smiled knowingly but then shook his head. 'Not the sort of chummy you mean – in that department, I gather she was a bit of what you might call an ice-princess.'

Blanding raised an eyebrow. 'A sex-tease, you mean?'

'No, not at all,' replied Palmer, blushing slightly. 'Poppy Summerfield was a thoroughly decent sort – an intelligent, sensible, friendly young woman with no side to her at all.'

'Yet you called her an ice-princess. What did you mean?'

The engineer took another sip of his coffee. 'I suppose,' he answered thoughtfully, contemplating the contents of his cup as he spoke, 'there was something distant and untouchable about her – I don't know, some sort of innocence if you know what I mean.' He gave an embarrassed laugh. 'Almost a touch of the angelic, you might say.'

At the phrase, Blanding thought of the girl's body lying, one cheek pressed against the sodden dark earth, the mittened right hand resting across and hiding the blood-caked face, foetus-like on the fence-side track. Once again there came back the vision of the toppled marble monument lying moss-encrusted and lichen-stained among the overgrown laurels in the corner of the Dorsetshire churchyard. 'She was certainly physically attractive,' he said after a pause. 'She had a boyfriend, I presume?'

'Here on the station, you mean?' Palmer shook his head. 'Not currently anyway, though I believe she'd been close to a couple of different chaps in the past – a nineteen-year-old pilot from the previous squadron through here, then almost straight after with an equally young Rhodesian navigator.'

'What happened to them?'

Impassively, Palmer raised his right hand and twisted his wrist into the thumbs-down gesture.

45

'Both killed?' Blanding frowned. 'But what about more recently? There must have been someone she was seeing. With her looks, I'd guess there were plenty of fellows interested.'

'No,' said Palmer, shaking his head. 'At least, not among any of the aircrew.'

'Why ever not for goodness sake? She was popular as well as pretty according to you.'

Not answering immediately, the engineer drew a silver cigarette case from one of the breast pockets of his battledress blouse. Flipping it open, he held it out. 'No, thanks, Pete,' said Blanding, shaking his head. 'But go on, tell me,' he asked, 'why weren't the aircrew keen to take Summerfield out? I'd have thought they'd be queuing up for the chance.'

Palmer drew out a cigarette and lit it. Leaning back in his chair, he inhaled deeply. 'Very simple,' he said, tilting his lips to breathe out a thin stream of smoke towards the ceiling, 'Poppy Summerfield was a chop girl.' Lowering his head and seeing the other's blank look, he smiled. 'Chop, my dear fellow, as in "turn up your toes", "cash in your chips" or simply "kick the jolly old bucket".'

For a moment, Blanding stared blankly at the speaker, but then a look of wondering incredulity rose in his face. 'Good God!' he burst out. 'What are you saying, Pete? That the girl was thought to have the evil eye or something of the sort? That she was jinxed?' Evoking no immediate denial, he forced a laugh. 'Come off it, Pete! You're having me on, aren't you? You must be, damn it! This is an RAF station for heaven's sake – not some one-horse Cretan village!'

Palmer smiled indulgently back at him through a haze of cigarette smoke. 'My dear Trott,' he said, 'you really are still so much the civilian, aren't you! Haven't you learnt yet, that for all its scientific know-how and technical expertise, the Royal Air Force is by far the most superstitious of our gallant fighting services?' Reaching over, he poured himself more coffee. 'I tell you,' he went on, 'that there are beliefs current in every aircrew mess, especially those of Bomber Command, that Caesar's legionaries or even Nelson's jolly Jack Tars would have blushed to confess to!'

'Surely not!' exclaimed Blanding, but then abruptly broke off, remembering the rabbits' feet, the St Christopher medallions, the scrofulous-looking collection of battered, one-eyed, almost fur-less old teddy-bears or other stuffed babyhood toys, items of female underclothing and the rest of the incongruous mascots and good luck

46

charms (or 'whammies' as they were popularly known within the air force) that so many of the aircrew flew with. Apart from those, there were the various ill-omens everyone knew of: getting photographed before a mission, the premature signing of a leave pass or the unfortunate killing of a bird during take-off – the latter sadly only too frequent an occurrence on an aerodrome situated in the midst of the fens, with clouds of partridges and green plovers flocking in at due season. Indeed, his recent quarrel with the accommodation officer had been over Gilbert's obstinate insistence on re-numbering some of the aircrew Nissen huts merely because some numbers were apparently regarded as unlucky. Blanding also knew of the impossibility of getting anyone at all to use the bed space, let alone the actual bed, once allotted to the unfortunate 'Thirty-Minute Murray', an eighteen-year-old wireless operator straight from training school who'd had barely time to lay out his kit before being ordered out on a small daytime nuisance raid or 'moling trip' over the Heligoland Bight – a sortie from which neither of the two machines taking part had returned.

'Of course,' resumed Palmer, 'the aircrews are considerably better educated than the majority of the population. Nevertheless, most aren't much older than schoolboys and don't live long enough even to complete the seventeen ops the Air Ministry regards as justifying the cost of their training, let alone the thirty of a fully completed first tour.' He paused to inhale his cigarette. 'Frightened witless by flack, searchlights and the thought of the prowling nightfighters, the poor devils have to fly through fog and freezing-cold darkness night after night in clumsy, slow-flying aircraft, surrounded by gallons of high octane petrol and loaded down with both incendiary and explosive bombs, knowing that, for all their experience or technical expertise, it's often just a matter of luck who survives and who doesn't – who returns home to a hot breakfast and clean sheets, and who ends up a cindered, unrecognizable corpse in a pyre of blazing wreckage. As a result, the most sophisticated war machines mankind has so far devised are sent into battle crewed for the most part by youngsters every bit as superstitious and fearful as painted savages padding through the jungle armed with nothing but a couple of sharp-pointed sticks.'

Blanding grimaced. 'And Summerfield?' he said. 'You say she was thought to be bad luck just because two men she'd been close to were killed?'

Palmer nodded. 'There's always one or two on most operational stations – girls to be liked and joked with, perhaps even taken to the cinema or a local dance on occasions, but not to become emotionally attached to.' He smiled grimly. 'Not if you value your life, that is.'

Blanding looked curiously across at him. 'Peter, you're a technical officer – a skilled engineer, up to date with all the latest wizardry. Surely you, of all people, don't believe such absolute damned balderdash?'

To his surprise, Palmer looked embarrassed. 'All I know,' he answered, colouring slightly, his eyes fixed on the ashtray as he stubbed out the remains of his cigarette, 'is that in the service you hear some mighty strange things from time to time – things don't appear to have any rational explanation and which can send the odd prickle up the spine. Anyway,' he added, looking up with a bashful grin, 'what was it that young Danish chap is supposed to have said? Something about there being more things in heaven and earth than are found in an RAF training manual!'

With a self-conscious laugh, the speaker pushed back his chair and began getting to his feet. Blanding did the same, and together the two men left the dining room. Having collected their greatcoats, gasmask satchels and Blanding's service cap from the duty orderly, they went outside to stand at the top of the front steps, looking away across the aerodrome towards the row of parked vehicles beyond A Flight hangars and the line of tiny figures still plodding across the open ploughland beyond the perimeter fence.

'Well,' sighed Palmer after a few moments, 'I'd better be shoving off, I suppose. There's the undercart of the kite that young lad Mackenzie managed to bog down last night needing to be stripped down and checked over.' He glanced round at Blanding, 'Oh, and that reminds me, Trott – be a good chap would you and see if you can hustle me along a couple of replacement machines as soon as possible. I'd like to have plenty of time to get them tuned up before the next show.'

'Next show!' exclaimed Blanding in dismay. 'Good God, Pete, but from what I've heard, I had thought the squadron was to be stood down!'

With a scornful laugh, Palmer began descending the steps to where his bicycle stood propped against the balustrade. 'I've told you before, my dear fellow,' he called back over his shoulder, 'whilst in the

48

air force, put not your trust in rumours nor yet in the tongues of the mighty, then verily you'll not be disappointed.' Slinging his gas-mask satchel around his neck, he pulled a crumpled forage cap from his coat pocket and adjusted it over his mass of white curls before bending to attach his bicycle-clips. Only when he'd mounted and was about to ride off did Blanding lean over and call down to him, 'Peter, what are the chances that someone here on the camp killed Summerfield?'

Obviously surprised by the question, Palmer raised his head and looked up at Blanding with a frown. 'Because of her reputation, you mean?'

'Yes – could some poor, misguided idiot have thought that he was chucking a Jonah overboard? You know what I mean – ridding us of the evil eye after this recent spate of heavy losses we've suffered?'

Palmer shook his head vigorously. 'No, I can't believe that – though there are plenty of odd crazies here on the camp, especially among the aircrews, there's no one absolutely off his head as far as I know.' He paused but then grimly added, 'But if you were right and it was indeed someone here on the station that attacked young Poppy, then God help him is all I can say! What is it the Good Book says? You, as a parson's son, ought to know. Isn't it something about it being better if he had never been born or that a mill stone had tied round his neck and he'd been chucked into the sea?'

So saying, Palmer began riding away, giving a parting wave back over his shoulder as he went. From beneath the lip of the portico, Blanding watched him go. Through the watery sunlight beyond, a multitude of similarly blue-clad figures were now moving about the camp on bicycle or on foot. On the breeze came the familiar cough and splutter of an aero-engine being started. As Blanding descended the steps and began walking thoughtfully back towards his office, the sound became a growling roar, rapidly increasing in volume as, one after the other, all four of the Lancaster's motors fired and burst into thunderous life.

CHAPTER THREE

Even without the distant roar of aero-engines being run up and tested, it was clear that the workaday life of RAF Frampton Wissey was beginning as usual. The routines of an operational bomber station were, in many ways, as fixed and inviolable as those of a medieval monastery, its inhabitants' lives being directed by rules every bit as strict and all-embracing as those laid down by the Blessed Benedict. However unusual it might, therefore, be to have police cars and a civilian ambulance out on the aerodrome, and whatever rumours and emotions were being stoked by the sight of the head-bent figures combing the ploughland beyond the perimeter fence, hundreds of personnel were now pouring from various billets and mess halls to take up their allocated tasks in hangars, workshops, offices and stores in accordance with King's Regulations, not to mention camp standing orders and the host of minor directives emanating almost daily from the adjutant's office.

As the author of the last category strolled back along the edge of the central camp road, his mind remained occupied with what Palmer had said about the dead Waaf's ominous reputation. Still considering the possible implications of Corporal Summerfield having been regarded as a 'chop girl', Blanding walked on as a succession of vehicles passed by: delivery lorries with provisions for cookhouses and bakery; road tankers laden with high octane petrol; heavy eight-wheeled trucks, red flags fluttering front and rear, heading out towards the semi-subterranean bomb-pits that lay scattered like prehistoric long-barrows at the far side of the airfield.

Pausing on the pavement, Blanding waited as a small convoy of Queen Mary type low-loaders rumbled by, carrying complete sets of propellers and replacement wings. Somewhat surprised at the amount of equipment being delivered, he crossed over to the administration block. Within the single-storied building, there was the same bustle of activity as outside, although in more muted form: a constant tread of feet along linoleum-floored passageways, an

50

incessant ringing of telephones and the muffled background clatter of typewriters penetrating the thin, prefabricated walls. Conscious of the amount of work awaiting him, Blanding strode along the central corridor until, passing the frosted-glass panes of the main records office, he glimpsed the ghostly forms of a group of female clerks whispering together among the filing-cabinets.

The sight checked him and he paused, peering in at the dim huddle of silhouettes. It was only too easy to guess the subject of the girls' conversation. The first rumours of what had happened to June Summerfield would have reached the Waafery, a requisitioned Georgian manor house just a mile or so from the camp at the nearer end of the village, a couple of hours before. The news would have spread round the building like wildfire, striking horror and fear into its over two hundred inhabitants as they woke to learn that some brutal attacker had violated their tightly-regulated world, pouncing out of the night to half-strip and beat to death a popular, pretty young corporal from the wireless section.

Wondering for the first time why Summerfield had contravened standing orders by apparently illegally creeping out of the sealed aerodrome after dark to take a shortcut back across the fields, Blanding turned away and walked thoughtfully on towards his office. Hardly, however, had he arrived and taken his place at his desk when his meditations were interrupted by the entrance of his senior clerk, bearing a thick wad of papers and files beneath his arm. 'Good morning, Mr Starling,' he said, ruefully eyeing the bundle the NCO was carrying. 'I see you've again brought plenty to occupy me as usual.'

'I'm afraid so, sir.' The grey-haired warrant officer laid his burden on the desk, then bent over it to separate a ribbon-tied collection of personal record files from the rest. 'The crew of H-Harry,' he explained, placing them immediately in front of Blanding,

'Ah, yes, of course.' Blanding absently tapped the small pile of blue folders. 'There's no news of the aircraft, I take it? Nothing at all from Group? No sightings or reports of radio messages received? No word from air-sea rescue?'

The clerk shook his head. 'I'm afraid not, sir.'

'Well,' sighed Blanding with a glance at his watch, 'that seems pretty straightforward then.' Taking out his pen, he wrote the word *Missing* on the front cover of each of the files, adding his signature and the date beneath. 'Right,' he said, 'you'd better phone the names and numbers of those concerned through to the Air Ministry straight away.'

'Very good, sir.'

For a moment, Blanding remained looking down at the files, each decorated with the eagle emblem and air-force motto, all appearing almost as virginally clean as when they and their human subjects had originally arrived on the station. During the murderous cull of aircrews over the last five months this brief little formality between his chief clerk and himself had become almost routine. Now, however, whether from lack of sleep or the shock of the early morning's gruesome discovery, he seemed to have a sudden vision of the process his signature had set in motion. In little more than a couple of hours or so, seven telegram-boys would arrive at seven different doors, the sight of the small yellow envelope in the outstretched hand striking a chill into the hearts of those who answered the long-dreaded knock or ring, and then trembling fingers would tear open the flap to read the same brief message of formal regret. For each recipient and for all those emotionally attached to the missing crew, the process would then continue its inevitable course: the initial searing pain being followed by the long drawn-out agony of waiting for news – days, weeks, even months crawling by without even knowing if the loved one were alive or dead, whether he were safely a prisoner-of-war, or merely another barely recognizable body buried in an obscure foreign graveyard – either that, or a frozen corpse drifting in a waterlogged dinghy somewhere out in the North Sea. Blanding closed his eyes. At least, he thought, if nothing else, the similarly shattering blow about to fall on Corporal Summerfield's family would be mercifully swift and certain, with no lingering hopes to prolong and intensify their suffering.

'Right,' he said brusquely, handing the files back to the chief clerk, 'have all these duly stamped and returned to Uxbridge. The rest of this bumf,' he continued, pulling the heap of remaining folders and papers towards him, 'is mostly routine, I take it?'

'I'm afraid there's another letter from the Reverend Rose, sir. This time it's an old lady dying in one of the farm cottages out beyond the main runway.' A barely perceptible smile softened the NCO's somewhat hatchet-like features. 'He wonders if the pilots might fly as quietly as possible over the house.'

'Oh really!' Blanding gave a weary sigh. He'd have to write something to appease the rector, he supposed – the old boy, after all, had prevailed upon a reluctant parochial church council to allocate some of the already scarce graveyard space for RAF use. Anyway, as he told himself, despite Palmer's gloomy warning, there was every chance of the station being stood down for a while. If so, then the Reverend Rose's aged parishioner might be allowed to depart this life without the incessant roar of aircraft in her ears or having fragments of ceiling plaster flaking down onto her face as a succession of heavily-laden bombers thundered low overhead on maximum boost. 'All right, Mr Starling,' he said, reaching over for the first of the day's disciplinary folders, 'I'll find time to pen the rector a short note.'

The clerk cleared his throat and coughed respectfully. 'What about Corporal Summerfield's records file, sir? I thought you'd want it to hand in case the civilian police wish to go through it.'

'Quite right.' Blanding nodded, wondering why such an obvious idea hadn't occurred to himself. 'Have it brought in to me just as soon as you can. Yes, and that reminds me,' he added, 'doubtless Summerfield would have shared a room at the Waafery. I think it therefore best that her personal effects are immediately removed and brought over here to the camp for storage. Please ring the chaplaincy and present my complements to the padre. Ask him to take a couple of the service police and get the job done straight away.'

'Very good, sir.' Starling went to the door. Once there, however, he paused. 'One last thing, sir – when would it be convenient for the new desk to be brought in?'

'New desk?'

'Yes, sir – the CO rang just before you arrived to say your assistant would be taking up her duties this afternoon.'

'What's that?' Blanding stared incredulously at the clerk. 'Assistant, you say?' Suddenly recalling the conversation with Chesterton at the foot of the control tower steps in the early morning and remembering his vague promise of additional help, he recovered his composure. 'I see,' he said with a frown, 'and this assistant I'm to be given? From what you say, I gather it's a woman.'

'That's correct, sir – Section Officer Taylor. She was posted here only last week.'

'Yes, indeed: from Holme-on-Spalding-Moor, I believe,' murmured Blanding, remembering the rather sour-faced redhead who had been conducting the debriefing of D-Dog's crew. 'Well,' he added coldly, turning to the first of the disciplinary folders, 'thank you for informing me.'

53

'And the desk, sir?'

Blanding shrugged. 'Whenever you think best, Mr Starling – I leave the matter entirely to you.'

After the clerk's departure, Blanding read the squadron commander's short, hand-written note affixed to the cover of Flight Sergeant Mackenzie's file. This done, he sat back and, removing his spectacles, began carefully cleaning the lenses with his handkerchief. Despite Chesterton's concern for his wellbeing, with the present lack of manpower and the continuing expansion of Bomber Command, he hadn't expected anything to be done about the matter of an assistant in the short term at least. That the CO had acted so promptly he found surprising, especially so soon after the devastating shock of coming across the Waaf's dead body. Nevertheless, touched though he was by his superior's thoughtfulness, Blanding didn't exactly rejoice at the thought of his new helper. Until now, the adjutant's office had been entirely his domain, and despite the obvious attraction of having at least some of the crushing workload lifted from his shoulders, he far from welcomed the idea of sharing it with anybody, let alone the rather disagreeable-looking young woman he'd seen earlier – especially, he thought gloomily, as she was bound to feel aggrieved at being transferred from her specialised work in the intelligence section to the humdrum daily drudgery of station administration.

The drumming roar of a Lancaster passing overhead brought his mind back to his duties. Thrusting Section Officer Taylor from his thoughts, he replaced his glasses and, opening Sergeant Mackenzie's file, bent to the task of reading through the young Scotsman's decidedly dismal operational record.

Having undertaken the usual first couple of sorties as a 'dickey' or second pilot, the twenty-year-old Andrew Mackenzie had been appointed skipper of the – in the circumstances – rather inappropriately named A-Able. Since then, after a couple of successful 'gardening' or mine-laying trips off the Friesian Islands, the quiet, unassuming son of a remote Tayside manse had somehow contrived to chalk up an unprecedented record of two 'boomerangs' or early returns in a row. The first time he'd apparently aborted his mission with an unaccountable magneto drop in both starboard engines; on the second occasion he'd high-tailed it for home with a malfunctioning hydraulic system. And now, taxiing out to the runway the previous evening, he'd allowed one wheel of A-Able to stray off the peri-track, bogging the heavily-loaded bomber down into the soft earth, and thus dangerously delaying the take-off of the aircraft lining up behind his own. As a result, he'd immediately been placed under open arrest by Wing Commander Birdie and his papers forwarded as an LMF suspect. If a board of inquiry upheld the charge, it meant the stripping of the young pilot's wings and badges of rank, and his transfer to another camp for latrine cleaning and other such menial, demeaning tasks – either that, or being sent on what was euphemistically termed as an 'Aircrew Refresher Course' at either Sheffield, Bournemouth or Brighton, where the so-called 'Lack of Moral Fibre' would hopefully be remedied by a rigorous diet of non-stop physical exercise and parade-ground drill.

"Keen as mustard - a conscientious and careful pilot, though perhaps rather lacking in self-confidence." Blanding glanced through the OTU chief flying instructor's comments, then sat and considered for a moment. Whatever sympathy he might or might not feel for a fellow child of the cloth, one bad apple, he knew, could quickly rot general aircrew morale, and, just as in the matter of removing a missing crew member's possessions, what had to be done were best done quickly. Without further ado therefore, he checked the CO's diary and then penned a note to Warrant Officer Dawson, requesting the attendance of Sergeant Mackenzie, along with his navigator and flight engineer the following afternoon at a station commander's board of inquiry.

The next disciplinary matter was pure routine: the local police had been called to break up a fight between one of the station airman and a minor Government employee in one of the village pubs – a conflict which resulted in the civilian concerned receiving treatment at the local cottage hospital. After skimming over the depressingly familiar details, Blanding wrote a further note to Dawson, ordering the man concerned to appear on defaulters' parade first thing next morning. As he did so, a Waaf clerk knocked and entered with a bundle of requisition forms and travel warrants requiring his signature.

'Just drop them in the tray, would you,' he murmured, turning his attention to a service police report detailing the latest incident concerning station coal stocks. Yet again the padlock on the store had apparently been forced and a sizeable amount of the scarce fuel 'liberated'.

'Excuse me, sir, but I've also got Corporal Summerfield's

records for you.'

'Ah, have you? Good!' Blanding blinked up at the pale-faced young Waaf, noticing with embarrassment that she'd recently been crying. 'Just drop the file there for now,' he murmured gruffly, nodding towards a space on the desk. Wondering if she'd been a particular friend of Summerfield, he began writing out his severest memorandum yet on the subject of coal. Finishing it, he dropped the paper into the typing tray and sat back in his chair. Before him lay the dead Waaf's personal record file, as clean and pristine as those of the crew of H-Harry. He gazed at it for a moment, then despite the mound of work still waiting to be got through, reached over and drew it towards him.

Immediately he lifted the front cover he found himself looking down at June Summerfield's face for the second time that day. Now, however, instead of the bloodstained, marble-still features turned away and half hidden beneath the mittened hand, the girl's living face looked directly up into his own from the small passport-sized photograph stapled to the upper right corner of the initial recruitment form. For a few seconds, he gazed down at her attractive features, so vibrant with life and apparently innocuous, feeling less able now than ever to credit Palmer's idea that the young woman in the picture had been regarded as a *femme fatale* – or 'chop girl' as the typically brutal RAF slang had it.

Glancing down the form to the details of next-of-kin, he made a note of her father's name, 'George Albert Summerfield', and then of the address, 'The Village Stores, Shefford, Bedfordshire'. This information he placed aside, ready for Chesterton's customary letter of condolence. He then turned back to the file and flicked on through the enclosed sheets, learning that Summerfield had obtained a School Leaving Certificate from Bedford Girls' Grammar School before joining the WAAF at the age of eighteen, and that, throughout her subsequent twenty-six month service career, her senior officers had without exception thought highly of her; also that she had passed out top of her class in basic training and qualified with distinction on her telegraphy course at the RAF wireless school in Blackpool.

He leafed on through the file until, suddenly pausing, he leaned forward and stared incredulously down at the page in front of him, seeing now at last why her name had rung a faint bell when he'd heard it from Dawson's lips. Before him, appended to the file, lay the girl's formal request to be considered for a commission, her

56

application endorsed and supported by both the head of her section and the 'Queen Bee', as the senior station Waaf officer was universally known – and there beneath, at the foot of the completed form, written by himself in red ink, appeared a date and the words: *Application withdrawn at applicant's own request.*

Another Lancaster rumbled low overhead, vibrating the metal window frames. Hardly conscious of the sound, Blanding continued to stare down at the typed sheet, a look of bewilderment on his face. According to the date, the application had been withdrawn less than two months before. Yet in that short time he had somehow contrived to forget the entire matter, including even the applicant's name. He couldn't understand it – his retention of detail had always been good, and even with the evidence of his own handwriting before him, it seemed impossible to believe that he'd ever seen this particular item of paperwork before. Obviously, as he told himself, what with the winter bombing campaign at its height, squadron losses mounting remorselessly and the general strain that he and everyone else on the station had been under at the time, it was not unnatural that one comparatively minor item should have slipped his mind. Nevertheless, so completely had he forgotten the matter that he experienced for a moment a tingle of something like fear at this unprecedented failure of memory.

Flipping back to the girl's photograph, he struggled in vain to remember ever having seeing her alive. At last giving up, he sat wondering what had caused the smiling, fresh-faced young woman in the photograph to change her mind about becoming a commissioned officer. Again, as out in the corridor earlier, he also asked himself why an apparently intelligent, trustworthy girl should have chosen to slip off camp during operations in clear breach of standing orders, and then had taken the additional risk of crossing the fields alone in the dark. Unable to think of a satisfactory answer to either question, he finally closed the file and, with an audible sigh, turned his attention to the latest hiccup in station laundry procedures.

Ten minutes later, the expected requisition order for the two replacement aircraft was delivered from the equipment officer. Remembering his promise to Palmer, Blanding immediately broke off what he was doing to phone Group headquarters and speak directly to the Head of Supply. He'd hardly replaced the receiver when there was a knock on the door and the CO entered, closely followed into the room by a thin-faced, gaunt-looking civilian in a limp brown suit, whose iron-grey hair, nicotine-stained moustache and generally doleful demeanour gave him somewhat the appearance of a rather down-at-heel shopkeeper or some local undertaker.

'Excuse the interruption, Alan,' said Chesterton as Blanding rose to his feet. 'This, Chief Inspector,' he continued, addressing his unlikely-looking companion, 'is Flight Lieutenant Blanding, our hard-working and quite invaluable station adjutant. Detective Chief Inspector Stanley,' he went on, turning back to address Blanding, 'has been placed in temporary charge of the investigation into Corporal Summerfield's death. I have told him you'll be happy to liaise with him and provide whatever facilities he and his team need.'

'Of course, sir. Very pleased to,' answered Blanding, eyeing the unlikely-looking investigator with misgivings. Obviously, he thought to himself, the Cambridgeshire Constabulary was suffering the same wartime manpower shortages as everyone else. Nevertheless, it seemed they weren't exactly rolling out the barrel over the matter of an obscure airwoman's death, placing in charge of the case some dried-up superannuated relic obviously brought back out of retirement and dusted down for the duration.

'Doubtless,' continued Chesterton, 'our own service police will be co-operating fully with the chief inspector and his team. I've already been in touch with the Provost Marshal's office, of course, and they've promised me that someone from the RAF special investigation branch will arrive tomorrow morning to oversee the service side of the inquiry. In the meantime, Alan, I want you to make yourself available to Chief Inspector Stanley and give him all the help he requires. That's partly the reason why I decided to appoint you an assistant.'

'I see – thank you, sir.'

During this short interchange, the elderly police officer had stood before the adjutant's desk, head tilted slightly to one side and for all the world like a creaky, old retainer respectfully awaiting his superiors' attention. Now, however, he stepped forward and picked up Summerfield's record folder. Blanding suppressed a tinge of annoyance. 'I notice,' said Stanley, raising a pair of surprisingly piercing pale blue eyes to Blanding's face, 'that you've already dug out the deceased's file.'

'I thought I should have it ready.'

'Good!' interposed Chesterton, nodding approvingly. 'You see, Chief Inspector,' he said, turning to his visitor with a slight smile, 'as I

58

told you, our adjutant here is very much on the ball. And that reminds me, Alan,' he resumed, turning back to Blanding, 'there's been nothing from Group so far regarding further operations. Obviously, I have informed Air Vice Marshal Harrison as to what has occurred, and I hope in the circumstances that the station will be at least temporarily stood down. If we are, I wish to address all off-duty male officers at twelve hundred hours in the mess bar. Please inform everyone concerned.'

'Very good, sir.'

'Right then, I'll leave the two of you to arrange things together.' Chesterton went over to the door. There he paused and turned back to face Stanley. 'Whenever you need to speak to me, Chief Inspector, I'm fully at your disposal, as is, I may add, every man and woman on this station.'

'Thank you, Group Captain.'

Chesterton looked past the policeman towards the window and the road outside. 'Find me the fellow who did it as fast as you can, Chief Inspector,' he burst out, distress working his face. 'Until the blighter is safely under lock and key, neither I or anyone else on the station will know any peace of mind.'

'We'll do our best, sir,' answered Stanley evenly. 'On that you can rest assured.'

Chesterton hesitated for a moment, but then turned and went out of the room, leaving Blanding facing the police officer across the desk. 'Please take a seat, Chief Inspector,' he said. 'I imagine you'll have quite a number of requests.'

'Not too many,' replied Stanley, pulling up a chair. 'All I need at present is a room and the use of a phone – that perhaps and a couple of desks and something to sit on.'

'Of course. I'll arrange for my chief clerk to put things in hand straight away. Just pass him a list of whatever you need.'

'Thank you. And now, Flight Lieutenant, perhaps you can tell me where can I find the deceased's personal effects.'

'Certainly.' Blanding smiled. 'In fact,' he said, 'I've already arranged for her things to be gathered up and stored here in the administration block.' Seeing a frown of disapproval rise in the other's face, he hesitated. 'I thought it best,' he added, 'as Corporal Summerfield would have been sharing a room at the Waafery, and I didn't want any items going astray.' He paused and then concluded rather lamely, 'It is, after all, standard RAF practice in the event of

59

death.'

'I see.' Stanley drew out a small notebook from an inside pocket and scribbled a few words. 'Now,' he continued, looking up, 'there's one other little matter you can perhaps help me with.'

'Yes, of course.' Blanding felt himself growing more tense and uncomfortable by the moment. There was something both in the policeman's manner and tone that gave him the feeling that he was the object of Stanley's cordial dislike.

'I understand,' went on Stanley, 'that air operations were being conducted from this station last night. If so, am I correct in believing that, for security reasons, the camp would have been sealed from mid-morning onwards, and that only you as adjutant or Group Captain Chesterton himself, could have authorized the departure of anyone during that time?'

'That's correct,' answered Blanding, somewhat surprised at the civilian's knowledge of Bomber Command procedure.

'And is it also true,' Stanley continued, 'that, for the same reasons, during operations all public telephone boxes are sealed, and that the only calls coming off the station would come through your own switchboard – and that, again without your express authorization, nobody could have rung out?'

'Yes.'

'Then perhaps you can tell me the exact time your telephone boxes were reopened this morning?'

Blanding nodded. 'That's easy,' he replied. 'I passed on the CO's orders for the camp to be unsealed at exactly 0532 hours. You'll find the time recorded in the station log. The service police would, therefore, have removed the locking straps from around the boxes shortly after that.'

'I see – so sometime just after half past five then.' Stanley made a further entry in his notebook.

'Why, if I might be allowed to ask,' said Blanding, intrigued by questions, 'are you so interested in our phones?'

'Because, Flight Lieutenant,' came the immediate answer, 'it seems that someone, either from one of the public phone boxes here on the camp or possibly from the kiosk down in the village, took the trouble to make an anonymous call to the local exchange, reporting the body and saying exactly where it was to be found.'

'Good God!' exclaimed Blanding incredulously. 'What time was this?'

60

Stanley consulted his notebook. 'At twenty-five to six.' He looked up and gave a dry smile. 'In other words,' he said, 'soon after the phone boxes here on the camp were unlocked and at almost exactly the same time as when Group Captain Chesterton's dog first drew his attention to what was lying just outside the perimeter fence.'

CHAPTER FOUR

As Group Captain Chesterton had so fervently hoped, the red scrambler phone in the ops building remained mercifully silent that morning, as did the pair of grey-painted Typex cypher machines in the communications room which, if an op were on, would now be hammering out coded details of targets, flight heights and courses, bomb, fuel loads and take-off times. Finally, just before eleven, a telephone call was received from Group Headquarters at Exning near Newmarket, officially congratulating the aircrew on their performance the previous night and standing the squadron down from operational flying for twenty-four hours.

Although this was not the indefinite stand-down longed for, the station immediately began to relax as the news spread. The bustle and noise gradually diminished in workshops and hangars, and all further flying was cancelled for the day. By the time Blanding set out to walk over to the officers' mess for the CO's midday meeting an unusual, siesta-like quietness had fallen over the camp, broken only by the raucous shouts and intermittent cheers from where an improvised game of football was in progress on the muddy patch of ground outside the NCO aircrew huts.

Reaching the point where the road forked off for the mess, Blanding paused to look out across the aerodrome. As forecast, the needle clamped to the slowly revolving drum of the barometer in its louvered white box on the control tower balcony had risen steadily since dawn, while overhead the sky had gradually cleared. For the first time in weeks, the expanse of runways and grass lay bathed in bright sunshine, and the large, tattered, grey windsock in front of the control tower barely stirred in a light southerly breeze. Out beyond the hangars and the parked aircraft of A Flight, the edge of the taxiway was once more empty of vehicles, while the dark ploughland behind the boundary fence stretched away, now equally bare of activity. Indeed, apart from a solitary Wolseley police car parked next to the guardroom and the RAF's blue ensign flying half-mast from the yardarm of the parade ground flagstaff, Blanding could see no external evidence whatever of the CO's horrific discovery of the early morning.

Turning on his heel, he strode on towards the mess. Nearing the building, he frowned to see a mass of bicycles piled untidily against the walls and pillars on either side of the porticoed entrance, much in the manner of those heaped around the porters' lodge of his old Oxford college. A feeling of enormous irritation swept over him at this blatant disregard of both station regulations and his own repeated memorandums on the subject of correct bicycle storage. Determined to deal with the matter before Chesterton's arrival, fists clenched, his anger rising, he hurried towards the front steps.

With every available male officer gathered to hear the CO's address, the mess foyer fairly teemed with uniformed figures, most sporting aircrew insignia on their chests and many wearing the name of one of the British dominions or of an enemy-occupied nation on their sleeves. Despite the evident relief at the temporary cessation of operations, it was immediately clear that everyone was very much affected by the fate of the young woman whose brutal death had occasioned this unusual gathering. There was none of the usual loud babble of talk and laughter in a variety of accents and languages – no ribald jokes, no rowdy horseplay. Permanent station officers and the cosmopolitan crowd of aircrew alike stood talking in grave, quiet groups, and an underlying sense of sadness pervaded the building – a feeling reinforced by a faint, ghostly rendering of *My Melancholy Baby* being played on a jazz trumpet behind the closed door of 'Fluff' Brewer's room overhead.

Often during the past months Blanding had marvelled at the capacity of the mainly youthful flyers to relax and enjoy every temporary reprieve from whichever of the various unpleasant deaths that statistically awaited approximately half of their number. Today, incensed though he was by the unsightly piles of bicycles outside, he couldn't help being touched by the gravity of these normally light-hearted youngsters, nearly all of whom had been risking their lives high over enemy territory just a few hours before. Torn as always between admiration for their courage and profound annoyance at their cavalier disregard of rules and regulations, he forced a passage between them. Having handed over his cap, coat and gasmask satchel to the duty orderly, he set off in search of the mess sergeant, a personage whose whereabouts habitually seemed to elude him.

'Ah, there you are, Tomkins!' he burst out, entering the latter's tiny cubicle a short while later. 'I've been hunting the entire confounded place for you!'

The white-jacketed NCO leapt up from puzzling over his bar-accounts, hastily stubbing out a cigarette as he did so. 'Yes, sir? Can I help?'

'Indeed you can – I want you immediately to detail a couple of men to move all the bicycles from the front of the building round to the racks at the side. You'll also instruct them to make a note of the serial number of each of the machines concerned, and then have the information passed to me.'

The initial look of surprise on the other's face transformed itself almost instantly into the same wooden blankness of expression that Warrant Officer Dawson's countenance had worn out on the airfield that morning whilst denying all knowledge of the illicit gap in the boundary fence. 'Move all the bicycles to the racks at the back of the building and pass all the serial numbers to you?' repeated the mess sergeant gravely. 'Very good, sir.'

Leaving the NCO to mutter darkly to himself over his scattered bar-receipts, Blanding made his way back through the throng in the corridor outside. Ahead, he spotted Wing Commander 'Batty' Kochanowski, the squat, balding captain of G-George's all-Polish crew. Trapped between the advancing German and Russian armies, Kochanowski had escaped from his homeland in 1939 with his wife and baby daughter in an antiquated biplane trainer to serve with the French Air Force. After the invasion and fall of France, he'd fled on to England and there joined the RAF, his exuberant personality, extraordinary courage and seemingly unappeasable zest for national revenge having survived double defeat, exile and, by now, almost five years of operational flying.

As usual, Kochanowski was in animated conversation with a group of fellow East Europeans, including the gangling Czech pilot of the Mosquito that had paused on the peri-track earlier. As Blanding endeavoured to squeeze past unnoticed, the Pole turned and eagerly sized his arm. 'Ah, dear Trott!' he exclaimed. 'My very good friend! You will help us, yes?' Thrusting his broad face close to the adjutant's, he continued, 'We like to know about this poor young lady the commandant found dead early this morning. The police, I think,

64

catch the one who did it soon?'

'I sincerely hope so, Wing Commander, but, of course, it's very early days yet.'

'But he *will* catch him, and then...' With a gleam in his eyes that matched his gold teeth, Kochanowski threw back his head and drew a stubby finger slowly across his throat, emitting a gargling croak as he did so.

'Quite,' murmured Blanding stiffly. 'After due process, of course.'

'Jew process?' The Pole looked confused. 'But they will be hanging him, yes?'

'Certainly – if, of course, he's found to be sane.' Excusing himself, Blanding hastily moved on, not wishing to embroil himself in a discussion of the niceties of legal sanity with one whose exuberant cry of 'So let's go kill Germans, gentlemen!' invariably closed pre-operational briefings at Frampton Wissey – someone who, from the evidence of the stray machine-gun holes in the belly of G-George and the lengths of balloon cable or telephone wire occasionally streaming from one of its wingtips after returning from a raid, apparently delighted in nothing so much as racing back across enemy territory at little more than roof-top height, with his gunners strafing searchlight and flak positions at suicidally close range.

Reaching the now crowded bar, he ordered a dry sherry. He'd hardly raised his head from signing the orderly's chit when he heard his name called. Looking round, he found Palmer pushing towards him, a pewter beer mug held above his head as he squeezed through the crush. 'Ah, there you are, Trott!' he said, eventually reaching Blanding. 'Nothing yet on either of those two replacement kites, I suppose?'

'Actually yes,' was the reply. 'I managed to speak to the head of supply. It's good news apparently: they're flying them here direct from the factory this afternoon.'

'Really! As quickly as that?' Palmer took a contemplative swig of his beer. 'Well, someone is obviously stirring themselves for some reason? I wonder what's in the air?' He took another rather thoughtful pull at his drink, then peered across the crowded room towards where Kelly and Chuck Fowler, the former's bomb-aimer, sat drinking alone together in the far corner. 'Come on,' he said, glancing at his watch, 'let's go and break the good news to our Aussie friends over there. From their faces, they both look as if they could do with a bit of cheering up.'

Reluctantly, Blanding followed Palmer over to where the two men, both wearing the lighter blue uniforms of the dominion air forces, sat facing each other across a low table littered with glasses. From their grim, unsmiling expressions, it seemed that the close shave with the night-fighter and the severe wounding of their navigator was still having its effect. He wasn't surprised, therefore, that neither man showed the slightest enthusiasm at the imminent arrival of their replacement aircraft. As Palmer announced the news, both continued to drink, staring down at the empty glasses on the table in front of them as if anxious to avoid his eyes. Although it was clear that the pair wished to be left alone, Blanding felt that, as station adjutant, it was incumbent on him to inquire after their injured crew member.

'According to the doc, Pete's still pretty crook,' Fowler replied almost tonelessly. 'He'd lost a hell of a lot of blood by the time we'd got down, and what, with the second big op he's just had, it's a toss-up whether the poor bastard will pull through.'

'I'm sorry to hear it,' murmured Blanding sympathetically. 'Anyway, I'll make it my duty to get over to see him as soon as I get the chance.'

'Really?' For the first time Pat Kelly looked up to meet the adjutant's eyes, his expression venomously cold. 'You are too kind, old boy!' he said, crudely mimicking and exaggerating Blanding's accent. 'Well, that should set poor old Pete up in no time, I don't bloody well think,' he continued, reverting to his customary manner of speech, 'having a visit from a stuffed-bloody-shirt of a barmy Pommy bastard like you!'

Taken utterly aback at this savage outburst, Blanding coloured. Before, however, he had chance to stumble out any sort of reply, a hush suddenly fell over the room. Turning round, he saw that Group Captain Chesterton had entered the bar, accompanied by Wing Commander Birdie and, as always, his heavily panting labrador.

'A trifle short on the social niceties!' repeated Blanding bitterly. 'Oh, come off it for God's sake, Peter!' he exclaimed, scowling across a table from which mess orderlies were busily removing the last of the lunch plates. 'The man was downright rude and you know it!'

'So what are you going to do?' asked Palmer with a grin. 'Call the chap out? What's it going to be then – boomerangs at dawn?'

Laughing, he took a sip of his coffee, but then lowering the cup, shook his head, his expression becoming suddenly serious. 'No, really, just forget it, Trott, for goodness' sake! Pat Kelly has always been very much your typical wild colonial boy, but there's no real malice in the fellow, I promise you. He's a decent enough sort for all his quite natural antipathy to authority, especially when it happens to be British. He just needs to be treated with kid gloves, that's all. Anyway,' he added, pausing to acknowledge a greeting from a couple of the station's civilian meteorologists who were leaving the next table in the company of a couple of Waafs, 'the poor chap's nerves obviously haven't settled down since that unfortunate brush with friend Jerry last night.'

'That may be,' answered Blanding coldly, 'but really, there's no excuse for gratuitous rudeness!'

'No excuse?' For a moment, Palmer leaned back and eyed his companion with a look of something like amused perplexity. Unbuttoning a pocket of his battledress blouse, he drew out his silver cigarette case. 'Presented to yours truly by dear old 149 Squadron when they were rotated on to Lakenheath,' he said, holding it up for the other's inspection. 'As you see, the chaps kindly had it specially inscribed.'

Wondering at this apparent abrupt change in the conversation, and with the memory of Kelly's rudeness still rankling, Blanding reluctantly leaned forward and began examining the design engraved on the lid. At first sight it appeared to be merely the ordinary RAF insignia and motto. Looking closer, however, he noticed that from the talons of the familiar eagle dangled a spanner and dripping oil-can, and on the motto scroll beneath, instead of the conventional *"per ardua ad astra"*, appeared the legend, *"per ardua ad nauseam"*.

'Very clever!' he murmured, smiling despite himself at the typically schoolboy-like humour. 'And very appropriate for you, Pete, with the amount of work you put in.'

'Appropriate for us all,' replied Palmer gravely, snapping the case open and then drawing out a cigarette. 'After the number of operations the past winter and the murderous culling the crews have undergone, one way or another we're all of us pretty well at the end of our own particular tethers. Now, with Poppy Summerfield's death coming on top of all that, I'd say there are quite a few on this station in need of a longish rest.' Pausing, he lit his cigarette and leaned back, meeting Blanding's eyes. 'And that,' he added, smiling sympathetically, 'includes even you, my dear good chap.'

Blanding frowned, but said nothing. Until now he'd never noticed just how nicotine-stained Palmer's fingers were; nor indeed the slight but distinct tremble of the hand that held the cigarette. Clearly, despite first appearances, even this apparently relaxed, easy-going man was suffering from the same high degree of nervous strain as everybody else.

'And if these last months have been hard enough for mere earthbound mortals like you and me,' continued the speaker, 'imagine then what it's been for the likes of Pat Kelly. Safe on the ground, we can only guess what the aircrew go through, setting off night after night, knowing that, chances are, one morning they won't be coming home. Under that strain, even the best can crack, especially towards the end of a tour when it seems that there's the chance that they might possibly survive after all.' The engineer paused to inhale. 'I remember,' he said, exhaling smoke through his nose, 'once finding an ex-Cranwell cadet from the same intake as myself, weeping uncontrollably because his pet mouse had just pegged it. Up to then, he'd flown forty-eight missions without apparently turning a hair, yet there he was, a well-respected senior flight commander with just a couple more ops to complete and with God knows how many ribbons on his chest, sobbing his heart out over a wretched dead mouse!' Palmer leaned forward and flicked a length of ash into the ashtray. 'Another time,' he went on, sitting back, 'I had another second-tour pilot come to my room and shake me awake at two in the morning to announce he'd received a heavenly visitation – the archangel Gabriel had apparently dropped by to announce his transfer to Coastal Command! I can see the poor devil now,' Palmer continued, 'sitting there on the end of my bed, telling me in all seriousness that the orders for his conversion course to Sunderland flying-boats were on their way to the Chief of Air Staff, endorsed apparently by no less a personage than the late Lord Baden-Powell.'

'God God!' exclaimed Blanding, genuinely horrified. 'Whatever did you do?'

'Congratulated him, of course,' answered his friend impassively. 'After all, the Sunderland's a mighty fine bus, safe and solid as the proverbial house, while the wretched Manchester the poor chap was condemned to fly was a virtual death-trap, what with those ghastly Vulture engines it had hardly power enough to lift the lousy crate much above ten thousand feet with a full bomb-load on board.'

'And what happened?'

Palmer shrugged. 'The inevitable, of course! Bought it over Cologne the following week in the first thousand raid – same show that finally did for my friend with the mouse.'

In the ensuing silence, the mournful sound of *My Melancholy Baby* resumed from the floor above. Blanding looked up at the ceiling and listened to the air traffic controller's playing for a few moments before turning back to his companion. 'You really think Kelly is cracking up then?' he asked.

'I'd guess so, yes,' answered Palmer, nodding. 'Didn't you see all those empty beer glasses lined up in front of him and Chuck, and that deadpan look in his eyes? The strain has simply gone on just a bit too long, I'd guess. Either that,' he added thoughtfully, 'or he's simply eating himself up with remorse, blaming himself for what happened to poor Ellis last night. As I say, Kelly's basically a warm-hearted sort of bloke, and he could well be thinking that he let his crew relax just a little too soon after re-crossing the Dutch coast and so not keeping quite as good a look-out as they might have done.'

Apart from the sound of crockery being cleared and the muffled tones of the trumpet overhead, there was a long silence before Blanding spoke.

'You may be right,' he answered. 'All the same, I still find his outburst inexplicable. Whatever else, I'd have thought Kelly to be the last person to crack up – he's always seemed an eminently tough-minded chap to me.' He paused, but then suddenly struck by a new idea, he looked earnestly across at Palmer. 'Peter,' he said, 'you don't think there could be anything other than that attack on his aircraft that's affecting him, do you?'

'Such as?'

'Corporal Summerfield's death perhaps.' Disregarding the other's look of surprise, Blanding continued. 'I'm merely wondering if they knew each other, that's all – though, of course, it's always possible I suppose that there might have been something between them both. Oh, I know,' he went on hurriedly before his listener could interrupt, 'what you said over breakfast about Summerfield's unfortunate reputation. All the same, she was an attractive girl, and being the sort of chap he is, it seems unlikely that someone like Kelly would have been put off by a mere bit of superstition.'

69

To his surprise, Palmer burst out laughing. 'I don't know if you know, Trott, but Kelly is a Roman Catholic. He regularly wears a St Christopher medallion round his neck, I hear. Apart from that, by all accounts he's a happily married man as well as a devoted father – apparently he always sticks a snapshot of his wife and young son on his instrument panel in the air. In fact, rumour has it he's faithfully promised his boy that he'll be back home in Brisbane for the kid's fourth birthday at the end of the year.' Pausing, Palmer suddenly frowned. 'Mind you though,' he resumed thoughtfully, 'now you come to mention it, I think that you might be partly right: the news about Poppy certainly won't have helped as I happen to know she was particularly chummy with D-Dog's crew. In fact, on a couple of occasions, I recall seeing her and a group of other Waafs playing darts with Kelly and his lads down at the Red Lion.' Palmer broke off and, stubbing out his cigarette, pushed back his chair. 'Anyway,' he said, getting to his feet, 'whatever it is that's eating our antipodean friend, I really must be off now. I've got to start having the guns and electronic gear stripped out of D-Dog ready for his new kite when it eventually decides to show up.'

Blanding remained sitting after Palmer had left. Like the majority of those gathered to hear the CO's address before lunch, he'd been mildly shocked at Chesterton's announcement that, at the request of the police all ranks, including officers, should hold themselves available for questioning during the initial investigation into Summerfield's death, and that nobody was to leave the camp without authorization. Now, however, after what Palmer had said about the psychological effects of operational flying, and having learnt from Chief Inspector Stanley that it was probable that the killer himself had telephoned to give the location of the girl's body to the authorities, he was suddenly struck by a new and terrible idea. It was just conceivable that one of the squadron aircrew might have attacked Summerfield in a moment of insanity sometime between briefing and take-off the previous evening, then returning hours later, bitterly regretting his deed, had phoned the local exchange soon after landing. After all, as he told himself, if the unremitting strain of operational flying could conjure up an archangel or reduce a decorated flight commander to weep over a dead mouse, then anything was possible - including perhaps demonic voices demanding the elimination of the station's so-called 'chop girl'.

Blanding grimaced. In the light of their sacrifices, the very

70

thought of one of the flyers being responsible for the Waaf's murder seemed almost blasphemous, and he hated himself for having even conceived the idea. Face clouded, he began to rise from the table.

'Excuse me, sir.' The mess waiter, the same pimply youth who'd been assisting at breakfast, approached him as he turned to leave. 'Here's the list you wanted.'

'List?' repeated Blanding angrily, gazing down at the incomprehensible columns of pencilled numbers on the paper he was handed. 'Good God, boy! What the devil are these now?'

'Bicycle numbers, sir.' Seeing the adjutant's blank look, the youth hurriedly added, 'They're from the mess sergeant, sir. You ordered the officers' bikes to be moved to the cycle racks and their numbers taken.'

At his words, Blanding remembered his earlier rage at the sight of the untidily stacked bicycles. Standing in the now almost deserted dining room with the pencilled list in his hand, a wave of horrified disbelief passed through him at the realization that, in less than two hours, he had completely forgotten his own instructions. 'Yes, of course,' he murmured, folding the paper and thrusting it into one of his tunic pockets, 'you're quite right – I did ask for these numbers. I'm sorry that I snapped at you like that. My mind, I am afraid, for the moment was occupied with something entirely different.'

CHAPTER FIVE

If anything, the mood of relaxation that had first made itself felt during the morning had deepened by the time Blanding left the mess. With what little wind there had been having now died away altogether and the general lack of activity around the station, Frampton Wissey's five hundred acres of requisitioned farmland had temporarily regained much of their original rural tranquillity. The football game outside the NCO aircrew quarters had long since finished, and with all ranks confined to camp, the players were now sleeping off lunch, reading, playing cards or writing letters to sweethearts, parents or friends. Apart from one or two figures moving along the cinder paths between the Nissen huts, the only signs of occupancy were the occasional thin streams of smoke rising vertically from the stovepipe chimneys protruding above their curved black-tarred roofs – that, and the faint plaintive tinkle of a Polish rear gunner's ukulele.

Beyond the huts, the airfield itself was enjoying similar peace. The parked bombers for the most part stood deserted and solitary on their pans of hard-standing distributed around the rim of the field, although one or two had ground engineers clambering over their wings or kneeling either side of the engine nacelles in a manner reminiscent of agricultural labourers thatching a rick. Reinforcing the pastoral mood, a blue-painted Fordson tractor was towing one of the Lancasters out to its distant dispersal position. Further away, another tractor was hauling a cluster of mowers across one of the grass-covered sectors between the pair of overlapping runways. The only actual flying activity in evidence was the station Anson communication aircraft ponderously waddling like some plump grey goose round the perimeter track, bound either on a navigational training exercise or some humble errand to one or other of 3 Group's half dozen similar stations.

Despite the peacefulness of the scene, and with this early first cutting of the grass – a hopeful sign that the winter bombing campaign was indeed at an end – Blanding remained troubled as he walked back towards his office. Following his failure to remember Corporal Summerfield's unaccountable decision to withdraw her application for a commission, his forgetfulness of his own instructions regarding the taking of the bicycle numbers had shaken him severely. All in all, he ruminated, what with the disproportional fury the sight of the unstacked bicycles had originally inspired, and then his subsequent complete amnesia regarding the matter, what Palmer had hinted appeared only too true: that the strain of the past months was indeed beginning to tell, and that, coming on top of a habitual lack of sleep and the unrelenting pressure of his duties, the shock of coming upon the girl's battered corpse had finally undermined his mental balance. In fact, the more he considered, the more it seemed that he was already well on the way to becoming indeed the 'barmy Pommy bastard' of Kelly's description.

Moodily, he strolled on. As things were going, he reflected gloomily as he paused opposite the administrative block, he could well be the next one offending others with savage outbursts of gratuitous rudeness or else boring them stiff with cranky talk of ley-lines, pyramidology and the Second Coming – or more likely, knowing himself, simply locking himself away like his unfortunate predecessor to compose reams of maudlin poetry with the aid of a whiskey bottle. Oppressed by these thoughts, he crossed the road and, pushing into the foyer, began heading along the central corridor towards his office. Suddenly remembering his new assistant, he found himself wondering when she might arrive. His speculations, however, were interrupted at that moment by the sight of a WAAF corporal seated on a folding-chair outside the room he'd allocated for the temporary use of the Cambridgeshire Police. She was a stocky, freckled-faced girl in her late teens or early twenties, bulkily clad in the brown overalls and leather jerkin of the airfield staff. As Blanding approached, she rose to attention.

'It's Jennings, isn't it?' he said, remembering her from the tour of inspection of the bomb-stores he'd made with Chesterton and the armament officer a fortnight before. At the time, she had been working in the fuze shed – the heavily sandbagged, metal-lined, low tunnel through which the convoys of bombs were towed on their trolleys to be armed before being loaded into the waiting aircraft.

73

'What on earth are you doing here?' he asked with a puzzled frown.

'It's the police, sir. They want to interview me because I shared a room with Poppy.' Blushing, the girl hastily corrected herself. 'Sorry, sir – I mean Corporal Summerfield.' She glanced at the door beside her. 'At the moment, they're talking to the officer in charge of the wireless section.'

'I see.' Impressed that Stanley had already begun his investigations, Blanding started to walk on, but then, thinking that he had been perhaps a trifle abrupt with the obviously upset girl, he turned back. 'I imagine this has been a terrible shock for you, Corporal,' he said. 'You and Summerfield were close, I suppose?'

'Well, in a way, sir, yes – although she tended to mix more with the girls in her own section.' The unexpected gentleness in the adjutant's voice had obviously affected the Waaf, for she gulped and lowered her face. 'Even now I can still hardly believe she's dead.'

'Quite.' Embarrassed, Blanding struggled in vain for some suitable words of consolation, wondering not for the first time how his stiff, rather chilly father had dealt with the inevitable bereavements among his parishioners. 'When did you see Summerfield last?' he asked as the girl, recovering herself, eventually again raised her head.

'Back in our room at the Waafery yesterday morning straight after breakfast, sir. She was packing up to go home.'

'To go home?' repeated Blanding incredulously. 'What the devil do you mean, girl, "go home" ?'

The abrupt change in his tone shocked the Waaf, and she looked at him in wide-eyed surprise. 'Poppy had a week's leave starting after coming off duty on Saturday evening,' she answered. 'She planned to spend it with her parents. You must know that, sir,' she added, sounding mildly reproachful. 'After all, it was you who signed her leave pass and travel warrant.'

'Did I?' Taken aback, Blanding glanced away down the empty corridor. Of course, all such documents had to cross his desk for final authorization, but what with the endless paperwork daily showering upon him from all sides, the signing of travel warrants and leave passes was a formality, something that he generally did without a second's thought. All the same, coming on top of his other recent lapses of memory, this third instance of forgetfulness troubled him. 'But I don't understand,' he said, turning back to the Waaf. 'You say Summerfield was packing up to go home on leave first thing yesterday

74

morning. But in heaven's name, why didn't she leave straight after work the day before, and what was she doing here on the station later in the next day, and why on earth should she have ended up creeping out unofficially through a hole in the fence some time during the night?'

'I'm sure I don't know, sir.'

The girl looked away, but not quite fast enough for Blanding to miss her expression. It was a look which, after years of schoolmastering, he knew only too well: the unmistakable shiftiness of eye and general embarrassment of someone with information to disclose, but who wished to hide it for the sake of some classmate or friend.

'Come on, Jennings,' he said, automatically adopting the same tone he had used a thousand times in the corridors and classrooms of Dulwich. 'What have you to tell me?' He paused. 'I should perhaps remind you, Corporal,' he resumed, his voice growing sharper, 'that this is a matter of murder. What reason might Summerfield have had for coming up to the station yesterday when she was officially on leave? And why, if she voluntarily chose to be here on the camp, should she later have illegally left it when operational flying was in progress?' He paused again, the obvious solution suddenly occurring to him. 'Would I be correct,' he said, 'in assuming that this was connected with some romantic attachment?'

Pink in the face, his victim shook her head. 'I really don't know, sir.'

'But you think it could have been? Am I to take it then that there was some special man in her life?'

With obvious reluctance, Jennings nodded. 'Yes, I think so, sir, but for some reason Poppy never mentioned him.'

'Really? Then how do you know she was seeing someone if she never told you so?'

'I don't know,' answered the girl unhappily. 'I just had the feeling, that's all. When I first knew her, Poppy was still grieving for a boy she'd been close to, a navigator who'd recently been shot down. But then, in these last months, she'd seemed so happy and serene, that I was certain she had found someone else.'

'Months?' Blanding's voice was now icy. 'Young woman, are you seriously asking me to believe,' he went on, his tone growing more schoolmasterish by the moment, 'that your roommate had been meeting some man regularly all that time, and that you really have no idea who it was?'

'I know it's hard to believe,' said the Waaf, growing bright red in the face, 'but it's true all the same, honestly, sir. For some reason, Poppy would never admit she was seeing anybody. She'd just laugh and change the subject whenever I pressed her. All I know is that sometimes she'd go away for an evening or a whole weekend when she wasn't on duty, then afterwards never say a word of where she'd been.'

Blanding was silent for a moment or two. 'All right, Corporal,' he said at last, certain that the girl was now voicing the truth, 'just make sure you tell all this to the police.'

'Yes, sir – of course, sir.'

'Very good, carry on then.'

Blanding walked thoughtfully on down the corridor, thinking to himself that his first instinct had been right after all: that Summerfield had indeed been involved with some man. But who had he been, and why had she been so careful to hide his name and to make sure the pair of them were never seen together around the camp? Could it have been Pat Kelly, whatever Palmer said about him being happily married and a devoted father? Australia was a long way off after all, and very likely D-Dog's skipper had not seen his wife and young son for a couple of years at least. Had Summerfield said nothing to her roommate because she was secretly seeing a married man, and thought that her roommate would disapprove of the liaison? Is that why she had stayed on the Waafery on the first evening of leave, and then had come up to the camp next day because, from the strong rumours of an impending raid, she'd guessed that her sweetheart would be flying that night and wished to join the usual crowd of well-wishers gathered beside the runway to wave the squadron off? Was it then, after D-Dog had finally roared away into the darkness, that she had slipped out through the gap in the fence, intending to go home and stay with her parents just a day later than she'd originally planned? Yet that didn't make sense either, he thought, for if that had been the case then surely she'd have wanted to wait to see her lover's aircraft landed safely before going home on leave. Anyway, the squadron had not begun taking off until nearly ten o'clock, and by the time it would have taken her to walk to the village and collect her luggage from the Waafery, it would have been well past eleven. There were no buses or any way of reaching the railway station by public transport at that hour, and even if she'd somehow managed to get a lift over to Ely to catch a late-night train, she still wouldn't have arrived at her parents' home until next day. What possible point, therefore, would there have been for leaving the aerodrome when her supposed sweetheart was still airborne, to say nothing of taking the risk of illicitly slipping out through the gap in the perimeter fence to take that fatal last walk across the dark fields alone?

Absorbed in his speculations, Blanding arrived at his office. As he opened the door, however, all thoughts of the dead girl's final movements vanished at once, and, reddening, he paused on the threshold, looking into the room in momentary confusion. During his absence, the promised desk had been carried in and placed at right-angles immediately adjacent to his own, and there, seated at it in front of him, head-bent over an open file, was the flame-haired Waaf intelligence officer who'd interrogated the crew of D-Dog.

Disconcerted, he remained in the doorway as the interloper looked up and then hurriedly rose to her feet. 'I'm Diana Taylor, sir,' she announced with a bright smile. 'I hope you don't mind,' she continued, following the new arrival's glance down to the folder lying open before her, 'but I saw Corporal Summerfield's service file on your desk, so I took the opportunity of having a quick glance through it whilst waiting for you to get back from lunch.'

'Indeed?' Frowning, Blanding entered and closed the door. He hung up his service cap, greatcoat and gas-mask satchel, taking his time so as to recover from the shock of finding his new assistant already ensconced – a likelihood that Corporal Jennings's revelations had driven from his mind just as completely as Kelly's rudeness had earlier done over the matter of the bicycles. Profoundly irritated by the woman's presumption in touching the file that Stanley had left for him to hand over to the officer from the special investigations branch who arrived the next day, and also by what he took as her implicit criticism of his late return from lunch, he turned back to face her. 'It's Mrs Taylor, isn't it?'

'Yes, sir, but please call me Diana.'

'Well, Mrs Taylor,' he continued icily, 'for the sake of the smooth running of this office and the efficient administration of the station in general, in future I wish nothing to be removed from my desk without my express authorization.'

The other's smile faded. Instead of apologizing as Blanding confidently expected her to do, Section Officer Taylor's face resumed the same sour, almost sulky look it had worn when he'd seen her debriefing Kelly's crew. Flicking the folder closed, she held it out. 'There!' she said. 'Do have it back then! Now, if you would kindly tell me my duties, I'd like to make a start.'

The dropping of the original 'sir' stung; so did the defiance in her tone. Nevertheless, conscious that she was a fellow officer, and that, whether either of them liked it or not, they somehow had to work together, saying nothing, Blanding went over to his desk. Hand still quivering with suppressed anger, he replaced the file in its original position, then taking his seat, surveyed the mass of papers awaiting his attention. Until that moment he'd hardly given a thought to what responsibilities he could usefully offload, and he was therefore temporarily at a loss as to what he could usefully give the woman to do. Uncomfortably aware of her eyes on him, tension increasing, he sat racking his brains for some task to occupy her. Mercifully, the answer suddenly came. 'Ah, yes,' he said, looking up with a sense of relief, 'as it happens, I do have a small job in mind for you.' Drawing from his tunic pocket the folded list the mess waiter had given him, he leaned forward and passed it across the adjoining desks. 'That's a list of bicycle numbers. I'd be grateful if you would track down the names of the officers to which they were issued, and then send each a short note, pointing out that their machine was left stacked against the front wall of the mess at midday in clear breach of standing orders. You'll please also remind them of the importance of correct bicycle storage.'

As he spoke, the cold look on Diana Taylor's face turned to one of bewildered incredulity. Seeing it, Blanding's tension came flooding back. 'I would remind you,' he said, his voice sharpening, 'that this war we're engaged in, Mrs Taylor, is only going to be won by absolute efficiency – and that demands strict adherence to all orders and rules, however pernickety or even unreasonable they might at first seem.'

'I see.'

Blanding felt himself growing decidedly hot round the collar. Had there, he wondered, been something supercilious in her tone? Although her expression appeared bland enough, there was, nevertheless, something about that rather wide mouth of hers and those greenish-grey eyes that gave him the uncomfortable impression that she was dangerously close to actually laughing aloud. Colour rising, he hurried on. 'As the vast majority of the personnel on this

78

station have been issued with bicycles, Mrs Taylor, I would have thought it was obvious to anyone of even moderate intelligence that they cannot be thrown down wherever people happen to...'

Voice suddenly trailing away, the speaker frowned, and then, turning in his chair, stared out through the window towards where, at that moment, a couple of service police were cycling slowly past in the direction of the guardroom, the pair whistling loudly as they went. As Blanding remained looking out after the gradually disappearing figures, she gazed bewilderedly across at his rapt profile. Finally, with the silence continuing and her superior obviously now lost in thought, Diana rose to her feet. 'Right then,' she said briskly, going over to the door, 'I'll go and fetch the bicycle issue list from the records office.'

'One moment please!'

Blanding had turned and was looking at her.

'Do you yourself use a bicycle, Mrs Taylor?'

'Yes, of course,' answered Diana, obviously surprised by the question. 'As you said yourself, nearly everyone does: it's the only reasonably quick way of getting about the camp.'

'Exactly so,' replied Blanding. 'Therefore, if for any reason you had to go across the airfield, to say nothing of taking a short cut from there back down to the village, you'd use your bicycle, would you not?'

'Yes, definitely – it's a long walk.'

Blanding nodded. 'Right, in that case,' he said, 'I have an additional task for you: when you're going through the bicycle issue list, first check to see if Corporal Summerfield was issued with a machine.'

'Summerfield?'

'Yes, that's right – if she had the use of a bike, I want you to find out its service and serial number, and then phone them through to the orderly officer. Instruct him to have the service police start tracking it down immediately. Also tell him that, if they find it, the machine is not to be touched on any account, but placed under guard and the matter reported directly to me.'

Almost at the same moment when it occurred to Blanding that Corporal Summerfield's bicycle should have been found lying somewhere in the vicinity of her body and that its absence added to the mystery of her death, a brand new Lancaster, naked as yet of squadron letters and with its turrets empty of guns, lifted from the runway of Armstrong-Whitworth's factory at Baginton, south of

Coventry where the Mark 2's were being assembled under licence. Banking over the blackened, flame-scorched ruins of the medieval heart of the city and the cathedral like some avenging dark angel, the black-painted bomber set course and growled away eastwards. Less than an hour later, as the faraway drone of its engines began to tinge the mid-afternoon quiet, the person whose telephone call had summoned this first of Frampton Wissey's two replacement aircraft raised his head and listened. With the sound of the approaching machine growing steadily stronger, he turned and glanced surreptitiously across at the figure sitting at right angles and disturbingly close to him at the pair of adjoining desks.

Having now traced the number of Summerfield's bicycle and phoned it through to the orderly room, Diana sat again bowed over the bicycle issue-list, combing down through the long columns of names. The light from the window fell across her hair, irradiating and highlighting its fiery-red tincture. As Blanding continued to regard her, his eye caught the gleam of the pair of rings on her left hand. Who and where was her husband, he wondered, and what had brought her to this obscure fenland aerodrome? Why exchange one of the prestigious northern bomber groups for Air Vice Marshal Harrison's decidedly Cinderella-ish 3 Group, with its dangerously outdated Stirlings and the lower-ceilinged, Hercules-powered version of the world-famous Lancaster – the two aircraft between them producing an even slightly higher than normal loss-rate among their long-suffering aircrews?

The crunch of marching feet and an NCO's shout from the roadway outside broke into his thoughts. Lowering his gaze, he returned to puzzling over the latest Air Ministry directive as a squad of airmen passed outside. Uncomfortably aware of his assistant's close presence, however, Blanding found himself unable to concentrate, and soon his mind returned to the question of her husband's identity. Most likely, he thought, he'd be another RAF officer, someone perhaps she'd met during her time at Holme-on-Spalding-Moor. If so, that could account not only for her transfer south but also for the sour look she'd worn when debriefing Kelly's crew, for in accordance with common practice, her previous CO might well have insisted on enforced separation immediately after nuptials had been celebrated, marriage between those serving on the same station being generally regarded as prejudicial to good order and discipline in a way that reasonably discreetly-conducted affairs were apparently not.

Any treasonable musings on the unfathomable working of the official mind on Blanding's part were forestalled at that moment by a brief knock on the door and the unexpected entrance of Chief Inspector Stanley, who was closely followed into the room by a ginger-haired, freckled-faced, rather horsy-looking young woman in police uniform. 'I'm sorry to disturb you, Flight Lieutenant,' said the grey-haired detective, 'but I'd like WPC Matthews here to start going through Corporal Summerfield's things. Your clerk tells me that the keys of the storage area are in your safekeeping.'

'Yes, indeed.' Extracting one of the many bunches of keys from the top drawer, Blanding turned to the adjacent desk. 'I'm sure, Mrs Taylor,' he said, addressing the occupant, 'you wouldn't mind breaking off work for a few minutes to show our visitors the way?'

'I'm sorry,' replied Diana, hardly glancing up, 'but as I haven't had chance yet to learn the layout of the administration block, I wouldn't be of much help to them, I'm afraid.'

Blanding felt himself redden. Momentarily lost for words, he stared at his assistant as she resumed checking down through the list of names. 'Ah, yes, of course,' he said, recollecting himself and hurriedly rising to his feet to cover his confusion. 'I was forgetting, Chief Inspector – my assistant is a new girl here at Frampton Wissey, I'm afraid, so I'd better come and show you the way myself.'

Proceeded by the policewoman, Stanley turned to leave. Pausing in the doorway, however, he looked back round at Blanding. 'I wonder, Flight Lieutenant,' he asked, 'if the lady officer might be allowed to accompany us all the same.'

'Section Officer Taylor, you mean?'

'Yes, if it's possible I'd like to have her with us. I think she could prove useful.'

'Indeed?' Frowning, Blanding turned to look back at Diana, who by this time had raised her head to face the figures gathered at the door. 'Well, in that case, Mrs Taylor,' he said to her coldly, 'you had better join us then. Now, I suppose, is as good a time as any to start learning your way about.'

With Stanley at his side and the two uniformed women following, Blanding conducted the small group through a maze of virtually identical passages, feeling an immense irritation at this interruption to his own and his assistant's duties. Mainly for the latter's benefit, he self-consciously announced the designated number of each section of corridor they passed through, while at the same time outlining the type of work being done in the various rooms, contriving all the while to sound absurdly to himself as if he were back at Dulwich, showing a bunch of new boys and their parents round the school house. Finally he halted outside a green metal door, on which was stencilled in red, OUT OF BOUNDS APART FROM AUTHORIZED PERSONNEL. Unlocking it with two separate keys, he opened the door and, reaching into the mothball-tainted darkness, groped for the row of light switches inside. 'Right,' he proclaimed, stepping aside to usher his companions into the now brightly-lit interior, 'welcome to the Glory Hole.'

'Glory Hole?' repeated Stanley, pausing in the doorway and peering in. 'It looks more like the blasted catacombs to me!'

In truth, there was a certain justice to the policeman's jaundiced remark. The long, narrow, concave interior was more like a section of curved tunnel than conventional storeroom, and with its airless, musty smell and the crude, wooden, bunk-like racks lining the sloping grey-painted metal walls on either side of a long central trestle-table, there was indeed something of the feel of a Roman necropolis about the bleak length of windowless space stretching beyond the door. Stuffed kitbags, battered cheap suitcases, cardboard boxes and respirator-bags lay in each of the labelled niches in place of shrunken cadavers and blackened bones. Dusty greatcoats and uniforms hung on coat-hangers along the front of the racks, half obscuring the stowage cavities behind, while the gold braid of flying insignias and cap-badges and tarnished gilt and silver buttons gleamed dully in the glare of the row of naked bulbs overhead.

'This is where we store everything either belonging to or issued to any dead or missing personnel,' announced Blanding, turning from securing the door behind them. 'Now, if you'll allow me to squeeze by, I believe I can quickly find what we're looking for.' Shouldering past the hanging garments, he led the way between the wide central table and the right-hand row of storage racks, brushing past the Number One best uniforms, caps and greatcoats of the crew of the unreturned H-Harry. After them came the still equally seemingly pristine items of clothing belonging to the twenty-one aircrew missing after the latest of the, as always, costly Berlin raids of five days before. Next to the last of these, two niches in from the end wall, he stopped before a label bearing the dead girl's name, rank and service number. In the alcove below were the usual small assortment

82

of battered cheap cases and stuffed canvas kitbags, while suspended from a hook at the front hung a wooden coat-hanger supporting a Waaf's Number One tunic and skirt.

Assisted by the two women, Blanding removed everything from the rack, spreading the items out on the table. While this continued, Stanley moved around the crowded space, fingering the hanging uniforms and peering up at the various labelled names on the racks, his expression and general demeanour as sombre and sorrowful as if he were examining the mutilated remains of those to whom the various items about him had originally belonged. 'Tell me, Flight Lieutenant,' he said, finally turning to look back across the table, 'what happens to all these things in here?'

'Well, first the padre and I, wearing our other hats of so-called appointments officers, normally go through them together. After we've separated private property from service issue, we glance at all letters, diaries and any other personal items to decide what to destroy and what to forward to the RAF's central depository at Colnebrooke for eventual return to next-of-kin.'

'For security reasons?'

Blanding nodded. 'In part, yes, but also, of course, to protect the feelings of the relatives of the person concerned. After all,' he added with a smile, 'we'd hardly want grieving parents confronted with a collection of saucy postcards or racy magazines, nor indeed a tearful widow to receive some indiscreet *billet doux* intended for one of our local barmaids.'

Not even a hint of an answering smile softened Stanley's cadaverous face. Indeed, if anything, the indefinable air of gloom that hung about the elderly detective seemed only to deepen at Blanding's well-intentioned attempt to lighten the atmosphere. Now once again, just as during their first meeting, the latter was acutely and uncomfortably conscious of being the object of the policeman's personal dislike.

Turning away, Stanley again briefly contemplated the array of laden storage racks and hanging uniforms before turning back to the trio across the table. 'I wonder, Miss,' he said, addressing Diana, 'if you would mind remaining and going through Corporal Summerfield's things with WPC Matthews here. You presumably know precisely what items of clothing the girl would originally have been issued with, and therefore you should be able to tell us exactly what is missing from among her things.'

'Yes, I'd be pleased to help,' answered Diana. 'But that is, of course,' she added, turning to look directly up into Blanding's face, 'only if Flight Lieutenant Blanding here feels able to spare me.'

Blanding met her mischievous grin with bewildered astonishment. Completely taken aback, colouring, he glanced away. 'That will be perfectly all right, Mrs Taylor,' he answered stiffly. 'As you know, the CO has instructed us all to give the chief inspector our fullest co-operation.'

'Good,' intruded Stanley, seemingly unconscious of this curious little interchange. 'Now, Matthews,' he continued briskly, addressing the policewoman, 'I think you know what's wanted: a full inventory of items. Put aside all notes, diaries, and any other such personal objects of the same sort, including any letters or postcards. Nothing, no matter how small, to be thrown away.'

Something of the stale, musty air of the storage room seemed to linger in the chief inspector's soul as he and Blanding returned through the maze of busy corridors. Tugging one drooping end of his moustache and with a more than usual melancholy in his lean, bony face, the detective walked in brooding silence, a shabby outsider in his crumbled brown suit among the blue-uniformed young male and female clerks who paused and stood aside to allow him and his equally unsmiling companion to pass.

Whatever dark thoughts had been stirred in Stanley's mind by Frampton Wissey's so-called 'Glory Hole', the frown on the face of the person beside him owed nothing, however, to the dismal sight of the dusty mementoes of the missing and dead, nor indeed to the pathetically small pile of Corporal Summerfield's possessions. Blanding's perplexity stemmed entirely from the living, from that teasing, mischievous grin his assistant had given him when turning to seek his permission to remain. Unexpected and completely unwarranted as it had been, it was, nevertheless, not so much the grin itself, but his own reaction to it that had shaken him most. Truth was as he now reluctantly admitted to himself, he'd rather enjoyed the ironic mockery in Diana's eyes – indeed, if truth be known, he'd had to struggle hard to prevent himself from actually smiling in response. Even worse, he now knew as a certainty what he'd been vainly trying to deny to himself for the last hour or more: that, despite himself, he was highly attracted by the independently minded, strong-willed young woman whom the CO had so innocently foisted upon him.

For Blanding, the position was horrifying. Section Officer Taylor was his subordinate; she was married; she was at least ten years younger than himself. Though to him each of these factors was a disqualification for any possible intimacy between them, it was the third, the difference in their ages, that rankled and worried him most. Having lived ever since coming down from university in worlds revolving around those far younger than himself, he was hypersensitively conscious of his comparatively advanced years. Being past forty, he was, in RAF terms, already an old man. As such, he felt his present position not only ludicrous, but potentially disastrous. If any inkling of his feelings became known, he'd become a public laughing-stock – a joke to everyone on the station, including almost certainly the young woman herself. Scowling at the very notion, he clenched his fists, resolving to crush, not only the feelings within him, but the slightest attempt at any future familiarity on Section Officer Taylor's part.

He and Stanley had just reached the door of the temporary police inquiry room, and the latter was turning aside to enter when Warrant Officer Starling appeared ahead, hurrying along the passageway towards them. 'Mr Blanding,' he called out as he spotted the adjutant, 'I was on my way to find you, sir. There's been a call from the guardroom. The service police have located Corporal Summerfield's bike.'

Chief Inspector Stanley's hand was already reaching for the handle of the door of the inquiry room as the words rang down the corridor. Checked by the announcement, he turned to listen as the clerk approached. 'I'm sorry to trouble you, sir,' resumed Starling, addressing Blanding as he reached him, 'but the men are waiting to know what to do. According to the instructions passed to them, the machine was not to be touched until you'd been personally informed.'

'Quite right.' Blanding glanced round at Stanley, but the policeman's face remained impassively grave. He turned back to Starling. 'And where precisely was the bicycle found?'

'Almost in the first place they looked, sir. It was in the racks outside the wireless section where Corporal Summerfield normally left it when on duty.' As if aware of his superior's discomfiture at the proximity of the civilian police officer, Starling now also glanced round at the chief inspector. Receiving, however, exactly the same neutral stare as Blanding had done, the NCO hurriedly turned back to the adjutant. 'So what shall I do, sir?' he asked. 'Instruct them to take it to the guardroom?'

Blanding shook his head. 'No, Mr Starling – tell the service police to leave it where it is for the time being, but to keep a guard posted on it. Inform them that either Chief Inspector Stanley here or I will give further instructions on the matter shortly. In the meantime, remind them that on no account is the bicycle to be touched.'

Waiting until the clerk was out of earshot before speaking, Blanding turned to address the policeman. 'I suppose,' he said, colouring slightly, 'that I ought to apologize for intruding into your territory, Chief Inspector. It merely occurred to me that any of our personnel returning to the village would normally be expected to use a bicycle. I therefore ordered a search to be made for Corporal Summerfield's machine, giving strict instructions as you just heard that, if found, it was not to be touched because of the possibility of fingerprints.'

'Whose fingerprints?'

Surprised by the question, Blanding coloured the more. 'I don't know,' he answered hesitatingly, 'the killer's, I suppose.' He paused. 'It's just possible that the person concerned might have brought the machine back onto the camp after the attack, perhaps in the hope of covering things up.'

'Covering things up?' Stanley's voice was dry as sawdust. 'Dumping the girl's body on an often-used shortcut route between the airfield and the village, then apparently ringing the telephone exchange to inform the authorities of its presence, doesn't exactly sound to me as if he was trying to cover things up to me – if anything, I'd have thought, the very contrary.'

Uncomfortably aware of a small bevy of Waaf typists watching them both through the corridor window opposite, Blanding looked down at his feet, feeling suddenly foolish. Confound the fellow, but Stanley was right, he thought: the notion of the murderer risking the guard patrols and actually coming on to the camp and wheeling Summerfield's bicycle back across the aerodrome to replace it in the racks outside the wireless section was plainly absurd, even if the man concerned could had known where the machine was normally left – and anyway, what possible point would there have been in returning the bike to its rack? 'Yes,' he murmured, raising his head to meet the policeman's eyes, 'I agree with you, Chief Inspector. As you imply, it's seems that, for whatever reason, Corporal Summerfield didn't use her machine when she left the camp.'

Stanley nodded. 'Yes, but all the same, your search for the bicycle was a good idea, and it's certainly an interesting question as to why the girl didn't choose to use it if she was indeed planning to return to the village last night.'

The unexpected note of approval in the policeman's voice came as a pleasant surprise. Now for the first time in their acquaintanceship, Blanding noticed what seemed like a slight warmth in the other's crooked smile.

'I wonder, Flight Lieutenant,' continued Stanley, reaching again for the door-handle, 'if I might possibly intrude on a little more of your valuable time. At this juncture, I feel that a short private chat between just the two of us might possibly prove extremely beneficial to my enquiries.'

CHAPTER SIX

'All right, Bob, leave off those witness reports for now and nip over to the guardroom. It looks like the service police have come across the girl's bicycle. See that it's placed under lock and key, ready for the fingerprint lads.'

As Stanley addressed the beefy, middle-aged plainclothes policeman who sat ponderously typing at the further of the pair of facing desks, Blanding looked about him with interest. Furnished with the same stark austerity as every other office on the station, everything in it – carpet, desks, chairs, metal filing-cabinets and anglepoise lamps – was standard RAF issue and thus replicated a hundred times over throughout the camp. Nevertheless, in their short occupancy, the Cambridgeshire Constabulary had somehow managed to set their mark upon the narrow, little ex-storeroom allocated for their use. Intangible though it was, the difference was there, and as he surveyed his surroundings, Blanding was reminded of visits before the war to foreign embassies to collect visas for his summer mountaineering expeditions, and of the curious sensation he'd always had on those occasions of stepping directly from one world into another and entering a territory with customs and assumptions alien to his own.

'Right, if you'd like to take a seat then.'

Stanley gestured towards the chair in front of the nearer desk, seating himself behind it as his detective sergeant heaved himself to his feet and then, taking a greasy-looking trilby hat from the top of one of the battered metal filing cabinets, disappeared out into the corridor. But instead of immediately commencing the interview, the chief inspector opened his desk drawer and drew out a battered old tobacco tin obviously utilized as an ashtray. He then felt round his pockets, producing and laying before him in turn a rather worn leather tobacco-pouch, a box of matches and a cigarette-rolling machine. 'So,' he began, bending to the task of packing the gadget, 'you've already had a word with the deceased's roommate, I understand.'

'With Corporal Jennings, yes,' answered Blanding, aware of addressing his remarks to Stanley's grey pate. 'I happened to meet her in the corridor when she was waiting to see you earlier this afternoon.'

'And what did you think?' Looking up, Stanley raised the tiny machine to his lips and licked along the length of protruding paper, his pale blue eyes fixed on Blanding's face. 'I mean,' he continued, rotating the miniature rollers to produce a thin, droopy, damp approximation of a cigarette, 'did you believe she really has no idea of the identity of the man Summerfield is meant to have been seeing?'

'Yes, I believed her.'

'Did you now.' A sceptical smile glided over the speaker's lips. 'Then perhaps,' he went on, leaning back to light his crude cigarette, 'you can enlighten me as to why a young women chose not to confide in her roommate over such an important matter as a boyfriend?'

'I don't know,' answered Blanding with a frown, 'but I suppose it possibly might have had something to do with her rather unfortunate reputation.'

'Reputation? Corporal Summerfield's reputation, you mean?' Sudden interest lit the elderly detective's face. 'I don't understand,' he said, eyeing the man opposite through a trail of smoke. 'According to your senior Waaf officer here and everyone else I've spoken to, she was a conscientious, intelligent and extremely popular young woman.' He gave a dry laugh. 'Indeed, a real angel by all accounts!'

'Angel perhaps,' answered Blanding, thinking again of that long-ago toppled statue in the Dorsetshire churchyard and of the smiling, attractive, open-faced girl looking out from the photograph appended to the front page of her records file, 'but a dark angel for all that, or so it would seem.'

'How do you mean?'

'An angel of death, Chief Inspector.' Feeling satisfaction at the effect of the phrase, Blanding quickly went on to recount what he had learnt over breakfast that morning from Palmer concerning the murdered Waaf's ominous reputation.

'Very interesting,' murmured Stanley as his visitor finished speaking. Pulling out his notebook, he jotted a few words in pencil. 'Nevertheless,' he said, again looking up, 'even if she was regarded as jinxed as you suggest, that still doesn't exactly explain why she should hide her boyfriend's name and keep the whole relationship secret from everyone, including even the girl she shared a room with.'

Turning to the window, Blanding gazed out at the parade ground where a squad of airmen was being drilled. As he watched the blue-coated figures moving in the jerky yet, at the same time, curiously elegant motions of the slow or funeral march, he found himself thinking again of Pat Kelly and of the crushed, almost beaten look on the Australian's face as he and his bomb-aimer had sat drinking together in the mess. 'I suppose,' he murmured, eyes still fixed on the distant marching figures, 'that Summerfield might have been seeing somebody she shouldn't have been.' He paused slightly. 'A married man for instance, someone whose name she was anxious to protect.'

'It's possible.' Stanley pondered a few moments. 'And yet,' he resumed, 'unless some love letters or something of the sort turn up among her things, apart from Corporal Jennings's intuition, is there any actual indication that she was involved with anyone at all?'

Blanding remained silent for a moment, but then, struck suddenly by a new idea, he burst out excitedly, 'Yes, but damn it, Chief Inspector, I think there just might be! Summerfield applied for a commission back in the autumn, but then, just a month or so ago, she withdrew her application without explanation – and until this moment, I really couldn't imagine why.'

'I don't understand,' said the policeman, frowning. 'Why should her deciding not to seek promotion have anything to do with a romantic liaison?'

'For the very simple reason,' came the immediate answer, 'that, with the exception of actively employed aircrew, taking commissioned rank invariably involves automatic transfer for all service personnel. Pursuing her application would have meant Summerfield being moved to another posting, and so having to leave behind whoever she was seeing.'

'I see.' Stanley scribbled again in his notebook and then sat a few moments meditatively smoking. 'You saw the body, Flight Lieutenant,' he said at last. 'I'd be interested to know what you thought.'

'About what?'

'The feet, for example. They were unmarked, completely clean apart from where they rested on the mud. What did you make of that?'

Blanding shrugged. 'That the poor girl was obviously attacked elsewhere, then subsequently carried to where she was found.'

'Yes, but carried from where? There was nothing discovered in the lean-to barn in the corner of the field: no sign of the missing clothing or whatever weapon was used, nor the slightest trace of a struggle.' Stretching across to his makeshift ashtray, Stanley stubbed out the now bedraggled remnants of his cigarette. 'Anyway,' he resumed, peeling a stray tobacco strand from his upper lip, 'wherever the attack took place, why lug a dead body all the way round the edge of a ploughed field to deposit it outside the airfield fence? A corpse, even that of a slim young woman like the deceased, is surprisingly heavy and awkward to carry. Why go to all that effort and also take the grave risk of being seen? One can understand a murderer taking pains to cover up his deed, but for him apparently to do the exact contrary doesn't appear to make sense at all.'

'Not unless,' answered Blanding thoughtfully, looking out again at the marching figures, 'that moving the body to such a prominent spot was some sort of gesture of remorse – an indication that the assailant perhaps never actually intended to kill the girl at all, and afterwards bitterly regretted his actions. That at least would fit with the telephone call made to the local exchange.' Breaking off, he sat furrowing his brow for a few seconds. 'Either that,' he resumed, still gazing fixedly out through the window, 'or, alternatively, it might have been the complete opposite, I suppose: that leaving the corpse beside the airfield and making the call were both acts of defiance, some sort of challenge to authority perhaps or even a macabre form of boast, rather like a cat dragging a dead sparrow back to deposit before its owner's door.'

'Either way, we're looking for some sort of madman then?'

'I would have thought so, yes,' replied Blanding, oppressed suddenly by the same dark thoughts that had occurred to him after hearing what Palmer had said over the lunch table about the physiological effects of operational flying. With over two hundred aircrew on the station, there seemed every chance that one of them had gone temporarily berserk – that some terrified youth, nerve-shattered and unhinged by his experiences over the Ruhr or Berlin, had somehow found the opportunity to attack June Summerfield sometime between briefing and take-off – presumably doing so in the insane belief that, by striking down the station chop girl, he was

91

ridding it of the person responsible for the recent much more grievous loss rate. If that was correct, then it necessarily followed that the half-stripping of the victim had been nothing more than a crude attempt to disguise the true nature of the attack. Conscious of the policeman's gaze fixed upon him, Blanding mentally went back over the known facts: the anonymous phone call; the girl's undisturbed underclothing; the moving of her body after death; the almost ritualistic way in which it had been left lying in a foetal position with the mittened left hand positioned over the forehead as if to protect the closed eyes. The more he considered, the more he began to be convinced that his first assumption had been in fact utterly wrong: that no violent sex-maniac was involved, and that the real cause of the murder was directly connected with the Waaf's curiously sinister reputation. If so, then it followed that the attacker was almost certainly a member of aircrew – though openly to volunteer such a horrendous suspicion to a mere civilian, police officer or not, was not something he'd willingly do.

'Well, Flight Lieutenant? Have you any other ideas you'd like to share?'

Blanding reluctantly raised his head. 'It's just conceivable, I suppose,' he said unhappily, 'that the killer never carried the corpse back towards the airfield at all. Rather, I wonder if he might have done the very reverse, in fact – attacked and killed the girl somewhere here on the camp itself, and then afterwards dumped her body outside the fence to make it look like the work of a passing stranger. That would, after all, explain why her bicycle was found still in its rack outside the wireless-room.'

'A nice idea,' answered Stanley with a tight-lipped smile. 'Unfortunately, however, there's one slight difficulty about it. There were no traces of cloth round the hole in the fence, nor indeed were there any cuts or scratches found on the deceased's head or legs. How could anybody have manhandled a half-naked corpse through that narrow gap without catching either the girl's tunic or his own clothing on one of the sharp wire ends? It would have been difficult enough, I'd have thought, to manoeuvre the body through without some part of it coming into contact with any of the cut strands in daylight with a firm surface underfoot – doing it on a pitch-black night whilst having to balance on greasy mud would be virtually impossible.'

Remembering how Dawson had to hold back the wire to allow him to pass through unscathed, and also how his shoes had skidded on the wet soil as he'd stepped out into the field, Blanding felt a huge surge of relief. 'I agree,' he burst out, nodding vigorously, 'it simply couldn't be done.' Relaxing, he leaned back in his chair. 'Then I take it, Chief Inspector,' he continued with a smile, 'that, if nothing else, we can at least safely assume that Corporal Summerfield wasn't actually killed here on the station?'

'Not unless,' replied the other dryly, 'there was more than one person involved – at least one to carry the corpse and another to hold back the wire.'

Smile disappearing, Blanding stared back at the speaker in scandalized surprise. 'Impossible!' he cried. 'The notion of even one of our men bludgeoning a Waaf to death is horrific enough; the idea that some gang or group was involved is absolutely out of the question!' He paused, but obtaining no response, burst out indignantly, 'Good God, Chief Inspector! May I remind you, this is an RAF camp, not the back streets of Glasgow or downtown Chicago!'

Stanley gave a slight smile but made no reply. From out on the parade ground there faintly echoed the barks of the drill corporal, while through the walls on either side came an almost constant clatter of typewriters and ringing of telephones. Finally, the policeman glanced at his watch. 'Well, Flight Lieutenant, this has all been most interesting, but now though you'll have to excuse me, I'm afraid. The autopsy is being conducted in Cambridge this afternoon, and I must get over there to receive the pathologist's report.'

'Of course.'

Still resentful at the notion that a group or even a couple of the station personnel might have been involved in the Waaf's murder – taking it, indeed, almost as a personal affront – Blanding rose to leave. He turned to the door, but then, struck by sudden idea, he paused and looked back at the still seated figure behind the desk. 'One little question, Chief Inspector – do we know yet when Summerfield was actually killed? Has the time of death been established?'

'Both your own medical officer and the police surgeon agree she died sometime yesterday evening, somewhere between ten and midnight. Of course, the pathologist may be able to give me a more accurate assessment.' Breaking off, Stanley crooked his head a little on one side and looked across at the figure beside the door with the merest hint of a smile. 'May I enquire, Flight Lieutenant,' he asked, 'if you have any special purpose or reason for wanting to know?'

'No, no,' answered Blanding evasively. 'I was merely being

93

curious, that's all.' He gave a slightly forced laugh. 'Well,' he said, opening the door, 'I'd better leave you to get off to Cambridge while I go and find out how things are progressing in my own quiet little corner of the war.'

Back in his own office, Blanding stared glassily down at the latest pile of group and ministry signals lying on his desk, mentally going back over the conversation with Stanley. Although in many ways, Corporal Summerfield's death seemed now even more mysterious and perplexing than ever, at least his fears that her murder had occurred on the camp and that one of the aircrew might have been responsible seemed to have proved groundless after all. As the detective had indicated, not only would it have been virtually impossible for anyone to have carried the body through the gap in the fence unaided without either scratching the girl's flesh or leaving traces of cloth on the sharp wire ends, but there was every likelihood that Summerfield had died well after the last of the Lancasters had taken off. If the original estimate of time of death was confirmed by the autopsy, then obviously none of those flying that night could possibly have been involved in her murder.

Thinking this brought Pat Kelly back to mind. With his rage at the fellow's rudeness long since cooled, Blanding now regretted having suggested that Summerfield might have been having an affair with a married man. Although according to Palmer, she and her friends had often socialized with the crew of D-Dog, there was not the slightest evidence that she and the aircraft's captain had been anything more than friends, and even to have indirectly hinted otherwise felt uncomfortably like a betrayal of a brother officer. Thinking this, he suddenly remembered the promise he'd made to Kelly and Chuck Fowler to inquire after the condition of their wounded compatriot, and partly to appease his conscience and partly from a sense of duty, he decided to telephone the RAF hospital at Ely at once for the latest medical report on Flying Officer Ellis.

Inevitably, the ward sister he was put through to was unwilling to say anything beyond that the patient was stable. Making clear his authority, Blanding insisted on speaking to a doctor. Overriding the nurse's protests, he was eventually put through to an exhausted-sounding senior registrar. Finally, having gleaned from him the information he wanted, he rang the officers' mess and had Kelly fetched to the phone.

'Yes?'

'Ah, is that you, Pat?' he said, adopting as breezy and informal a tone as he could muster. 'It's Alan Blanding here. I thought I should ring to tell you the good tidings. I've just been on the blower to the hospital about young Ellis. I'm happy to say that apparently there's been a great improvement in the last few hours. It seems he's got through a couple of ops, and there's now a better than even chance of him not only recovering, but of actually keeping his leg.'

There was silence for a moment, then Kelly's voice came down the phone, sounding oddly hollow and flat. 'That's good.'

'Well, he's still not yet out of danger remember,' resumed Blanding, disconcerted by what seemed a strangely lukewarm response, 'but at least he's relatively stable. Anyway, as soon as he's able to receive visitors, the hospital promises to give me a ring. When they do, I'll arrange for you and the rest of the crew to be able to get over to see him.'

'Right.' There was a slight pause, then, 'Thanks, mate.'

'Not at all, my dear fellow – only too pleased.'

Frowning, Blanding replaced the receiver. Though the confrontation between them had been got over, the Australian's curiously blank, lifeless tone of voice and apparent lack of enthusiasm at the news was disappointing to say the least – as was his failure to even acknowledge, let alone apologize for his extraordinary rude outburst before lunch. Had he been in love with Summerfield after all, Blanding wondered, and was he now mourning her, forcing himself to repress his grief because of his married state? Or was it simply, as Palmer suggested, that the near-fatal attack on his plane had profoundly affected an already battle-weary man? Either way, it seemed that Kelly was deeply depressed and thus in no mental condition to fly, and ought therefore to be at least temporarily grounded.

Blanding considered writing a note to Wing Commander Birdie to that effect. Knowing, however, how touchy the squadron commander could be about anything concerning his aircrews (there had been an extremely unpleasant reaction to an earlier note of his regarding the flyers' often quite deplorable standards of dress), he decided against it. Instead, turning his attention to the waiting pile of signals, he opened the topmost – an official ministry circular stressing the importance of all vehicles adhering to station speed limits. Hardly had he time to glance at it, however, before the door opened and Diana entered.

At the back of his mind, Blanding had been preparing himself for this meeting ever since leaving the Glory Hole. Determined to present as cold and offhand a front as possible, he hardly glanced up as she came in. 'Ah, good! There you are at last!' he exclaimed. 'Finished going through Summerfield's things, have you? Good! Well, in that case you'd better push on with sorting through those bicycle numbers if we're going to get those notes out to everyone concerned this evening.'

'Very good, sir.'

Perversely, though her response had been exactly what he thought he'd wanted, Blanding found her polite acquiescence disappointing. Determined to get on with his own paperwork, however, he carefully reread the first signal. Having scribbled a reminder to himself to have more traffic notices posted, he then turned to the second. Before opening it, however, he stole a furtive glance at Diana, who was now seated at her desk, combing down once again through the bicycle-issue list. Doing so, he felt his resolve weaken, and, inwardly cursing himself as a fool, self-consciously cleared his throat. 'I take it,' he remarked, 'that you found everything in order with Corporal Summerfield's things?'

Clearly surprised at the interruption, his new assistant looked up. 'Yes,' she answered, 'everything was as expected. Summerfield's service cap, greatcoat and respirator bag are missing, along with the skirt, stockings and shoes she'd have been wearing.'

'What about letters and diaries? Any of those?'

Diana shook her head. 'No diary, no – just some sort of jottings book filled with odd bits of poetry and prose. The only letters we found were a few rather scrappy notes from her mother and a postcard from a Waaf radio operator up at RAF Scampton that she apparently trained with at Blackpool.'

'None from any boyfriend then?' Blanding frowned. 'That suggests that if, as her roommate believes, there was some man currently in her life, she must have been in close contact with him – yet no one here on the station seems to know who he is.'

'Well, I suppose the pair of them could have been very discreet for some reason,' replied Diana. 'Or perhaps the man concerned doesn't belong to the air force at all – he could be a local civilian.'

Blanding considered. 'Yes, that's possible,' he answered, 'but who then would he be? With the military call-up, I wouldn't have thought there were many men left in this area of appropriate age.' He paused and then shook his head. 'No,' he went on, 'I'd guess that if she was seeing someone from off the camp, the chances are that he was an American – after all, this whole area is so heavily dotted over with their bases that it's often jokingly asserted that East Anglia is the newest state of the Union!'

'Yes,' answered Diana, 'but why in that case not tell her roommate? After all, having a Yank for a boyfriend is normally considered quite a feather in a girl's hat.'

'I suppose that's right,' murmured the other, nodding thoughtfully. 'As you say, if he's really one of our Atlantic cousins, then why all the mystery?'

This short interchange had somehow relieved the tension. Leaning back in his chair, Blanding folded his arms. 'So,' he said with a smile, 'you and WPC Matthews discovered nothing unusual then? Corporal Summerfield remains mysteriously ordinary, does she – a typical Waaf, indistinguishable from all the rest of our valiant young ladies in blue?'

A look of something very like irritation flashed across Diana's face. 'Not quite,' she replied somewhat curtly. 'Among her things we found a bundle of brass-rubbing impressions.'

'Brass rubbings?' repeated Blanding with surprise. He scratched his chin reflectively, 'Well, yes, I suppose that brass rubbing would be considered a fairly unusual off-duty pastime by the majority of our personnel. Mind you,' he continued, 'due to the predominance of the wool trade, East Anglia was once the richest region of England. As a result, it possesses some of the finest church buildings and ornamental tomb-tablets in the kingdom.' Aware suddenly that it sounded as if he were quoting verbatim from a local guidebook, he gave an embarrassed smile. 'Fact is,' he said, colouring, 'brass rubbing used to be a bit of a hobby of my own at one time. As a schoolmaster before the war, I quite often took parties of boys up to the Norwich area for brass-rubbing weekends.'

Diana raised her eyebrows in mock surprise. 'Really?' she said with an ironic smile. 'So you were a schoolmaster? Amazing! I should never have guessed!'

Somewhat to his own surprise, Blanding found himself laughing in response, and then went on to talk for a few minutes about his former life. His companion listened with apparent interest, but then, as he finally broke off, her face grew thoughtful. 'You know,' she said, 'I've an idea that those brass rubbings may be a clue to whoever Summerfield was seeing.'

'Really? Why?'

'Simple – when I looked through her file, Summerfield hadn't listed brass rubbing as one of her interests on her initial recruitment form. Apart from that, I found no unused sheets of paper or lumps of graphite among her things. With general wartime shortages, I imagine it's not easy to get hold of those sort of things these days, especially in a remote rural area like this. Therefore my guess is that she must have obtained them from somebody who has a stock of such materials from before the war, and that brass rubbing was something the two of them did together.'

Interesting though Blanding found the idea, there was no time for further discussion, for just at that moment there was a tap at the door and Warrant Officer Starling entered. 'Excuse me, sir,' he said, addressing Blanding, 'but the new aircrew replacements have just arrived – will you see them now?'

'Replacements?' repeated Blanding vaguely, his thoughts still on what Diana had just said about the rubbings.

'Yes, sir – the signal came in more than two hours ago.'

'Really?' Hurriedly, Blanding scrabbled among the heap of still unread messages on his desk. Finding the correct one, he scanned the brief details. 'Right then,' he said, looking up, 'if you'd kindly wheel them in, Mr Starling, we'd better see what we've been given.'

The group of young men who entered a few moments later seemed a typical novice or 'sprog' crew direct from the Lancaster 'finishing school' as the specialist final operational training unit was commonly known, although there was a far higher proportion of officers among them than normal, with half of the new arrivals commissioned instead of the usual one or two at most. All were in their late teens or early twenties, and despite a tediously long journey south from Yorkshire on grossly overcrowded and slow-moving trains, youthful enthusiasm shone in their faces. As they lined up before his desk, it felt to Blanding as if he were back at Dulwich, conducting a meeting between himself and a batch of newly appointed house prefects, all earnestly eager to please.

'Eight of you?' he remarked with surprise. Although the Lancaster Mark 2 had provision for a ventral or belly gunner, in all but the all-Canadian 6 Group the downward-pointing guns had long ago been removed, and crew numbers thus kept down to the standard

98

seven.

'Who's the odd man out?'

'Me, sir – Pilot Officer Martin.'

Noticing the navigator's winged badge on the youngster's tunic, Blanding immediately understood: he was the replacement for the wounded Ellis, and therefore almost certainly destined to make up Kelly's crew. 'Well, gentlemen, welcome to Frampton Wissey,' he said, smiling, 'though I'm afraid you arrive at a rather unusual time. At the moment, the civilian police are conducting an investigation into a serious matter concerning one of our Waafs. You'll doubtless hear the details soon enough. Apart from that, the station is on an twenty-four hours stand-down, and there is every chance of it being extended indefinitely.'

Looks of bewildered concern rose on the faces before him.

'As you doubtless know,' he continued, 'Bomber Command is due to pass into the control of General Eisenhower's staff in just a matter of days, and we're fairly confident that your squadron will be rested and re-equipped before the commencement of pre-invasion operations.'

'You mean, sir, we won't be flying operationally?'

'Not in the immediate future, I imagine.' Blanding looked along the row of young men, noticing the curious mixture of dismay and relief in their expressions. 'Anyway,' he resumed, 'transport will now convey you and your kit to your respective messes. Once you've been allocated your billets, you'll be taken to meet Wing Commander Birdie, your squadron CO.'

Coming to attention, the youngsters turned to leave. At the door, however, they paused, raising their heads to listen – through the late afternoon silence came a faint but growing growl of engines. 'Your own aircraft, gentlemen, I believe,' announced Blanding, 'the last one of our replacements flying in direct from the makers. If you hurry, you'll be in time to see her land.'

With an avuncular smile, he watched the group hasten out, eager as schoolboys to see the arriving bomber. As they disappeared, he looked round to find his assistant staring at the now empty doorway, and then, as he watched her, he saw her give what seemed like a shudder. 'Mrs Taylor, is everything all right?' he asked with concern. 'You appeared to shiver just then.'

Snatched from her reverie, Diana blushed and hastily turned back to perusing the bicycle issue-list. 'Sorry,' she replied with an evasive laugh, 'it was nothing – just someone walking on my grave.'

CHAPTER SEVEN

As if convulsed by a charge of electricity, the sleeper jerked from unconsciousness. With a terrified cry, he sat up in bed, sweeping the air before his face in an attempt to ward off the wolf that held him fast by the throat. Desperate to tear the slavering jaws from his neck, he flayed about wildly, toppling the bedside light and sending his alarm clock spinning to the floor.

The crash and splinter of glass brought Blanding to his senses. Recollecting where he was, he lowered his arms but remained sitting up, peering into the pitch-darkness of the blacked-out room and listening intently. There was not, however, the slightest sound, not even the usual companionable tick of the clock, and after a moment he collapsed back onto the pillow, his entire body drenched in sweat and his heart pounding. Shaken, he lay staring at the ceiling, wondering the cause of this horrific nightmare. Presumably, he told himself, it was the shock of the discovery of the girl's body the day before. Coming on top of weeks of overwork and fatigue, the sight of the corpse lying limp and motionless in the early morning light with its frozen grimace of horror had obviously affected his already strained nerves. For a full half-minute Blanding continued to lie gazing upwards as the residue of fear gradually seeped from him, and then, propping himself on an elbow, he leaned over and groped for the fallen lamp in the darkness. Righting it, he switched it on and, having put on his spectacles, found that his wristwatch showed that it was not yet quarter to two.

'God damn it!' he groaned aloud. Craning over, he despondently surveyed the fallen clock that lay face downwards on the floor amidst slivers of glass, knowing that with wartime shortages it would be difficult if not impossible to obtain a replacement. Although the window behind the blackout blind had been left slightly open and the radiator beside him felt stone cold to the touch, the little room seemed overpoweringly stuffy and hot. Now fully awake, he was sorely tempted to try to divert his mind with some reading. Remembering though that he was expected to appear alert and fresh at the CO's disciplinary parade that morning, he turned off the light and, snuggling back down under the blankets, determinedly closed his eyes.

Sleep proved impossible, however. Itching and sticky with perspiration, Blanding lay at the mercy of his circling thoughts. There was still that latest hiccup in the new station laundry procedure to clear up; the notices regarding station speed limits and the latest blackout regulations had yet to be posted – finally, in the afternoon, there was to be the inquiry into young Sergeant Mackenzie's series of early returns. Technical evidence would almost certainly be needed for that, and rack his brains as he might, he couldn't now remember if Palmer had been officially instructed to attend or not. On top of all that, the officer from the special investigations branch was due to arrive in the morning, and doubtless would be requiring one of the guest rooms for his stay. Had the station accommodation officer been informed, Blanding wondered? He profoundly hoped that he had – as it was, that wretched man Gilbert had been acerbic enough over dinner the previous evening about the arrival of eight replacement aircrew in late afternoon without the usual prior notice from the adjutant's office.

Goaded by the recollection of that particular conversation, Blanding rolled over to lie once more looking up towards the ceiling. Again, as so often of late, he feared that he was mentally cracking up. This was followed by the same painful thought that had tormented him previously: that the CO was already well acquainted with his recent lapses of memory and sudden outbursts of anger, and that the real reason for the appointment of Section Officer Taylor as his assistant had been his perceived inability to cope. The idea made him squirm. Half raising himself on the pillow, he stared into the darkness, terrified of failure and its consequences – ignominious transfer back to some glorified clerkship at the Air Ministry, or simply perhaps to be discharged as unfit for further duty and end up having to return to Dulwich before hostilities were over, an object of pity to boys and fellow members of staff alike. Mercifully, these torturing imaginings were interrupted that moment by a sudden sharp double bark from somewhere in the darkness outside, followed by a prolonged quavering howl.

So loud and close was the sound that Blanding sprang up in bed, immediately certain that this blood-curdling cry had prompted both his nightmare and terrible awakening a few minutes before. Some wretched dog was obviously loose about the station, he thought, baying the moon from sexual frustration or some unfathomable misery of a canine kind. As the barking resumed, Blanding tore off the blankets and scrambled from bed. Carefully avoiding the broken clock and the shattered glass, he blundered towards the window and lifted the blackout blind.

Despite the pale misty moonlight, the roadway outside was bathed in shadow. All that could be made out was the roof of the Naafi building opposite and the silhouette of the water tower behind. For a few moments, he remained gazing out into the night, wondering whose dog it was. Not prohibited by King's Regulations (it came under section '1845: Sanitation', he thought), there were plenty enough on the station, as many members of aircrew kept them, theoretically having obtained the CO's permission, as mascots or pets. Indeed, with Chesterton such a dog-lover himself and unwilling to refuse his permission or give up his own animal, it had been as much as Blanding could do to prevent his fellow officers from actually bringing their four-legged friends into the mess – his uncompromising stand over the matter adding to his general unpopularity and doing much to confirm his reputation as a pernickety, cold-hearted martinet.

Again, but now from a little further away, came the harsh double bark, followed by the same mournful howl as before. The dog sounded lost and miserable, and, as Blanding returned to bed, it occurred to him that it may have belonged to one of the crew of the unreturned H-Harry, and, being instinctively aware of its master's fate perhaps, was now broken-heartedly wandering the night, yowling its misery to the empty sky. If true, he thought as he snuggled down under the bedclothes, it might perhaps be a mercy to the unhappy animal (and certainly to everyone on the station) if someone could put the wretched creature out of its pain. Hardly had this thought struck him, when the double bark was again repeated somewhere close outside, followed by the familiar prolonged howl.

It was too much. Grieving pet or not, Blanding was determined to have some peace for what little remained of the night. Switching on the bedside light, he scrambled out onto the floor and, dressed only in his pyjamas, lurched through the interconnecting

103

door into his office. Going over to his desk, he rang straight through to the guardroom and spoke to the duty sergeant. 'Look, I don't care a tuppenny-damn how few men you've got!' he exploded. 'I'm not having some confounded cur kicking up a damned racket half the night! You'll kindly send a couple of pickets out to round it up this moment, and I'll have the name of its owner on my desk first thing in the morning.'

Having delivered himself of this, but still furious at the NCO's unaccountable reluctance to muster a search party, Blanding returned to the inner room, profoundly wishing now that he'd driven over to spend the night at his cottage as he'd originally planned. Glancing at the dishevelled bed, he felt loath to lie back down in the stuffy darkness. Instead, he decided to go outside for a breath of fresh air, at the same time perhaps attempting to capture the dog himself if the animal should venture his way. Pulling his greatcoat over his pyjamas and putting on his slippers, he passed back through the office and out into the corridor. Outside the door, however, he paused and considered for a moment before returning inside. Going over to the office safe, he unlocked it and took out the service revolver and the box of .38 ammunition always kept there. He loaded the gun and slipped it into his greatcoat pocket before again hurrying out into the corridor.

Along the dark passageway ahead, a faint ray of light shone from the glass-panelled door of the signals room. As he reached it, Blanding automatically glanced in to see the duty Waaf cipher clerk hunched at her desk beside the shadowy Typex machines, her features illuminated by the hooded gleam of a single anglepoise lamp. There was something about her slumped attitude and the look of desolation on her pale face that caught his attention, and, pausing, he continued to peer in through the glass at the bowed figure, certain he'd recently seen this particular girl before. Then suddenly it came to him where that had been: she'd been one of the pair of unauthorized spectators who'd slipped in to sit at the back of the operations room during the final stages of the wait for the two unreturned aircraft the previous morning – indeed, it had been her muffled sobbing that had so irritated the station CO.

Obviously, thought Blanding as he continued to gaze in, the poor girl been close to someone on board one of the overdue planes, and from her present expression it seemed clear that whoever it was must have belonged to the crew of the missing H-Harry. Not wishing to intrude on her grief, he turned and crept on down the deserted passageway, thinking as he went of the number of attachments there must inevitably have been over the years between various Waafs and different members of aircrew. How often, he wondered, had other young women waited in drizzling grey dawns for never-returning sweethearts or friends? Corporal Summerfield again came to mind – she'd lost two such men on flying operations, and yet had apparently suppressed her grief and uncomplainingly continued her duties as before, including presumably often taking her turn at night duty in that very signals room. The notion was strangely humbling, and Blanding suddenly found himself thinking, not only of the murdered girl but of all the other Waafs – drivers, flight mechanics, aircraft fuellers, armourers, parachute packers, batwomen, clerks, cooks and radio operators – whose cheerful demeanours and dedication to their work was so much taken for granted, and yet were so vital both to the morale as well as the efficiency of the station. With his mind thus occupied, he reached the unlocked side entrance to the administration block and stepped out into the early morning darkness.

Conscious of the weight of the revolver at his side and the chill of the dew-wet turf at his ankles, he began moving round the outside wall of the building, half expecting at any moment to come face to face with the dog that had disturbed him. There was no sight or sound of it, however, and emerging from the shadows at the back, he stopped and gazed out across the airfield, momentarily forgetting his search and his already damp feet.

As so often in this flat eastern landscape, sunset the previous evening had been spectacular: wide cloudless skies transforming by degrees through a sky-spanning blazing red down into deepening purple and on into final blackness. Such beauty had to be paid for, however. Within an hour of darkness, a rapid drop in ground temperature brought moisture smoking up from the fenland ditches and dykes to smother the entire region in a shallow, ground-clinging layer of radiation fog. This now stretched across the aerodrome, the hangers and control tower protruding island-like into the moonlight, and with the cockpits, dorsal turrets and the upper sides of the fuselages of the parked bombers peeping above the motionless vapour like the nostrils, eyes and backs of huge amphibian creatures wallowing in some primeval swamp.

After the stuffy closeness of his bedroom, the night felt

pleasantly cool. Glad to be outside, Blanding set off towards the dim shrouded shapes of the small collection of aircraft parked in front of B Flight hangars. Away through the mist came the muted chimes of the church clock. This was followed by a short faint burst of staccato barking away in the distance from some neighbouring farm. Expecting an answering bark from the dog that had disturbed him, the walker stopped and listened. There was no sound, however, and after a few moments he continued on towards the dark shapes of the Lancasters ahead.

Reaching the first, he paused beneath its nose, turning to look up at the crescent of light glowing through the mist. Although the term 'a bomber's moon' had been a common journalistic expression in the early war years, experience had soon proved that bright nights were much more the friend of the roving nightfighter than the clumsy, slow-flying bombers. Both the RAF and Luftwaffe had learnt to their cost that, without a strong escort of fighters, the bombers needed all the protection of darkness they could get, and now, with the development of electronically guided 'blind bombing' techniques, raids were no longer normally carried out during the main lunar passage. By tomorrow night, thought Blanding, gazing upwards with satisfaction, that strip of moon would be thicker and brighter still, and the light it cast, together with the clear skies of the anticyclone, was an almost certain guarantee against further operations for at least the next seven days – by which time Bomber Command would have passed into the overall control of General Eisenhower's invasion committee. There was, therefore, every chance that the Reverend Rose's aged parishioner would be allowed to depart this life in peace; also that Pat Kelly and the crew of D-Dog would have the time to rest and recover their shattered nerves after the near fatal attack on their aircraft; and that the enquiries into June Summerfield's death could continue without risk of the ordered routines of camp life being shattered by the clattering cipher machines' imperious call to arms.

A profound sense of well-being ran through Blanding at this thought. Moving further under the Lancaster's fuselage, he stretched up an arm to stroke its condensation-wet belly, running the palm of his hand along the smooth wet aluminium of the bomb-doors and then wiping his brow as if baptising himself with the ice-cool sweat of the shrouded warplane. Refreshed, he moved over to rest against one of the aircraft's huge canvas-shrouded wheels. Leaning back upon it, he gazed up through the faintly luminous mist towards the sickle moon. So tranquil was the scene, so magically lovely, that it was hard to believe that mankind was battling across half of the war-torn globe, nor indeed that, just twenty-four hours earlier, the station had been preparing to land back its homeward-bound bombers – and that, hours before the call-sign of the first had been received, one of the young female operators who normally would have sat crouched in the wireless room, listening out for the tapped-out recognition signals, had been savagely struck down and killed somewhere out in the dark fields between the camp and the village.

Folding his arms, Blanding relaxed against the curve of the huge tyre, feeling calmer and more at peace than for a long time. Above him, the moon shimmered down through the mist. Gazing up at that seeming bright talisman of peace, he thought suddenly of Diana Taylor's mischievous smile when she'd turned to him in the storage room, feeling as he did so none of the anxiety at what, at the time, had seemed like dangerous over-familiarity. On the contrary, folding his arms, he luxuriated in the memory. Volatile and unsettling as the woman was, he'd enjoyed her company immensely. Indeed, it was solely because of her he hadn't returned to his cottage that night, choosing instead to stay on in the mess after dinner and endure the accommodation officer's sardonic comments as well as boisterous games of Flare Path and what had seemed like interminable choruses of 'Here Comes the Muffin Man' echoing from the bar as the usual beer-drinking contests continued – all in the hope – vain as it turned out – that his new assistant might venture up from the Waafery for a pre-bedtime drink.

Once again, he found himself wondering who and where Diana's husband was, and the reason for her transfer south. He also wondered what had provoked her expression of dismay when those young replacement aircrew had hurried out of the office to witness their arriving bomber, and the reason for that defensive look when he'd inquired what the matter was. With his assistant occupying his thoughts, he suddenly found himself remembering her comments on the possible significance of the brass rubbings found among Summerfield's things. Although he'd said little at the time, he'd been impressed by the inference she had laid on them; and now, thinking about it again, he was even more inclined to agree that the dead girl's interest in medieval tomb tablets had most likely been encouraged by whoever she'd been secretly seeing. After all, as he told himself, it was extremely unlikely that she'd have embarked upon such a solitary and

107

unusual pastime without the encouragement of somebody else; also, as Diana had pointed out, from where could she have obtained the scarce paper and other materials necessary except from someone who already possessed such things from before the war?

Thinking this, he finally rejected the possibility that Pat Kelly had been the Waaf's mysterious boyfriend. Whatever exotic wonders Australia possessed, medieval tomb brasses were not among them – anyway, it was hardly credible that a rebellious nonconformist like Kelly should, since arriving in Britain, have developed an interest in the kingdom's feudal past. For much the same reason, he dismissed the idea that Summerfield might have been originally encouraged in her hobby by either the dead Rhodesian navigator or the nineteen-year-old pilot she'd been close to. Instead, there came into his mind an image of the blonde-headed Waaf corporal cycling country lanes in the company of some earnest local young schoolmaster or curate, the two searching out obscure medieval churches as he himself had often done with various parties of his Dulwich boys in pre-war days.

Quite naturally, his thoughts moved on from this pleasing picture to the matter of Summerfield's bicycle. Why hadn't she taken it with her when she'd left the station? Indeed, if she'd arranged to meet her boyfriend on her first evening of leave, why bother to come up to the camp in the first place? Could it have simply been that she'd intended to meet some friends for mid-morning coffee in the Naafi, and then found herself trapped when the station was sealed in preparation for the night's raid? With the phoneboxes padlocked and all access to the outside world denied, she'd have had no way of cancelling her planned assignation, and so might well have felt driven to risk illicitly leaving the camp after dark to keep her tryst – perhaps not taking her bicycle with her in case it hindered her from slipping through the gap in the fence unnoticed.

There was a certain pleasing logic to this idea, yet the flaw was obvious. With the simultaneous approach of the anticyclone and the main lunar passage, it had been virtually certain that an attack would be ordered prior to the enforced temporary cessation of operations. Indeed, the station had been rife with rumours of an impending raid long before the Typex machines had leapt to life with the usual stand-by signal. How, in that case, could an intelligent young woman have allowed herself to get unnecessarily marooned?

Momentarily defeated, Blanding turned his mind back to his conversation with Chief Inspector Stanley. As the policeman had remarked, what sort of madman, having brutally struck down the girl, would have carried her body back across the fields to lay it down like that of some sacrificial victim just outside the airfield fence? And why, having left the corpse on a well-used shortcut track, had he then apparently taken the additional risk of informing the local telephone exchange of its location? It just didn't make sense – not unless, he suddenly thought, the killer had been no stranger at all, but, in fact, none other than Summerfield's unknown lover himself.

Gripped by this now seemingly obvious explanation, and wondering why it hadn't occurred to him before, Blanding straightened and excitedly took a step forward. That surely had to be the answer: the killing of Corporal Summerfield had been the tragic result of a lovers' tiff, a case of a *crime passionnel* – the man concerned turning on the girl for some reason and savagely clubbing her down in a fit of jealous rage. Convinced of his new-found theory, the likely scenario now rushed though his mind: the arranged meeting taking place in some nearby outhouse or barn where paraffin and farm machinery was stored; the ensuing quarrel; the raised voices; the increasingly bitter words, then the enraged lover grabbing at some implement and bringing it viciously down on his victim's forehead – this in turn followed by a moment of stunned silence and then the attacker falling perhaps on his knees before the prone form, fearful and appalled at what he'd done, yet somehow still cool and controlled enough to half-strip the body in an attempt to make the whole thing look like a botched sexual attack. Finally, the grief-stricken killer carrying his victim's bloodstained corpse back towards the often-used gap in the airfield fence, presumably partly to distance himself from the deed and partly because he was unable to stomach the thought of her being left to rot in some obscure fenland ditch or drain. Now a further idea occurred to him: perhaps the reason why Summerfield had postponed her departure in the first place had been because she'd decided to end the relationship and had wished to announce her decision before going on leave – and it had been that painful announcement that had triggered the fatal attack. And yet, mused Blanding, beginning to pace restlessly to and fro beneath the Lancaster's wing, if that was true, and Summerfield had really planned to end her mysterious liaison, then surely she'd have confided her intention to her roommate. Apart from that, it was curious the other girl hadn't spotted any of the usual signs of a deteriorating relationship – indeed, according to Corporal Jennings,

June Summerfield had never seemed more happy and fulfilled as during these last few months.

Lost in speculations and struggling with the difficulties of his theory, until that moment Blanding had been only dimly aware of faint cries and shouts in the distance. Now, however, he was abruptly jerked back to the present by a sharp double bark, followed by the same long, drawn-out, ululating howl as before. The sounds came from nearby, somewhere it seemed in the mist between where he stood and the rear of the now almost invisible administration block. Further away, men's voices were calling to one another: clearly one of the pickets had finally stumbled upon the dog and they were now driving it in his direction.

Stepping out from under the aircraft's wing, Blanding drew the revolver from his pocket. He had no wish to shoot the animal if he could avoid it. On the other hand, if it wouldn't allow itself to be captured, he was determined to put the poor creature out of its misery with one carefully aimed shot.

Ahead, much closer than before, came an excited double bark from out of the fog, followed again by the long mournful howl. Straining to listen, Blanding began to hear through the mist what sounded like heavy panting and the noise of running feet. Cocking the pistol, he raised his arm. As he did so, to his astonishment there materialized before him not the expected dog, but the form of a man looking back over his shoulder as he ran. 'I say...' he faltered, so taken aback that he could hardly struggle out the words. 'Halt there! Halt or I fire!'

The runner came to a complete stop and stood looking towards him, a blurred dark shape in the mist. Then to his amazement, whoever it was then fell onto his hands and knees, and came scurrying forward on all fours, growling and snarling up at the raised gun. Blanding froze, finger on the trigger. Then before he could recover, the figure leapt to its feet and ran off past him into the mist, disappearing among the parked Lancasters, uttering a final wolf-like wild howl as it went.

So unexpected and bizarre had the incident been that Blanding stood stock-still with the gun still raised. Stunned, hardly believing what he'd just witnessed, he remained frozen for a second or two before recollecting himself. He then turned and attempted to chase in the direction in which the figure had vanished. In his slippered feet, however, running proved impossible, and, after a few

110

clumsy steps, he stopped and, pointing the revolver upwards, fired off a couple of rounds. A few moments later a pair of greatcoated airmen emerged from the mist, each armed with a pickaxe handle and both puffing prodigiously.

'What's happened, sir?' gasped the first as he ran up. 'Was that you who fired those shots? Did you manage to hit the blooming thing?' Coming to a stop, the two men peered about them in the darkness, obviously expecting to see the body of the animal they'd been pursuing.

Blanding's brain was working fast: with the airfield shrouded in fog, it was unlikely their quarry could be caught. Nevertheless, both discipline and security demanded that something be done. 'Right,' he said, addressing the still panting airmen, 'that wasn't a dog; it was someone playing the damned fool. Clearly, there's some sort of joker or lunatic loose about the station. Both of you remain here,' he called, starting to stride back towards the administration block, 'and watch over these aircraft. I'm going to have the guard turned out and the entire camp searched.'

CHAPTER EIGHT

'Fun and games last night, I hear!'

Squadron Leader Palmer looked up from his plate and grinned as Blanding slumped down on the opposite chair, pale, puffy-eyed and unusually late for breakfast. 'My dear fellow, what in heaven's name has been going on?' he demanded with evident amusement as the new arrival groped for the coffee-pot. 'Rumour has it you spent the small hours indulging in a spot of impromptu pistol practice on the airfield, and then had the entire guard rousted out to chase after some non-existent dog!'

'It wasn't a ruddy dog!' responded Blanding sourly, grimacing as he sipped his coffee, now decidedly tepid. 'Nor was it non-existent! Some damn-fool joker was out creeping around the camp, barking his blasted head off and howling like a banshee!'

With mist still hanging across the aerodrome and no apparent chance of further operations in the near future, the dining room of the officers' mess, although more crowded, had much the same relaxed atmosphere as the previous day. Most of the breakfasters had already finished eating and were lingering over their coffee, some absorbed in newspapers, others, including the station padre and medical officer, gathered at one table, endeavouring by combined effort to solve the day's *Times* crossword puzzle. The majority, however, especially the younger, sat chatting and laughing together in noisy groups, cigarette smoke wafting and intermingling above their heads.

Sipping a little more of his coffee, Blanding blearily surveyed the scene. Fluff Brewer, he noticed, had now rejoined society. He was seated among the four commissioned aircrew replacements, his rubicund cheeks and huge, blond handlebar-moustache incongruous among their earnest, clean-shaven, young faces. From his laughter and the motions of his hands, he was obviously regaling them with tales of his Battle of Britain days in speech doubtless heavily laced with the already slightly archaic RAF jargon of the early war years. In complete contrast, Kelly sat smoking alone at the table immediately behind, his expression every bit as bleak and unsmiling as the air traffic controller's had been twenty-four hours before. At the sight of him, Blanding's thoughts went back to their telephone conversation the day before. Remembering the pilot's oddly flat reaction to the good news about his wounded navigator, he immediately made up his mind to voice his concern about Kelly's mental state to Group Captain Chesterton directly after that morning's defaulters' parade.

'So you didn't manage to catch this nocturnal prowler of yours then?'

'Unfortunately not,' grunted Blanding, bending to his bowl of stewed prunes. 'Still,' he resumed, swallowing and looking up, 'I've already written an official report of the incident – I did so the moment I got back to my room after dismissing the guard. Whoever the damned blighter was, I'm determined to have him brought to book in double-quick time.'

Pushing his plate aside, Palmer leaned back in his chair. 'Really, my dear chap,' he said with a languid smile, 'I wouldn't bother if I were you.'

'Not bother?' repeated Blanding incredulously, fatigue bringing an edge to his voice. 'Not bother when some confounded idiot is wandering around the station, kicking up an infernal racket half the night!'

'That's right,' answered the engineer placidly. 'Be a good fellow and let the matter drop.'

Blanding was flabbergasted. 'Look, Peter,' he said, his tone changing, 'I'm not a complete fool: I, of course, realize it was most likely just some sort of idiotic prank or piece of stupid horseplay. Nevertheless, it could have been something serious – sabotage for example.'

'Saboteurs going about barking like dogs!' The engineer laughed. 'Hardly likely I'd have thought, old chum, not unless, of course, our friends of the Wehrmacht have taken to parachuting in the mentally afflicted! Perhaps you're thinking of a German agent dropping a spaniel in the works?'

'It's all very well making a joke of it,' responded Blanding, goaded as much by Palmer's laconic drawl as his good-humoured levity, 'but what if the individual concerned is completely off his

113

head? In case you've forgotten, we had a Waaf attacked and battered to death just the night before last! Are you seriously saying then that it's not important to know if there's a dangerous maniac loose about the place?' Pausing, he glanced down the table to where Wing Commander Kochanowski and three of his fellow Poles were excitedly discussing an article in the *Daily Mirror*. 'Don't you see,' he resumed, lowering his voice, 'if only to eliminate him from police enquiries, we need to know the man's identity.'

Extracting his cigarette case from a top pocket, Palmer shook his head. 'No, I promise you, Trott, you're barking up the wrong tree.' He laughed at the inadvertent pun. 'Sorry!' he said. 'Just a wee slip of the tongue.' Then his smile vanished and his face was suddenly serious. 'Look, Trott,' he said, leaning forward, 'I know you're a zealous and conscientious officer, a credit to the service and all the rest of it, but really, on this occasion take an old sweat's advice and leave the matter alone. I can guarantee that your noisy friend of last night had nothing whatsoever to do with poor Poppy Summerfield's death.'

Blanding looked at his friend curiously. 'Obviously you know who the fellow was, Peter,' he said as Palmer drew a cigarette from his case and lit up, 'and you say he's no danger. All the same, as adjutant, I need to know what's going on and who the man is.'

Imperturbable as ever, Palmer breathed out a thin plume of smoke and shook his head. 'No,' he answered, 'with all respect, Trott, I really don't think you do. Take it from me, it's best for the person concerned and for the morale of the station in general that the incident remains officially unnoticed. I'm sure,' he continued with an amiable smile, 'neither of us wishes to add unnecessarily to the casualties of this ghastly war, nor to load additional problems onto someone who has more than he can easily digest on his plate as it is, and who I may say quite voluntarily and of his own volition came and offered himself as a willing victim to strains and dangers that you and I are thankfully only spectators of.' He took another drag on his cigarette and then, rather unexpectedly, grinned. 'But changing to happier matters,' he went on, 'how are you finding the lovely Mrs Taylor? I hear Buster has appointed her your assistant, you lucky dog!' He burst out laughing. 'Sorry,' he said, eyes twinkling, 'honestly, I promise – just another unfortunate slip of the tongue!'

Blanding stared stonily back, struggling not to smile, irritated at the abrupt change of subject and still rather resentful at not being taken into the other's confidence regarding the identity of the person who had disturbed his night, yet at the same time secretly enjoying the new topic of conversation.

'Go on!' urged Palmer, now grinning broadly. 'Tell your old Uncle Pete the truth – what's your opinion of our mysterious young lady from 4 Group? Something a wee bit cold and stand-offish about her, wouldn't you say?' He eyed Blanding through a veil of cigarette smoke with evident amusement before adding with an arch smile, 'Or perhaps that hasn't been your experience?'

There was something so infectious about Palmer's good-natured banter that, just as in the glory hole the previous day, Blanding felt dangerously close to laughing in response. At that moment, however, the Tannoy speaker over the door crackled into life. As it did so, all conversation in the dining room faded and every face turned towards the source of the sound.

'Flying Officers Ash and Fletcher to report to the briefing room immediately. I repeat, Flying Officers Ash and Fletcher to report for pre-flight briefing straight away.'

As the speaker clicked off, two figures rose from a table in the far corner, hurriedly wiping their mouths with their napkins. Through a subdued hush, Fletcher and Ash left the room, the looks of nervous expectation and unconcealed curiosity on the faces who watched them depart strongly reminding Blanding of schoolboys when one or more of their number are unexpectedly picked out and summoned to a housemaster or headmaster's study. 'What's going on?' he asked, turning back to Palmer as the door closed behind the two officers.

His companion shrugged. 'Tampa call, I imagine,' he answered, glancing out at the foggy airfield. 'Those two are Mosquito boys; someone, it seems, wants a special meteorological sortie flown.'

'Why?'

'God knows!' Palmer smiled. 'Perhaps dear old Butch and his High Wycombe pals have a little something else up their broad-ringed sleeves – some extra trifle more to keep friend Jerry amused.'

'Another op you mean!' exclaimed Blanding in horror. 'Surely not, not during the start of the main lunar passage!'

At that moment, Kochanowski's voice boomed down the table. 'Balloon goes up you think, Squadron Leader? Soon I and my boys go again, yes?' Broad face exuberant, gold teeth gleaming, the Pole leaned across the table towards them, brandishing his fork. 'If so, come fly with the Polskies! You're invited – and you also, Trott, my good friend!' He gave a chortling laugh 'Together we make plenty more bloody noses and cracked heads!'

'Bloodthirsty bastard!' murmured Palmer with a grin as Kochanowski turned back to his compatriots. His smile faded, however, and was replaced by a look of concern as he noticed Blanding's expression. 'For heaven's sake, Trott, don't look so damned worried! I was only joking. It won't be our lads going: it'll be the Yanks, I bet you my bottom dollar. Now they have the new Mustang long-range fighter as escorts, they'll be wanting to use this spell of clear weather for another of their big daylight shows.'

The initial shock of the Tampa call having worn off, Palmer's apparent confidence seemed shared by the majority of his fellow breakfasters. On the surface at least, the atmosphere in the dining room now seemed as relaxed as before. The padre and his companions were once more absorbed in the crossword; the Poles had started to argue noisily about something to do with Monte Cassino; Pilot Officer Steenbok's South African accents rose above the babble of voices, indignantly demanding the return of the day's Jane strip-cartoon – and with his twisted, lop-sided body leaning across the table, Fluff Brewer was once more the laughing cavalier, regaling the grave little group of young Puritan Ironsides about him with jocular accounts of 'splendid kites', 'wizzo prangs' and 'dicey shows' in those hard-pressed battles high over a smoke-shrouded Dunkirk and the Kentish hop-gardens of four summers before.

The characteristic cough and staccato bark of a starting Merlin echoed dully across the misty airfield. As the second engine fired and boomed into life, Blanding paused on the path and peered towards the distant Mosquito. Among the Lancasters outside B Flight hangars, the small, unarmed, twin-engined reconnaissance aircraft looked puny and insignificant. Yet, as he knew, within less than an hour it would be deep inside German airspace, flying at such a speed and altitude that it was almost invulnerable to either anti-aircraft fire or fighter attack. Much as he personally disliked flying, sure he would hate the mix of boredom and physical discomfort it involved, Blanding felt a spasm of envy. Those two young men who'd been snatched from breakfast were, in the words of the psalmist, preparing to take 'the wings of the morning' and soar like gods above the face of the enemy, leaving him behind to his blinkered, mothlike existence amidst an unending welter of paper.

These rather mournful ruminations were interrupted that moment as a gaggle of half a dozen Waafs swept past him on bicycles, giggling loudly at some joke among themselves. Shaken from his reverie, Blanding hurriedly turned and began striding on towards his office. As he did so, from behind him came a succession of wolf-whistles and ribald shouts. Frowning, he paused and looked round to see a hoard of blue-coated figures emerging from the doors of the NCO aircrew mess hall behind. Exchanging shouted suggestive remarks with the passing girls, the airmen spilled out into the misty sunlight in their greatcoats and rakishly-inclined forage caps – the very epitome, it seemed, of the light-hearted young warriors so beloved of cinema newsreels. Observing them as they poured, laughing and shouting, out through the door, Blanding found it hard to believe what in reality he knew the majority to be: the physically and psychologically exhausted veterans of a five-month-long winter bombing campaign that, not only having fallen far short of what it had been expected to achieve, had also cost the lives of almost half of those taking part. Most were hardly out of their teens, yet often so nerve-strained and stressed by their experiences over Berlin and the Ruhr that they suffered the ulcers and gastric problems of middle-aged businessmen, some even already having premature streaks of grey in their hair – youngsters who, even if they survived the war, would carry the emotional and mental scars of what they'd been through for the rest of their lives, often manifesting itself later in the form of alcoholism, domestic violence and broken marriage. Among these, as he knew from talking with the chaplain and MO, were a number of airmen who'd already witnessed once too often the sight of another aircraft helplessly pinned by the probing searchlights or cartwheeling down like a blazing torch among the flashing barrages of exploding shells, and who now gibbered, moaned and shrieked in their sleep like those shell-shocked survivors of Passchendaele and the Somme he'd known back in his Oxford days – men who, trembling as if with fever, had now to force themselves to clamber back into the condensation-dank bellies of their aircraft at the beginning of each new operation, doing so only out of loyalty to their crewmates or simply from the fear of being publicly branded a coward.

With the shouts and laughter of the youngsters in his ears and the continuing roar of the Mosquito warming its engines in the distance, Blanding walked on. As he did so, his thoughts returned to

117

the extraordinary incident out on the airfield early that morning and the outlandish behaviour of whoever had emerged from the mist to drop on his knees and yelp and snarl at his pointing revolver. As Palmer had more than hinted, the man was almost certainly a member of aircrew himself – presumably one of those nerve-damaged causalities of the past winter, venting his pent-up tension and terror with all that insane howling and dog-like barking. If true, thought Blanding, then the bizarre response to the sight of the outstretched gun in the hand of authority was as understandable as that of those wretched French poilus of 1917 pitifully baaing like sheep as they'd trudged up past their GHQ towards the vast slaughter-yards of Verdun. It almost accounted for the duty sergeant's curious reluctance to mount a search party – almost certainly he knew of the man and wished to protect him from public humiliation. But was the person concerned safe, that was the question? Had Palmer been right when he'd asserted that, whoever he was, he had no connection with June Summerfield's death? Blanding was inclined to believe he was: Palmer was an affable, likeable man, just the sort to be confided in. Beside that, his work as senior station technical officer brought him into daily contact with ground staff and aircrew alike, which therefore put him in an ideal position to know what was happening throughout the camp in a way that he, a mere ex-civilian, desk-bound administrator, was quite unable to do. Beside that, there was also the time factor to consider: according to both the police surgeon and the station MO, Summerfield been killed some time between ten and midnight, when, apart from Sergeant Mackenzie's bogged-down A-Able, every serviceable bomber on the station was airborne and already well on its way out across the North Sea, taking their aircrews with them.

Pausing on the pavement to allow a grey-painted Church Army mobile canteen van to pass by on its way out towards the distant hangars with its daily comforting cargo of hot sweet tea and 'wads' for the airfield staff, Blanding finally made his decision. He would trust Palmer's judgement and not hand in an official report of the early morning incident. Instead, he would mention the matter informally to Chesterton after the morning's disciplinary proceedings, whilst at the same time acquainting him with his worries concerning Pat Kelly. This decided, Blanding crossed over to the administration block, and, pushing through the swing doors, headed along the main corridor, wondering as he passed the door of the police inquiry room what, if anything, had been unearthed by the autopsy; also whether Chief Inspector Stanley had yet made any progress in establishing the identity of Summerfield's mysterious boyfriend.

Although there was still more than half an hour to go before the first of the defaulters were due to be marched in front of the station commander, the airmen concerned were already assembled in the passage outside his office. Conspicuous in their number-one uniforms, they stood talking in whispering groups, one or two of the bolder spirits giving an occasional low whistle or muttering a furtive aside as female clerks scurried past. At the adjutant's approach they all fell silent, however, pressing back against the walls with downcast eyes, meek and docile suddenly as a group of noviciate nuns. Guessing that Dawson had slipped away for his customary 'cuppa' with the rather motherly cipher room Waaf sergeant, Blanding scowled. Conscious of his lateness, however, and eager to get to his office, he strode on between them without a word.

'Good morning, sir.'

Raising her head, Diana looked up with a smile as Blanding entered. 'I hope you don't mind,' she continued, 'but I thought that I'd make an early start on drawing up a list of aircrew entitled to home leave. It should speed up the process when the squadron is finally stood down.'

'Ah, yes, good! Yes, please carry on, Mrs Taylor.'

Annoyed with himself at arriving a second time to find his assistant already ensconced at her desk, Blanding hung up his cap, coat and respirator bag. Out on the airfield in the early morning, and then again after parting from Palmer outside the mess, he had wondered what this next meeting with her would be like. Now, despite the friendliness of her greeting, there was still the same formal constraint in her manner as there had been after the departure of the aircrew replacements the day before. Disappointment ran through him keenly – combining, perversely, with a measure of relief.

'I take it,' he said, going to his desk, 'there's been no word on the matter yet from Group?'

'About the squadron being stood down? No, sir – nothing so far.'

From beyond the window came the sound of the Mosquito finally taking off, its bellowing roar momentarily shaking the metal window frames. Hardly had its engines faded into the distance when there was a knock on the door, and Warrant Officer Starling entered with his usual quota of documents and folders. Blanding put his signature to the various urgent papers placed before him. Then, as the clerk left, he turned back to Diana. 'Look,' he said, 'I've got CO's orders this morning, and then I'm due to attend an LMF inquiry directly after lunch. That means, I'm afraid, that, for today at least, I'm going to have to leave most of this routine paperwork to you.'

'Not to worry,' answered Diana, smiling. 'If I need any help with anything, I'll call Mr Starling in.'

'Right-oh.'

Although this time she'd not used the formal 'sir', Blanding again sensed an underlying constraint in his assistant's reply. Not knowing how to break through it, he turned back to his desk. In the topmost wire-tray lay his hand-written report of the nocturnal happenings out on the airfield. Reaching over, he took it out, folded and refolded it, and then began rather absently tearing it up, allowing the tiny pieces of paper to flutter confetti-like down between his fingers into the basket at his side. Finishing, he looked round to find Diana regarding him with a look of puzzled inquiry. 'It was nothing important,' he explained hurriedly, his colour rising, 'just a report on an incident here on the camp in the early hours – a small matter that, on second thoughts, I consider best forgotten.' He paused slightly. 'The strains that all of us, particularly members of aircrew, have to live with, produce their inevitable consequences, I regret to say. An operational station cannot always be run with strict adherence to the rulebook.' Even to himself, he again sounded absurdly formal, almost as if he were delivering a training lecture. He gave a self-conscious smile. 'I'm merely saying that fighting a war demands a certain degree of flexibility from us all.'

'I'm sure you're right.'

Even in the tiny moment between her speaking and turning back to her work, Blanding glimpsed that same flash of ironic mockery in Diana's eyes he'd seen in the storeroom the day before, but this time, the warmth in her smile was undeniable. Looking across as she again bowed over the aircrew lists, he experienced a huge sense of relief, and remembering what Palmer had said about her supposed coldness only increased his feeling of well-being. Furtively, he continued to observe her for a few seconds before forcing himself to begin opening the morning's post. Hardly, however, had he begun reading a disappointing if predictable reply from the local manager of the local bus company regarding his repeated request for late-night transport back to the camp from Ely on Saturday nights, before the telephone rang beside him.

It was Chesterton's voice. 'Ah, good, Alan! You're there! Have you all the bumf ready for this damned disciplinary parade?'

'Yes, sir, of course,' he answered. 'It's all ready for me to bring along.'

'Right – in that case, I'd like you to come to my office straight away.'

'Very good, sir.' Blanding replaced the receiver and turned to meet Diana's eyes. 'That was the CO,' he said with a frown. 'For some reason, he wants to see me at once. That means I'm going to have to leave the rest of these letters to you.' Taking the thick bundle of personal files and charge sheets Starling had heaped on his desk, he got up and went over to the door, but then hesitated. 'God knows what's happened now,' he said, turning back to meet his assistant's gaze, 'but from his tone, I'd say something else has definitely cropped up to upset the old man.' He paused, thinking suddenly of the Tampa call and Mosquito crew snatched away from breakfast. 'I only hope,' he added gravely, glancing towards the window, 'that there hasn't been an order for another operation.'

'Or an attack on another of the girls.'

A look of horror crossed Blanding's face. Until that moment the possibility of such an occurrence hadn't occurred to him. Now as it did so, he experienced a sudden feeling of dread. Glancing towards the wastepaper basket in which lay the scattered pieces of his torn-up report, he suddenly found himself remembering again the early hours out on the airfield: the fog-shrouded fens, the dark shapes of the bombers in the misty moonlight and of the demented howling and barking of whatever tormented soul had been wandering loose about the station.

CHAPTER NINE

'Ah, yes! Come in, Alan.'

Pipe in hand, Group Captain Chesterton sat at his desk beneath a sort of shrine to his flying career. This comprised a wall-mounted propeller of ancient vintage, between whose four paddle-like blades hung a collection of framed sepia photographs. In one, an amazingly boyish but nevertheless instantly recognisable version of the station commander stood leaning against the nose of a rickety, high-wing monoplane, cradling some variety of spaniel in his arms. In another, a squadron of almost equally primitive-looking machines was drawn up among palm trees and tents, with a herd of grazing camels in the background and what appeared to be the Great Pyramid of Giza dominating the horizon. A third featured a bulbous-nosed, twin-engined biplane flying over one of the Khyber forts, with the snow-capped mountains of Afghanistan stretching away into the far distance beyond.

It was not, however, his commanding officer nor the familiar photographs, nor indeed the elderly labrador bitch in her usual place in the basket beneath the corner table, that caught Blanding's eye as he came through the door. His attention was wholly taken up by the two men standing beside Chesterton's desk. One was Chief Inspector Stanley, garbed in the same dowdy brown suit as the previous day, his face as melancholy and grave as when he had poked around the dusty recesses of the Glory Hole. The other was his seeming antithesis, a dark-haired, bushy-moustached, bright-eyed little man of thirty or so, immaculately dressed in RAF uniform with the rings of a squadron leader on his well-tailored sleeves.

'The chief inspector you already know, of course,' said Chesterton, introducing his visitors, 'while Squadron Leader Walker here is the officer sent by the special investigation branch. Needless to say, he'll be co-operating closely with the Cambridgeshire police during his enquires. I trust that suitable arrangements have been made for his accommodation.'

'Yes, sir,' answered Blanding, heartily relieved that it wasn't either the news of an impending operation or another murderous attack on one of the station Waafs that had prompted this early summons, and equally that he'd remembered to seek out and speak to the mess steward after breakfast. 'A guestroom is being prepared at this moment,' he said with a confident smile. 'I've also instructed Warrant Officer Starling to have the office next to the chief inspector's made available for the squadron leader's use.'

'Good,' murmured Chesterton, nodding approvingly. 'Anyway, I called you in a few minutes early, Alan, because it's been decided that a further attempt must be made to find Corporal Summerfield's missing items of clothing as well as whatever weapon was used by her assailant. The plan is that Squadron Leader Walker and the station police will begin a thorough search of the camp this morning while their civilian colleagues again concentrate on the surrounding fields. With that in view, I thought we might send as many airmen as we can spare to assist in combing the fields and dragging the nearby ditches and dykes. Perhaps you'd arrange with the duty officer to have that put that in hand at once.'

'Yes, sir, of course. If you'll excuse me, I'll go and see about it straight away.'

'One moment, Alan, before you do so there's something else you ought to know.' Chesterton paused and lowered his head. 'Chief Inspector Stanley has the result of yesterday's autopsy. I'm afraid that the information he brings puts an even darker and more distressing slant on this whole ghastly affair.'

As the CO made no attempt to continue, but merely continued staring gloomily down at his desk, Blanding glanced questioningly round at Stanley. The elderly policeman cleared his throat. 'As was obvious from the preliminary examination, the deceased received a heavy blow to the right temple, delivered by a sharp metal object – very likely, it's thought, some type of agricultural implement as traces of mud and what looks like engine grease were discovered embedded in the wound. However, though the blow was hard enough to crack the skull, and would certainly have rendered the victim unconscious for a few seconds at least, medical evidence shows that the blow itself was not the actual cause of death. Rather, it appears that the girl literally died of fright.'

'Of fright?' repeated Blanding incredulously. 'Good Lord, Chief Inspector! Is that medically possible?'

'So it would seem,' answered Stanley evenly. 'According to the pathologist, the deceased suffered from a rare heart complaint occasionally found among young people known as hypertrophic cardiomyopathy. Basically, it's a thickening of the heart muscles. To anyone suffering from the condition, any sudden great shock or exertion can mean instantaneous death.'

Blanding frowned. 'But I don't understand,' he said, shifting his gaze from Stanley to the uniformed figure at his side, 'surely such a thing would have shown up at Summerfield's medical examination when she originally joined up.'

'Apparently not,' replied Squadron Leader Walker, his clipped tones in marked contrast to Stanley's soft-rolled East Anglian accent. 'We've checked with your MO. According to him, hypertrophic cardiomyopathy is undetectable with a stethoscope. Apart from a slight shortness of breath, sufferers of the condition neither feel or show any symptoms whatsoever. Therefore both they and their doctors usually remain completely unaware of the danger. On the other hand though, it seems that the condition is immediately obvious to any pathologist opening up the chest.'

Turning away, Blanding looked out across the still-misty expanse of grass and runways stretching away beyond the window, thinking again of the frozen look of horror on the dead Waaf's face. It was only too easy to imagine the last thing the terrified girl would have seen: the upraised billhook, hatchet or whatever had been used in the attack, and behind it, pale in the darkness, the demented features of her assailant. His speculations of the early hours now came rushing back. Had Summerfield's attacker been indeed no other than the unknown man her roommate believed she'd been secretly seeing? Had he, goaded perhaps by her wish to end the clandestine relationship, lashed out in an almost instantly regretted moment of rage? Thinking this, he now remembered the victim's torn-open blouse and the oily smears on the skin beneath. Suddenly confident of his theory, he turned back to the burly figure seated behind the desk.

'Sir,' he said, addressing Chesterton, 'if what the chief inspector tells us is true about Summerfield's heart condition, then it seems at least possible to me that her attacker never actually intended to kill her at all, and that those oily finger marks and bruises on her chest might well have been the result of some crude attempt at resuscitation.'

To his surprise, the station commander nodded. 'Yes,' he answered, 'that seems to be the pathologist's opinion also. Apparently, as well as that, there's evidence to show that efforts were made to staunch the head wound.' He paused and frowned darkly. 'But I'm afraid, Alan, what you've heard isn't the whole story; the chief inspector has yet to tell you what else the autopsy disclosed.'

As Blanding turned back to Stanley, the barest hint of a smile creased the policeman's lugubrious face. 'It would appear, Flight Lieutenant,' he said, 'that, despite my original doubts, you and the deceased's roommate were quite correct in your assumption that Summerfield had been involved with some unknown man. According to the pathologist, she was well over two months pregnant when she died.'

'Pregnant!' exclaimed Blanding, taken aback. Dumbfounded, he stared at Stanley for a moment, then shook his head in dazed belief. 'Good God!' he murmured flatly. 'That's something I hadn't bargained for at all.'

'Quite,' rejoined Chesterton heavily from behind. 'It's an eventuality that hadn't crossed any of our minds.'

A short silence followed, broken only by the crash of boots and harsh tones of Warrant Officer Dawson's voice outside in the corridor and also by the sound of the labrador beginning to scratch herself vigorously in her basket beneath the table. In front of her master's desk, the three visitors stood saying nothing while the station commander himself turned and gazed abstractedly across at the photograph of the King on the opposite wall. 'Anyway, Alan,' sighed Chesterton, breaking off his brooding contemplation of the gaunt, rather melancholy-faced figure in air marshal's dress uniform to turn back to Blanding, 'you had better hurry along now and get that search party organized. After that, you and I must then try somehow to get through this wretched defaulters' parade.' He shook his head sorrowfully. 'Though heaven only knows,' he added, 'how either of us are meant to apply our minds to such things after having heard what the chief inspector has had to tell us!'

'Well, spit it out for God's sake, man! What is it that the confounded fellow is supposed to have said?'

Partly from the effect of his broken night, partly from the tidings brought by Stanley, Blanding had indeed found it hard to

125

concentrate for the last fifty minutes or so. As usual during these twice-weekly disciplinary proceedings, he sat at the station commander's right side, passing over the appropriate personal file to him as Dawson marched in each of the defaulters in turn. Today, however, as the various charges were read and the usual depressing and often sordid details of petty thefts, drunkenness, instances of minor insubordination and unlawful absences were gone over, his mind kept straying back to the autopsy findings and to the news that, in one moment, had shattered his previous convictions regarding the likely reasons for Corporal Summerfield's death. So it had continued until the angry impatience in Chesterton's voice cut through his thoughts, abruptly bringing him back to the matter in hand. Raising his head, he now blinked up at the unnaturally flushed face of the uniformed figure standing rigidly at attention next to the station warrant officer in front of the desk, and waited in anticipation for the man's reply.

'Come on then, damn you!' Chesterton's mottled cheeks grew darker. 'What in God's name did this civilian say to provoke you into starting the fight?'

Head erect, Leading Aircraftman Phillips, a lean, wiry northerner, raised his eyes a fraction to the brassbound propeller-boss above his interrogator's head as if endeavouring either to distance or elevate himself above what he was about to say. 'He called me a ruddy penguin, sir.'

'What's that? Speak up, man! What did he call you?'

'A penguin, sir.'

'I see.'

Chesterton lowered his gaze and sat tapping Philips' open file with heavy-jowled gravity. Like all four men in the room, he was well acquainted with the apparently innocuous epithet. Four years before, bitter at having been strafed and bombed for days on the Dunkirk beaches by the Stukas and Heinkels of Goering's Luftwaffe with rarely, if ever, a sight of the squadrons of high-flying Spitfires and Hurricanes (plus a few of the almost useless Defiants) being desperately employed in their defence, the returning troops of the BEF had used the term unsparingly on any unfortunate airmen they happened to meet. As a provocation to fisticuffs, the insult couldn't be bettered, the reference to the flightless bird being a pointed reminder that the majority of RAF personnel were wholly employed on ground duties, and thus, in the main, lived relatively safe, comfortable lives compared with those of soldiers and sailors on active service. To anyone wearing air force blue without flying insignia on his chest, the taunt thus came as almost an imputation of his manhood, especially so as within the RAF the term had originally been used disparagingly for Waafs as *'flappers who did not fly'*. For someone like Phillips, a skilled instrument fitter working on operational aircraft and witnessing at first hand the enormous losses among the bomber crews, to be equated with a waddling, rather ridiculous-looking seabird rubbed salt on what inevitably was already an extremely sensitive spot indeed.

'So what you're saying is this,' resumed Chesterton, looking up again at the man in front of him, 'you innocently took yourself off for a peaceful early evening drink at the Red Lion. There this civilian, for no reason at all, gives you this gratuitous insult – is that really what you're asking me to believe?'

If anything, Philips' face flushed even redder. 'Well, not exactly, sir, no,' he answered hesitatingly. 'As I told you, he was there in the pub with one of them land army girls.' He paused slightly before reluctantly adding, 'So I said something to him.'

Chesterton scowled darkly. 'Said what exactly?'

'I told him, sir, in a manner of speaking, that I didn't much care for it, not to his having an arm round the young lady's waist.'

Perplexity rose in the commanding officer's face. Leaning back, he gazed up at Phillips' immobile features for a moment or two without speaking. Then bending forward, he flicked back through the airman's personal file to the first page. 'I notice from this,' he said, putting on a pair of spectacles and peering down at the typed details, 'that you claimed membership of the Church of England when you first joined up as an Halton apprentice in 1938. You haven't in the meantime, I take it,' he continued, looking back to the airman, 'converted to a Seventh Day Adventist, Anabaptist, Christadelphian or member of any other of the more singular and stricter of the nonconformist sects – either that, or become a Mohammedan?'

'No, sir,' came the steady, if somewhat bewildered reply.

'So,' continued the questioner, 'we can therefore assume that this public display of affection was not an affront to your moral or religious sensibilities, Phillips?' Receiving no response to this clearly rhetorical question, Chesterton pressed on. 'Then may I ask, was the lady concerned a particular friend of yours?'

'No, sir.'

127

'Or friend of anyone you know?'

'No, sir – I'd never seen the lass before.'

'Indeed? And I presume the young woman herself wasn't objecting to having this man's arm round her waist?'

'No, sir.'

Since the start of proceedings, it had been obvious to Blanding that Chesterton was still upset by the news that the chief inspector had brought. Throughout all the marchings in and out, the questionings, answerings and awardings of punishments and admonishments, he'd been far more irritable than usual, and during this interchange with Phillips there had grown an increasingly dangerous edge to his voice. Now, at the airman's final admission, his fury finally boiled over. Face crimsoning, he glared fiercely up at the figure before him and then struck the desk a resounding blow with his clenched fist. 'Then, by all that's holy,' he roared, causing the sleeping dog in the basket to sit up, yawning and blinking, 'what the devil was it to you if the fellow had his arm round the girl or not? If he chose to sit hugging Mickey-damned-Mouse or his own great-grandmother, that was entirely his own concern and no bloody business of yours! Good God, man,' he went on, glowering up at the unfortunate fitter, 'isn't that exactly the sort of thing that we're bloody well meant to be fighting this confounded war for?'

Face expressionless, yet somehow expressive of a sullen obstinacy, Aircraftman Phillips remained staring over the station commander's head at the varnished surface of the wall-mounted propeller. Equally poker-faced, Dawson stood stiffly at attention beside him, clipboard clasped rigidly beneath his left arm.

Outburst over, Chesterton remained glaring at Phillips for a few seconds longer before slumping back in his chair with an exasperated sigh. 'All right,' he said wearily, 'so it comes to this then. For reasons best known to yourself, you apparently didn't like the look of this man ...what the devil was the fellow's name again?'

'Price, sir,' interposed Blanding, reading out the details from the charge sheet. 'Edward Albert Price, aged twenty-four, unskilled labourer, temporarily employed by the War Agriculture Committee.'

'So you didn't like the look of Mr Price's face for some reason,' resumed Chesterton. 'As a result, you made a completely uncalled-for objection to his being in the pub with the girl. Quite understandably, he insulted you in return, whereupon you started the fight which ended up with the wretched man having to receive treatment in the outpatients' department of the local cottage hospital.' The speaker paused. 'That's what basically happened, is it?'

'Yes, sir.'

'And you've no excuses?'

'No, sir.'

'Very well.' Chesterton glanced once more through the airman's personal file. He then sat back and steadily regarded Phillips. Ever since when, as a seventeen-year-old flight cadet straight out of school, he had first clambered into the nacelle of an ungainly and grossly underpowered old Maurice Farman biplane, it had been upon the diligence, devotion and expertise of skilled fitters like Phillips that his life had often depended. Throughout a training programme that regularly killed off nearly forty per cent from each successive batch of eager young hopefuls, and then during his subsequent service in France, his ground crew had helped strap him into his seat at the start of each flight and then waited for his return, often as amazed as genuinely thankful to see him safely home. Though now vastly expanded into a huge industry of destruction, the RAF remained a sort of family in Chesterton's eyes – and looking up at this representative of the swirls of so-called 'erks' who cycled out every morning to struggle for hours in often arctic weather to keep the bombers serviceable, he gave a grudging, fatherly smile. 'Well, it would appear, Phillips,' he said, 'that both Squadron Leader Palmer and your own flight sergeant consider you a generally reliable and conscientious man. In the light of their good report and your excellent record until this unfortunate episode, I'm prepared to be lenient this once. You'll be confined to camp for twenty-eight days with extra duties. In addition, the sum of eighteen shillings and ninepence will be docked from your pay to make good the breakages caused to the fixtures and fittings of the Red Lion – you understand?'

'Yes, sir. Thank you very much, sir.'

'Right then, cap on and dismiss, but let me not see you here in front of me again.' Shifting his gaze, Chesterton nodded at the warrant officer. 'Mr Dawson, march him out if you please.'

Thankfully, with Phillips' dismissal, the disciplinary parade was finally at an end. As the door closed and Dawson's barks faded away along the corridor, Chesterton relaxed, leaning back in his chair to draw out his pipe and tobacco-pouch from a side-pocket. 'Well,' he grunted, glancing round at the man besides him with a weary smile, 'I think we both know what all that was about, don't we?'

'The reason for Phillips starting the fight?' Blanding looked up from making a note of the punishment awarded. 'No, sir, I don't think I do,' he replied, 'though I'd definitely say he was hiding something – something, I imagine, to do with the unfortunate man he picked on.'

Chesterton laughed and blew down his pipe-stem. 'No,' he said, 'I don't think it would have mattered who the fellow was – it could have been Charlie Chaplain or King Farouk for all that friend Philips cared!'

'I don't understand, sir,' answered Blanding, frowning. 'He looked no sort of bully to me. If it wasn't something about this man Price who provoked him, and if he really didn't know the girl as he claims, what possible reason on earth could he have had for picking a quarrel?'

'None at all, rationally speaking,' replied Chesterton, filling his pipe-bowl. 'What, I guess, our friend was suffering from was nothing but simple, old-fashioned jealousy brought on by sexual frustration, the inevitable consequence of incarcerating hundreds of virile young men miles from nowhere.'

Long used to the expressions of tight-lipped schoolboys, and, despite what the CO had said, still certain that the airman had been holding something back, Blanding made no reply. Noticing his sceptical look, Chesterton smiled. 'My dear Alan,' he murmured good-humouredly between sucks as he began lighting his pipe, 'there's too much of the schoolmaster about you – you look too deeply into things. A lifetime in the service has taught me there's no suppressing the Old Adam, however much bromide we may add to his canteen tea!' He chuckled through a cloud of tobacco smoke. 'I'm afraid, until in its wisdom, His Majesty's Air Council adopts a policy of recruiting only eunuchs for the service, the consequences of frustrated male sexual desire is a cross that we of the Royal Air Force must continue to bear.'

Even as he spoke the final words, Chesterton's smile vanished and an expression of something like pain flashed across his battered broad face. Heaving himself to his feet, he went over to one of the windows and gazed out across the airfield. For almost a full minute he remained without speaking, pipe in mouth, a smoke-hazed bulky silhouette against the pale sunlight. 'Damn it!' he sighed at last. 'I have still to write to that poor girl's parents. It would have been bad enough anyway, but now, with this news about her pregnancy, the deuce only knows what the hell I'm meant to say!'

Still sitting behind the desk, Blanding made no reply as

Chesterton remained a few seconds gazing disconsolately out across the misty expanse of runways and grass before turning back to face him. 'You know, Alan,' he said, 'when I first saw that girl's body lying there outside the fence yesterday morning, I naturally assumed she had been attacked by some drunken lout from the village – either that, or some wandering tinker or didicoy.' Grimacing, he shook his head. 'Now, having heard what the autopsy revealed, I'm not nearly so sure. I've this quite awful feeling that someone actually from here on the station was responsible – some poor weakling of a married man who presumably wasn't up to facing the music when Summerfield announced that he'd put her in the family way.'

In his characteristically blunt manner, Chesterton had largely voiced Blanding's now modified explanation for the Waaf's death. He nodded. 'I agree, sir. It looks as if the man she was involved with was responsible, and as you say, he's most likely to be married: that's the only reason I can think of to explain why Summerfield was so careful to keep the relationship hidden. All the same, there's no reason to think that he's someone actually here on the camp. He could just as easily have been some civilian she'd met in the village.'

Taking his pipe from his mouth, Chesterton shook his head. 'Much as I would wish to believe that, simple statistics say otherwise, I fear. There are well over a thousand men here on the station. How many other young males live in the immediate locality? A few dozen at most, and who would they be? Ignorant farm labourers for the most part, much like the chap, I imagine, that Phillips got himself into a fight with – hardly the sort of fellows that an intelligent, well-educated young woman like Corporal Summerfield would willingly have chosen for a beau.' He paused and meditatively reapplied a match to his pipe while, from outside, came the sound of the now-returning Mosquito landing back on the airfield. 'No,' he resumed as the engine sounds faded, 'I'm afraid we have to face it: the man involved is almost certainly one of our own men. What happened, I presume, is that the girl came up here to the camp on the first day of her leave in the hope of being able to settle matters with whoever she'd been secretly seeing before going home to break the news of her pregnancy to her poor parents and write a formal letter of resignation from the WAAF. Obviously some God-awful row developed between the two of them; she might well have threatened to tell everything to the fellow's wife. Anyway, whatever the reason, he must simply then have lost control and struck her down with whatever lay close at hand, and stunned and frightened she died of this heart condition she unknowingly suffered from. Scared out of his wits by what he'd done, the man then desperately tried to revive her. Failing to do so, of course he panicked and decided to it make it look as if she was the victim of an attempted rape, smuggling her body off the camp through the hole in the boundary fence sometime during the night to make us think that the assailant had been some passing stranger.'

It was now Blanding who shook his head. 'No, with all respect, sir, at least one part of your theory cannot be true: Summerfield couldn't have actually been killed here on the station. As the chief inspector pointed out to me yesterday, nobody could have got through that gap in the fence after dark whilst carrying a corpse without either that and his own body coming into contact with the sharp wire ends. Having no free hand to ward them off, they would have bound to have scratched the girl's flesh as well as picking up traces of his own and Corporal Summerfield's uniform.'

As he spoke, his listener's expression gradually lightened, but then, as he broke off, Chesterton again frowned. 'Yes, I agree,' he murmured. 'As you say, the man couldn't have carried the body out through the fence on his own, but it's always possible I suppose that whoever he was found some chum willing to assist him – somebody to hold back the wire mesh to allow whoever was carrying the body to pass through the gap unscathed.'

'No, sir! That I refuse to believe!' protested Blanding. 'Murder's a hanging matter. So for that matter is aiding and abetting it. Is it really credible that the assailant could have found someone, friend or not, willing to risk imprisonment, let alone the gallows, by helping to cover up the killing of anyone, to say nothing of a person as well-known and apparently universally popular as June Summerfield appears to have been?'

'I suppose not.' Chesterton gave a heavy sigh. 'Well, anyway let us just hope you're right.' Looking back round at Blanding, he shook his head sadly. 'I tell you, Alan, the very thought of any one of our chaps here being involved in the girl's killing sickens me to my stomach!' Turning back to the window, he resumed gazing broodingly out across the airfield in silence until there came a tap at the door and a white-jacketed orderly entered the room, wheeling in a laden tea trolley.

CHAPTER TEN

As was customary when there were no air operations pending, Blanding stayed on to take morning coffee with the station commander. He always welcomed these twice-weekly sessions as they gave him the chance of acquainting his superior with any problems he'd recently encountered concerning the smooth running of the camp. It was also an opportunity to gain the CO's support for various small improvements and innovations he'd made, including the latest of the recent changes in laundry procedures and the original installation of the station bicycle racks.

For his own part, Chesterton valued these informal chats equally: not only did they help him 'keep a finger on the pulse' as he put it, but made a pleasant break from the inevitable isolation of command. On these occasions, once business was over, he'd invariably unbutton his tunic and relax, recounting amusing or moving incidents from his Royal Flying Corps days or his later between-wars service in the still-fledgling RAF. At such times, sitting there laughing and talking, he appeared as what he essentially was: a genial, avuncular man, perhaps lacking the drive and ambition for higher command, yet someone who, despite the occasional irascible outburst and an obstinate, Canute-like insistence on pre-war standards of dress and decorum, was almost universally regarded throughout the station with genuine respect and affection.

Today, however, despite Blanding's assurances as to the unlikelihood of any of his men being responsible for what had happened to Corporal Summerfield, the Waaf's death and the circumstances surrounding it continued to weigh heavily upon Chesterton. Apart from a grunted inquiry as to how the other was getting on with his new assistant and if she was settling into her work, he said hardly a word as the pair of them drank their coffee together. For the most part he sat chewing on his pipe, his expression exactly matching that of his dog who, after gulping down the couple of biscuits she'd been thrown, sat soulfully watching her master from beneath the table.

Not even back in January and February, at the height of the winter bombing campaign, when mounting losses were severely undermining morale, and when the daily quota of those visiting the MO included abnormally large numbers of aircrew suffering from stress-induced gastric complaints (as well as a few cases of what was suspected as deliberately contracted venereal disease), had Blanding seen his commanding officer so gravely affected. It was almost as if, in his contemplation of the Waaf corporal's fate, Chesterton was at last confronting those successions of violent deaths and hideous mutilations that had been integral to his life ever since first reporting for pilot training at the old Brooklands racetrack and aerodrome. Either that, or he was simply lamenting the loss of the comfortable certainties and assumptions of the Victorian world into which he'd been born, seeing perhaps the murderous attack on a pregnant young woman as symptomatic of the brutalization two world wars were wreaking upon Western society, allowing the bombing of helpless civilians in their workplaces and homes, and in turn, reducing him to a sort of middle-rank manager, helping to implement a ruthless, systematic and virtually industrialized process of wholesale destruction and slaughter.

Either way, unwilling to burden him further, Blanding mentioned nothing about the disquieting events of the early hours. Nor, with the unlikelihood of further operations in prospect, did he refer to his worries concerning Pat Kelly's state of mind. Instead, he decided to raise both matters with Wing Commander Birdie straight after the LMF inquiry that afternoon. Hurriedly finishing his coffee, he gathered up his papers and withdrew, leaving Chesterton still sitting meditatively sucking on an empty pipe beneath the array of fading, yellowing photographs.

Closing the door quietly behind him, Blanding turned to head back along the crowded main corridor towards his own office. As he did so, among the clerks and typists approaching, he noticed a couple of young sergeants with flying insignia on their chests. There was nothing particularly odd or unusual about the sight of junior aircrew in the administration block, and he would have walked on past without a second glance if they hadn't snapped smartly to attention as he reached them.

Even among the overwhelmingly youthful community of the station, the pair looked very young, hardly older indeed than many of the boys he'd taught back in Dulwich. Though their faces were vaguely familiar, Blanding guessed they were comparatively new to Frampton Wissey, and that, like the eight equally juvenile aircrew replacements he'd welcomed the previous day, they'd only recently arrived from their training unit. Reluctantly he paused, expecting to hear some trivial complaint about lost post or the station's temporary lack of clean laundry – either that, or else to be inflicted with an equally irritating request for information as to the likely length of the present stand-down and the chances of being granted home leave. 'Well?' he asked sharply, disliking being buttonholed in this way. 'What is it you both want?'

It was the shorter of the two who answered, a short, spare, wiry, red-haired youth, whose single-winged flying brevet with its encircled initials AG denoted him an air gunner. 'We're from Sergeant Mackenzie's crew, sir,' he said, a pink flush on his heavily freckled face. 'We've just been to your office looking for you. We were wondering if you could spare us a wee word before the inquiry this afternoon.'

Like Mackenzie himself, the speaker was clearly a lowland Scot – a Glaswegian, Blanding guessed from the accent, and one, as his colouring and physiognomy indicated, almost certainly of Celtic descent. His front teeth were badly chipped. These, together with his unhealthy pallor and stunted frame, brought a vision of grim granite Gorbals tenements and poverty-stricken backstreets and the rusting, weed-strewn shipyards of pre-war Govan or Clydebank.

'A word about what exactly?'

His blush growing deeper, the young Scotsman hesitated a moment before bursting out, 'It's just that we wanted to say that Andy Mackenzie is nae a bad pilot, and we would as soon gang along wi' him as wi' another.'

'That's right, sir,' joined in his comrade, whose battledress blouse sported the insignia of a wireless operator. In contrast to his companion, he was a stocky, broad-shouldered youth, and his voice had the familiar soft burr of a fellow west countryman. 'We're happy to bide along with Andy.'

Normally such a blatant attempt to influence the outcome of an official inquiry would have infuriated Blanding, and he'd have given the perpetrators short shrift for their pains. There was, however, something touching about the nervous concern on these boyish faces. Despite himself, he gave a slight smile. 'Really, I don't

135

know what you think any of this has to do with me?' he said. 'Your skipper's future isn't in my hands – it's a matter to be decided jointly by your squadron commander and Group Captain Chesterton.'

Again it was the Scot who answered, blurting out, 'Aye, sir, but you have influence with yon CO. If you were minded, you could talk him into giving Andy another chance.' Giving Blanding no opportunity to interrupt, the youth pressed desperately on. 'There's nothing wrong wi' the skipper, sir – he's just a wee bit nervy and anxious at present. That's how he came to let the port wheel stray off the taxiway the other night, and why he turned back those two times. We all trained together at the Heavy Conversion Unit and the Lancaster finishing school, and we know him just fine. Honestly, sir, Andy will be okay if he's only given the chance.'

'That,' answered Blanding, frowning severely, 'is for the air force to judge, not you, young man! You may take it from me that the CO and Wing Commander Birdie know their business, and that their ruling will be in the best interests, not only of Sergeant Mackenzie himself, but of everybody else, including both of you.' He paused, but then, seeing the looks of disappointment on the two boyish faces, his expression softened. 'Anyway,' he continued more gently, 'I'm sure you wouldn't want anyone in charge of your aircraft who isn't up to the job. What A-Able needs, I'd have thought, is a skipper who'll give you the best chance of getting through your first tour safely.'

'Och,' burst out the young Scot with scornful impatience, 'with Andy or anyone else, in the end it'll be most likely the same for us! Chances are we're all of us for the chop, sooner or later – and Mike here, me and the rest of the lads would as soon gang down wi' the skipper we've got as wi' another!'

Uncouth though their expression was, and so typical of the fatalistic attitudes prevalent among most bomber aircrew at that stage of the war, the words nevertheless had an almost classical nobility for Blanding, and he regarded the youth who'd spoken with new respect. From his almost jockey-like dimensions, it was only too easy to guess his crew position even if this weren't betrayed by his air-gunner's brevet. It would almost certainly be in the cramped Frazier-Nash turret protruding between the Lancaster's pair of boomed elliptical tail fins. Huddled in that exposed, Perspex–glazed confinement (from which most gunners removed a centre panel to improve their view) and wielding a quartet of woefully inadequate rifle-calibre .303 Browning machine-guns, there this youngster would

136

remain in isolation for hours on end, hardly able to move in his bulky, heavily padded flying gear, chewing caffeine tablets to ward off the deadly drowsiness induced by a combination of continuous engine-roar and stultifying, freezing cold, his neck heavily smeared with lanolin against the soreness caused by his constant scanning of the darkness about him – this boy was a rear gunner, then, an 'arse-end Charlie', first target for any fighter attacking from the rear, and of all the 'poor bloody infantry of the air', as the bomber crews mockingly termed themselves, statistically second only to the pilots themselves as least likely to survive an operational tour. Yet for all that, here he was, this stunted, pallid product of the slums, this poor Irish-Scots Catholic, prepared nevertheless to lessen his already slim chances of outliving the war by standing staunchly by the son of a Presbyterian manse.

Beside him, the wireless operator now joined in enthusiastically. 'That's right, sir. Jock here speaks for the whole crew. We want to stick with Andy and take our chances with him.'

'All right,' said Blanding, reluctantly relenting, 'I'll acquaint the station commander with your wishes. Nevertheless, remember what I say: whatever he and Wing Commander Birdie eventually decide will be in the best interests of yourselves and your skipper – on that, you can rest assured.'

'Aye, sir, of course. Thank you very much, sir.'

Youthful gratitude shone in both faces. Saluting, they turned and hurried away as if fearful the adjutant might change his mind and call them back. As they went, Blanding saw one nudge the other, and the pair exchange covert grins. With a pained half-smile, he watched them disappear, knowing that, either from cowardice or pity, he'd not spoken the truth. Though increasingly composed of such youngsters, the RAF was neither club nor school, and certainly did did not exist for the well-being, happiness or personal fulfilment of its members. That afternoon Mackenzie's lamentable performance – those unprecedented two 'boomerangs' in a row, followed by the near disastrous bogging-down of a fully-laden bomber during the commencement of operations – would be objectively analyzed, and the decision regarding the young pilot's future would be decided solely on what was considered the best interests of the service. What that would be, Blanding had little doubt: Mackenzie's personality and competence would almost certainly be judged inadequate for operational flying, and before colours were lowered that evening in all likelihood he'd already be off the station and on his way to one of the euphemistically termed 'refresher courses'. That or worse – transferred to another camp with his battledress stripped of rank and flying insignia, his papers, even his pay-book, boldly stamped with the initials LMF – in the harsh biblical terms of his father's church, a pariah, a leper, a diseased minor limb or other appendage plucked out and removed from the main body for the good of the whole.

Turning away, he walked thoughtfully on, those misplaced looks of triumph on the youngsters' faces still vividly in his mind. During his time at Frampton Wissey, he'd learnt that the comradeship of a bomber crew was invariably close. Nevertheless, until now he hadn't fully appreciated the potential strength of that bond. As the young air gunner and wireless operator had just demonstrated, it could transcend not only the barriers of religion and class, but even of self-preservation itself – almost as if, flying through freezing darkness, cocooned within the frail womb of the aircraft, drawing on the same life-giving oxygen system through umbilical-like tubes, they became united as one interdependent blood brotherhood.

Lost in these thoughts, Blanding suddenly paused. Until that moment, he'd confidently believed that the assault on Corporal Summerfield must have happened outside the camp simply because, as he'd asserted to the CO, it was impossible to conceive the assailant being able to find anyone willing to risk liberty or even life by helping to cover up the deed. Now he realized the fallacy of that view. It had been based upon the assumption that, except within fairly narrow parameters, people invariably acted from self-interest, choosing those courses of action most likely to guarantee their own well-being, comfort and safety. War, vile and inhuman though it was, taught quite otherwise, however: that mankind was ultimately neither logical nor pragmatic, and was at times driven by urges, not only unnecessary for propagation and the survival of the species, but often directly inimical to those ends. Daily it demonstrated that, for a flag or a political creed, men and women could rise above their inborn terror of physical pain and personal annihilation, either risking death during the frenzy of battle or by coolly and deliberately choosing some especially hazardous duty. It followed, therefore, that, if an abstract allegiance or simply a wish for excitement could prompt thousands of youngsters to volunteer for the perils of wartime flying, then personal loyalty to a friend easily might transcend fear of mere legal sanctions. If the person who had struck Corporal Summerfield down belonged to one of the bomber crews, then potentially at least he'd had six others to aid and abet him in the concealment of the crime – men bound to him by the strongest of ties, whose natural repugnance and horror at the killing would have been at least partly mitigated by their constant anticipation and experience of violent death – and that all the more so if the victim had been regarded as a 'chop girl', whose involvement with a comrade indirectly appeared to threaten the lives of the whole crew.

As he stood in the busy thoroughfare, clutching the pile of defaulters' personal files and charge sheets to his chest, all Blanding's earlier suspicions now came rushing back. Was it possible, he wondered, that the police surgeon's rough estimate of the time of death had been wrong, and that one of the station aircrew had been responsible for Summerfield's death as he'd originally thought? Had the girl been attacked, not after the bombers had taken off, but earlier, when the squadron was still on the ground? Could it have been that, faced with returning home to announce to her parents that she was pregnant and knowing that she must therefore resign from the WAAF, she'd managed to make her way out to her lover's plane, doing so perhaps with the desperate intention of shaming him in front of his crewmates into acknowledging his unborn child? And had he, already tense with pre-operational nerves and goaded beyond patience by her repeated entreaties, finally lost control and lashed out wildly with some heavy, sharp object conveniently at hand, perhaps the aircraft's fire axe – the raised implement, the fury in his face and the blow itself combining to inspire the terror that had stopped the victim's heart and left her face contorted in horror? Blindly panicking after failing to revive her, had he then implored the aid of his comrades to dump her body outside the perimeter fence? Then later, suffering the inevitable guilt pangs, had either the killer himself or another of the crew contacted the local exchange to inform the authorities where the dead Waaf lay sometime after safely returning from the operation next morning?

Even as this scenario ran through his head, Blanding could see its patent absurdity. To begin with, there was victim's own personality: from everything he'd learnt, June Summerfield had been an intelligent, well-balanced young woman – someone who, without fuss, had gone quietly on with her duties after the death of the two men she'd been close to. Surely, therefore, the last sort of person to be harassing the father of her unborn baby and creating an hysterical

139

scene in public. Apart from that, there was also the simple matter of opportunity: even though an unauthorized person might have been able to make his way out to an aircraft at dispersal, from the time the crew-truck arrived to the moment when its engines were started and it began taxiing out to join the queue of planes awaiting take-off, its ground staff would have been in constant attendance. Beside that, the very notion of a corpse being half stripped and then lugged unnoticed across a busy airfield even in darkness was plainly ridiculous, especially as the men involved would have been encumbered at the time by clumsy, fur-lined flying-boots and thickly padded in multiple layers of clothing.

Bizarre and fanciful though the concept undoubtedly was, Blanding nevertheless found himself unable to dismiss it completely. There had to be a link, he felt, between the girl's pregnancy – and the enforced discharge from the WAAF this entailed – and her subsequent death. There was also something about the timing of the anonymous phone-call and the manner in which the body had been left that gave him the feeling that he'd moved a tiny bit nearer to discovering the truth of what had happened to Corporal Summerfield.

There were the files and charge sheets to be returned to the clerks' office; there was the usual mass of paperwork awaiting his attention; above all, Diana was having to deal with everything on her own in the office. Torn between his wish to see how she was coping and a similarly overpowering urge to check with Stanley to see if the pathologist had verified the original estimated time of death, Blanding remained standing a few moments longer in the maze of busy corridors. Then, remembering that most of the afternoon would be taken up with the LMF inquiry and that he'd therefore have little opportunity of consulting the chief inspector later, he reluctantly turned and began retracing his footsteps back down the passage in the direction of the police inquiry room.

There was no one waiting outside to be interviewed, and when Blanding knocked at the door, a gruff voice immediately invited him to enter. To his relief, he found neither Squadron Leader Walker nor any of the station personnel present within. The same burly figure in civilian clothes sat laboriously typing at the further of the pair of facing desks as the previous day, while the only change in the decor and furnishing of the cramped little ex-storeroom was that now a large-scale Ordnance Survey map of the area hung on the wall directly above Stanley's chair.

With WPC Matthews standing besides him, open telephone directory in one hand, the chief inspector was seated beneath the map, poring over what obviously were the brass rubbing impressions found among the dead Waaf's things. As Blanding appeared in the doorway clutching his bundle of charge sheets and personal files to his chest, the detective glanced up with a look of irritation. Seeing who his caller was, however, he leaned back in his chair and, carefully peeling the latest bedraggled home-made cigarette from his lips, regarded the intruder with a quizzical smile. 'Ah, good morning once again, Flight Lieutenant – and what, pray, can we do for you?'

Conscious of the typing having stopped and his entrance causing a momentary hiatus in activity, Blanding flushed. Sensing that this was not the best moment to be inquiring into further details of the autopsy findings, and also feeling constrained by the presence of Stanley's assistants, he decided to postpone his questions until a more opportune time. 'I merely dropped by, Chief Inspector,' he answered evasively, 'to check that the number of our men placed at your disposal for today's search was sufficient. If you need more, you have only to ask.'

A smile, knowing and ironic, flickered momentarily across the elderly detective's face. As fast as it had come, however, it disappeared, and Stanley gravely inclined his head. 'Thank you,' he replied, 'but I think we have enough searchers for the present. If more are required, Squadron Leader Walker will doubtless arrange it through you or Group Captain Chesterton.'

'Yes, of course – well in that case, I'll allow you to continue your investigations in peace.' Thankful for the opportunity to escape, Blanding hurriedly turned to leave. Hampered, however, by the bundle of files and papers in his arms, he had to struggle to open the door. As he was doing so, Stanley called out from behind, 'Actually, Flight Lieutenant, to tell you the truth, I don't think there's much likelihood of us finding anything, not even if we had the help of the entire Brigade of Guards!'

Startled, Blanding paused and looked round.

'There are just too many dykes and ditches in this area to conceal whatever weapon was used,' explained the speaker, seeing the adjutant's look of surprise. 'Same goes for the deceased's missing items of clothes – if they've been weighed down and dropped into water, we'd be lucky to come across them if we searched every day for the next six months!'

Emboldened by the companionable confidentiality of the policeman's tone, Blanding's glance strayed towards the brass rubbings on the desk. 'I take it,' he said, nodding towards them, 'that you're trying to establish from where these impressions were taken?'

'Yes, indeed,' grunted Stanley, stretching across the papers to stub out what remained of his cigarette. 'In fact,' he continued, sitting back, 'WPC Matthews here was about to start telephoning round the local clergy when you came in. If we can only discover which churches contain the actual brass plates, then we can send someone round to see if anybody remembers the deceased asking permission to take their impressions. By that means, we might be able to get a description of anyone who might have been with her. Trouble is,' he continued, frowning down at the papers in front of him, 'we need some accurate way of describing these things.' He gave a dry laugh and glanced back at the caller. 'I don't suppose, Flight Lieutenant,' he said grinning, 'that the RAF, even with its multitude of trades and specialisations, is able to provide me with an expert on medieval tomb brasses?'

All his former coldness had now disappeared, and catching the humorous glint in his eyes, Blanding smiled in return. 'Well,' he answered, turning to heap the burden he was clutching onto the filing-cabinet besides the door, 'as it so happens, I've a slight knowledge of the subject myself. If you'll allow me, perhaps I can be of some use.' Squeezing past the young policewoman, he bent over the desk and began examining the topmost of the long sheets of waxed paper.

On its broad surface, rather like a black-and-white photographic negative, appeared the effigy of a young knight and his wife beneath an heraldic shield. Clad in plate armour, with a sallet-type helmet on his head, visor raised, and with a long sword at his side, the curiously thin and elongated warrior was depicted kneeling in prayer. In identical pose, his equally juvenile spouse knelt obliquely facing him, wearing a butterfly head-dress and a low-cut gown whose collar and cuffs were trimmed with fur. In no way were the quaintly stylized figures unusual or strange. Both their pious meekness and extreme youth were, as Blanding knew, merely the artistic convention of the age – the figures being nothing more than a formalized expression of a poetic ideal. Similar images of chivalric humility and wifely devotion were, he was aware, emblazoned on dozens of medieval tombs, commemorating those who in life had

142

doubtless borne little or no resemblance to such strangely unworldly representations of themselves. Nevertheless, examining the carefully-made rubbing with the irregular thump and clatter of the typewriter continuing at his back and with the low, pulsating sound of a large formation of American heavy bombers passing high overhead, Blanding found himself strangely touched by the poignancy of the crudely depicted young couple, so many hundreds of years dead and belonging to a world so infinitely remote from his own. He continued to peer down as the roar of aero-engines gradually faded into the distance, feeling a vague but growing sense of familiarity with the rubbing in front of him: somewhere he'd seen that particular pair of kneeling figures before, but where that had been and when, and in what particular circumstances, he was utterly unable for the moment to remember.

'Mean anything to you?'

Stanley's question broke into his thoughts. 'Not much,' he murmured, 'though this armour here,' he went on, tapping the rubbing with a forefinger, 'with these large elbow-cops and the jointed sollerets is definitely mid- or late fifteenth century, as indeed seems the woman's head-dress.' Straightening, he turned back to face the policeman. 'But knowing the approximate age of the tomb won't be of much help, I'm afraid, Chief Inspector. As you doubtless know, East Anglia is dotted all over with ancient churches, and this particular tablet could be in any one of them. What I'd therefore suggest,' he continued, bending back to flick rapidly through the rest of the rubbings, 'is that you take the whole collection over to the county museum in Cambridge. If they don't show up in their records, then contact the Royal College of Arms – from the shield devices, they'll be able to give you the locality of the family seats concerned. It will take a few days perhaps, but once you have those, it should be easy to trace the churches in which the actual brasses themselves are located.'

A look of admiration lit Stanley's face. 'Good Heavens, Flight Lieutenant! You amaze me! You turn out to be a ruddy mine of information!'

'Not at all,' protested Blanding, blushing profusely. 'It's just that brass rubbing used to be a hobby of my own at one time. As a schoolmaster before the war, I found it a useful way of interesting the boys in our medieval past.'

'Indeed? So you were a teacher then?' Stanley leaned back

and, folding his arms, regarded the man standing above him with much the same look of wry amusement as Diana had done the previous day. 'And this establishment you taught at – would I be correct in assuming that it was some sort of private school?'

'Yes,' replied Blanding, colouring the more. 'I was a senior housemaster at Dulwich College in south London.'

Throughout his conversation with Stanley, the detective sergeant's amateurish typing had continued in a fitful manner behind his back. Now, however, as Blanding uttered the final words, the irregular clatter of the keys came to an abrupt halt. At the same time, the young policewoman, who until then had stood listening with respectful attention to everything said, visibly stiffened and looked round at him with what seemed like an expression of cold disapproval on her thin, freckled, rather horsy face.

Sensing the sudden change in the atmosphere in the room, Blanding seemed to feel a similar cold chill go through himself. Before he had chance to get out a word, however, the chief inspector hastily intervened. 'Right, Matthews,' he said, briskly rolling the collection of brass rubbings into a bundle and passing them to the policewoman, 'you heard what the gentleman said. Phone the county museum and arrange for these to be shown to them. If they can't help, then get on to this Royal College of Arms down in London.' As she turned to leave, Stanley gestured towards the chair in front of his desk. 'Please take a seat, Flight Lieutenant,' he said, smiling. 'There are one or two other little matters I'd like to consult you on – that's of course if you're able to spare me a few more minutes of your valuable time.'

'Yes, of course,' murmured Blanding, still dazed and dismayed by the reaction to his mention of Dulwich College and his position in the school. Uncomfortably aware that it might have sounded like showing off a social superiority, he took the seat, inwardly cursing himself for his stupidity and profoundly wishing that he'd had the good sense to mention nothing about his pre-war life.

Whatever hostility the reference to the school had evoked in his subordinates, Stanley was apparently not touched by it. Indeed, as if keen to relieve his guest of any embarrassment, he was again all smiling affability. Having dispatched his sergeant in search of a pot of tea, he began talking about his connections with Dulwich. It seemed that he knew the area well as his late wife had been born in the area, and he had many happy memories of long ago stays above her father's

144

ironmonger's shop on the Brockwell Park end of the Croxted Road. 'But now, Flight Lieutenant,' he said, suddenly breaking off from his reminiscences, 'might I inquire the real reason for your visit?' He smiled broadly. 'It was, I imagine, something more important than inquiring as to the number of men on this morning's search.'

Relaxed by the conversation, Blanding smiled in response. 'Well, as it happens, Chief Inspector, you're quite right. Passing your door, I thought I'd slip in check to see if the autopsy report confirmed the original estimate of time of death.'

Head slightly on one side like some thin-necked wading bird, Stanley regarded him thoughtfully, beginning as he did so to tap round his pockets. 'Yes, I remember,' he said, taking out and laying before him the now familiar tobacco pouch, matches and cigarette-making machine, 'that yesterday you were rather keen to learn the time of the deceased's death. Now here you are, asking about it again.'

Meeting the policeman's gaze steadily, Blanding gave a slight shrug. 'I'd merely like to know, that's all.'

A sceptical smile crossed Stanley's face. Saying nothing, however, he opened his desk drawer to take out a sheet of typed paper. 'Well,' he said, consulting it with the aid of a pair of wire-rimmed spectacles, 'the pathologist's estimate generally agrees with that of the police-surgeon. According to him, death most likely took place somewhere around eleven that night – certainly no earlier than ten in the evening or much later than midnight.'

'And that's quite certain, is it? There's no chance of a mistake?'

'I very much doubt it,' replied Stanley dryly, folding his glasses and slipping them into his top pocket. 'Unless something like an unusual high or low temperature happens to affect the normal cooling-down rate of a body, the time of death can be gauged pretty accurately on the whole – the standard calculation is, I believe, that it cools at a rate of one and a half degrees Fahrenheit per hour.'

Having not only been awake throughout the entire period, but also having read the hourly met reports coming into the operations room, Blanding had first-hand knowledge of the conditions prevailing on the night of Corporal Summerfield's death. The tail end of a low-pressure system had been passing over at the time. The resultant weather had been similar to the forty-eight hours preceding it: miserable, drizzling-wet with light westerly winds and heavy cloud cover maintaining an even ground temperature. The pathologist's estimate was therefore, he concluded, almost certainly correct, and that the attack on the girl must indeed have taken place well after the last of the Lancasters had taken off as he'd originally thought. It therefore seemed to follow that nobody flying that night could possibly have been involved in the girl's death, and that the whole unlikely scenario he'd conjured up out in the corridor had been nothing but his own absurd imaginings.

As he was thinking this, Stanley returned the pathologist's report to the drawer. Instead of immediately closing it, however, the policeman drew out a large, leather-bound notebook from the drawer. 'You're an educated man, Flight Lieutenant,' he said. 'You could therefore perhaps do me another small favour. This jottings or commonplace book was discovered among the deceased's things. I'd be grateful if you'd glance through it, and give me your response.'

'Of course – only too delighted.' Remembering Diana mentioning such an item the previous afternoon, Blanding took the proffered book. Turning it over, he briefly admired the quality of the tooling on the cover before flipping it open to find written on the flyleaf in a juvenile hand:

June Margaret Summerfield,
Form IA,
Bedford Girls' Grammar School,
Bedfordshire,
England,
Great Britain - Europe - the World - the Universe
bought with the pocket money given me by Dad, Mum and Auntie Meg for
passing my school entrance exam

24th May 1936

Although she'd been so often in his thoughts since coming across her half-stripped body, until this moment June Summerfield had been a somewhat nebulous figure to Blanding: a pretty, if unexceptional face in a tiny official photograph; the sociable young woman of Palmer's description; the girl whose smile the station commander had remarked on – 'just one more', as he'd facetiously phrased it when speaking to Diana, 'of our valiant young ladies in blue' – differentiated from the two hundred or so other Waafs on the station only by a curiously sinister reputation and an unusual interest in making brass rubbings. Now though, looking down at the hand-written inscription, he glimpsed something of the spirit and the strength of the personality who'd originally penned the words.

146

Curiosity whetted, he turned over the first page, intrigued to discover what particular extracts of poetry and prose the eleven-year-old pupil had chosen to copy into her book.

> *I remember, I remember,*
> *The house where I was born,*
> *The little window where the sun*
> *Came peeping in at morn;*
> *He never came a wink too soon,*
> *Nor brought too long a day*
> *But now, I often wish the night*
> *Had borne my breath away!*

It was with surprise that he found himself looking down at the familiar opening words of the first adult poem he himself had loved. To find that somebody else at a similar age, and she a girl, had been attracted by the doleful poignancy of Thomas Hood's famous lines came as a mild shock. For a few moments, he sat regarding the carefully rounded handwriting, trying to envisage the childhood and youth of the village shopkeeper's daughter who'd won a place at her local grammar school, guessing that she'd suffered much the same sense of isolation and loneliness in her small Bedfordshire community as he in his equally obscure little Dorset abode.

Turning on, he noted the more expected choices: Blake's 'The Tiger' and Ariel's cowslip song from 'The Tempest', together with some well-known biblical extracts. Nevertheless, the later inclusion of two of Shakespeare's darker sonnets, Robert Frost's 'Stopping by Woods on a Snowy Evening' and Keats's 'Ode To a Nightingale' all bespoke that same melancholy awareness of mutability and inevitable loss that had been so much his own experience of adolescence. Pausing in his reading, he again envisaged the growing girl, marooned in the drab mid-Bedfordshire landscape amidst an interminable acreage of cabbages and brussels sprouts.

'Interesting, Flight Lieutenant?'

Stanley's question broke into his thoughts. Glancing up, he found the policeman had paused in the task of smoothing a charge of tobacco between the rollers of his cigarette-making machine and was regarding him closely.

'Yes, indeed.' Bowing back to the book, Blanding observed the handwriting growing increasingly firm and distinctive as he thumbed on, and also the inclusions becoming ever more diverse and sophisticated as girlhood gave way to young adulthood. Now there was 'Prufrock' and some other poems by T. S. Eliot, as well as a number by John Donne and other seventeenth century poets, including some particular favourites of his own. But then, as he turned to the last completed page, he gave an exclamation of surprise, and stared incredulously down at the final prose extract the Waaf corporal had copied out.

> The course of Fate moves the sky and the stars, governs the relationship between the elements and transforms them through the reciprocal variations; it renews all things as they come to birth and die away like generations of offspring and seed. It holds sway, too, over the acts and fortunes of men through the indissoluble chain of causes; and since it takes its origins from unchanging Providence, it follows that these causes, too, are unchanging. For the best way of controlling the universe is if the simplicity immanent in the divine mind produces an unchanging order of causes to govern by its own incommutability everything that is subject to change, and which will otherwise fluctuate at random. It is because you are in no position to contemplate this order that everything seems confused and upset. But it is no less true that everything has its own position which directs it towards the good and so governs it.

'Is everything all right, Flight Lieutenant?'

Blanding blinked up to meet Stanley's gaze, who now sat smoking, eyes fixed intently upon him. 'Yes,' he replied evasively, his mind still reeling from the shock of what he'd stumbled upon, 'it's merely that I've come across something I didn't expect – an extract from the writings of Boethius.'

'Boethius?'

'Anicius Manlius Boethius, Chief Inspector,' murmured Blanding, glancing down again at the copied-out words in wondering disbelief, but at the same time determining already to hide the full extent of his shock from his watchful interrogator, 'the fifth-century stoic philosopher, who wrote his *De Consolatione Philosophiae* whilst in prison awaiting execution during the reign of the Ostrogothic Emperor Theodoric.'

'Indeed?' Stanley took a thoughtful drag on his cigarette. 'And this work is very obscure, I take it?'

'The Consolation?' Blanding shook his head. 'By no means,' he answered. 'In fact, our two perhaps greatest monarchs, Alfred and Good Queen Bess, translated it into the vernacular, as so, of course, did Chaucer. Indeed, so important was the work regarded in the Middle Ages that Dante set it among the twelve heavenly lights of the sun. Nevertheless,' he added, frowning down again at the page, 'it isn't exactly what I'd term commonplace reading these days, and I find it surprising that even a comparatively well-read young person like June Summerfield should ever have come across the work. Nor,' he went on with a slight grimace, 'can I help thinking that there's something horribly ironic in the fact that both she and the book's author met such curiously similar fates – one struck down by a blow to the forehead by person or persons unknown, the other dragged from his cell to be bludgeoned to death by soldiers of the imperial guard.'

Without immediately replying, Stanley turned to the window and gazed thoughtfully out at the deserted parade ground. 'Flight Lieutenant,' he said, at last looking back round, 'when I questioned Warrant Officer Dawson yesterday over the finding of the body, he mentioned that you didn't appear to recognize the deceased. I therefore concluded that you'd had no personal contact with Corporal Summerfield – I take it that is correct?'

Conscious of a new, careful formality in the policeman's tone, Blanding nodded. 'Yes, I don't remember ever having met her, though I suppose I would have passed her often enough around the camp.'

'And you never had cause to communicate with her in any way?'

'Directly, you mean?' Blanding shook his head. 'No, there was no necessity of my doing so.'

'And you taught at Dulwich College before the war?'

Startled by this abrupt change of subject, and wondering where the questioning was going, Blanding again nodded. 'Yes,' he replied with a frown, 'that's correct.'

Stanley rubbed his chin thoughtfully. 'I don't suppose,' he said, 'that you've ever come across any of your old pupils or fellow ex-members of staff during your time in the RAF? There's not, for example, apart from yourself, anyone here on this station connected with the school?'

'With Dulwich College?' Again Blanding frowned. 'No, nobody at all. But whyever do you ask? What has any of this to do with the investigation into Corporal Summerfield's death?'

Not replying, Stanley reopened the desk drawer and drew out a second volume: a battered, yellow cloth-bound book whose cover had been extensively repaired at some time with strips of red sticky tape. 'This also,' he said, opening and then holding up the title-page in front of his face, 'was also found among the deceased's things.'

Intrigued, Blanding leaned forward and peered at the held-open page. As he did so, his face immediately cleared. 'Ah yes, of course!' he cried out in delighted recognition. 'That's a copy of W. V. Cooper's 1902 translation of the *Consolation* – Summerfield must have copied the extract from it.'

'So it would appear,' murmured Stanley dryly. 'That particular passage has been carefully underlined.' Lowering the book, he flipped back to the flyleaf. 'And this, I imagine,' he said, once again raising the volume and turning it towards the man sitting across the desk, 'you find equally familiar.'

Blanding gave a gasp and stared almost unbelievingly at what was now being held up before his face. There, affixed to the inside cover, was the familiar Dulwich College bookplate with its motto and elaborate baroque crest, over which two ruled lines in green ink had been drawn. The tag 'ex libris' had been similarly scored through, and above in the top left corner there was written in slightly faded pencil: 'Sale price 2d'.

Dumbfounded, he continued to stare at the held-open page, realizing now only too clearly the reason for the questions about Dulwich College and why that frisson of hostility had passed through the room at the mention of his connection with the school. Dimly, as if from a distance, he heard Stanley's voice. 'Well, Flight Lieutenant,' he was saying, 'how do you explain how a book, sold off from the library of the same boys' public school in which you taught, should ever have found its way among the possessions of one of your own station Waafs?'

CHAPTER ELEVEN

'Look, would you mind if I went off for lunch now?'

As if startled out of a daydream, Blanding raised his head and blinked at the questioner. Little more than a quarter of an hour had passed since returning to find Diana still hard at work where he'd left her when originally summoned to the station commander's office. Nevertheless, from the look of dazed perplexity on his face, it seemed to her that the short interval between her giving him the various messages she'd taken during the course of the morning and him then turning his attention to the latest batch of official signals was still enough time for him to somehow contrive to forget her existence completely. He now seemed quite bewildered to look up to find her sitting at the adjacent desk. 'Lunch?' he murmured vaguely as if hearing the word for the first time. Hastily recollecting himself, he glanced at his watch. 'Ah, yes, of course!' he exclaimed, forcing a smile. 'Off you go – and thank you once again for so efficiently holding the fort here all morning on your own.'

Diana gave a light laugh. 'I only hope,' she said, getting to her feet, 'that I didn't make too many mistakes, that's all – and if I didn't, it's only due to all the help Mr Starling gave me.' As she went over to collect her coat from beside the door, Blanding's gaze returned to the pile of dispatches before him. Despite his best efforts to absorb their contents, his thoughts remained wholly dominated by his recent conversation with the chief inspector. So staggering had the revelations been – so inexplicably strange and uncanny – that even now, thirty minutes or so after leaving the inquiry room, he still felt almost as appalled and disorientated as when Stanley had first held up the battered ex-library copy of the *Consolation* to display the Dulwich College bookplate inside. Indeed, having had time to consider the implications, his initial bewilderment was now overlaid with a sense of fear – a terror not so much at the thought of his

151

imminent arrest (although that possibility certainly he knew couldn't be discounted), but rather what he'd learnt seemed to suggest about his own present state of psychological health.

Even without his unfortunate predecessor's example as an awful warning, Blanding had always known of the psychological dangers of his work. During training, he and the others on his course (mostly small-town solicitors, accountants or ex-public schoolmasters like himself) had been repeatedly warned of the possible effects of the isolation and overwork endured by most station adjutants, especially among those serving on operational bases. Long indeed before Kelly's extraordinary outburst the day before or Palmer's warning over coffee later, he'd been only too painfully aware of his deteriorating mental condition. The frightening lapses of memory, his general irritability as well as an obsessional desire to implement every minor rule and regulation were, as he realized, all obvious symptoms of stress. So indeed were the succession of nosebleeds and dreadful bouts of insomnia he'd recently suffered. Everything from his insistence on correct bicycle stowage to his tinkering with the camp laundry procedures could be seen as a classic form of neurosis, stemming in all likelihood from a deep need to try and impose order on a world in which he was helpless to prevent the destruction of so many of its younger inhabitants. Equally, his repeated attempts to penetrate the riddle surrounding June Summerfield's demise were most likely a further unconscious response to the murderous toll of aircrew over the winter – almost as if, in seeking to explain her mysterious death, he might somehow make sense of the savage losses the station had suffered. Now, however, after coming across that particular Boethius extract in the Waaf's jottings book, and then, before he'd recovered from the shock of that, having been almost immediately confronted by his old school bookplate, it felt as if he had at last reached – if not actually crossed – some invisible boundary or frontier between sanity and madness. Insane and utterly irrational as it seemed, he'd left the police inquiry room with the overpowering sense of having been somehow involved and deeply influential in the life of a young woman he'd never met – either that or, crazier yet, Corporal Summerfield had been in some way an extension of himself, a doppelgänger as it were, living a separate existence but moving towards her death along a parallel course to his own.

'Aren't you coming as well?'

Diana's voice broke into his meditations. Raising his head, he

152

found his assistant standing beside the door, greatcoat and service cap on, and with the strap of her gasmask satchel thrown casually over one shoulder. Not immediately understanding her question, he stared blankly back at him for a moment before shaking his head. 'No,' he answered, dropping his eyes, 'I think I'll skip lunch today — there are one or two trifling matters I need to try to sort out in my mind.'

Instead of turning away as he expected, Diana continued to regard him with what seemed like a look of concern. 'Pardon me for saying,' she said, 'but you seem as if you've heard bad news. Is this anything to do with being called away to the CO's room this morning?' She paused slightly, and then said anxiously, 'Don't tell me that another Waaf has been attacked!'

'No, no,' answered Blanding hurriedly. 'It's nothing like that — merely that I had a rather disquieting interview with Chief Inspector Stanley after defaulters' parade.' Unwilling to continue, he broke off, but as Diana remained beside the door, regarding him inquiringly, he reluctantly forced himself on. 'It appears,' he said with a slight grimace, 'that among Corporal Summerfield's things there was an ex-library book from Dulwich College — as you can imagine, that puts me in a somewhat awkward position.'

Diana frowned, but then, almost instantly, shook her head, 'Because you were once a member of staff there, you mean? No, I don't see that!' she went on. 'Summerfield could have got such a book anywhere — very likely she picked it up at some jumble sale or from a second-hand bookshop. What with the paper shortage and the destruction of so many of the publishers' warehouses during the Blitz, books are in short supply these days, and people are only too thankful to grab whatever they can get.'

'I know,' replied Blanding heavily, 'but all the same, it's an odd coincidence you must admit, Summerfield having a book from the very same school I used to teach at.' Removing his spectacles, he wearily rubbed his eyes. 'What with that incident here on the camp in the early hours,' he continued, 'I had a somewhat broken sleep last night. Now this, coming on top of that and everything else, has rather thrown me I must admit.'

'That's quite understandable.' As if endeavouring to think of something else she might add, Diana hesitated before reluctantly turning to leave. Pausing before the door, she seemed to consider for a moment before turning back to the seated figure at the desk. 'Look,'

153

she said gently, 'why don't you join me for lunch? You'll feel a lot better after having something to eat, and you really need to keep up your strength for this inquiry you've got this afternoon. Anyway,' she added quickly, 'we need to go over some of these administrative procedures together. I really can't keep calling on Mr Starling all the time – the poor lamb has enough of his own work to do.'

'I suppose that's right,' agreed Blanding reluctantly, one part of him briefly marvelling at the notion of the grim, hatched-faced Starling as a blithe skipping lamb. He briefly frowned down at the papers in front of him before again raising his head. 'Well, it seems I'm being given no choice,' he said, getting to his feet with a wan smile. 'In that case, I'd better take you up on your invitation then.'

A light south-westerly breeze had sprung up during the course of the morning. This, together with the sun's warmth, had dispelled the final traces of the previous night's mist, and there was once more an almost summer-like feel to the air as Blanding and Diana left the administration block. With no operations in prospect, the camp retained much the same feeling of tranquillity as the day before. Comparatively few people were about, and apart from occasional brief clatter of machine-gun fire from where armourers were carrying out calibration tests at the butts, the only sign of the station's normal high level of activity was the drone of a solitary Lancaster on circuit – presumably either the newly-joined crew returning from their local familiarisation flight or a recently repaired machine undergoing a routine airworthiness check.

The rumble of the descending aircraft's engines was as natural and familiar to Frampton Wissey as the distant gunfire or the intermittent bleating of sheep. Hardly aware of any of the sounds, the two figures strolled leisurely through the sunshine towards the officers' mess, Blanding answering his assistant's questions as they went. After the turmoil Stanley's disclosures had created in his mind, the mild interrogation came as a welcome relief. Like the grammar of Latin and Greek, service administration had its own fixed certainties and rules, and instead of wresting with the nebulous and intangible in vain, Blanding found it soothing to turn his attention to the relatively straight-forward and concrete.

Gradually, he began to unbend. Moving on from such everyday items as travel documents, movement orders and requisition forms, he began speaking of more general matters,

154

including his worries concerning the huge number of problems his new laundry procedures had thrown up. To all this, Diana listened intently, even volunteering to look into the matter herself. Talk thus continued until they arrived at the mess, ceasing only as they mounted the front steps and pushed through the revolving door into an almost deserted foyer. Apart from a murmur of voices from the bar and the click of balls in the billiards room, the whole building seemed oddly quiet. Due to the relaxed mood of the camp and the almost total lack of flying activity, breakfast had been unusually prolonged that morning. Consequently, there were few takers for early lunch, and when the two newcomers entered the dining room they found themselves among the first arrivals, and were thus able to find a table on their own next to one of the long windows.

On the walk over, absorbed in answering Diana's questions, Blanding's thoughts had been taken up with the details of their joint duties. Now, however, in accordance with the tradition that no so-called 'shop talk' was permitted within the mess, the subject of work was denied him. As a result, he could think of little to say, and after a few trite comments on the weather, conversation lapsed and an awkward silence fell. Around them came the clink of cutlery and the murmur of voices from the handful of diners scattered about the room, while faint and ghostly from a gramophone upstairs there wafted the liquid tones of Deanna Durbin, singing 'Ave Maria'.

Careful to avoid his companion's eyes, Blanding turned to the window to watch the now recently landed Lancaster taxiing back towards dispersals. Sunlight gleamed on its brown-and-green camouflaged upper surfaces, the bulbous H2S radar housing beneath its black-painted belly, and the highly-polished Perspex cockpit canopy, astrodome and gun-turrets flashing as they caught the light. For a few moments longer, he followed the bomber's cumbersome progress round the peri-track, then, raising his head, gazed broodingly away across the fens towards where Ely Cathedral rose like an ancient grey dreadnought in the distant haze.

'You're not still worrying about that old school book?'

Glancing back to face her, Blanding found Diana regarding him quizzically. 'Yes,' he answered with an embarrassed smile, 'I suppose I am.'

'Well, I really don't think you should,' insisted the other. 'There's bound to be some perfectly innocent explanation.'

'You think so?' murmured Blanding, sounding unconvinced.

155

Turning back to the window, he stared out towards the distant cathedral for a few moments more before again looking round. 'But you see,' he said with a pained look, 'it isn't just that. There are other things as well.'

'What sort of other things?'

There wasn't time for an immediate reply, for at that moment the first course arrived in the hands of the silver-haired steward. With ponderous, almost ecclesiastical solemnity, bowls of lukewarm tinned tomato soup were placed before them, the server finally bowing slightly and then backing away as if having presented the most exotic of dishes. With a wry smile, Diana watched him withdraw before turning back to Blanding. 'Well?' she asked. 'What are these other things then?'

Giving himself time to compose his reply, her companion bent to take a spoonful of the tepid liquid. 'You remember,' he said, wincing slightly at the taste and pausing to dab at his lips with a napkin, 'there was also a leather jottings book among Summerfield's possessions? Anyway, before springing that ex-Dulwich College library book on me, Chief Inspector Stanley asked me to glance through what she'd copied into that.'

'Yes?'

'Well, in a way,' resumed Blanding with a frown, 'I suppose most of the poems and prose extracts included were what any well-read youngster might have selected. But then, reading on, I was struck by the fact that the pieces used were, without exception, things I have particularly loved myself.'

Diana shrugged. 'So you and Summerfield happened to share the same tastes in literature – there's nothing, I'd have thought, particularly odd about that.'

Though Blanding met her eyes steadily, his look remained troubled. 'But you don't understand,' he answered, 'the similarity of taste was almost uncanny. I know this sounds completely crazy, but towards the end it felt almost as if I'd been doing the choosing.' He paused slightly and looked down. 'And there was something about one particular item,' he said, as if frowningly addressing his soup, 'the very last thing copied into the book, that I didn't mention to the chief inspector – something I felt too scared to tell him – something I can hardly believe myself.'

'Go on.'

'On the last used page, Summerfield had transcribed a passage

156

from Boethius' *Consolation of Philosophy*.' Blanding lifted his head and looked inquiringly across the table. 'I don't suppose you're personally acquainted with the work?'

'Never even heard of it, I'm afraid,' replied Diana with a rueful laugh. 'Though I did moderately well at school – modern languages was my forte – I wasn't at all what you might call a scholar. But go on,' she urged, seeing Blanding's look of disappointment, 'tell me – what was it about this particular extract that you didn't dare tell the police?'

'Well,' he answered, 'first, I suppose I found it odd that someone of Summerfield's age and background should have chosen to quote from Boethius at all. As you've just demonstrated, the *Consolation* isn't exactly commonplace reading these days, and the meditations of a middle-aged Roman administrator wouldn't, one would have thought, be of enormous interest to most modern youngsters – especially a sociable young woman like Summerfield. But what I found really so strange,' he continued, 'and the thing I couldn't bring myself to tell Stanley is that the extract she had happened to select from it is one that has special meaning for me – in fact, it's the very same passage that my tutor pointed out to me when my mother died during my first year at Oxford.'

Diana bent and thoughtfully sipped her soup. 'This particular extract?' she asked, eventually once more raising her head. 'I assume it's an important one, and that's the reason he drew your attention to it?'

'Yes, of course,' replied Blanding, nodding vigorously. 'Indeed, in my view, it encapsulates the central argument of the book – that all events have their purposes, and that human existence is not subject to random chance, but lies in the control of a merciful, all-wise Providence. In other words, that some mysterious, invisible hand directs the entire course of the universe for good, and thus the lives of us all.'

For the first time in their conversation, there was a sparkle of animation in the speaker's tone and expression, and just for a moment, worries forgotten, he was carried away in his enthusiasm for the intellectual idea. In contrast, a shadow seemed to flicker across his listener's face, and just for an instant Blanding seemed to glimpse something almost hostile in her eyes. But then, almost before he had time to requester the fact, her look softened. 'Well,' she said gently, 'surely there's your answer then – if the passage is as important as

157

you say, Summerfield most likely copied it out from some sort of religious anthology.'

'No.' Blanding shook his head emphatically. 'I forgot to tell you but that ex-Dulwich College library book among her things was Cooper's 1902 translation of *The Consolation*. Apparently she transcribed the passage directly from that as the words are underscored. Anyway, those lines are not, in fact, some oft-quoted passage – merely one part of a long, reasoned argument. So,' he asked as if demanding an answer, 'how, in God's name, could she then have happened to alight upon that particular excerpt?' He paused, but then, without giving Diana a chance to respond, almost instantly resumed. 'And that isn't all,' he cried out, 'apart from selecting that one special passage that means so much to me personally and also having a library book from the very same school I taught at, there's also the matter of her brass rubbing collection. As I mentioned to you yesterday, brass rubbing used to be a hobby of my own before the war.'

Perplexed, Diana leaned back a little in her chair and regarded him curiously. 'I don't understand,' she said with a frown. 'So what exactly are you saying by all this?'

With a heavy sigh, Blanding lay down his spoon. 'I don't really know,' he answered, removing his spectacles and rubbing his eyes. 'Just, I suppose, that I feel there's too much of me in Corporal Summerfield's life altogether: it's almost as if the girl had been part of me! But how could that be?' he demanded, replacing his glasses. 'How could I, a perfect stranger, have possibly influenced her in any way – someone I never met, a person whose name I couldn't even remember?' He paused briefly before bursting out in undisguised anguish, 'Good God! I don't know if I am going mad or not, but I tell you this – if I were the one responsible for investigating her death, and I knew what I had recognized in that jottings book and in Corporal Summerfield's life generally, I'd now be arresting myself!'

'Hallo, you two! Mind if I join you?'

Startled by the sudden intrusion, Diana and Blanding looked round to find Palmer approaching, a broad grin on his face. Formally dressed to give evidence at the forthcoming inquiry, the station engineer was wearing a neatly pressed tunic uniform in place of the rather scruffy workaday battledress blouse he habitually wore. 'The name's Peter Palmer,' he said, addressing Diana with a friendly smile as he reached the table, 'and you, I imagine, must be the famous

158

Section Officer Taylor. We've not met before, but I gather from the grapevine that you'd been appointed assistant to our grossly over-worked adjutant here.'

The newcomer's arrival not only put an end to any further discussion on the implications of the dead Waaf's literary tastes and off-duty pursuits, but heralded the start of a minor invasion. While Blanding and Diana had been talking, a steady flow of officers, both male and female, had been entering the dining room; and now, instead of the comparative isolation in which he was usually left to eat, Blanding soon found himself one of a fast-growing group. Palmer had hardly finished introducing himself before a couple of the civilian meteorologists joined them. Even more surprising, Fluff Brewer limped over in the company of a figure wearing the uniform of a First Lieutenant of the United States Army Air Force, but sporting (with Presidential permission) RAF wings. Despite his youthful good looks and languid easy-going charm, 'Tex' Crawford was a Harvard graduate as well as a much-decorated second-tour pilot, who, despite having lost a number of toes from frostbite during a four days winter sojourn in an open dinghy in the North Sea, was (at his own insistence) one of the few remaining Americans still flying with Bomber Command, after having originally enlisted in the Canadian Air Force as early as 1940. He was also someone whom Blanding had had reason to speak severely to on a number of occasions regarding the bringing of dogs into the mess, the lanky, loose-limbed Texan being virtually inseparable from Lulu – the miniature black poodle that invariably peeped out of his bicycle basket as he peddled around the camp, service cap rakishly pushed back on his head.

In accordance with the holiday-like atmosphere about them, talk flowed freely as lunch proceeded. Disconcerted though he'd initially been by the new arrivals, Blanding gradually began to relax. There was an infectious gaiety about both Palmer and Crawford, and Fluff Brewer's darkly humorous stories soon had him laughing along with the rest. The oppression he'd felt after his interview with Stanley had, in part at least, been mitigated by voicing his thoughts to Diana, and the merriment around him now came as an additional relief, and somewhat to his surprise, he even found himself enjoying the banter directed against himself.

It was clear, however, that Diana was the real centre of attention. Although he couldn't help feeling a twinge of jealously at the way the others, especially Crawford, seemed able to laugh and joke so easily with her, Blanding took pleasure in her obvious enjoyment of the occasion. Nor, looking across at her, could he help contrasting her present relaxed good humour with the tense, sour-faced young woman he'd seen debriefing Kelly's crew. He noticed, nevertheless, that she was careful to avoid all mention of her private life, and deftly sidestepped the more personal questions she was asked. Once again he found himself wondering the reason for her transfer south, and who and where her husband was; and also the cause for that cold, hard look he'd glimpsed when outlining Boethius' essentially optimistic philosophy.

Like some ghostly presence, however, June Summerfield continued to haunt his thoughts. Shocking though the discovery of her half-naked corpse had been, the experience had not affected him quite the way her jottings book had done. The body lying slumped on its side in the wet mud had been something external and separate from himself, a sodden rag doll arbitrarily thrown down as it were across his path. What, however, the young Waaf had copied into her jottings book had not only brought her to life for him, but the inexplicable parallel of their reading habits and hobbies as well as her possession of the ex-Dulwich book, had made it feel as if she were someone to whom he was in some way spiritually linked. It was, therefore, with a different kind of relief when, over coffee, talk turned to the subject of the continuing police investigation and the large-scale search that had been going on all morning in both the camp and the adjacent fields.

'Apparently they haven't been able to find a thing,' stated Palmer in reply to a query from the younger of the two meteorologists, an earnest-faced, thickly bespectacled, balding man in his early thirties. 'I was just talking to one or two of our chaps who've been taking part. They'll be going on again with the search this afternoon, but there's been no sign yet of either her missing clothing or whatever the weapon used in the attack.'

'Well,' intervened Crawford, looking up through the window, 'at least the guys should have good weather for it. With this anticyclone, I doubt if there's much chance of any more of your goddamned English rain for a few days at least.'

'I wouldn't be so sure,' remarked the meteorologist, glancing across at his older colleague as if for confirmation. 'From the reports we've been getting this morning, it seems there's a whole new series of depressions moving in from the Atlantic. If so, we're due for another good dose of rain and heavy cloud in the near future.'

Like the rest of the group, at these words Blanding automatically glanced with some foreboding up at the sky, as yet still clear. As he turned back to the table, Palmer caught his eye. 'Talking of near futures, Trott,' he said smiling, 'you and I better be getting our skates on – this wretched inquiry of Buster's is due to commence in less than half an hour.'

'Good God, yes!' exclaimed Blanding, consulting his watch. 'I hadn't realized quite how long I've been sitting here.'

'Isn't this to do with the lad who managed to bog down his aircraft the other night?' inquired the younger meteorologist as Blanding gulped down what little remained of his coffee. 'What's going to happen to him?'

'To Mackenzie?' Since the mention of the search, Fluff Brewer had lapsed into brooding silence, and had sat, head bowed, meditatively twirling one end of his bushy moustache. Now, however, he gave the questioner a caustic smile, 'Ordered to pack his bags, I expect – rumour has it that Jumper Birdie is after that kid's blood. As squadron CO, he has to answer directly to Group for his aircrews' performance, and two boomerangs in a row and a failed take-off won't exactly have improved our Kiwi friend's chances of adding another damned ring to his sleeve!'

'I say, that sounds unnecessarily cynical, old boy!' intervened the elder meteorologist, turning to look down the table at the crippled air traffic controller with an expression of barely concealed distaste.

'Oh, does it?' responded Brewer, twisting round in his chair to face the civilian, his blue eyes venomously cold. 'Then I'll tell what else may sound cynical, old boy,' he said, derision ringing in his voice as he stressed the sobriquet. 'Whatever happens this afternoon – whether the poor lad is stripped of his wings and publicly demeaned, and ends up cutting his throat in some lavatory cubicle, or if he and his unfortunate crewmates are sent off to get the chop on the very next damned op, it's all much the same in my book, old boy: either way, it'll be every bit as much cold-bloodied murder as whatever happened to young Poppy Summerfield the other night!'

CHAPTER TWELVE

'Right, Sergeant – the board is ready for you now.'

There was none of the stiff ceremonial and ritual of a court martial: no shouted orders, stamping of feet or prisoner's escort, no intimidating row of seated officers in full dress uniform. A station commander's board of inquiry was a quiet, unostentatious affair, little more indeed than a formally conducted interview supported by the evidence of whatever witnesses or technical experts were considered necessary. Normally held to investigate accidents involving the loss of or damage to aircraft, its function was generally limited to ascertaining either the cause of mechanical failure or degree of any possible pilot error. In the latter case, the worst the individual involved could expect was a severe reprimand and the possible endorsement of his flight logbook – serious perhaps to an ambitious peacetime officer, but ludicrously inconsequential to 'Hostilities Only' volunteers nightly risking death in the skies over enemy-occupied Europe. So crucial and potentially devastating, however, could the outcome be for any unfortunate LMF suspect that, for all the apparent informality of the occasion and the far from unkindly tone of his summoner, the youngster addressed was unnaturally pale, and he looked up with something akin to terror in his face as the station adjutant entered the room.

As Sergeant Mackenzie clambered rather unsteadily to his feet, Blanding glanced round the bleakly furnished little overspill office that was normally used by one or other of the station commander's two female civilian secretaries. Despite (or even possibly because of them) a couple of recruitment posters on the walls and a dusty, small cactus plant on the window-ledge, the otherwise bare little chamber had all the dismal appearance and atmosphere of a rather down-at-heel dental surgery waiting room. A-Able's navigator and flight engineer sat smoking nervously on straight-backed chairs opposite the door, both studiously looking down to avoid the intruder's eyes. Similarly head-bent with a smouldering cigarette dangling from his lips, Peter Palmer was seated in the far corner, doodling in the tattered old copy of *The Aeroplane* magazine he'd brought over from the mess.

'You other gentlemen will be called when needed,' announced Blanding before turning back to the young Scot, who now stood looking past him into the corridor as if expecting to be marched straight out through the door to meet a firing squad. 'Well, Sergeant,' he said gently, 'if you'd like to follow me across to the station commander's room.'

Group Captain Chesterton was sitting behind his desk in exactly the same position as during the morning's disciplinary parade, although now he had Wing Commander Birdie seated on his left. Despite his comparatively elevated rank, the latter was a man still only in his late twenties, strikingly good-looking with swept-back hair black as a raven's plumage, his chiselled features spoilt only by the somewhat hard set of his mouth. Eldest son of a wealthy New Zealand sheep farmer, before the war he'd reputedly been a successful show-jumper and amateur steeplechase jockey as well as a lively and popular member of the Christchurch social scene. Since then, having completed two operational tours (including a series of desperate, almost suicidal, daylight attacks on the gathering German invasion fleet in the late summer of 1940 – his Blenheim light bomber being one of only two out of the entire squadron to survive a low level sortie to Boulogne) as well as losing a beloved younger brother during the Burma campaign, war had stamped its grimness into his face, and as Mackenzie was led into the room, he looked down at the desk and scowled.

In contrast, Chesterton greeted the new arrival with an avuncular smile. 'Ah good, Sergeant!' he exclaimed. 'You've remembered to bring your logbook, I see.' He gestured towards the chair positioned immediately before the desk. 'Park yourself there while I take a quick shufti through it.'

The hand that passed the book over visibly trembled, and as the CO began leafing through the pages, occasionally pausing to ask some detail or other about his flying instruction in the southern United States as part of the Arnold Training Scheme, Mackenzie gazed fixedly across at the propeller that hung like some twisted St Andrew's cross directly above his questioner's head. Blanding, who had taken a seat at the opposite end of the desk to Birdie, observed the young pilot sympathetically. From the rigidity of his bearing and his almost palpable anxiety, clearly Mackenzie was extremely tense. He was also someone, thought Blanding, who in physical appearance curiously reminded him of someone he had until then almost forgotten: a former pupil of his, a bright, rather dreamy and artistic boy named Francis Nelson, who'd left Dulwich shortly after both his parents were killed in a road accident just a year prior to the outbreak of war.

'Right,' said Chesterton, passing the logbook across to Birdie, 'let's begin then, Sergeant, by hearing your reasons for deciding to turn back the first time.'

Unlike in the morning, when the succession of defaulters had been paraded before the desk, Blanding's attention remained now wholly concentrated on the matter in hand, and he listened carefully as Mackenzie began to speak. Whatever his temperamental unsuitability, the youngster was obviously desperately anxious to continue operational flying, and whether he would be allowed to do so largely depended on the answers he now gave. The knowledge of this temporarily drove all thought of June Summerfield from Blanding's mind. However she'd obtained the ex-Dulwich College library book and by whatever strange chance she'd happened to alight on that particular passage from the *Consolation* that meant so much to him personally, the girl was now dead – while the nervous youth in front of him was very much alive, blushing and stumbling over his words as he struggled to explain two aborted sorties, followed by the near-disastrous bogging down of a fully-laden bomber during the commencement of a third.

Chesterton led the questioning, going over each of the abandoned flights in detail and making notes of heights, times and the various headings flown. Mackenzie's two crewmembers were brought in to confirm the facts, and then, after they'd been dismissed, the station engineer was called. Then came a long detailed technical discussion, which Blanding found himself occasionally unable to follow, with Palmer stating that although, as reported, there had indeed been a pronounced magneto drop in both A-Able's starboard motors on the first sortie, and a leak in the hydraulic system of the rear turret during the second, neither occurrence was highly unusual or normally regarded as justification for aborting an operation. Nevertheless, as he listened, Blanding found himself trying to imagine how it must have felt to Mackenzie, sitting alone at the controls, heading into the dark unknown with an untried crew and a malfunctioning aircraft. What in the circumstances would have been his own decision, he wondered? To continue on towards the enemy coast with the possibility of failing engines or a turret jamming, or simply – as the young Scot had done on both occasions – to jettison the bomb-load over the sea and high-tail it home to face the consequences? What became increasingly clear, however, was that both so-called 'boomerangs' were due to a combination of inexperience and lack of confidence on the fledgling pilot's part. Equally obvious was that the subsequent bogging down of A-Able on the edge of a greasy taxiway in rainy darkness had been no wilful or cowardly act, merely the unfortunate blunder of a highly keyed-up and over-anxious young man.

With increasingly kindly feelings, Blanding sat observing the pale-faced occupant of the chair. In a sense, he'd seen him many times before: he was the boy who lived with self-doubt, the serious, hard-working pupil, driven to push himself beyond his limits. He was also, he guessed, someone who, lacking a natural flair for leadership, generally preferred to have some other, more forceful personality to lead the way. That latter luxury was now denied him, however. In the RAF, whatever his rank and those of his crew, the pilot was automatically captain; thus Mackenzie was solely responsible for the safety of his aircraft, and on him alone rested the final choice between pressing on or turning back. Added to that, since March 1942, Bomber Command had dispensed with the luxury of second pilots – indeed dual control was not normally fitted in any of the British 'heavies' apart from the already somewhat antiquated Stirling. As a result, the only actual 'on the job' training the pilot of a Halifax or Lancaster received was flying a sortie or two as an observer or so-called 'second dickey' with a seasoned crew. Consequently, youngsters like Mackenzie, many not out of their teens and hardly old enough to have passed their driving tests (although these had been suspended for the duration of the war), were given command of a four-engined bomber and sent out over enemy territory with virtually no operational experience at all.

'Thank you, Squadron Leader,' said Chesterton as Palmer finished giving his evidence, 'that all seems very clear. I don't think we need detain you any longer from your duties.' He waited until the station engineer had closed the door, and then, leaning forward, looked directly into Mackenzie's eyes. 'Well, Sergeant,' he said, 'I have just one or two questions left to ask.'

'Yes, sir.'

'Tell me – is it your wish to remain with your squadron?'

'Aye, sir, it is,' answered Mackenzie with the barest tremor in his voice.

Chesterton nodded gravely. 'And if,' he went on, speaking with slow deliberation, 'this board were to recommend that you be allowed to continue as an operational pilot, do you feel adequate for the job?' He paused slightly. 'Capable that is of coping with the strain of flying through enemy airspace with the lives of six other men in your hands?'

Mackenzie gulped slightly and raised his eyes to the antiquated propeller. 'In truth, I don't really know, sir,' he struggled out, 'but I'd like to be given the chance to prove I'm capable.'

'Right.' Chesterton's voice was suddenly crisp. He glanced round at Birdie who had remained broodingly silent throughout the proceedings. 'Do you have any questions, Wing Commander?'

'No, sir.'

Chesterton nodded. 'Well, in that case, Sergeant, that will be all for the present. If you would like to return to the waiting room, your squadron commander and I shall now discuss what we've heard.' After the door had closed behind Mackenzie, the CO drew out his pipe and began packing the bowl thoughtfully. 'So,' he said, turning at last to Birdie, 'what are your immediate thoughts then, John?'

The New Zealander shrugged. 'That the little runt's a complete wash-out – he obviously scared half to death.'

Not immediately replying, Chesterton lit his pipe and then began leafing through the pilot's personal file. 'It says here in these reports that he's keen and conscientious,' he said, 'and I must say, that concurs with my own impression.'

Birdie gave a dismissive snort. 'That's all very fine, sir,' he answered, 'but the boy lacks any backbone at all. He should never have been passed as suitable for operational duties in the first place.'

'And yet he seems desperately eager to continue flying.'

'That may be,' retorted the New Zealander, 'but quite evidently he simply isn't up to the job. The sooner he's kicked off the station the better for everyone concerned, including the poor little devil himself!'

Chesterton sucked his pipe in silence. From his frown and the perplexity in his face, it was clear that he was having to struggle between sympathy for the youth and support for his squadron commander. 'Well, Alan,' he asked, suddenly looking round, 'what's your opinion? I take it you concur with the wing commander's view?'

Blanding could feel Mackenzie's future hanging in the balance: he need only shrug or give the slightest nod of assent and Mackenzie's chance of remaining with the squadron would be gone for ever. On the other hand, to do otherwise, to argue for his retention from mere sympathy would be grossly irresponsible. Thankfully at that moment he remembered his promise to the two youths who had buttonholed him earlier. 'Well, sir,' he answered, 'I would only say this: after this morning's disciplinary parade, I was approached by A-Able's wireless operator and rear gunner. They asked me to inform you that they and the rest of the crew have complete faith in Mackenzie and wish to continue with him.' He paused slightly. 'It's also the feeling I got while listening to his navigator and flight-engineer just now.'

'I agree,' replied Chesterton, nodding judiciously, 'and that's obviously an important consideration. If his crew wish to stick by him, who are we to say they shouldn't?'

'Holy Christ!' burst out Birdie, his face flushing. 'With all respect, sir, we're not running a ruddy Sunday school here! The fact remains, Mackenzie's scared half out of his wits: to let others fly with him is as good as to sentence them to death. You might as well take a pistol and shoot the whole bloody lot now as send them blundering back out across the North Sea in the charge of a frightened child!'

Chesterton looked pained. 'And if we do chuck him out, what happens to him?'

'Christ knows!' came the instant retort. 'That's not my business, thank God. I've a war to fight and the lives of the rest of my lads to consider.'

'Fair enough,' murmured Chesterfield appeasingly. He sat a few moments sucking on his pipe, brooding in a curling blue haze of smoke. 'All right,' he said eventually, 'I think it comes to this: you, John, are adamantly for throwing Mackenzie out, and I, of course, totally respect your position. On the other hand, bearing in mind the faith his crew still have in him and his stated wish to continue flying, I feel the boy should be allowed that chance. However,' he added hurriedly, seeing a look of dark displeasure rise on the New Zealander's face, 'I'm not willing to pull rank on his occasion. Therefore, with your permission, I'll ask Alan here to give the casting vote.'

Birdie peered coldly round at Blanding, but then nodded. 'All right,' he said with obvious reluctance, 'I agree. Let him decide.'

As if hypnotically drawn, Blanding turned to stare across the desk at the now empty chair, thinking of the look of apprehension in the eyes of the person who had recently sat there. Trying to push his sympathy aside, he wondered how he'd feel if he were to cast his vote for retaining Mackenzie, and then A-Able and its whole crew were lost on the very next operation. But then he remembered the bright crescent moon shining down through the mist in the early hours. If there was little or no possibility of further raids in the near future and every likelihood of the squadron being rested and re-equipped before the invasion, then surely it would be needless cruelty and waste to destroy what remained of an insecure young man's sense of self-respect, especially if Fluff Brewer had been right and there was the strong possibility of the boy ending up taking his own life. Making up his mind, Blanding turned back to the CO. 'Sir, I think I tend to agree with you: Mackenzie ought to be given a further opportunity to prove himself.'

Clearly relieved, Chesterton smiled. 'Well, that's the decision then: he gets one last chance – but if he doesn't match up, then it's off the camp for him in double-quick time.' He paused and glanced round at Birdie, but the squadron commander made no reply, though from his expression his feelings were patently obvious. 'All right, Alan,' resumed Chesterton, turning again to Blanding, 'would you kindly ask Sergeant Mackenzie to step back in.'

Although he was icily polite, it was clear that Wing Commander Birdie was inwardly fuming as he and Blanding left the CO's office. Obviously he regarded the decision regarding Mackenzie as gross interference with the running of his squadron, and was plainly furious that the views of a mere administrative officer should have swayed the issue. Deeming it, therefore, not to be the best time to be expressing a view on the psychological condition of another of his pilots, Blanding said nothing about his worries concerning Pat Kelly. Instead, making the excuse of wishing to check on the room used by the witnesses, he turned aside, leaving Birdie to stalk away down the passage, doubtless eager to find someone on whom to vent his feelings about 'interfering bloody pen-pushers' and 'desk-bound damned sycophants'.

As expected, the now deserted little room stank of stale cigarette smoke. Going straight over to the window, Blanding unlatched the metal frame and pushed it open. Doing so, he heard laughter, and, peering out, was in time to see Mackenzie and his crew heading away past the NAAFI. They moved in a noisy, jostling group, for all the world like a pack of schoolboys celebrating a victory on the games field or some unexpected escape from the hands of wrathful authority. Blanding watched them until they disappeared around a corner while Birdie's dire predictions on their likely fate echoed in his ears. Whatever the present phase of the moon and however long the squadron was stood down, eventually they'd be sent out again to risk their lives. Now, due to him, thought Blanding, they'd go in the hands of someone who doubted his own capabilities – an anxious, highly-strung youth who, for all that he'd declared about wishing to remain an operational pilot, could well have secretly longed for that particular cup to be taken from him. By supporting Chesterton's view that Mackenzie should be given a further chance to prove himself something that he most likely could never be, had he not only pressed the poisoned chalice back into the youngster's hands, but as good as countersigned the death warrants on both him and the six others of his crew?

The idea sent a shudder through Blanding. In an effort to rid himself of the thought, he turned from the window and quickly began going round the room, emptying ashtrays and straightening chairs. Finally, noticing the old copy of *The Aeroplane* still lying open, face downwards, on the corner table where Palmer had left it when summoned to give his evidence, he went over and picked it up. As he did so, his heart gave a jerk and, tilting the magazine towards the light, he stared down mesmerized at the open page.

Two sketches had been doodled in pencil across a large advertisement for aviation tyres. One was of the living June Summerfield, a head-and-shoulders portrait of the Waaf corporal in uniform, her rather widely-spaced eyes, the curly hair beneath the peaked service cap and her slight grin all instantly recognizable from the photograph appended to her personal file. The other and slightly larger sketch was of her dead body lying huddled in a foetal position outside the airfield fence, just as it had appeared to him when he had turned from clambering out through the narrow gap in the wire.

Thoughts reeling, Blanding continued to gaze down at the doodles, all his unease concerning Sergeant Mackenzie temporarily forgotten. Through the turmoil of his mind, one vision above all filled his mind – that of Palmer sitting across the breakfast table from him on the morning of the dreadful discovery, wolfing down great spoonfuls of cornflakes, the very epitome of vigorous good health and purposeful energy. Then he remembered the nicotine-stained fingers and the tremble of the hand holding the cigarette when Palmer had spoken so feelingly later about the strain everyone on the station had been under these last months. Aware suddenly of how little he knew about his friend, Blanding hurriedly went over the obvious facts: Palmer was unmarried and lived a bachelor's existence in the mess, and was, for all his affable humour and languid charm, essentially a loner like himself; he was also a long-serving regular officer, someone who, by his own admission, believed in the superstitions so integral to service life – above all, he was a senior member of ground staff who, after the last of the Lancasters had roared away into the rainy darkness that Sunday night, would have had both time and opportunity to rid the station of its so-called 'chop girl', while at the same time perhaps disencumbering himself of an inconveniently pregnant young woman.

Raising his head, Blanding looked out through the window towards the distant hangars, vividly remembering again the smears of dirt and grease on the dead girl's blouse and skin; he also recalled what Dawson had said about her recently having been where machinery was stored. He continued to gaze towards the huge camouflaged sheds for a few moments more. Then finally making up his mind, he turned for the door and went out, and, still clutching the magazine in one hand, began striding purposely back along the corridor, face every bit as cold and rigidly set as Wing Commander Birdie's had been ten minutes before.

'I'm sorry, but I really don't understand why you're quite so upset.' Raising her head from the open page, Diana smiled up with a look of slight puzzlement at the person who had so peremptorily slapped the periodical down in front of her. 'I realize, of course, that Squadron Leader Palmer is a friend of yours,' she went on, 'but honestly, there seems nothing particularly sinister about either of these drawings to me. People doodle things all the time, and surely it's perfectly natural that they should sketch whatever's on their mind.'

'I know that,' burst out Blanding, almost angrily, 'but don't

170

you see?' he said, pointing down. 'That drawing of the corpse there is just too good!'

'Too good?' Diana repeated, bending to re-examine the sketch in question. 'It's accomplished certainly,' she murmured, frowning down at the page, 'as indeed both of them are. Obviously, the squadron leader is a talented artist.'

'No! No!' cried Blanding impatiently. 'You misunderstand – that isn't what I meant. It's just that the sketch is too damned accurate. How in God's name could anyone have got all those details right unless he'd actually seen the body himself?'

'That's easy,' answered Diana, looking up with a smile. 'Obviously the artist got the particulars from someone else. Apart from yourself, Warrant Officer Dawson, the CO and the medical officer later, quite a few other people here on the camp, including some of the station police, would have seen Summerfield's corpse before its removal – any one of them could have supplied the necessary details. Anyway,' she added, rotating the magazine to face Blanding, 'take another good look at the sketch and see if it's really so exact as you say.'

Grim-faced, Blanding leaned forward and peered down at the page. Almost the instant he did so, his face lightened, and he glanced up at his assistant with a shamefaced grin. 'You're perfectly right,' he exclaimed, straightening. 'Now I look again, I see that Peter has got at least one detail wrong.' He jabbed with a forefinger at the drawing. 'This hand here, sheltering the eyes – you see, it's bare? It hasn't got a mitten on.'

'Mitten?'

'Yes, Summerfield was wearing one of a pair of rather amateurishly knitted pink mittens.'

Frowning, Diana twisted the page back round and once again leaned forward to study the sketch. 'But why on earth was she wearing mittens?' she asked. 'From what I remember, it was wet and overcast that night; it certainly wasn't very cold. Apart from that, all Waafs are issued with a perfectly respectable pair of leather gloves, so whatever was she doing in uniform, improperly dressed?'

'God knows!' murmured Blanding. 'But surely that's not the point. The main thing is that you're right, and that I quite overreacted to Palmer's doodles. As you say,' he said, going round to his own desk, 'there's nothing particularly sinister about either drawing. Anyway,' he added with a rueful laugh as he sat down, 'leaving sketches of his victim lying around is, I imagine, just about the last thing a murderer is likely to do.'

All his former stiff awkwardness in Diana's presence had, by this time, largely disappeared. His admittance to her over lunch of his fears regarding the discovery of the ex-school library book among Summerfield's possessions and the inclusion of the Boethius extract in the Waaf's commonplace book had created a bond between them. Indeed, it had seemed to him the most natural thing in the world to hurry back to the office to show her Palmer's drawings. For her own part, Diana appeared equally at ease with him. Closing the magazine, she brushed a wisp of hair back from her eyes and, turning, smiled at the figure in the adjacent desk. 'So,' she asked, 'what happened at the inquiry? You haven't said a word about it yet.'

Blanding's brow darkened. 'Well,' he answered, not quite meeting her eyes, 'it's been decided to give young Mackenzie another chance.'

'Is that good? You seem worried.'

'I really don't know,' replied Blanding. 'Certainly the lad looked hugely relieved when given the news. And then later from the window of the witnesses' room I spotted him and his crewmates heading off to celebrate, all obviously thinking they'd been damned lucky.'

'But you're not so sure?'

Blanding shrugged unhappily. 'Fact is,' he said heavily, 'I had the casting vote. It was me that allowed Mackenzie to stay on, but whether I was right or not, who can tell? Wing Commander Birdie certainly didn't think so – in his view, I've as good as sentenced all seven of the crew to death.'

Diana's face momentarily clouded, but then she suddenly brightened. 'Oh, yes, talking of aircrew, I was forgetting!' she exclaimed. 'There's been a call from the RAF hospital in Ely. Apparently you rang yesterday to inquire after the condition of Flying Officer Ellis, and asked to be informed when he was able to see visitors. Anyway, it seems that he now is.'

'Really? That's excellent news! We must inform the rest of his crew.'

'I've already done it,' answered Diana. 'And I've also arranged for them all to go over and see him this evening.'

As his assistant returned to her work, Blanding surveyed the surprisingly small amount of paperwork awaiting him in his pending

172

tray. The news from the hospital had come as a welcome relief for, despite everything else on his mind, ever since separating from Birdie outside the CO's office he'd had the nagging feeling that he really ought to have risked further inflaming him by mentioning his worries about Pat Kelly. Now, however, he was glad he hadn't: whether the Australian and his crew had been friends of the murdered girl or not, he thought, and however badly the nightfighter's attack had shaken them all, the visit to see Ellis at the hospital that evening would certainly do much to restore their morale. Nevertheless, for all that, he still felt a strange sense of oppression – presumably, the inevitably consequences of the inexplicable revelations of the morning combining with the unease he felt over his decision regarding Sergeant Mackenzie.

'You know,' he sighed, glancing at his assistant, 'for two pins I'd ring the CO and get his permission to drive over to the hospital to see Ellis myself this afternoon. I haven't been off the camp for what feels like days, and I could do with a change of scene.'

'Well, why don't you?' encouraged Diana, raising her head. 'Most of the routine work has been got through, and there's nothing very pressing at the moment.'

'I suppose that's right,' murmured Blanding, swivelling round to look out into the sunshine. 'And after all, I did promise I'd go over to see young Ellis as soon as I was able.' Struck by a sudden new thought, he turned back to meet his companion's eyes. 'Tell you what,' he blurted out, 'why don't you accompany me to Ely? If nothing else, it'll at least give you the chance to learn something of the locality.'

A smile lit Diana's face, but then almost immediately disappeared. 'No, I couldn't possibly,' she said, hurriedly bowing back to her work. 'I've got to check through these requisitions that Mr Gilbert sent over.'

Normally such a rebuff would have silenced Blanding. The mention, however, of the accommodation officer's name roused his hackles.

'For goodness sake,' he exclaimed, the memory of the man's gratuitous rudeness the previous evening rankling anew, 'surely you can leave the fellow's confounded forms for now! I doubt if a few hours delay in the ordering of a few dozen pillowcases and whatever else he wants will greatly effect either the squadron's efficiency or the general progress of the war! Anyway,' he added, determinedly picking up the phone, 'now I think of it, you've the perfect excuse for playing a little hookey – visiting young Ellis will, after all, allow you to complete your debriefing of D-Dog's crew.'

CHAPTER THIRTEEN

It was with a feeling of guilty unease that Blanding folded back the canvas roof of his small red Morris 8 tourer. There was something about doing so, a consciousness perhaps of transforming a utilitarian mode of transport into a pleasurable toy, that reinforced his sense of irresponsibility at leaving the station during the working day. Nevertheless, after being confined so long in a stuffy office, he felt the chance of travelling in the open air with the wind in his face was too good to miss, especially when he'd be sharing the experience with somebody else.

It was only after he and Diana had turned onto the central camp road that he realized just how conspicuous they were in the open vehicle. As they headed towards the main entrance, heads turned in their direction, some with mild curiosity, others with knowing grins. Nor did it feel any better when they halted in front of the guardhouse barrier and Sergeant Williams emerged to stand over the car as if collecting the fares for a fairground ride. After their names and the details of the journey had been recorded, it was, therefore, with considerable relief that Blanding was able to swing the little, three-geared Morris out onto the main road and accelerate away in the direction of Frampton Wissey.

Some of his own embarrassment seemed to have communicated itself to Diana, for she said nothing as the camp disappeared behind. In silence, they descended the gentle half-mile slope leading into the village, passing the white-painted gates of the Waafery as they entered the little waterside huddle of houses and shops. Following the riverbank as far as the bridge, they turned and drove out over the Wissey into the open, flat fenlands beyond. Dark arable land now stretched away on either side, huge unfenced fields bordered by ditches and spindly popular trees, the almost unrelieved monotony of the landscape broken only by the occasional ruined

175

wind-pump or the gaunt frame of an eel-trapping sluice standing silhouetted above the drained marshes like some monstrous rusty guillotine.

Whether their enforced proximity or the novelty of the situation had created an awkwardness – or simply that travelling with the slipstream buffeting their faces inhibited conversation – neither of them spoke as they sped westwards across the open plain. Greatcoat collars turned up against the headwind, peaks of their service caps pulled down low over their eyes, they both remained sunk in their own thoughts as they followed the dipping telephone wires along the empty road towards where, on the low hump of land ahead, the towers and pinnacles of Ely Cathedral rose against the declining sun.

Normally Blanding enjoyed driving: it was an opportunity for him to relax and allow his mind to wander, something that had always offered a temporary escape from the stifling confines of both school and service life. Now, however, he experienced none of that customary freedom. Rather, sensing the unease of the woman beside him, he felt his own tension grow, and as he drove, he increasingly cursed himself for ever having insisted on her accompanying him on what increasingly already felt like a doomed little excursion.

'Who do you think all those men are?'

Diana's sudden question came as a huge relief. Roused from his gloomy ruminations, Blanding glanced across towards where his passenger was pointing. Dwarfed by an immensity of landscape and sky, a long row of bowed figures was strung out across the field ahead. His first thought was they were part of the police search for Summerfield's missing clothes and for whatever weapon had been used to strike the girl down. Realizing, however, that they were already much too far from the aerodrome for this to be possible, he slowed the car. 'They appear to be hoeing,' he muttered, squinting against the glare of the sun as he peered towards the bent figures. 'Surely they're just a large gang of workers weeding sugar-beet, turnips or some other root-crop.'

'Funny looking farm labourers!' responded Diana, leaning forward and shielding her eyes. 'One's wearing plus-fours; at least two are wearing trilby hats; and another has on what looks like a University of London scarf!'

Intrigued, Blanding brought the Morris to a halt besides the field and then turned to look again at the straggling line of workers.

Now that he had chance to observe them properly, he could see at once why they'd caught Diana's attention. Apart from the unconventionalities – even eccentricity – of their clothing, there was something decidedly odd about their behaviour in general. Instead of slogging on with the dogged perseverance of the typical landworker, at frequent intervals one or other of the stooping forms would straighten and pause – sometimes, he noticed, even casually casting his implement aside and strolling over to chat for a while with one or other of his neighbours. One individual in particular appeared forgetful of the task in which the group was engaged. A knotted white handkerchief protecting his head, his spectacles glinting in the sunlight, he remained continuously upright, leaning on his hoe whilst vigorously waving an arm above his head as if addressing a political rally or some open-air revivalist meeting. Whilst this oration continued, Blanding noticed that those each side either continued their dilatory labours or else went on with their conversations, seemingly as oblivious of the haranguing to which they were being subjected as of the huge acreage stretching out ahead of them all. 'Do you think they possibly could be prisoners-of-war?' he asked doubtfully, glancing round at Diana.

'Hardly!' she laughed. 'Not in those clothes! Anyway,' she added, leaning across to peer past his shoulder, 'I can't see any guards.'

A small canvas-topped brown van stood parked in the field gate entrance ahead, and drawn up on the verge just beyond it a black Austin saloon. As Blanding let in the clutch to drive on, two figures could be made out standing beside the car. One was a bowler-hatted official carrying a briefcase, the other clearly some sort of foreman or overseer – a tall, willowy, leather-gaitered countryman with drooping grey moustaches and a corduroy cap pushed well back from his heavily tanned face.

'E.W.A.E.C.?' murmured Diana, reading aloud the letters prominently displayed on the van door as they passed. She wrinkled her nose. 'I don't understand – what do those initials stand for?'

Certain he'd come across them very recently, but not sure for the moment where, Blanding stared ahead at the fast approaching outskirts of the city, going back over in his mind the huge volume of paperwork that had passed beneath his eye during the last couple of days. Then suddenly the answer came. 'E.W.A.E.C.,' he announced, glancing triumphantly round, 'is a rather clumsy acronym for a certain government body – something I believe called in full the Emergency War Agricultural Executive Committee or simply the War Agricultural Committee.' He laughed. 'I happen to know simply because one of our airmen – a certain Aircraftman Phillips – recently contrived to get himself into a fight with one of its employees.' Smile suddenly disappearing, Blanding broke off and then, slowing the car, craned round to look over his shoulder towards the row of now already minuscule figures in the field behind. 'I remember now,' he muttered, frowning as he turned back to the wheel, 'that there was something decidedly odd about the whole affair. As one might expect, a girl was involved. Nevertheless, although the CO wouldn't believe it, I'm sure Phillips was holding something back – something or other, I imagine, about the person he attacked that, for some odd reason, he was unwilling to divulge.'

Like the vast majority of the airfields it served, the RAF hospital at Ely had been built since the outbreak of war. Largely comprising a series of long, prefabricated huts interconnected by roofed walkways and asbestos-clad heating pipes, and presided over by a water tower identical to the one at Frampton Wissey, it lay a couple of miles north of the sleepy little community on the main King's Lynn road. Its military credentials were obvious from the moment the Morris swung in through the main entrance. There was a crisp, clean look of efficiency to everything from the burnished brass nozzles of the rolled-up, white-clayed hoses on the gatehouse wall to the geometrically neat layout of the well-tended lawns and shrubberies on either side as the little red convertible began following the prominently marked signboards round to the main car park.

The final stages of the journey had been conducted in the same silence as the start. Once the gang of amateurish-looking labourers had vanished behind, Diana gradually seemed to withdraw into herself once more. Although Blanding tried to interest her by recounting the details of the mysterious altercation between the two men at the Red Lion, her replies had been monosyllabic, and by the time he negotiated the narrow city streets, he was once more feeling almost as stiff and uncomfortable in her company as when they'd first left the aerodrome. Not a word was said as they got out of the car and began making their way to the visitors' entrance. Diana walked with her head down, the peak of her cap hiding her face, and it was only when she glanced up to thank him for holding open the door that

Blanding noticed her expression. It was tense, and in her eyes he glimpsed something of the same look that he'd seen earlier that afternoon when summoning Sergeant Mackenzie before the inquiry board. With a joyous surge of relief, he realized at that moment that he'd completely misread the situation: his assistant's initial hesitation in agreeing to accompany him to Ely and her subsequent silence through most of the journey had been neither aloofness nor embarrassment in his company as he'd feared – rather, he guessed, it had been nothing more than a quite understandable apprehension of what they were likely to have to confront within the pristine-clean wards and corridors of the building they were now entering.

As might be expected, the majority of patients in wartime RAF hospitals were casualities of flying, and some of them had been almost literally through the fires of hell. Apart from the large quantities of petrol which planes carried, doped fabric, glycol and hydraulic fluid were all highly inflammable, and their crews had often to bale out or scramble from the wreckage through a virtual blowtorch of flame. For the badly burnt survivors, the subsequent treatment was excruciating – loose skin scraped off and the raw flesh beneath sprayed with tannic acid to form a cement, and then the patient left to lie suspended in a cradle for weeks, doped with morphia and regularly dipped into brine baths, his eyes smeared with a protective coating of gentian violet. Although great strides had been made in plastic surgery since its first use on the hideously disfigured victims of the Somme, the science was still very much in its infancy, and those eventually returning to duty after its application bore unmistakable testimony to the sufferings they'd undergone: their purplish-blotched, curiously static faces and claw-like hands being, like that of the crippled, twisted body of Frampton Wissey's senior air traffic controller, a constant reminder to all around them of the horrific risks the aircrews ran.

'Haven't you ever been in one of those places before?' asked Blanding gently, checking his companion's progress with a light touch on her elbow.

'Just once or twice,' she murmured, looking away.

'Well, don't worry,' he answered reassuringly. 'You'll be fine – the main thing is to try to look them all in the eye.'

Inside they were met by a smiling VAD nurse, a girl no older than the majority of the Waafs back at the camp. Guided by her, they preceded through a succession of passages smelling strongly of polish and chemicals. Blanding had often had cause to visit the hospital as part of his duties and, as always, he braced himself for horrid sights. Nevertheless, when a heavily-plastered form was trundled towards him in a wheelchair, the arms propped rigidly in front and suppurating wounds on hands as shrivelled and black as those of a pharaoh's mummy, it was all he could do to follow his own advice and force himself, as they passed, to meet the eyes gazing up out of the two holes in the gauze-covered face with what he hoped was an encouraging smile.

Following the nurse, he and Diana entered a long, silent ward. Most of the blinds were drawn, and in the dimness the majority of the pyjama-clad figures occupying the beds lay unmoving beneath what seemed a small forest of metallic drip-feed support stalks. Even the few patients who turned their pale faces towards them or raised a hand in greeting seemed mere shades of those boisterous young men who had poured forth out into the sunlight from the NCO aircrew dining hall after breakfast that morning.

'This is Flying Officer Ellis's room,' announced their conductress, pausing outside one of the private side-wards. 'You must understand,' she went on, 'that his right thigh was badly shattered and that the surgeons have had to more or less completely rebuild the leg. You may go in and see him for a few minutes, but I must warn you that you're likely to find him still rather confused.'

The prone figure made no move as Blanding and Diana entered. He lay on his back, hips and thighs heavily plastered, one bandaged leg raised and supported by straps hung from a grey-painted metal frame. He appeared to be sleeping, but as the visitors cautiously approached the bed, he seemed to sense their presence. Opening his eyes, he turned his head a fraction and blinked up at them in mild surprise.

'Hallo, old chap,' said Blanding gently, smiling down at the ashen face. 'So how are you feeling then? A little better?'

There was no immediate response. As the nurse had warned, it was obvious that Ellis's mind was still befuddled from either the effects of the anaesthetic itself or the various sedatives he'd received since the second of his two operations. Clearly confused by the question and unable at first to recognize the speaker's identity, he stared blankly up at him for a second or two before finally managing a weak smile. 'Thank you, sir. Can't complain,' he murmured, 'still a trifle groggy though.'

Blanding had spoken to Diana about the young Australian as they drove over, perhaps in an attempt to fill a silence, perhaps to explain his particular interest in the young man. Unlike most of their rougher-hewn intake from the antipodes, Ellis came from a professional family, his father being an eminent lawyer in Melbourne. Usually only the faintest timbre of his native accent could be discerned in Ellis's voice but under stress, and Blanding had heard him in furious political discussions in the mess, the purer strains of his childhood accent emerged like a guard dog rushing out of its kennel. Ellis had a keen nose for injustice but never on his own behalf. Blanding told her about Ellis's education at a private school in Melbourne in the hands of British-born teachers, from whom he'd inherited many of the speech patterns and idioms of the minor English public school. At seventeen Ellis had run away to sea, having tracked down an old clipper making its last voyage from Sydney to California. By the time the ship reached San Francisco Ellis had been turned into a useful hand aboard and a friendly deck officer had even shown him the rudiments of the sextant. He had then hitchhiked and jumped freight trains across the States, to then take ship once more to Liverpool, where, now old enough, he had finally signed up, not in the Royal Navy but as a volunteer for aircrew in the RAF. This surprising choice was due to a twenty-minute joy ride in a crop sprayer thanks to a friendly pilot somewhere in the American mid-West. Although regarded as somewhat of a curiosity by his compatriots, he was, nevertheless, a skilled navigator, and as such, respected throughout the squadron. Like most of his calling, he was somewhat introspective and bookish. Only a month before, indeed, Blanding had come across him in the mess on a Saturday evening, reading Rilke in translation, and the pair had then spent the subsequent hour discussing tendencies in European poetry, after which Ellis had told him a few stories about life on a square rigger. For Blanding, it had been a pleasant interlude from the grim tedium of his duties, and thinking back to that conversation now, he smiled down at the wan face on the pillow with genuine warmth and affection. 'I must say,' he said, 'it's very good that the doctors have managed to patch up your leg – it won't be long, I'm sure, before they have you up on your pegs again, jitterbugging the night away in Piccadilly and Leicester Square.'

There was no answering smile this time from the patient: Ellis merely gazed up at him blearily, blinking as if trying to focus his eyes. Uncertain if the youngster was doubting his well-meant tone of breezy confidence, and that he already knew that weeks of painful physiotherapy lay before him before he'd even hobble a step, let alone dance, and that he'd never again walk without the aid of an artificial support, or simply that he was still too doped to take in properly what he was saying – whatever it was, Blanding felt suddenly crass and awkward. To cover his embarrassment, he hurriedly introduced Diana. 'This is Section Officer Taylor,' he announced as she carried a chair over to the bed. 'She was responsible for interrogating the rest of your crew when they were carting you over here in the blood-wagon.'

Slowly turning his head, Ellis looked up as Diana seated herself at his shoulder. He continued to stare up at her face as if unable to see her clearly before finally murmuring, 'I don't seem to remember having ever having seen you before – though I'm sure I would if I had.'

'I'm new,' answered Diana, smiling down. 'I've just been transferred down here from 4 Group.'

'From 4 Group!' repeated the youth with a touch of wondering incredulity. 'Strewth,' he went on, a grin gradually lighting his face, 'that's hard luck! Someone in postings had obviously got it in for you and no mistake – whisking you away like Cinderella from the ball to plonk you down here among us simple, web-footed, fenland folk!'

'Maybe,' responded Diana, laughing, 'but now, would you like to tell me about the attack on your aircraft? The reports I got from the rest of your crew were somewhat confused and contradictory, so I'd appreciate hearing what happened from you.'

'I can't remember very much,' stated Ellis after thinking for a few moments, his expression suddenly sombre. 'Someone, I think it must have been Chuck Fowler, gave me a shot of morphia soon after I was hit. I was hardly conscious of anything after that – I just have a vague memory of being carried back and strapped into the crew-cot, and then of Chuck and I think one of the other blokes bandaging me up. I must have passed out completely then for I can't remember a dicky bird until we'd landed and I was being lifted out into the blood wagon.'

'What about the attack itself though? What do you remember of that?'

As if struggling to bring his thoughts into order, Ellis looked up past Diana's head. 'According to my estimates,' he said, 'we'd safely crossed the coast about ten minutes before, but what with the cloud below, I hadn't been able to get a good fix since clearing the target so I decided to try for a sextant shot on a couple of stars. I was just sticking my head into the astrodome when I felt the kite suddenly judder. Next thing I knew something with the force of a mechanical shovel seemed to kick me from behind and then I was down beside the chart table. I couldn't move a muscle due to the g-force. I suppose the skipper had the kite in a dive at that point. I must have been still plugged into the intercom as I could hear voices shouting above the din, and then the skipper was bawling for everyone to shut up as he chucked the crate around. Then, when we finally levelled out, I began to feel the pain in my right leg – it felt like a devil was shoving a red-hot poker into the very marrow of the bone!' Closing his eyes, the speaker lay silent for a moment as if reliving the agony he'd undergone. At last he again looked up to meet Diana's eyes. 'And the other blokes?' he asked, a sudden anxiety in his voice. 'Are they all right? That's not what you've come to tell me, is it?'

'They're fine. Rather shaken and worried about you, of course, but all physically okay.'

'That's good.' Reclosing his eyes, Ellis lapsed into silence for a few seconds before, with an effort, he raised his head from the pillow to across at Blanding with plaintive eyes. 'All of them, everyone on board, they were all okay? Is that really true, sir?' he asked. 'With all the shouting, I was sure someone else had been hit as well.'

Smilingly, Blanding shook his head. 'No, as Section Officer Taylor has just told you, apart from yourself, no other person on board was hurt. Anyway, you needn't take my word for it – you'll soon see for yourself. It's been arranged for the rest of the crew to visit you this evening.'

'That's good,' murmured Ellis with obvious huge relief, allowing his head to fall back onto the pillow. 'It's just,' he explained, looking up again into Diana's face, 'that I keep having such ruddy awful dreams: I'm back in the plane, pinned down there half under the chart table, unable to move, everything shaking and trembling around me, and all the time there's some dreadful shouting and cursing going on and the screaming bellow of the engines – it makes me scared about dropping off to sleep.'

Reaching over, Diana took his hand and gently squeezed it. 'That's quite normal,' she said soothingly. 'After what you've been through, you're bound to have nightmares for a while. They'll disappear as your nerves settle.'

'So everything is all right then? Nothing you're keeping from me?'

'No, of course not,' answered Diana, smiling. 'Everything's fine, I promise. You're safe now and being well looked after; your family in Australia will be informed of what happened, and in just over an hour your crewmates will be arriving to visit you – so now try not too worry about anything, and just get as much rest as you can.'

Dusk was already falling as Diana and Blanding left the main hospital block and began walking back towards the now deserted car park. Both had been affected by the visit, and neither spoke until they'd reached where the Morris stood virtually alone. 'Poor kid!' murmured Blanding, pausing beside the car to look back through the gloom towards the buildings they'd just left. 'All that dreadful anxiety is due to delayed shock, I imagine. I only hope this visit by his crew this evening will set his mind at rest.'

As he spoke, there came an urgent, repeated double ringing of a bell; a moment later an RAF ambulance swept round the corner to draw up in front of the main entrance. As the two onlookers watched, in the dimness they saw the rear doors opened and a stretchered figure lifted out onto a trolley and wheeled inside. 'You know,' sighed Blanding as the ambulance was again slammed shut and the vehicle began moving away, 'being here at the hospital, I can't help thinking about that other boy this afternoon – I wonder if young Sergeant Mackenzie would have been quite so keen to continue operational flying if he could have seen that half-lamed, nerve-shattered youngster back there, let alone all those dreadful burn cases.'

Diana looked round at him sharply. 'People,' she said, 'have to make their own choices. And anyway, Sergeant Mackenzie isn't a boy, and neither for that matter are you a teacher anymore. You're no more responsible for what might or might not befall him and his crew than you are for whatever happened to Corporal Summerfield the other night.'

Taken aback, Blanding stared at the speaker in dumb surprise. 'Come on,' she said briskly, turning to the car before he could struggle out a word. 'It's getting cold. We'd better get this roof up before it gets too dark to see.'

Together they erected the hood and then clambered into their seats. Despite Diana's impatient outburst, the experience of the hospital visit had re-established the bond between them, and in the dew-damp dark confines beneath the taunt canvas there was a

184

curious feeling of intimacy. Having started the engine, Blanding held his wristwatch beneath the dashboard light. 'Look,' he said, 'I don't know about you, but I don't feel like driving straight back to the camp. What say we try to find somewhere that'll serve us a pot of tea? Who knows, if we're lucky we might be offered the odd crumpet or even perhaps a few baked beans on toast.'

Diana looked away across the car park. 'I'm sorry,' she said quietly, 'but I'm not really in the mood for that sort of thing just now.' She looked back round, her face a white blur in the darkness. 'But if you wouldn't mind awfully, I'd like to visit the cathedral for a moment or two.'

'The cathedral?' repeated Blanding, considerably surprised. Perhaps because of the impatient, almost angry expression when he'd spoken of Boethius' ideas over lunch, he'd naturally assumed that his apparently self-assured and confident assistant was committed entirely to an entirely secular, material world. 'Yes, of course,' he murmured, engaging reverse and starting to back the Morris out of the parking bay, 'and, if I put my foot down, we might be just in time to catch the beginning of choral evensong.'

CHAPTER FOURTEEN

'Right, if you'd both like to follow me quietly as you can, so as not to disturb the service any more than you absolutely have to.'

Now that the great west door had closed behind the latecomers, the darkness seemed total. As if to prove that the disembodied voice that whispered peevishly out of the cavernous blackness had a corporeal existence, the elderly sidesman briefly raised his torch, shining its thin, yellowish beam up from beneath his chin so that his gaunt, whiskery face appeared suddenly before them like that of some hideously illuminated imp or gargoyle.

From the moment when the Morris, the twin slits of its hooded headlights glimmering feebly through the dusk, turned out of the hospital gates for the return journey, its occupants had increasingly felt as if they were being transported backwards across time. Apart from a pair of dangerously weaving cyclists and a solitary US military police jeep, they passed nothing at all on the main road back into Ely, where the streets themselves were as quiet as in the age of the horse. Above all, however, it was the almost complete absence of light that gave the impression that war had rolled away the centuries. The blacked-out city lay as if the Age of Enlightenment and all the subsequent achievements of science had been but a dream, and that its inhabitants had returned to a simplicity of existence not enjoyed since Oliver Cromwell and his burgeoning young family had occupied the modest half-timbered house overlooking the cathedral green. Now though, as Blanding and Diana followed the wavering beam of their conductor's torch across the worn nave flagstones, with the verses of the psalm *Dominus illuminatio* echoing in the inky blackness overhead, it felt as if they'd travelled a lot further back than the late Lord Protector's day, and were now moving in the time when Norman monks had first erected the abbey church – or long before that even, when Etheldreda of the East Angles had originally fled her

186

husband's embraces to establish a religious foundation on the small island of firm ground among the marshes and reed-beds.

'For in the time of trouble he shall hide me in his tabernacle; yea, in the secret place of his dwelling shall he hide me, and set me up upon a rock of stone.'

By this late stage of the war, the danger of air raids had largely receded. Nevertheless, there remained always the possibility of a hit-and-run raider, some lone wandering Dornier or Heinkel, skimming in low over the coast to catch a shimmer of light shining up from one of the cathedral's huge uncovered windows. Thus even beyond the arched entrance to the choir, where candles glimmered in the small glass bowls dispersed along the tiers of facing stalls, the darkness was such that at first only the faces and hands of choristers and officiating clergy could be made out above the flickering little pools of light.

Although not a regular churchgoer, Blanding had often attended evensong in Norwich Cathedral during his pre-war brass rubbing weekends, enjoying the sombre beauty of setting and service as much an aesthetic as a religious experience. On such occasions, he and his party of schoolboys had invariably been part of a tiny congregation, comprised for the most part of worshippers decades older than themselves. Despite what he'd read about hugely increased church attendance since the outbreak of war, it was therefore still somewhat of a shock, after he and Diana had been led in across the marble flooring and shown up to a pair of canonical stalls, and his eyes had had time to adjust to the shadowy dimness, to realize that the seats below and either side of them were tightly packed with young uniformed figures. This being bomber country, unsurprisingly the majority wore RAF blue, although among them was a fair sprinkling both of khaki and US Army beige. Those clad in the latter appeared taller, more broad-shouldered and certainly a lot more smartly dressed than their British counterparts. Yet for all that, in Blanding's eyes, there seemed some sort of innocence – or was it naivete – about these youngsters so recently transported across the Atlantic from the land of plenty. Conscious that in a matter of weeks many of those same smooth, boyish faces and well-fed bodies could well be exposed to withering fire on one of the as yet unknown invasion beaches, he peered at them through the gloom, experiencing the same curious mix of envy and guilt he always felt back at Frampton Wissey when welcoming the latest batch of aircrew replacements to the station.

187

Since clambering into the adjoining stall, he'd been acutely conscious of Diana's presence at his side. Now, as the psalm ended and the congregation seated themselves for the first lesson, he felt the brush of her elbow against his own. Glancing surreptitiously round at her shadowy profile, he found himself again wondering about her desire to visit the cathedral. Clearly, she'd found the hospital visit an ordeal, and, with a sharp stab of jealousy, he imagined that the nerve-shaken Ellis as well as the sight of other badly wounded other patients, had stirred fears for her husband's safety.

Around them, he could make out a number of female figures: a bespectacled Waaf sergeant he vaguely recognized from visits to Group HQ; an auburn-haired ATS subaltern and, seated directly opposite, a smartly dressed pair of what he guessed were members of the American Women's Army Corps; and now, as they and the rest rose for the singing of the Magnificat, his thoughts strayed back to the dead June Summerfield. Had she also, he wondered, occasionally attended evensong in the cathedral while off duty? Might she indeed have sat in this very same stall, not only seeking consolation for the loss of the two men she'd been close to, but searching for some explanation or meaning for the deaths, not only of them, but of the many other missing aircrew members she'd inevitably have known during her time at Frampton Wissey?

The thought seemed to bring her close – indeed, it was almost as if her ghostly presence hovered somewhere in the darkness around him. With the service continuing with its familiar words and long-learnt responses, Blanding's mind was free to wander. As he automatically knelt, stood and sat in turn, he found himself thinking of his and the dead girl's shared hobby of brass rubbing; also of her unaccountable possession of the ex-Dulwich College library book and the surprising similarity of their literary tastes. Separately, he told himself, each of those things could be mere simple coincidence. Putting them together, however, and then adding the carefully copied-out transcription of that particular Boethius extract that meant so much to him personally, finally now convinced him that it could have been no such thing: that impossible though it seemed, there must have indeed been some connection between himself and the doomed young Waaf, some bond, mysterious yet tangibly real, linking him, the stiff, shy, almost middle-aged ex-schoolmaster to the pretty, popular, blond-headed corporal from the wireless section.

But what that link could possibly be, he simply couldn't

imagine. Certain, nevertheless, that it had to exist, he stared down over the heads below him across towards the choir stalls where the hands and faces of men and boys glowed Rembrandtesque above the flicking little bowls of light. In all likelihood, he thought, the solution was perfectly obvious if not downright simple if he could only but think what it was. It might also, he told himself, explain all those other perplexing conundrums surrounding Summerfield's death: the reason why she had postponed going home after coming off duty that Saturday afternoon, apparently choosing instead to spend her first day of leave hanging about the station; who the father of her unborn child was, and why she'd been so careful to conceal his identity; whether there was a link between her pregnancy and enforced resignation from the WAAF and her seemingly inexplicable decision to allow herself to become unnecessarily marooned within the sealed-off camp that Sunday, only later, as it seemed, to risk slipping illegally off the aerodrome after dark that evening; the curiously tender, almost ritualistic way in which her battered, half-stripped corpse had been left on the ground on the short-cut just outside the perimeter fence so as to be found early the next morning – above all, the precise nature and cause of the horrific attack that had stopped her vulnerable young heart and left her face blooded and contorted in a rictus of horror.

'Lighten our darkness, we beseech thee, O Lord; and by thy great mercy defend us from all perils and dangers of this night; for the love of thy only Son, our Saviour, Jesus Christ.'

The priest's words echoed in the vast dark emptiness. As they did so, Blanding continued to stare down at the illuminated faces of clergy and choristers, his fists clenched, his features working as he struggled in vain, standing there at the edge of the candlelight, for an answer that seemed to hover for moments tantalisingly somewhere just beyond his grasp.

'Come on now! Stop tormenting yourself for a moment and eat your supper up before it gets cold!'

For the last half minute or so, Blanding had sat swirling round the depleted contents of his beer-glass while gazing fixedly down into it as if attempting to fathom the depths of some crystal ball. Now, at the speaker's words, he broke free of his reverie and, embarrassed, looked up to meet her eyes. 'It's just,' he replied, 'as I told you when we were leaving the cathedral, I'm now absolutely certain that June

Summerfield and I are somehow linked – and yet having pummelled my brains throughout most of the service and once again in here, for the life of me I still can't see what that connection could possibly be.'

'One way or another, I'm sure the answer will eventually come,' answered Diana, smiling. 'In the meantime, I suggest you concentrate on your meal – it's a pity to let good food go to waste, especially after all the trouble they went to in producing it for us.'

Despite the somewhat fearsome depiction of a mounted Cromwellian trooper brandishing a blood-smeared sabre on the sooty signboard over the street door, the Association was a homely mix of inn and lodging house. Hidden away behind the city station, and situated so close to the platforms that it fairly trembled at the passing trains, the quaint, old hostelry was patronised by passengers and staff alike as a welcome alternative to the stark and somewhat forbidding railway company cafeteria. In contrast to its unheated rival, a large coal fire glowed in the low-beamed main saloon, where the proprietor presided in shirt-sleeved splendour behind the bar, aided by his peroxide-blonde wife. At that moment, both were engaged in conversation with a cluster of regular customers, including a couple of black-waistcoated porters. So warm and inviting was the atmosphere that, apart from a prominently-displayed Spitfire Fund collecting box and a tattered poster warning of the dangers of loose talk, there might have not been a war going on at all. This was equally true of the delicious dishes of roast beef and Yorkshire pudding that had appeared as if magically conjured out of the peacetime past and placed before the blue-uniformed couple facing each other across the table in the room's little side-alcove or snuggery.

As Blanding bent again to his plate, Diana pensively sipped her cider. 'I've been thinking a lot about Summerfield too,' she said, lowering the glass, 'but for me, it's that pink mitten you mentioned that, for some reason, keeps going round in my head. As I said back in the camp, I can't understand why on earth she should ever have worn such awful, ugly items after being issued with a smart-looking pair of proper leather gloves.'

Taking another forkful of beef, Blanding chewed thoughtfully. 'The point about mittens,' he said, clearing his mouth, 'and the reason, I imagine, they were invented in the first place, is that they leave the wearer's fingers free to work on intricate tasks. Apart from that, I suppose, at a pinch they can always be worn for extra warmth beneath conventional gloves.'

'Maybe,' responded Diana, 'but neither of those alternatives seems to make much sense in this case. In the first place, Summerfield would hardly have wanted to knit a jumper or croquet a shawl while crossing the fields after dark to meet this mysterious lover of hers. Secondly, her service gloves were still among her things back in the Waafery so she wasn't wearing them under those – and anyway, it wasn't as if it were cold that evening, just rather damp, so what was the point of having anything on her hands at all.'

With a weary sigh, Blanding pushed away his still unfinished plate. 'Yes, damn it,' he exclaimed, 'mittens or gloves, the whole thing doesn't make sense at all. And then there's this mysterious lover as you call him! We still haven't the foggiest idea who the fellow was, or why on earth she should have been so careful to keep his identity secret.'

As he broke off, there came the sound of a heavy lorry turning into the road and drawing to a stop almost directly opposite the blacked-out window beside them. The engine was turned off, and then almost at once there came a couple of loud metallic slams. These were followed a moment or two later by sound of boots on pavement outside and the rattle of the street door being opened behind the pair of overlapping velvet curtains that served to screen the light from the street outside – then, as if emerging on stage, a couple of lanky, black American soldiers pushed into view between the heavy folds of material. The appearance of these broadly grinning newcomers in their crisp white forage caps and officer-like tunics caused all conversation round the bar momentarily to cease – but then, an instant later, landlord, his wife and customers alike were exchanging enthusiastic greetings and handshakes with this obviously well-known and highly popular pair.

On leaving the cathedral, Blanding had inquired of a passing policeman where visitors might obtain a bite to eat. Of the various alternatives suggested, he'd chosen this out-of-the-way inn. Now, as the two new arrivals began a jocular account in broad Kentucky accents of a horrendously slow journey across the country from the Liverpool docks, it occurred to him that the pair had most likely chosen this particular hostelry for reasons not unlike his own – its backstreet obscurity being an almost certain guarantee against being confronted by others of their compatriots in uniform, though not from a general wish for privacy as in his case, but an understandable reluctance to avoid confrontation with potentially belligerent fellow

191

nationals. Thinking this, Blanding was suddenly struck by what seemed like a flash of inspiration. Leaning across the table, he excitedly half-whispered to Diana, 'Could that be the answer, do you think? Could Summerfield's lover have been a soldier from one of the local American black transportation or airfield construction units? Was it because of his skin colour that she was careful to hide his identity?'

Diana considered for a moment, but then shook her head. 'No, I don't believe it,' she answered emphatically. 'Apart from the obvious fact that most soldiers, black or white, are unlikely to be interested in tramping round a lot of draughty old churches in search of brass rubbings, there's the way that coloured GI's are regarded in this country. As you just saw, they're generally popular with the British public – often more so indeed than some of their white counterparts who can seem a trifle too full of themselves at times.'

'Yes, that's all very well,' protested Blanding, 'but surely you're not saying there isn't racial prejudice here?'

'No, of course not, but nevertheless, in matters of race, our history is very different from that of the United States, which still even segregates their army. God knows, though British merchants played a leading part in the establishment of the Atlantic slave trade, we've never actually had slaves in this country – at least, not since feudal times. If we're divided socially, it's by class, not race. Apart from that, outside London and a few of the larger seaports, until the arrival of large numbers of American troops during these last two years, most people in this country – apart that is from service personnel having served overseas – had never actually ever seen a negro in the flesh, and the only ones they would have heard of would have been Paul Robeson, Jessie Owens and some of the more famous heavy-weight boxers. As a result, coloured soldiers are still often viewed as exciting and exotic by the British people, as well as being representatives of a downtrodden people to be supported and sympathized with. On top of that, rightly or wrongly, black GI's have a reputation for being well-mannered and gentle. Consequently, going out with one here isn't generally regarded as it would be even in the most liberal areas of the United States – that is, as something so demeaning and shameful that a girl would try to conceal it from her friends. No,' continued Diana, 'whatever made Summerfield so careful to hide her relationship from everyone, I'd say it had to be something far more unacceptable and shocking to those around her

192

than a matter of skin colour – but what that could have been, I can't begin to think.'

'Yes, well,' murmured Blanding, nodding thoughtfully, 'even if I can't quite fully accept your rather rosy view of interracial relations in this country, I don't suppose any girl out here in the wilds of East Anglia could get into a cinema or a dance with a coloured man without being noticed – and if she were a Waaf, the news would be all round her station in no time at all. Apart from there being no such rumours regarding Summerfield, there aren't any actual US bases within walking distance of RAF Frampton Wissey. Therefore she couldn't have been in daily contact with any sort of American, black or white – apart, of course, from Tex Crawford.' Breaking off, he sighed heavily. 'I don't know,' he went on, 'but like so much else about Summerfield's death, we seem to keep going round in circles round this question of her lover, and yet we never seem to get a step nearer to establishing his identity!'

Diana leaned back against the high settle and took a thoughtful sip of her drink. 'We could, of course,' she said, 'always try to narrow the search down by attempting to put ourselves in her place –'

'How?'

'Simply by trying to see things as she saw them, and feeling them as they must have felt to her. For example, how do you think she'd have reacted to losing two men she'd been close to among the bomber crews?'

Blanding shrugged. 'I don't know – felt grief, I suppose.'

'Yes, of course,' answered Diana impatiently. 'But what else might she had felt, especially after the whispers began?'

'Whispers?' Blanding was totally at a loss for a moment, but then, realizing what the other was implying, he stared at her in amazement. 'For heaven's sake,' he burst out, incredulity in his voice, 'surely you're not suggesting that the girl might have actually believed that ridiculous idea about herself being jinxed?'

'Of course – why not?' answered Diana with a slight shrug. 'After all, none of us is very logical in the end, especially about anything where sex is involved. And anyway,' she added, 'women are especially good at blaming themselves.'

Blanding thought for a few moments before shaking his head. 'But even if you're right,' he said, 'and Summerfield actually started to believe all that silly chop girl nonsense about herself, and, as a result,

193

was burdened by a misplaced feeling of guilt as you imply, what would have been the implications?'

'Well, certainly these I'd have thought,' answered Diana. 'Consciously or unconsciously, she'd have wished for a relationship with someone she felt safe with – or, to put it the other way round, with someone she felt would be safe with her. In other words, somebody not obviously at risk of being shot down and who wasn't likely to burden her with more death on her conscience as well as grief to bear. Therefore, I'd say that the man concerned would have to be a local civilian or, if he were an RAF serviceman, at least someone safely employed on the ground.'

'That's a very interesting insight, and somehow very convincing,' murmured Blanding, nodding thoughtfully. 'However did it come to you?' Receiving no answer, he swallowed what was left of his beer, and then, looking up from his glass, he glimpsed something in Diana's face – an expression that seemed to hover somewhere between fear and guilt, and one that caused a sudden idea to rush upon him. And in that instance, as if in a mirror, he saw his realization register in his companion's eyes. 'Your transfer down here?' he struggled out, but then, breaking off, he lowered his glance. 'Look,' he resumed after a painful pause, forcing himself again to look up, 'you don't have to answer this if you don't want to, of course, but your transfer down here – had it anything to do with your husband?'

Diana turned and looked away towards the noisily laughing group at the bar. 'Roger was killed over Bochum nearly two years ago,' she said in a flat, almost matter-of-fact low tone. 'Apparently his Halifax collided with another over the target.'

'I'm so sorry,' murmured Blanding, staring down into his empty glass.

There was another long pause before Diana resumed. 'For months after that,' she said, turning her gaze back from the bar, 'I continued my duties mechanically, just as Corporal Summerfield and thousands of other grieving lovers and spouses must have done during these last years. People were kind, but still I made a sort of island of myself. Soon I stopped going to see Roger's parents, and then even my own – I just wanted to hide away and to go quietly on with my work which was in photographic interpretation.' She paused. 'But then, early last spring, almost indeed at this same time of the year, I started going out for the odd walk or cycle ride with one of Roger's friends. His name was Harry, and he and Roger had been out

194

in Rhodesia together for flying training.' Diana paused again slightly before going on. 'Anyway,' she said, 'over the next weeks, the two of us gradually drew closer, though I think it was still nothing more than friendship for both of us. But then, all at once, the relationship changed; and then, to cut a long story short, we went off for a weekend leave down in London together and became lovers – but then again, shortly after that, just a matter of weeks later – on the 24th of July to be exact – Harry and his crew were sent off on that first of those big Hamburg raids, the one when they used 'Window' for the first time to block the enemy radar-controlled anti-aircraft guns. It worked wonderfully, you'll remember – the German radar was temporary blinded by the strips of silver foil that were dropped, and almost all our aircraft came back safely.'

'But not Harry's plane, I take it?' murmured Blanding gently.

'Oh, yes, it came back all right,' answered Diana, 'but it had been badly damaged by one of the very few successful German fighter attacks of that night. A couple of the crew, the radio operator and rear gunner, had been badly wounded, so Harry felt he must try to land. Anyway, the plane overshot the runway and caught fire, and though they managed to cut almost everyone out, Harry was badly burnt in the crash, and he and one of the other survivors died just a week or so later.'

Bewildered, Blanding stared at her for a moment, and then, all at once, it felt if his heart was turning to ice within him. 'And you,' he said slowly, 'would have gone to see him in that week, of course: that's how you come to have been to an RAF hospital a couple of times before today.' Pausing, he saw the slight nod of Diana's head. 'My God,' he exclaimed bitterly, 'what a pompous, insensitive sort of ass I must have sounded this afternoon, advising you to try to look the patients in the eyes! No wonder you didn't want to accompany me over here to another damned hospital, and also that's why, of course, you wanted to go to the cathedral after seeing Ellis!'

'I wanted to be able to tell you, but I was afraid of breaking my cover.'

Not understanding, Blanding shook his head. 'Cover?'

'My cover as a married woman,' came the answer. 'A person off-limits – someone not available for a romantic attachment, someone to be left severely alone.'

Blanding stared at her, but then, once again, the full truth seemed to rise up and rush upon him. 'You don't mean,' he gasped, 'what you said about Summerfield applies equally to you? Good God, surely you're not saying that the same sort of rumours began about yourself?'

'That I was a chop girl?' Diana nodded and smiled wanly across at him. 'Yes, the whispering started very quickly after Harry's death – it's so simple, you see, what with the high loss rate suffered in Bomber Command and everyone, ground personnel as well as aircrew, generally living on their nerves. A girl gets close to a couple of men who get killed, and then perhaps she just happens to speak to someone whose aircraft is shot down that very night, and suddenly she's a dangerous sort of Eve – a malign siren who always manages to kill the thing that gets close to her, someone who it's fatal to get attached to and even dangerous to know. Then almost as quickly as the stories begin – and that's the worst part – the girl in question actually starts half-believing the rubbish herself.' Diana paused and remained silent for a time before struggling on. 'Anyway, that's why I applied for a transfer south: I wanted to get away from everyone who knew me and my history. Hidden away down here in 3 Group where nobody knew me, I felt I could begin again. And with these,' she continued, holding up her left hand to display her wedding and engagement rings, 'I had safeguards to protect myself from all attentions – or rather perhaps, to protect others from getting close to me.' She forced a stiff, unhappy smile. 'And so, Alan,' she went on, 'now you know my little secret – and also understand perhaps why it isn't only you who feels a link with June Summerfield, and wishes to find out what awful thing it was that happened to her that night.'

CHAPTER FIFTEEN

The crowing of a cockerel rang through the damp silence.

Not certain for the moment where he was, Blanding lay a few seconds, eyes closed, face buried deep in the pillow, but then, as the raucous loud heralding was repeated, he rolled over onto his back and, blinking the sleep from his eyes, groped for his spectacles on the bedside cabinet. Putting them on, he blearily looked up through the rain-dribbling panes of the window above his head to see that the previous day's weather forecast had been correct, and that, as the younger of the two civilian meteorologists had predicted, an unyielding layer of dark cloud now completely blanketed the sky.

After dropping Diana off at the Waafery, he hadn't returned to the camp as originally planned. Instead, on an impulse, he had driven straight over to his rented cottage at Jubilee End, an isolated hamlet lying some six miles southeast of Frampton Wissey on the edge of what, before the First War, had been a prosperous estate. Due to the death of its presumptive heir under the machine-guns at Loos in 1915, followed by that of his younger brother from dysentery (helped on by the thrust of a Turkish bayonet) on the infamous march from Kut the following year, the land had long since been broken up and sold off as separate farms. Now the coppices once used for the rearing of game-birds were wild and overgrown, while the great house itself lay partly boarded up and partly occupied by a signals unit belonging to FUSAG, General Patton's phantom 1st American Army Group, a force created almost literally out of the air – or at least, from radio waves – as part of Operation Fortitude, whose task was to delude the Germans into thinking that the coming Allied invasion would take place in the Pas de Calais. Although the skies overhead seemed constantly a-murmur these days with the sound of aircraft and the surrounding roads often clogged nose-to-tail with military traffic, the tiny hamlet with its three-house redbrick terrace of labourers' cottages and the tumbledown farmyard opposite lay apparently untouched by the war. The lane running between them led only to one of the blocked-off entrances of the walled-in park (within which, much to the amusement of the locals, scores of dummy rubber tanks and plywood artillery pieces had recently been laid out in rows). The little habitation was thus being left to enjoy an almost medieval tranquillity midst all the elaborate and clandestine preparations for coming battle.

The find of the cottage had been a joy to Blanding – one indeed of the few real pleasures of his war service. With memories of playing in the village brook and of wandering the woods above his father's rectory as a child, part of him had always hankered after the rural life. Brought up on a diet of Wordsworth and Coleridge (supplemented later by the poetry of Edward Thomas and Robert Frost), he'd thus regarded his pre-war existence in the sprawling wastes of South London as a mere transitional stage, a temporary exile as it were before returning to what he fondly regarded as his proper roots. Thus to move into the small end-of-terrace cottage with its low ceilings, lack of electricity and the primitive earth-closet at the bottom of the garden had felt like a spiritual homecoming.

Over the winter, he'd taken much trouble with its furnishing, purchasing various articles at local auctions to supplement the items placed in storage after his father's death. He'd also brought up from London his entire collection of papers and books. As well as prevailing on a reluctant owner to have the sanitation arrangements modernized, he'd used whatever periods of time he could escape his RAF duties to redecorate the cottage throughout and also to clear and plant the garden, generally doing all in his power to make the cramped little dwelling and its quarter acre of stony soil as comfortable and pleasant a sanctuary as possible from the grim realities of service life.

From its coop in the neighbouring garden, the cockerel crowed loudly again.

Though it was still very early, Blanding felt surprisingly awake. For the first time in weeks he'd slept deeply and well, and for a few moments more he remained staring up at the drizzling overcast sky with a profound sense of satisfaction. The evening before had been delightful, a blessed balm after the strains and perplexities of the day. Between Diana and himself he'd felt a growing bond, tell himself as he might that, widow or not, she remained utterly beyond

198

his reach – a single green isle in a vast ocean of grey that time would inevitably sweep him past, a mirage that must necessarily vanish as he drew nearer. Nevertheless, for all that, he couldn't suppress a flood of happiness at the remembrance of their time in Ely together, a sensation he was determined to revel in and enjoy to the full, however fleeting and illusionary.

Full of nervous excitement at the thought of his next meeting with his assistant, and far too awake now to linger longer in bed, he scrambled out from under the blankets, and, pulling on his trousers, hurried downstairs in bare feet. Passing through the heavily book-lined front parlour, he went out into the kitchen and put on the kettle to boil. As the water was heating, he went and opened the back door, and, standing there beneath its low, green-lichened lintel, he gazed out with proprietorial pleasure at the already burgeoning rows of spring cabbage, leeks and runner beans. Enjoying the cool caress of the thin drizzle drifting onto his naked arms and chest, he remained staring across the wet soil, thinking of the often huge disparity between external appearance and intrinsic reality, and of the quite extraordinary difference between the attractive and apparently utterly self-confident sharer of his duties and the isolated, private, inner woman, haunted by the irrational and, seemingly, ridiculous notion of herself as some sort of harbinger, if not actual instigator, of death.

Leaving the back door open, Blanding thoughtfully returned to wash and shave at the sink. Ablutions completed, removing the crisply ironed shirt hanging over the back of the kitchen chair, he returned upstairs with it to dress. It was only when struggling to fasten his collar stud that he happened to catch sight in the mirror of the life-sized facsimile of a mail-hooded Angevin knight displayed on the wall behind. It was easily the largest and most impressive of his brass rubbings, and the one of the few of his extensive collection he'd ever bothered to mount. As he twisted the obstinate stud into place, he continued to gaze at the rubbing's reflection in the glass, vividly recalling as he did so his visit to the police inquiry room the day before, and the sight of June Summerfield's equally carefully transposed likeness of the meekly kneeling couple beneath the heraldic shield.

Until that moment, his mind had been occupied almost entirely with thoughts of Diana. Now, however, he found himself thinking again of the young Waaf corporal and the mystery surrounding her death. Face abstracted, he turned away from the

199

mirror and, still in shirtsleeves, went back out through the door onto the landing and crossed over to the severe little cell of a room opposite that he chose to call his study. He'd not been inside for a week, and on entering, he saw that, uncharacteristically for him, he'd left its one small window ajar. As a result, rain had blown in and wetted the typescript notes and manuscript sheets of his half-completed history of the Ostrogothic kings – a project he'd been researching whilst at Dulwich, but which, like so much else in his life, he'd been forced to lay aside at the outbreak of war.

Frowning at this latest sign of his increasing forgetfulness and considerably annoyed with himself at the oversight, Blanding closed the window. He then went over to the ornately carved German desk that had originally belonged to his father and, standing before it, began surveying the series of deep shelves erected immediately above. He'd always been neat – almost compulsively so – and although packed with variously sized boxes and files, everything on the shelves was clearly labelled. It was, therefore, merely a matter of seconds before he spotted the folders in which he kept his brass rubbing collection and, next to them, the large cardboard box containing the stock of unused materials along with the many booklets and pamphlets garnered and used on his pre-war school cycling expeditions.

Although Summerfield's rubbing of the knight and his lady had seemed curiously familiar when when he examined it the day before, he was certain he'd never actually made a copy of it himself. Not to waste time, therefore, he didn't bother to check through the rubbings themselves. Instead, lifting down the bulky ex-soap carton, he seated himself at the desk and, dipping in, began leafing through his large assortment of local church guidebooks. Hardly aware of the lowing of a cow from across at the farmyard opposite or of the sudden excited clucking of hens being fed in the neighbouring garden, he flicked on through the crudely printed pages, moving rapidly from one limp-backed, cheap, slightly musty-smelling little publication to the next. Twenty minutes passed and he was already thinking of giving up the seemingly hopeless task and returning to finish dressing when, turning a page, he suddenly came upon the very thing he was looking for: a tiny photographic reproduction of the same kneeling knight and lady. Beneath was printed: *Tablet memorial of Sir John and Matilda (Maud) de Rodbourne, c.1470,* and next to it in the margin, pencilled faintly in his own handwriting: *A rather unusual and compelling little tablet – nicely preserved and well worth transposing at some future date.*

Opening the top middle drawer of his desk, he groped through its contents for his magnifying glass. A few frustrating seconds passed before he discovered it pushed to the back and wedged behind a wad of outdated garage receipts. Making a mental note to clear and re-tidy the drawers as soon as he had a chance, he extracted the glass. Then, bending over the open page, began to examine the photograph under the lens, clearly recalling as he did so that one and only occasion when he'd seen the original of the blurred little image before.

It had been an unusually warm day back in the early summer of 1936 Blanding remembered, about the very same time indeed, he thought, that the young June Summerfield must have been purchasing her commonplace book with the money she'd received from her aunt after winning a place in the local grammar school. Taking packed lunches with them, he with his party of schoolboys had set out from Norwich on the almost deserted main Bungay Road that Saturday morning with the intention of taking rubbings in various churches just over the Suffolk border. Eventually, with task completed and having refreshed themselves with cream teas, the group had turned homeward. It had been then, whilst cycling back on a roundabout route through the country lanes in the late afternoon those eight years before, that they'd chanced upon the church in one of the smaller villages – a surprisingly large and beautiful example of perpendicular Gothic architecture, standing well back from the road and largely screened behind churchyard yews and elms. It was a gem of a building, all the more impressive because of the obscurity of its setting, and, on an impulse, he'd immediately dismounted and led his mildly protesting charges inside.

After the heat of the day it had been refreshingly cool within the impressively lofty nave. Even the boys, he remembered, had been struck by the double row of painted medieval figures carved out of the ends of the protruding hammerbeams overhead – the wood so dried and the colour so faded that the horizontal statuettes appeared like greying ghosts peering down at them through the veil of the centuries. Beneath the gaze of those immobile faces, with the dust motes dancing in the slanting streams of light, he'd gone over to sit in one of the narrow, high-backed pews and began thumbing through the fourpenny guidebook he'd taken from the rickety and worm-eaten little display table next to the main door. It was then, in a silence

201

broken only by the bright twitterings of birds outside and the occasional low whispers and giggles of his juvenile companions about him, that flicking over a page, he'd first come across the photograph of the church's solitary and surprisingly striking medieval brass tablet.

There had been, he now seemed to recall, some difficulty in locating the actual plate. Eventually, one of the younger boys had discovered it set into one of the floor slabs in the dusty pumping recess behind the nineteenth-century organ. It being far too late in the day to seek permission to take a rubbing, he'd scribbled the note in the margin of his purchased guide as a reminder to do so as soon as he had an opportunity. The following year, however, as previously arranged, he'd taken his party to the Wroxham and Cottishall areas. After that, what with the Munich crisis and then Hitler's army later taking total control of Czechoslovakia, there had been no other such school expeditions. As a result, he'd not seen or thought about that particular brass tablet again until vaguely recognizing Corporal Summerfield's reproduction of it on Chief Inspector Stanley's desk the previous day.

Bending over the photograph and staring down through the glass at the oddly elongated pair of figures, kneeling opposite and each seemingly complementing the other, Blanding was again struck by the almost tangible link between himself and the dead Waaf. Both Summerfield's discovery of the hidden-away memorial in an out-of-the-way church and her choosing to make a rubbing of it seemed yet another impossible coincidence – a falling-together just as extraordinary and improbable as not only her possession of an ex-Dulwich copy of Boethius's *Consolation* but also copying out from it that very same extract that his college tutor had pointed out to him all those years before. Again, just as back in his office after the disquieting interview with Chief Inspector Stanley, Blanding had the eerie and quite irrational feeling that the doomed young woman with the fatal heart defect had been in some way an extension of himself – that she, the so-called 'chop girl', the imagined harbinger of death, had trodden almost literally in his own footsteps and, driven apparently by the same impulses as himself, had somehow managed in her tragically brief life to live a parallel existence to his own and to achieve some at least of those things he'd himself planned to do.

'Mr Blanding, sir? Are you upstairs?'

Startled from his thoughts by the voice suddenly calling from below, he glanced up, and then, hurriedly rising from the desk, went out onto the landing. Still occupied with the mysterious bond between himself and the dead girl, an abstracted look on his face, he descended the twisting flight of stairs to encounter the broad, ruddy features of the woman grinning cheerfully in at him through the open back door.

One of the unexpected pleasures of renting the cottage had been his relationship with the rather elderly couple next door. The Lutons were open and friendly country folk, and, as soon as the bespectacled young townie moved in, they'd taken him under their wing. On the day of his arrival, they had appeared on his doorstep with fresh milk and home-baked bread, and ever afterwards, Jim, local handyman and jobbing gardener, had given him practical advice on the upkeep of both house and land. In her turn, Elsie kept an eye on things whenever he was away on duty, making sure that the cottage was regularly dusted and that there was always food in the larder on his return. Although he knew their kindness was as natural and spontaneous as the couple themselves, and that, by his presence, he helped fill the gap left by their youngest and only as yet unmarried daughter having recently been transferred to an ATS searchlight battery guarding one of the south coast invasion ports, there nevertheless remained an element of unease in Blanding's mind: a fear that their generosity was partly inspired by the uniform he wore – that he, in his wingless blue tunic, was the undeserving beneficiary of the courage of the fighter pilots of 1940 or those of the bomber crews whose machines could be heard almost nightly droning their way back and forth from the North Sea.

'Oh, there you are!' burst out Elsie as Blanding's bespectacled face appeared. 'I saw the back door open so I knew you was up. I knocked a couple of times, but reckoned you must have your nose in another of them dusty old books.' Laughing, she stepped inside the house. 'Any rate,' she resumed, holding out a covered dish, 'I've brought round a couple of rashers, a spot of black pudding and a freshly laid egg. Sit yourself down at the table when I puts 'em to fry – Hitler or no blooming Hitler, you can't be going back off to the camp on an empty belly in all this rain!'

As Blanding meekly did as instructed, the speaker turned and disappeared out into the kitchen. 'Ah, I see you've found that shirt I washed then?' she called back through the doorway. 'It came out nicely even if I do say so myself.'

'Thank you, yes,' answered Blanding, relieved that the news of Corporal Summerfield's death had obviously yet to reach the remoteness of Jubilee End. 'It's the one I have on at this moment, in fact. But really, Mrs Luton,' he added, 'you shouldn't have put yourself to all that trouble – I left it soaking in the sink to rinse through later myself.'

'Another of them wretched old nosebleeds?'

'I'm afraid so, yes – as you doubtless must know from the noise of the car, I slipped back here to change late on Sunday night and then drove straight back to the camp.'

Apart from the hiss and sputter of frying bacon and the sound of the now increasingly heavy rain outside, there was silence for a few moments before Elsie called out again. 'Did you see all them Yankee bombers yesterday morning? Must have been hundreds of 'em passing overhead at one time! It was a regular Piccadilly Circus up there above! It's just been on the news: seems they were going out after them ball-bearing factories again.' The speaker snorted. 'Times our lads and them Yanks have been over to that place, you wouldn't think there was more than a few old piles of rubble left to knock around!' The war was an endless topic of conversation for Elsie: she took a sceptical interest in it, cataloguing triumphs and defeats as if they were slightly absurd happenings in some nearby village or town, yet along with the large majority of her fellow citizens even at the very darkest of times, always with the comfortable certainty of ultimate victory. She'd been young in one war and was now late middle-aged in another, and it often seemed as if all her tears and compassion had been drained by what she still habitually referred to as the *Great 'Un* – that all-overtaking cataclysmic slaughter that had killed both the old squire's sons and robbed her in turn of all three of her older brothers. Nevertheless, sometimes in a glance or look Blanding sensed she could tell when squadron losses had been particularly heavy, and on such occasions, he could feel her unspoken sympathy. 'Aye, and I saw 'em coming back again in the afternoon,' the voice from the kitchen continued, 'but there were a good few less of them poor Yankee lads as set out! As I says to Jim, there's a darn more sting left in old Jerry than ever them wireless folks lets on.'

Elsie's talk had taken Blanding's mind back to those moments the previous day when, bent over Summerfield's brass rubbing, he'd been dimly aware of large formations of heavy bombers throbbing overhead. In turn, this now prompted again the same two questions he'd been wrestling with when her voice had rung up the stairs – how could the young Waaf corporal have stumbled across that same memorial tablet as himself, and what unlikely chance – if chance it was – could ever have prompted her to visit such a distant and obscure country church to make the rubbing?

'Heard your car come in last night,' came Elsie's voice from the kitchen. 'Was it work that kept you so late?'

'In a way, yes,' Blanding called back. 'I had to go over to visit a young officer at the RAF hospital at Ely. I invited my new assistant to accompany me, and while there, we decided to stop off for a bite to eat.'

Perhaps because of the slight gap before he'd answered or that his tone seemed unusually matter-of-fact – whatever it was, something in his reply obviously caught Elsie's attention. She didn't answer at once, but then, appearing a few moments later in the kitchen doorway carrying a steaming plate, she asked with a smile, 'And this new assistant of yours – would I be right in thinking she's a young lady?'

Embarrassed, yet at the same time pleased by the question, Blanding nodded. 'Yes, as it happens, she is,' he answered, blushing slightly.

'Well, that's nice,' said Elsie, placing the dish before him. 'It's good that you should have a bit of fun for a change. Though, of course,' she added, 'it's a pity you should have missed your friends.'

'Friends?' Taken aback, Blanding looked up at her blankly. 'Whatever friends do you mean?' he asked.

'Your two air force chums as come round visiting last night. A very polite, well-spoken young man – a squadron leader I think he said he was. And along with him was a tall, dark-haired sergeant who didn't say much – a right old Taffy Welshman from the way he talked.'

With effort, Blanding controlled his emotions. Despite his shock at Elsie's news, he was determined not to betray the slightest surprise. 'This squadron leader?' he asked with apparent casualness. 'Was he a rather short, dapper little man with a large, bushy moustache?'

'That's him – a very nice gentleman, well spoken and very nicely turned out; he asked ever so polite if I thought you'd mind if they both could wait in the house till you got back.' Clearly a perceptive woman, Elsie hesitated, catching the look in Blanding's face. 'I hope, sir,' she added with sudden anxiety, 'I haven't done wrong.'

Not wishing to upset the woman unnecessarily, Blanding shook his head. 'No, of course not, Mrs Luton – you could, after all, hardly have left any of my friends sitting outside in their car.' He contrived a smile. 'So,' he asked with forced casual lightness, 'did you have a chance to talk with either of them?'

'Oh yes,' answered Elsie with obvious relief, 'we all three of us had a right good old chat. They were both very interested in your life here, especially about what other visitors you've had.' She grinned knowingly. 'Of course, them being young men and chums of yorn, I knew what they really wanted to know: if you often brought any lady friends back here.'

Blanding forced another sickly smile. 'Really? And what did you say?'

'Don't worry – I didn't give you away,' answered his neighbour, smiling maternally. 'Just hinted that you were a bit of a dark horse. As I said to Jim, I knows you wouldn't've wanted 'em thinking you lived like some old hermit hidden away out here on your own.'

'Quite.' Frowning, Blanding took a forkful of the bacon as Elsie disappeared back into the kitchen to make the tea. He chewed thoughtfully for a few seconds. 'So how long did they both stay, Mrs Luton?' he called out towards the kitchen door.

'Oh, I don't know,' came the answer. 'Must have been a good hour and more before they brought the key back round and said they couldn't wait any longer. They were sorry to have missed you, but the squadron leader said you wasn't to worry none – I was to tell you that he'd definitely be seeing you back on the camp today.'

After the woman had left, Blanding remained staring down at his almost untouched meal, hardly hearing the heavy rain that now continued to fall. Since leaving the police inquiry room the previous morning – indeed from the moment when Stanley had first held up the open first page of the ex-school library book, or even before that, when he'd first mentioned his connection with Dulwich College – he knew he was suspected of Summerfield's killing. Indeed, he'd more than half expected to be placed under arrest at the end of the interview, and had been greatly relieved to have been allowed to return unhindered to his duties. Not only had there been the damning evidence of the book itself, but he knew that each of his original suspicions concerning Palmer applied equally or even more so to himself. Like the station engineer, he was a loner – a private, self-contained bachelor, a person with both time and opportunity to have attacked Corporal Summerfield after the squadron had taken off. Apart from that, he was also an officer whose prominent position in the station community and disparity of rank could well be the explanation for the Waaf's strange reluctance to reveal her lover's name. With the passing hours, however, and the intervention of the Mackenzie inquiry – above all, after the evening spent with Diana – his initial fear of arrest had gradually seeped away. It was, therefore, all the more a shock now to find out that, not only was he obviously still under suspicion, but so much so that Walker and Evans had apparently taken the trouble to make the twelve-mile round journey to visit him, and then, once here, had sat an hour or more alone inside the house, vainly awaiting his return.

An hour alone in the house!

Blanding suddenly found himself thinking of the open window of his study and the wetted manuscript sheets lying on the low table beneath. Next moment, he was remembering the unexpected difficulty he'd had locating the magnifying glass in the normally tidy middle desk drawer. A cold chill rushed through him. Leaving his barely touched breakfast, he rose to his feet and hurried upstairs, where, starting with his bedroom, he began quickly going through cupboards and drawers. Now he saw all the obvious signs of disturbance he'd missed earlier – the pile of laundered shirts not lying exactly parallel in the chest-of-drawers, the uneven hang of the normally carefully-hung suits and jackets in the wardrobe, the door of the bedside locker left slightly ajar.

Face set like a mask, his hands trembling from a mix of tension and mounting rage, Blanding turned and went out across to his study, already knowing with an absolute certainty that, during his absence, not only had his next-door-neighbour been closely questioned as to his private affairs, but that after she had so trustingly left them to wait downstairs alone for his return, his two unexpected visitors had made a complete and systematic search of his home.

CHAPTER SIXTEEN

Through the inverted fan of swept windscreen, the airfield came into view, a barren expanse of concrete runways and peri-track, dismal and deserted beneath the drizzle. Apart from a square-nosed fifteen-hundredweight Bedford truck splashing out towards the control tower through a haze of spray, nothing moved. The parked bombers were dark brooding silhouettes in the distance, the chequered red-and-white mobile control caravan the solitary bright blur of colour in all the vast watery greyness. Further along the road ahead, dominated by the camouflaged water tower, rose the principal camp buildings where, beside the main gate, a pair of white-belted station policemen stood watching the Morris's approach from beneath the roof of the guardroom veranda.

Still fuming with anger, Blanding had left Jubilee End, impatient to seek out Walker to demand an apology for what he regarded as a gross violation of his private world. Within a mile of the cottage, however, he found himself stuck behind a convoy of American trucks. Lacking the horsepower to accelerate past, he was reduced to sitting beneath the stares of the cluster of helmeted heads regarding him morosely over the rear vehicle's tailboard. The whole experience was curiously dispiriting: great dollops of water thrown up by the massive wheels splattering derisively across the windscreen at intervals, his gum-chewing audience gazing down with what seemed Olympian disdain as he impotently hammered his horn. Frustrated, he soon ceased his useless hootings, and resignedly followed on at the back of the slow-moving procession with a steadily growing sense of apprehension.

During basic training, it had been forcibly impressed on him and all in his intake that the government had bought their services for every one of the twenty-four hours of the day, and that during every minute of that time, off-duty or on, each remained constantly subject to military law. Presumably therefore, he told himself, the authorities had as much right to search his private quarters as any Nissen hut or barrack room on the camp. Added to that were the undeniable links between Corporal Summerfield and himself – those extraordinary coincidences and parallels that he couldn't even begin to explain, and which increasingly now seemed to haunt his life. With growing foreboding, he drove on towards the ominous waiting figures outside the guardroom. As he turned off the road to draw up in front of the lowered barrier, one of the pair stepped forward. Half expecting to be politely but firmly ordered out of the car, he wound down the window and held out his identity card.

'Good morning, sir.' Stooping before the driver's window, the rain dripping from the peak of his service cap, the police corporal gave the proffered document a cursory glance. 'There's a message for you, sir,' he said, stepping back and saluting. 'Squadron Leader Walker would like you to call on him as soon as convenient.'

'Indeed?' Blanding looked up through the windscreen towards where the sodden ensign hung like a limp rag from the parade ground flagstaff. 'All right, Corporal,' he said, turning back the figure beside the car, 'in that case, you'd better ring the gentleman concerned to say that I'm on my way over to see him at this very minute.'

Strangely enough, with the interview now in immediate prospect, all Blanding's former nervousness had disappeared. In fact, as he drove on between groups of greatcoated figures scurrying through the wet, he found himself actually relishing the thought of the coming confrontation. Apart from giving him the opportunity to vent his bottled-up anger, there was every chance of learning from Walker the latest discoveries regarding Summerfield's death, and therefore perhaps finding the key at last to the mysteries surrounding it. Having arrived outside the administration block and parked in his allocated space, he joined the host of damp-smelling clerks and typists filing inside, and then, once inside, hurried towards Walker's office. Reaching it, he knocked at the door and, bending close to it, listened intently. Unable, however, to hear anything above the bustle and voices of those passing behind him along the corridor, taking a deep breath, he pressed down the handle and stepped inside.

As befitted his rank, the room allocated to the representative of the RAF's Special Investigations Department was comfortably large, and, on entering, Blanding was disconcerted to find himself intruding on what at first glance seemed like some sort of inter-police conference or briefing. Dominating proceedings, Walker himself was centrally ensconced behind a desk immediately facing the door, while seated at right angles to him sat Chief Inspector Stanley, arms folded, his head bowed. In front stood Sergeant Evans and Stanley's portly plainclothes assistant, together with a weasel-faced, rather shrivelled little man in civilian dress, whom the newcomer guessed was some sort of technical expert employed by the Cambridgeshire Constabulary.

'Ah, there you are, Flight Lieutenant!' exclaimed Walker with a flash of white teeth as the door opened. 'Thank you for attending so promptly – do please come in and take this seat over here.'

Although Stanley briefly raised his head, Blanding noticed that the elderly policeman didn't quite meet his eye. His head slumped forward once more, leaving him once again looking like some sleepy, old, superannuated clerk – either that, he thought, or an aged judge wearily enduring the tedious courtroom hours through some long, hot summer afternoon. In complete contrast, Walker, however, was the same bright, smiling, immaculately dressed figure as the previous day. 'I asked you to drop by,' he began as Blanding self-consciously took the seat indicated directly in front of the desk, 'as there are a few loose ends that I and the chief inspector feel sure you can help us with.'

Uncomfortably aware of the audience of three standing in the manner of dock guards at his back, Blanding stiffened. 'Before you begin, Squadron Leader,' he answered coldly, 'I wish to complain about your quite unwarranted intrusion into my home last night.'

Unabashed, Walker merely nodded and scribbled a few words on a writing pad. 'Your complaint is formally noted,' he said looking up, 'but you appreciate that we're investigating a very serious incident?'

'Of course.'

'Then I hope you'll similarly understand when I now ask you to pass your car keys over to Sergeant Evans.'

'My car keys?'

'If you'd be so kind.'

Disconcerted, Blanding stared back at the smiling, moustached figure. Unable, however, to think of any objection to the seemingly incomprehensible request, he drew the required objects from his pocket and, swivelling round, handed them to the clearly embarrassed NCO.

'Right, off you go then, Sergeant, and take the other two with you.'

Walker waited until the door closed behind the three before turning back to Blanding. 'Well, Flight Lieutenant,' he resumed, tapping his fingertips together as if closing the stops on some invisible musical instrument, 'now you've had twenty-four hours to consider, may I ask if you've managed to come up with any explanation of how the late Corporal Summerfield came to have an ex-school library book from the very same institution you formerly taught at?'

Blanding shook his head. He'd already decided that he didn't like Walker, and he was damned, he thought, if he was going to start revealing to some self-satisfied, conceited little popinjay the extent of his unease, not only about the book itself, but all the other disquieting links between himself and the dead girl. 'As I told the chief inspector yesterday, sir,' he answered coldly, 'I've not the slightest idea how such an item could ever have come into her keeping.'

Walker jotted a further note. 'Next,' he continued, 'there's the matter of the brass rubbings. You and the deceased both pursued that same pastime it seems. Another curious coincidence, wouldn't you say?'

Blanding gave a slight shrug, but made no reply.

'Then perhaps,' resumed the questioner with an increasingly infuriating smile, 'you can do a little better at explaining why you chose to go off-station during operations on Sunday night – and then didn't see fit to inform Chief Inspector Stanley here of this curious nocturnal departure whilst discussing the sealing of the aerodrome with him next day.'

Startled by the utterly unlooked-for questions, Blanding coloured and glanced across at the person in question, but the elderly policeman remained head-bowed, his eyes closed.

'As you doubtless appreciate,' went on Walker, 'we know exactly how long you were off camp that night. According to the guardroom log, you left just after midnight and didn't return for another ninety-five minutes. May we be told what you were doing all that time, and what, if anything, did you take out of the station with you?'

The implications were plain, and, with a sickening jolt, Blanding now suddenly understood the reason why his car keys had been required. The suspicion was clearly that, some time after striking Corporal Summerfield down and then having failed to revive her, he'd smuggled her body through the main gate (presumably under a blanket on the rear seat as the Morris 8 didn't possess the luxury of a boot or any sort of rear storage locker). He had then, it was presumed, transported it by road round to the field beside the aerodrome, finally carrying the corpse in his arms along the edge of the ploughland to deposit it outside the airfield fence. Obviously, even as he and Walker were now speaking, the car was being painstakingly searched for bloodstains or any other grisly evidence of its hearse-like role. 'Well, Flight Lieutenant?' came the interrogator's voice, breaking into his thoughts. 'May we be told the reason for this midnight outing of yours?'

'As I informed the station commander at the time,' answered Blanding curtly, 'I had a severe nosebleed and needed to slip off home to change as I had no clean clothes with me on camp.'

Walker gave a thin smile. 'Ah, yes, of course – and that, one supposes, was how a bloodstained shirt was found soaking in the kitchen sink by your obliging next-door neighbour.' Pausing, he leaned back in his chair and regarded Blanding narrowly across the outspread span of his fingers. 'I trust you don't think this offensive, Flight Lieutenant,' he added after what seemed an intolerable silence, 'but a jury might think a nosebleed a very convenient way for explaining away bloodstained clothes.'

Blanding felt his anger growing. Determined nevertheless to hide his feelings, he said nothing, clinging fast to the idea that if either Walker or Stanley had anything more than mere suspicion against him there would have been a reception party awaiting his arrival home the previous evening – and that, at the very least, he would have found himself spending the remainder of the night in the company of an officer escort.

'But now,' recommenced the questioner, 'there's another little matter I'd like to discuss. I believe you use the small storeroom behind your office as temporary sleeping quarters when duties keep you late – and at such times, I imagine this building is completely deserted apart for yourself?'

Unable to the guess the new direction of the questioning, but glad at least of a chance to contradict something at last, Blanding shook his head. 'Not quite,' he answered coldly, 'there's always a cipher clerk on duty in the signals room.'

'Ah, of course!' exclaimed Walker, folding his arms with a self-

212

satisfied smile. 'As you say, there's always a cipher clerk on duty at night – and she, of course, would be one of the Waafs drawn from among members of the wireless section.'

Blanding flushed at the implication. 'If you're suggesting I met Corporal Summerfield at such times,' he retorted angrily, 'I utterly deny it. As I told the chief inspector here, I don't remember ever having met the girl.'

'So I gather,' answered Walker evenly. 'It also appears you weren't even able to recognize her name when first coming across her body, although I notice that you yourself had personally amended her file when she withdrew her commission application.'

Thinking that this doubtlessly successful ex-barrister or whatever the infuriating little man in front of him had been before the war had not missed a trick, Blanding again made no reply. 'So anyway,' continued Walker, raising his voice as rain suddenly began lashing heavily against the window behind his head, 'to return to this matter of accommodation, you rent a remote country cottage, where as the good Mrs Luton hints, it would seem that you regularly entertain whole bevies of young ladies...'

'That's absolute damned nonsense!' interrupted Blanding, his temper now finally spilling over. 'God damn it, the woman only said what she did because you and Sergeant Evans had the cheek to pass yourselves off as friends of mine, and she didn't want you thinking I live as I do – that is, as a rather quiet, bookish, bachelor recluse.'

Seemingly impervious to embarrassment, Walker merely shrugged. 'Be that as it may,' he answered with a smile, 'the fact remains that you have a hideaway cottage where you have opportunity to conduct all kinds of liaisons, while here again on the camp you possess yet another convenient little pied-à-terre – one that not only gives you a complete run of this block throughout the night hours and would allow you secretly to meet whatever Waaf wireless clerk is on duty in the signals room, but which also must, I imagine, necessitate your use of the '*Officers Only*' lavatory situated down the corridor just a few doors away.'

Bewildered by the final reference, Blanding stared incredulously at the speaker. 'I don't understand, Squadron Leader,' he said reddening, 'what on earth has the lavatory got to do with anything?'

'Only this,' answered Walker with the same apparent amiable smile, 'that when the service police searched this building after your departure yesterday afternoon, they checked on what you, as an ex-schoolmaster, must surely know is one of the commonest places for amateur concealment: I refer, of course, to the overhead cistern of the lavatory in question. Although nothing was actually still on top, from the disturbed dust on the lid it was clear that it had recently been used to hide certain female garments.'

'Female garments!' Mind reeling, Blanding gazed at his interrogator in dazed disbelief. 'Good God!' he struggled out. 'You're surely not suggesting that Summerfield's missing clothing was actually hidden here within the administration block? That's impossible surely? For heaven's sake, why should you think such an extraordinary thing?'

'Simply because of this,' answered Walker imperturbably, reaching into his desk drawer, 'which was found to have slipped down and wedged itself between the back of the cistern and the wall.' As he spoke, he drew out and then held up and stretched out before him what was clearly a grey lisle stocking of the type normally issued to Waafs for everyday wear.

Staggered by the implications, Blanding watched in stunned silence as Walker bent to return the stocking to the drawer. As he did so, from behind came a tap on the door, and a moment later Sergeant Evans re-entered the room. Going over to the desk, the now distinctly wet-looking Welshman stooped to whisper something in Walker's ear, at the same time handing his superior a small brown envelope along with the keys of the Morris.

'Thank you, Sergeant,' said the recipient. 'If you'd care to wait outside, I'll call you back in if you're required.' As the door closed behind the NCO, Walker opened the envelope and carefully extracted the tiny object it contained. Holding his hand up towards the window, he squinted at whatever it was he held horizontally between forefinger and thumb. 'Ah, yes!' he murmured with evident satisfaction. 'Another little feminine item of interest: a woman's hairgrip with an actual strand of hair attached.' He turned triumphantly to Blanding. 'Apparently it was found lying on the floor next to the front passenger seat of your car – a rather unusual discovery wouldn't you say in a vehicle belonging to this harmless, bookish, bachelor recluse you purport to be?'

'I wonder, Squadron Leader,' interrupted a voice, 'if you'll excuse the interruption, if I too might be allowed to see this new piece of evidence.'

So unexpected was the intrusion – in fact Stanley's presence had almost been forgotten – that both Walker and Blanding looked round in shocked surprise to find the detective had at last raised his head and was regarding the RAF investigator with baleful pale-blue eyes.

'Yes, of course,' blurted out Walker, colouring. 'I'm most terribly sorry, Chief Inspector. Here you are.'

Taking the hairgrip, Stanley switched on the desk lamp and then, having put on his reading glasses, bent and began examining the object closely beneath its glare. 'The deceased's hair was blond, Squadron Leader,' he said at last, removing his spectacles and sitting back, 'while this strand of hair has a definite reddish tint.' With the merest hint of a smile, he glanced round at Blanding. 'At a guess, I'd say this grip belongs to the flight lieutenant's assistant who, I believe, accompanied him over to the RAF hospital at Ely yesterday afternoon as part of their joint duties – a young lady whom, I'm pleased to report, looked positively blooming with health when I passed her out in the corridor earlier.'

Like all enclosed institutions, RAF Frampton Wissey was prey to an unceasing flow of rumour and gossip. Thus, when Blanding entered his own office some fifteen minutes later, it was evident that news of his interrogation and the examination of his car had proceeded him. As he opened the door, Diana glanced up with an look of huge relief – an openness of expression matched only by the equally unmistakable flash of disappointment on Warrant Officer Starling's face as he looked round from counting out a number of coins onto one corner of the assistant adjutant's desk.

Pleasing as Blanding found the former's response, that of the latter irritated him enormously, especially as it seemed at first glance as if he'd actually caught the man in the very act of laying a wager on his likely arrest. Although the money turned out to be merely the cash received from station funds for the damage done during the recent fracas at the Red Lion, Blanding remained aggrieved, and quickly despatched the intruder with a demand to see what he well knew to be a couple of long-lost files. Only after Starling's dismissal was he able to confide to Diana the upshot of his interview with Walker and then to inform her of his early-morning discovery of the obscure and rather perplexing source of Summerfield's brass rubbing. It was, however, the revelation of the possible site of the Waaf's missing clothing that raised the greatest speculation between the two of them. If the overhead cistern of a lavatory just a few yards away from where they were seated had indeed been the place of concealment of the garments in question, then that seemed definite proof that the murderous assault on the girl had taken place within the camp itself, and that her assailant and presumably erstwhile lover was, just as Group Captain Chesterton had gloomily predicted, one of his own personnel.

'But why in that case doesn't anyone know his name?' protested Diana. 'To keep an affair hidden for any length of time within an RAF camp is virtually impossible, I'd say. Then again, even if we accept the idea of an amazingly discreetly-managed affair leading to some sort of *crime passionnel*, that still leaves the question of how her attacker was able to find anyone willing to help him smuggle Summerfield's body through the airfield fence late on Sunday night. No,' she added, shaking her head, 'I still don't believe that she was going out with anyone here on the station, and that stocking they found was nothing to do with her.'

'But if it wasn't hers,' replied Blanding, 'then whose was it for goodness' sake, and what on earth was such an item doing in a male officers' lavatory?'

His companion shrugged. 'God knows!' she answered. 'Some silly sort of sexual trophy perhaps. Anyway, however it came to be there, for me the lid of an overhead lavatory cistern seems somehow too childishly obvious a place for a killer to choose – it's what's used in school adventure stories for hiding things, not by real-life murderers trying to conceal the evidence of their crimes. And then again, even if Summerfield's greatcoat, skirt and the rest of her missing clothing were indeed originally concealed up on that cistern as suggested, to where have they since been moved?'

Diana's question was still hanging in the air when there was a knock on the door and Warrant Officer Dawson entered, bringing his usual clutch of guard-duty, fire-picket and punishment rosters for official approval. This morning there was, however, something new in the NCO's face – a wary, restrained knowingness, an unspoken, awkward embarrassment – that told Blanding that Dawson was fully acquainted with the previous night's search of his cottage and his subsequent grilling at Walker's hands. With renewed irritation, he took the proffered lists and began scanning their contents. Catching sight of Leading Aircraftman Phillips's name on the punishment list, he automatically glanced across to see what extra duties had been allocated to the obstinately tight-lipped defaulter of the previous day.

'*Serving behind the bar and generally assisting the chief steward in the sergeant's mess, including the removal of empty bottles as well as some light cleaning duties.*'

'Light cleaning duties?' exclaimed Blanding in shocked disbelief, raising his head to look up incredulously. 'Can this really be correct, Mr Dawson?' he demanded. 'The removal of a few bottles and some light cleaning duties for Aircraftman Phillips – a man who, I remind you, was confined to camp for knocking seven sorts of bells out of some harmless civilian?'

The only too familiar look of obstinate blankness rose on the warrant officer's face, and he made no reply.

Blanding frowned.

'Well, Mr Dawson, I must say I find this uncharacteristic leniency of yours very curious,' he continued after a few moments silence, 'as curious indeed as I originally found Phillips's explanation of the attack itself.' Breaking off, the speaker regarded the man before him narrowly, acutely remembering as he did so the same look of studied blankness on the station warrant officer's face when standing rigidly at attention beside the lanky defaulter during the CO's questioning the day before. 'You wouldn't, I suppose, Mr Dawson,' he resumed, leaning back and placing his fingertips together, 'have any idea yourself what actually lay behind the affair?'

'No, sir – none at all.'

Ever since being first commissioned, Blanding had been conscious of much the same sort of exclusion he'd felt as a school housemaster – that conspiracy of silence, in which pieces of information were deliberately kept back from him by his own subordinates. Irritating as the practice was, he normally shrugged it off, telling himself that, just as with schoolboy prefects, it was necessary to trust to the discretion and good sense of senior NCO's. This morning, however, his feathers were still ruffled by Walker's questioning, and he determined not to allow Dawson to put anything over on him at all. 'Really? No idea at all, you say?' In unconscious emulation of his own recent tormentor, he leaned a little further back in his chair and steadily regarded the studiously blank face of the figure before him over the span of his spread fingers.

'Come now, Mr Dawson,' he went on with a cold smile, 'what was it that caused Phillips to quarrel with this man Price down at the

Red Lion? From your recommended punishment, whatever it was, it's clearly something you feel a certain sympathy with.' He paused, but receiving no reply, continued, his voice neutrally flat. 'Of course, as you doubtless realize, Mr Dawson, it would be no trouble for me to amend your suggested punishment roster so that friend Phillips finds himself spending every off-duty moment for the next fourteen days in the main cookhouse, peeling his way through a veritable Himalayan range of potatoes.'

Clearly caught, Dawson glanced uneasily round as if to check the closed door behind him before looking back to Blanding. 'Don't do that, sir,' he pleaded. 'Phillips is not a bad lad, and has never been in any serious trouble before. Anyway, truth to tell, sir, the fellow he had the bust-up with was just one of them ruddy conchie bastards, strutting like regular barnyard cock around the place with some silly little tart of a land-girl on his arm.'

'Conchie?' Puzzled, Blanding shook his head. 'I don't understand, Mr Dawson – what does this term conchie mean?'

A look of astonishment rose in the warrant officer's face. 'Conchies, sir? You must know – conscientious bloody objectors! There are whole gangs of the yellow-spined buggers labouring on some of the farms around here – that's if you'll excuse the language, ma'am,' he added hurriedly, turning and glancing apologetically down at Diana.

'Conscientious objectors?' In his mind's eye, Blanding suddenly saw again that long line of incongruously dressed and obviously amateurish labourers silhouetted against the declining sun as they stretched away across the wide field. He gave a wry smile. 'Well, Mr Dawson,' he said, 'thank you so much for informing me – and in the light of what you say, I think we can safely leave your proposed punishment roster the way it is.'

As the door closed behind a clearly relieved Dawson, Blanding turned triumphantly to his assistant. 'Well,' he said grinning, 'if nothing else, at least a couple of minor mysteries seem to have been cleared up. Philips, I imagine, was reluctant to admit to blatant prejudice before the CO, and was therefore unwilling to say anything about being provoked by Price simply because the man was one of these so-called conchies. Also that curious gang of men we saw on our way over to Ely yesterday must themselves have been conscientious objectors, presumably all employed by the War Agricultural Committee or whatever the name is.'

Instead of responding directly, Diana turned towards the window. 'Maybe more than just those couple of mysteries have been cleared up,' she murmured thoughtfully, gazing out at the wet roadway. She paused for a moment before turning back to meet Blanding's eyes. 'As you just saw from Mr Dawson's attitude, being a conscientious objector doesn't exactly make you popular in wartime, especially among members of the fighting services. If therefore a Waaf started a relationship with one, she'd be strongly advised I'd have thought to mention nothing about him to any of her service friends or colleagues.'

Blanding blinked at her, not immediately taking in the implication of what she'd said. 'Surely you're not suggesting,' he said slowly with a look of growing incredulity, 'that Summerfield's lover might have been another of these conchies himself?'

'Why not?' came the answer. 'It certainly fits – most conscientious objectors are educated men, I imagine, who not only might well be attractive to a bright, intelligent girl like June Summerfield, but also could well be interested in rather esoteric hobbies like brass rubbing. And if he actually was a conscientious objector, that would certainly explain why she was so very careful to conceal his identity from her service friends.' Diana paused and, colouring slightly, looked away. 'And there's also another reason why Summerfield's lover could have been a conchie: it would have meant that he represented someone safe – that is, not someone who was going to fly off one night to get himself killed on account of her.'

'My God,' murmured Blanding, rubbing his chin, 'but I think you might just be right! And if nothing else, your theory certainly deserves investigating.'

Still dazed by the novel idea, he groped for the telephone and, picking it up, went to dial. His glance happening to fall again on the pile of coins on Diana's desk, he paused however and sat a moment, staring fixedly across at the money, the receiver still clamped to his ear.

'On second thoughts,' he said thoughtfully, replacing the unused instrument on its rest, 'I think we might leave both Squadron Leader Walker and Chief Inspector Stanley out of the picture for the present. Instead,' he continued, glancing at his watch as he rose to his feet, 'I think you and I ought now to do our adjutantly duty by taking that money there straight round to the landlord of the Red Lion. There's still an hour or more before opening time,' he added, smiling down at the puzzled face looking up at him, 'plenty of time I'd have thought for a grateful proprietor to inform us as to what he knows about the unfortunate Mr Price and any others of his ilk locally employed by the War Agricultural Committee.'

CHAPTER SEVENTEEN

'Look, Alan! That's the same van we passed yesterday! This has got to be the right place!'

As the Morris turned off the bridge, Diana pointed ahead towards the small, canvas-roofed vehicle with the now familiar initials boldly stencilled in red across the cab door. It stood parked outside a typically East Anglian wood-framed thatched cottage, painted in ochre and set well back from the road on a slight eminence overlooking the river, the smoke from its tall red brick chimney curling about the roof and drifting out on the damp air to hang like a translucent veil above the sluggish brown waters of the Wissey.

Inhibited by his questioners' uniforms and clearly fearing that an 'Out of Bounds to all Camp Personnel' notice was about to be peremptorily slapped on his premises, the landlord of the Red Lion had been considerably less than forthcoming at first on the subject of locally-employed conscientious objectors. According to him, they generally kept to themselves and avoided using public houses in the immediate area, especially those patronized by members of the armed forces. 'They mainly operate in teams,' he eventually divulged after being repeatedly pressed, 'though I believe a few odd blokes are attached to individual farms. If you want to know any more, I suggest you speak to old Bert Winstanley – he's what they call the committee ganger for these parts and supervises all war ag work in the area. After his wife died a couple of years back, he moved into a cottage just a few miles downstream from the village. If you both was to drive straight over there now, I'd bet a pound to a penny you'd catch him home for his midday bite.'

The sight of the parked van seemed to confirm the publican's opinion, and drawing the Morris to a stop behind it, Blanding switched off the engine. Though the rain had temporarily ceased, everything was still soggy and moist, and the muddy path squelched underfoot as Diana and he began making their way up to the cottage between well-tended vegetable beds. Reaching the front door, they knocked and waited in the dank, dripping silence while from within came the muffled tones of a radio announcer reading the news. Eventually they heard the sounds of footsteps and the door opened to reveal the same lean, wiry, melancholy-faced man with drooping grey moustaches they'd seen speaking to the official beside the road the previous day. Standing before them now in thick country tweeds, with high starched collar and tie and a large-linked watch-chain looped across the front of his waistcoat, and wearing well-polished leather gaiters and boots, he appeared even more than ever the epitome of a traditional country land-agent and overseer.

'Mr Winstanley?'

'Yes, I'm Bert Winstanley – how can I help?' There was a look of cautious suspicion in the hazel eyes that looked from one to the other of the two uniformed figures on his doorstep. Only after they had apologized for this lunchtime intrusion and explained that they had come on semi-official business concerning the contracted labourers he supervised on behalf of the War Agricultural Committee were they invited inside. 'I'll try to answer your questions,' said their host, ushering them into a gloomy if spotlessly clean front parlour, resplendent with a piano bearing silver-framed family photographs and a potted fern, 'though I can't imagine what you want to know. Them townies I get sent me are a cack-handed crowd for the most part, though generally pleasant and willing enough – that's, of course,' he added gravely as his visitors seated themselves on a horsehair sofa, 'if you can only stop 'em blathering on about politics and religion! I can tell you, there's all sorts among 'em,' he continued, drawing up a narrow, high-backed chair to face them, 'Quakers, Christadelphians, Plymouth Brethren and Elimites as well as those who call themselves the Particular People.'

Unexpectedly, he gave a rusty laugh. 'I've one of them last lot working along with my present gang – a fellow who used to be a lawyer's clerk before the war, and don't he just rattle on like Jeremiah from morn till night about Armageddon and what the poor little brute cares to term as these latter days!'

Blanding nodded sympathetically, thinking back to the long line of figures in the field the day before, and seeing again in his mind's eye that curious individual with his glasses flashing in the light and the knotted white handkerchief on his head, standing silhouetted against the lowering sun, waving an arm like some ranting soap-box orator above the stooped backs of those hoeing on either side.

'What we're interested in, Mr Winstanley,' intruded Diana, 'is whether you know of any among your charges who might possibly have formed a relationship with one of our Waafs from RAF Frampton Wissey.'

At her words, their host frowned, and his face took on again that same look of wary distrust with which he'd first regarded his visitors. 'Look, miss,' he answered sternly, 'you'll pardon me for saying, but if this is to do with a paternity suit or the like, I won't be able to help you, I'm afraid. Most of them conchie lads can't use a bagging hook properly to save their lives, and it would break your heart to see 'em try to swing a scythe, but in my sight, they've as much right to their opinions as the next man, however crack-brained and daft they be. Isn't that what we're meant to be fighting this war for, and why I myself was out there in Egypt and Mesopotamia with the Norfolks during the last lot? Anyway, I'm the Committee ganger, not its blooming nursemaid – nay, nor its beadle either! Whatever them boys get up to after doing their Government time is their own matter entirely in my view, and none of mine.'

Measured and politely as the words were spoken, there was, nevertheless, a world of obstinate independence in the speaker's voice. Sitting facing this suddenly grim-faced, elderly widower, Blanding was again reminded that it was from under these same wide East Anglian skies that Cromwell had recruited what he called his plain, russet-coated captains and all those implacable men of conscience who, marching under the banners of the Eastern Association, had broken the might of arbitrary royal authority at Naseby and Marston Moor.

Flushing slightly, Diana shook her head. 'I'm sorry, Mr Winstanley, you misunderstand – I promise you, the RAF has nothing whatever against Waafs forming relations with whom they like off-duty. It's just that you might have heard that one of our girls was found dead outside the airfield fence on Monday morning.'

'Aye,' murmured the countryman, lowering his gaze and nodding gravely, 'I did hear something about that.'

'Well,' continued Diana, 'there's reason to believe that she was struck down with a blow from a blunt instrument with traces of earth upon it, possibly an agricultural tool, whilst taking a shortcut route across the fields after dark the evening before to visit a boyfriend –

223

someone who obviously has to live relatively close to the camp, and who, it's thought, might well be employed by your committee.'

Without immediately replying, Winstanley rose from his chair and went to the window. 'This young man she's meant to have been going to see hasn't yet come forward then, I take it?' he murmured reflectively, after staring broodingly out towards the river for a short while in silence. 'And if he hasn't done so by this time, then it similarly follows he must be strongly suspected of having done the killing himself.'

'That's correct,' intervened Blanding, deciding that it was best to be open with this obviously intelligent man. 'It's for that reason we came over to see you, Mr Winstanley. If only to eliminate any such person from suspicion, we need to know if there are any government conscripted labourers, either billeted in lodgings or employed anywhere within walking distance of the aerodrome.'

There was silence for a few moments, and then the figure at the window gave an audible sigh. 'Well,' he said heavily, returning to his chair, 'I suppose it would be neither right or sensible of me to hide the facts in the circumstances – anyway, reckon you're going to find them out for yourselves soon enough.' The speaker paused while he reseated himself. 'I can tell you now,' he continued, 'that there's only one person in the area of your camp employed by the committee – a willing, handy, likeable sort of lad that I put on extended placement down at Hollow Bottom Farm after old man Edwards had a heart attack a while back. The farm can't be much more than a mile from the aerodrome as the crow flies, and young Frank's been there – let me see now – since Lady Day last, so that would make it exactly twelve months from this Friday just passed.'

'A year!' exclaimed Blanding, glancing round to exchange a significant glance with Diana. 'And this place, Hollow Bottom Farm,' he asked eagerly, turning back to the sombre-faced figure in the chair, 'can you indicate exactly where it is situated, Mr Winstanley, and how my assistant and I might most easily find our way to it?'

Armed with a carefully drawn sketch map provided by their host, he and Diana left the cottage ten minutes later. Hurrying back to the car, they restarted the engine and began making a rapid three-point-turn in the narrow road, observed by Winstanley who, grim-faced and unsmiling, stood watching them leave beside his front door. Obviously struck by some sudden idea, however, he suddenly came hurrying down the path, shouting out and waving urgently just as the

224

Morris began driving off.

'What was that he was calling out?' asked Diana as Blanding settled back in his seat after waving back at the figure beside the garden gate.

'God knows!' exclaimed the other, accelerating towards the bridge. 'I couldn't quite hear. Some nonsense or other about not going down to the farm dressed the way we are!' He laughed. 'For goodness sake! The fellow sounded exactly like my mother when I wanted to go out and play as a child! Does he seriously think that now, when perhaps we are close to the truth at last, we're going to bother to go back to the camp to hunt out gumboots and old clothes before confronting whatever muddy horrors await us at Hollow Bottom Farm?'

'I wonder, Alan, if this is really such a good idea after all?' murmured Diana as the Morris splashed its way along a puddled lane. 'Wouldn't it be simpler and perhaps a lot more sensible altogether if we went back to the station and reported what we've discovered to the proper authorities?'

Whatever the reason – the grey blanket of sky above, the almost continuous hiss of water beneath their wheels as they traversed the bottom of the shallow fold of ground lying just north of the airfield, or simply the physical effects of having hardly eaten a thing all day – Blanding's initial enthusiasm had waned considerably during the short drive, and his passenger's words only mirrored the doubts increasingly crowding upon him. Nevertheless, he shook his head. 'By the proper authorities,' he replied tartly, 'I take it you're referring to our good friend, Squadron Leader Walker? If so, no thank you very much – not after having him and Sergeant Evans poking around my home last night without so much as a by-your-leave, and then his having the additional cheek to submit me to the third-degree this morning! Anyway,' he went on, 'what have we actually discovered? Nothing really – all this stuff about Summerfield being involved with a conscientious objector is mere conjecture on our part; there's no actual evidence behind it at all. Chances are, this young fellow Frank or whatever his name is, never met Summerfield in his life. If so, we'd both end up looking complete fools in front of both Walker and Stanley if we were to drag them over to the farm on some wild damned goose chase.'

'Well, if you're absolutely sure,' answered Diana doubtfully.

'Anyway, if we're really going to the farm, then we should branch off here at this fork to the left. After that according to the sketch map, it then should lie directly before us.'

Sure enough, they turned off the road to find a gateway blocking the far end of an even narrower, muddier and more puddled lane. Beyond it, a ramshackle collection of barns and outbuildings stood huddled round a sloping yard together with a rather dull, grey, modern-looking bungalow-type farmhouse – while at the low crest of the fields above and seeming surprisingly close at hand, rose the oddly homely and reassuring silhouette of the station water tower and the huge curved roofs of B Flight's hangars.

'Slide over onto this seat and drive on though when I've opened the gate,' said Blanding, drawing the Morris up before the pool of muddy yellow water that had accumulated around the gateway. 'There's no sense in both of us ruining our shoes in this god-damned Slough of Despond!'

Thinking that there might, after all, have been a certain wisdom in Winstanley's advice not to visit Hollow Bottom Farm dressed as they were, Blanding clambered from the car. Hitching up his trousers, he began cautiously wading forward to the accompaniment of a ferocious outburst of barking from a large hairy grey dog chained up outside the nearest outhouse – presumably, he thought, the same noisy animal whose distant barks in response to the striking of the church clock he'd heard when out on the aerodrome in the early morning. Reaching the gate, he lugged the sagging framework open, closely observed by a few bedraggled chickens and a couple of unpleasantly hissing geese, the latter having come rushing down the slope, wings spread, honking loudly, to meet him. Having waved the Morris on through, he dragged the gate back into position, and was engaged in re-securing the unwieldy structure with a length of sodden twine when, above the barking and hissing at his back, he heard a male voice raised in anger.

Turning in surprise, he saw that Diana, having driven up to the front of the farm house, had climbed out of the car, and now stood confronting a thickset, unshaven man in his middle or late sixties. Wearing mud-caked overalls and a grubby woollen hat, this individual stood bucket in hand behind the low wall of the farmhouse terrace, shouting furiously down the slope at her. 'Whatever you want,' he bellowed, 'you can just bugger off and take that blooming heap of rusty junk with you!'

Blanding stared at the scene dumbfounded. Even during basic training, he'd always found the blue-grey air force uniform treated with respect – at least, by the civilian population. Indeed, after the summer of 1940, when the people of south-east England had witnessed the whirling contrails of the fighter battles overhead, and they and the entire nation had hung on the daily-announced tally of victories and losses as if to the score of some vast celestial cricket match, the RAF had been almost universally regarded with something approaching adulation. Therefore now to see a Waaf officer addressed as if she were some trespassing tramp or gypsy-woman was as shocking as it was unexpected. Recovering from his initial astonishment, and with his indignation rising, Blanding turned from the gate and hurried up the yard towards the gesticulating figure, eager to interpose between him and the object of his wrath. 'Mr Edwards, isn't it?' he called out as he approached. 'I'm the adjutant up at the camp, and this lady you're addressing is my assistant, Section Officer Taylor. We've come here merely because we want to …'

'I don't care what the hell you want,' bellowed the irate farmer, turning towards him. 'There's not another thing you blood-sucking bastards are getting out of me!'

Astonished, Blanding paused beside Diana and stared up at apparently deranged man behind the wall. As he did so, a slight, thin, grey-haired woman in a bedraggled apron emerged from the house to join the burly figure on the terrace. 'John, calm down,' she pleaded, putting out a hand to touch the man's arm. 'Remember what the doctor said about not getting all upset again and getting another attack! Why not just let the gentleman say what he wants?'

'Gentleman!' exploded the farmer, raising and rattling his metal bucket towards Blanding as it were some sort of tribal fetish designed for the warding off of evil spirits. 'I tell you, I'd hang every last one of these blue-bellied bastards if I could! His lot are worse than a whole ruddy cartload of Mussolinis and Hitlers, what with their hell-cursed compulsory purchase orders and so-called Defence of the Realm Acts! After they've taken my best-drained wheat acres for that blooming aerodrome of theirs, and just left me with the lower slopes, do you think I'm going to let them have another square damned foot of soil! They'll have to stamp me beneath their bloody jackboots before I'll let 'em take another inch of what little that bunch of thieving damned fascists have left me!'

227

Understanding now the man's apparent irrational anger at the sight of air force uniforms – and at the same time, belatedly, the reason for Winstanley's shouted warning as they were driving away – Blanding took a step forward. 'Look,' he said, trying to sound as reasonable as he could, 'the RAF doesn't need any more of your land, Mr Edwards, I assure you – we have plenty enough for our purposes. We merely wish to have a few words with the worker consigned you by the War Agricultural Committee.'

'With young Frank, you mean?'

Up until now the figure behind the low wall had been as belligerent and bristling with fury as his dog who, throughout the whole exchange, had remained continuously barking, leaping and tugging frantically at its chain. Now, however, the man's expression seemed suddenly to change to something like fear, and, as he blurted out his question, he darted an apprehensive glance towards the large barn at the top end of the yard.

'So our young friend is up there, is he?' said Blanding, following the farmer's glance. 'Right, I think in that case we'll go and make ourselves known to him – you keep well behind me,' he added, dropping his voice as he turned to Diana, 'as whoever is up in that barn, could well have a pitchfork or even a loaded shotgun at hand.'

'You come back here, you thieving pair of bloody scroungers! Come back or I'll turn the dog loose!'

With the old man's threats from behind mixing with the mollifying urgings of his wife, Blanding began striding up the yard, Diana close at his elbow, the elderly couple following more slowly in their wake. As he approached, Blanding saw that one of the barn's huge pair of double doors stood open, revealing an ancient-looking motorcycle propped against a wall and also the battered front end of an orange-coloured Fordson tractor. From behind one of the latter's jacked-up front wheels, a pair of legs clad in mechanic's overalls protruded, while within arm's reach of whoever was working beneath the machine lay an array of variously-sized tools neatly placed in order of size on a square of sacking. Catching the first faint oily whiffs from the shadowy interior, Blanding found himself suddenly remembering the greasy, dark marks on the dead Waaf's torn-open blouse and chest, and also the smell of paraffin when he'd sniffed her uniform jacket. Suddenly certain that his quarry was finally lying there just a few feet in front of him, clenching his fists, heart beating faster, he increased his stride.

228

As the noisy procession neared the building, the brown-clad legs under the tractor began to flex and move as whoever was lying beneath began wriggling back from under it. Next moment, a young man in his early twenties with tousled fair hair and heavily oil-smeared face sat up and stared at the approaching figures. With a look of stupefied amazement and clutching a massive wrench in one hand, he stumbled unsteadily to his feet to face the foremost and taller of the two uniformed figures who had momentarily paused in the doorway. As he did so, the second figure – a female, he noted – came forward to stand beside the first, while from behind, the farmer and his wife came hurrying up to add to the knot of spectators.

'What's going on?' said the young mechanic in surprisingly educated tones, looking in bewilderment from the one to the other of the two visitors, all the while holding the huge wrench defensively up in front of him with both hands like an iron club. 'With all that barking going on, I thought the feed lorry must have come a day early...' Voice suddenly fading, he broke off, his eyes fixing intently on the lanky male figure in blue standing against the light a few yards in front of him. Taking a step or two forward, he leaned forward and squinted at the lean, bespectacled face beneath the peaked blue service cap. 'Good God!' he burst out, astonishment shaking his voice. 'Is that really you, Mr Blanding? For heaven's sake, sir, whatever are you doing here, and how come you're in RAF uniform?'

Confused by the oddly familiar voice, Blanding stared back at the oil-smeared countenance in the shadows before him – and then suddenly, despite the dark smudges disguising the youngster's face, he recognized with almost physical shock who stood before him. Almost as he did so, in what seemed like one extraordinary moment of dazzling realization, there rushed upon him the answers to so many of the mysteries that had plagued him ever since first coming across June Summerfield's body: how she'd chosen the very same extract from Boethius' *Consolation* that had been pointed out to him years before by his old university tutor; the reason that the sold-off copy of an ex-Dulwich College library book had been found among the dead girl's possessions – also, how the young Waaf corporal could possibly have managed to seek out and find that obscure corner of an isolated country church to make a rubbing of the very same brass memorial plate that he'd planned to transcribe himself. 'Nelson?' he burst out, stepping forward with confused looks of pleasure, bewilderment and anxiety contending in his face. 'Francis Nelson, my dear fellow –

equally, I can ask from where on earth you've sprung from, and what in the name of God you're doing here in such an unlikely place?'

Brightly lit by large overhead skylights, the long, narrow, mainly uncarpeted room had obviously originally once been some sort of hayloft, and as Blanding followed Diana and their guide into what was now an attractive, if rather Spartan combination of living room and artist's studio, he paused before the almost completed painting on the easel immediately facing the door. For a few moments, he stared back at the gravely beautiful and instantly recognisable features of the semi-naked young woman smiling out of the canvas at him with those characteristically wide-spaced eyes. With an effort, he turned from the portrait to glance round the various other items in the room: the squat, pot-bellied heating stove, the same battered, old red-velvet-covered sofa on which the subject of the painting was reclining and the disparate collection of sketches, charcoal drawings, various-sized paintings and other *objets d'art,* including a few odd-shaped pieces of dried wood, decorating the otherwise plain wood-planked walls. Doing so, he spotted without surprise a mounted version of the same brass rubbing that had been lying on Chief Inspector Stanley's desk displayed high up in the far corner of the room. Going straight over to it, he peered closely up at the now only too familiar pair of kneeling figures. 'This knight and his lady,' he said, turning to meet the eyes of his ex-pupil who, now divested of both his overalls and his oily disguise, stood next to the stove, wearing a roll-neck green sweater and a baggy pair of brown corduroy trousers, 'is, of course, taken from that medieval brass plate that we came across on our afternoon cycle ride back to Norwich all those years ago – and you, my dear Francis, I now dimly recall were the boy who actually found the memorial?'

Obviously pleased at his ex-master's recollection, the young man beamed. 'That's right, sir,' he answered, nodding. 'I'll always remember searching the church along with the others, and then finally discovering the brass set into one of the floor-slabs at the back of the organ. By then it was getting late and you said we'd better be riding on, but because it seemed so singular and attractive a design, I determined to go back one day and make a copy of it.'

Blanding nodded and, turning back to the mounted rubbing, again regarded the pair of praying figures above his head. 'And, of course,' he said, as if directing what he was saying to the head-bowed couple on the wall, 'when eventually you did return, you didn't go alone, did you? Someone accompanied you and made a rubbing of her own.'

'That's right,' burst out the other in considerable amazement. 'June, my girl friend from up at the camp, came with me – we both made copies, but how on earth did you know?'

Not answering the question, Blanding continued to stare up at the rubbing. Just as he'd guessed when first struggling in the darkened cathedral to see the link between June Summerfield and himself, the solution was glaringly simple and only too obvious now that he'd solved it. As he should surely have realized, there had to have been some intermediary between himself and the dead girl – someone connecting him to her, and that someone being a sort of Pygmalion-like extension of himself. Since he was a childless ex-schoolmaster, that person could, he now saw, only have been one of his old pupils – some boy he'd been particularly close to and whom he'd so strongly influenced as to make into some sort of personal representative, a person whose taste in literature and so much else, including an interest in the taking of brass rubbing, had been shaped and moulded by himself. Also, of course, it also had to be someone to whom he'd have passed on his college tutor's recommendation to read that particular passage from Boethius, just as he surely must have when the seventeen-year-old Francis Nelson lost both his parents in a car crash – someone who, in his own turn years later, must have almost literally handed the baton on, passing the battered old copy of the *Consolation* he'd doubtless originally bought in a school library sale over to a Waaf corporal – a young woman still grieving over the loss of two aircrew she'd previously been close to.

As if unwilling to remove his eyes from the kneeling shapes above him, Blanding continued to gaze up at the wall for a few moments longer before turning back to meet the young man's puzzled face. 'Francis,' he said gently, 'there wasn't opportunity for you to answer my question back in the barn, but would you mind explaining now how you come to be here?'

'You mean, how did I become a conscientious objector?' Nelson smiled. 'Well, sir, if you remember, after I left Dulwich, I went on to one of the London art schools on a bursary provided by the Freemasons – my father had been a long-time member and they were very generous. But as you can imagine, things at the time were far from easy for me psychologically. I had no brother or sister, and felt

231

very much alone in the world, what with both my parents so recently dead. In the end, I suppose I must have suffered some sort of breakdown. Anyway, whatever the reason, I gave up the art course and wandered off down to Cornwall with the crazily naïve idea of setting up as a painter in St Ives. Luckily for me, whilst in the West Country, I came across a sort of commune composed mostly of ex-soldiers and their wives who had come together at the end of the Great War to live their own way– they ran a fruit and flower farm, as well as a small haulage business on libertarian principles. From them, I learnt about engines and machinery as well, I suppose, as a loathing of everything to do with war and the military life. The upshot was, despite my detestation of Hitler and his Nazis, I registered as a conscientious objector when called up. Eventually, after working on various War Ag Committee labouring gangs around East Anglia, I was sent down here to help Mr Edwards after his heart attack. He and his wife are not bad sorts when you get to know them. In fact, they treated me like second parents, letting me have these rooms to live in and allowing June to come over to stay here with me whenever she could escape her duties – even giving us the use of the motorbike that had belonged to their son-in-law who had helped work the farm before he and their daughter emigrated to Canada after most of the land was requisitioned.'

'I see – and the motorcycle, of course, allowed you to go off on your brass-rubbing trips?'

'Yes.'

Nothing more was said for a few moments, but then Diana, who until then had been sitting on one arm of the sofa, listening to everything being said, suddenly broke the silence. 'Frank,' she said, 'I hope you don't mind me calling you that, but have you any idea why Mr Blanding and I came over to see you today?'

Nelson nodded. 'Yes, I think so,' he answered, turning to her with a look of what suddenly looked like defiance. 'It's about June, I imagine. I always said someone would be bound to come when the RAF found out about us both, even though I don't think we broke any law, military or civil. Anyway, with the baby coming and June having to leave the services, I don't suppose there's anything that either you or anyone else can do about it.'

Blanding saw Diana make as if to reply, but then instead, saying nothing, she turned to look towards him, distress evident in her eyes. Either Nelson was the best actor in the world, he thought, or else he genuinely had no idea what had happened. 'Francis,' he asked gently, stepping towards him, 'tell me – do you have any idea of June's whereabouts at this moment?'

Once again, Blanding saw a look of bewildered astonishment cross his ex-pupil's still-boyish face. 'Yes, of course, I know,' he answered with sudden coldness. 'And you also must know, sir, I imagine – she's on official leave. She's gone to her parents' home in Bedfordshire to break the news of the baby to them and also to write her letter of resignation – the one, I imagine, which brought both of you over here today?'

Something in the faces of both the two figures with him in the room checked the speaker, and his voice tailed away. He turned and glanced quickly round at the head-bowed woman on the arm of the sofa, and then back to the tall gangling uniformed figure standing before him. As he did so, Blanding stepped forward to confront the young man's already stricken eyes. Then, just as back that evening in his dimly-lit study in Dulwich six years before when breaking the news of the death of both his parents to the adolescent boy, it suddenly seemed to Blanding as if he were standing outside himself, observing both him and his victim from somewhere above them both, as again, for the second time in both their lives, he forced himself to speak.

CHAPTER EIGHTEEN

From somewhere out in the dark fields came a brief scream – the cry of some small hunted animal, rabbit or hare, the sound plaintively loud in the dank stillness. Quiet for a few moments, and then the whooping call of a tawny owl rang from the roofless ruin of a barn in the farmyard across the lane, the bird's repeated cry resounding eerily out across the blacked-out hamlet.

So emotionally gruelling, and yet so strangely fascinating, had the discoveries of the day been that, at the close of duties that evening, it had seemed the most natural thing in the world for Blanding to invite Diana back for supper at Jubilee End. With night now fallen, a fire crackling in the hearth, the occasional patter of the recently returned rain on the parlour windows, the mellow glow of the globular-shaded oil lamp on the white-scrubbed tabletop, the cottage was finally that cosy sanctuary from war and all the bleak anonymities of service life he'd always planned. Yet despite that and the fine bottle of pre-war claret unearthed from the larder to accompany Mrs Luton's homely meat-and-onion pie as well as the opening of a long-prized tin of Australian sliced peaches, there was a subdued melancholy about both him and his guest as they sat over the remnants of their meal, each still haunted even now all these hours later by the look of disbelieving horror and shock on the face of the young man as the news was gently broken to him that he had lost, not only his lover, but his future wife and child.

'What beats me,' sighed Blanding, emerging from the reverie, 'is how such an unlikely pair ever came to meet in the first place. As a conscientious objector, young Nelson would hardly have been welcome in any of the local village whist drives or barn dances, I imagine. Same goes for Summerfield in a way – living in the Waafery and on duty for long hours up at the aerodrome, she can't have had much opportunity for mixing much in the civilian world beyond the odd chat in one of the local shops or an occasional boozy evening spent down at the Red Lion with the crew of D-Dog or any other of her service chums.'

'According to what Frank told me when you'd gone off down to the farmhouse to phone the chief inspector,' answered Diana, 'it seems that, after the second of her airman boyfriends was shot down, June got into the habit of going off on her own for long solitary walks when off-duty. On one of these, she apparently happened to come across Frank harrowing one of the fields, and he, noticing her watching from the gateway, stopped off to talk when next coming round on the tractor.' Pausing to sip her wine, the speaker continued. 'And anyway,' she added thoughtfully, 'were they really so unlikely a pair? For all the differences in their backgrounds and occupations, both were intelligent and well-read – and each in a way was mourning his dead.'

'I suppose that's right,' murmured Blanding, nodding. 'As you say, loss was something they shared.' In a silence broken only by the mournful cries of the owl and the quiet hiss of the pressurized lamp at his elbow, he meditatively swilled round what little remained of the liquid in his glass. 'But another thing that seems extraordinary to me,' he began again, looking up to meet Diana's eyes, 'is that not the slightest whisper of Summerfield's death apparently ever reached Hollow Bottom Farm.' He gave a slight shrug. 'Still,' he mused, 'being the sort of people they are and living out there in the back of beyond, I don't suppose old man Edwards and his wife see anyone much from one day to the next.'

'And anyway,' added Diana, 'even if the milk collection driver or any other of the farm visitors had happened to mention that a Waaf had been found dead up at the camp, it wouldn't have rung any alarm bells with them at all. As far as both they and Frank were concerned, June had returned home on leave straight after coming off duty on Saturday afternoon as she had told them she would. As far as all three of them were concerned, the only slightly odd thing was that she hadn't yet been in touch – but there again, according to Frank, they explained that by telling themselves she was probably waiting for the right moment to break the news of her pregnancy to her parents and also to tell them of her wedding plans with a man that she, until then, had never dared mention.'

'Yes,' sighed Blanding heavily, 'and there, you put your finger right on the very heart of the problem, damn it! Not only does the mystery of the girl's death remain, but now, after we've at last solved who her mysterious lover was and also managed to explain those apparently uncanny links with myself, the whole affair seems, if anything, even more impenetrable and incomprehensive than before.' Breaking off, he drank down what remained of his wine and then got to his feet and, going over to the fireplace, took a couple of logs from the hearthside basket and tossed them onto the glowing embers. For a few seconds he stared fixedly down at the flames before turning to again address the slim seated figure at the table. 'Why, for goodness sake,' he burst out, 'instead of going back to Bedfordshire as planned, should Summerfield have stayed on at the Waafery that Saturday evening and then cycled up to the aerodrome next morning to get herself unnecessarily marooned when it was sealed – especially as the station had been abuzz with rumours the past couple of days about a forthcoming operation? You know,' he went on as he returned to slump down in his chair, 'whether we like it or not, I'm afraid you and I just have to accept that young Poppy Summerfield was far from being the guileless innocent she appeared.'

'Why do you say that?'

'Because it's only too obvious, that's why. According to the chief inspector, she rang her father's shop from one of the public call boxes on the camp on the Saturday morning with some cock-and-bull story about extended duties, meaning she wouldn't now be arriving home for a couple more days or so. Instead, without a word to young Nelson, she stayed on at the Waafery that night and then cycled back up to the camp next morning, presumably to see someone else.'

'Someone else?' Diana frowned. 'Another man, you mean?'

'What other explanation can there be?' answered Blanding bitterly. 'She was a damned pretty girl after all, and I bet there would have been plenty among the ground staff at least who wouldn't have minded one jot about her spooky reputation. Anyway,' he continued, 'despite her seemingly virginal image, you must agree she hardly lived like some anchorite nun during her time at Frampton Wissey, did she? We know that she had intense relationships of some sorts with at least two other men before ever clapping eyes on Nelson. Given that and all the opportunities and temptations of an attractive young woman working among a mass of single men, it seems far from inconceivable – highly likely I'd have thought – that she was secretly seeing at least one other man apart from the supposed father to be of her child.'

'Oh, come on, Alan!' burst out Diana indignantly. 'That's absolutely unfair and you know it! Yes, of course, as a sociable young person, it's perfectly natural that June should have developed friendships with members of the opposite sex – given the circumstances, it would have been very odd if she hadn't. Equally, it's only to be expected that, with the heavy losses among the aircrew, any relationship with one of them would have had a special poignancy and intensity of its own. Nevertheless, whatever was between her and those two boys who were killed, whether the most platonic of friendships or passionate of affairs, either way, it doesn't mean she was some silly, flirtatious, little mopsy – and certainly not the devious, two-timing Jezebel of your imagination! Anyway, apart from the fact that she wanted to keep the baby and planned to get married,' she went on, 'we have the evidence of Frank's portrait – after examining that this afternoon, can you really believe the subject was really the sort of girl you suggest?'

'Ah, yes,' answered Blanding, shaking his head, 'but you're forgetting: the artist was very much in love with his subject, and that therefore his view of her could hardly be regarded as objective. Nor for that matter,' he added sorrowfully, 'are you and I entirely impartial either. Both of us, for different reasons, have identified a little too closely with Summerfield perhaps, and that may be preventing us from accepting the most plausible explanation of what happened to her.'

'Which is?' Diana's eyes flashed defiantly.

Again Blanding sighed. 'That she was involved, as I say, in a liaison with somebody beside poor Nelson – what other reason could she have had for allowing him to believe she had gone home when, in fact, she'd stayed on in the immediate area? She was clearly hiding something from him, and what other thing could that have been apart from another man? No,' continued Blanding, 'my opinion of what happened to Summerfield that night remains basically unchanged – that pregnant and faced with having to leave the service, she used that final weekend to meet this person to explain why she was returning home to resign, causing whoever he was to strike out at her in one terrible, instantly-regretted moment of jealous rage – a fury probably made all the more bitter perhaps by his discovering that his rival was nothing more than a despised conscientious objector – presumably, the confrontation taking place in one of the workshops or hangars where there was oil and grease about the place as well as was some

237

sort of tool or implement to strike her down with.'

To his chagrin, Diana laughed. 'And where also, I suppose,' she answered playfully, 'a violent quarrel could take place without some mechanic or anyone else overhearing, and also where the subsequent attack and the half-stripping of the victim's body would have been completely unnoticed to the hundreds of personnel about the camp! And then after that, of course, the attacker would have been able to rely on the sympathetic help of friends – friends crazy enough to risk carrying a half-naked corpse across an airfield during the course of an operation, when apart from the chance of running into any one of the ground crews awaiting the return of their particular aircraft, there was every chance being spotted by those on duty up in the control tower!'

Blanding scowled, but then, catching sight of Diana's teasing smile, he gave a shame-faced grin. 'All right,' he answered, 'but when you can think of a better explanation for Summerfield's unaccountable behaviour those last couple of days of her life, you tell me – I'll be very interested to know. What was this thing she was hiding from the person she was meant to be in love with and why couldn't she tell him about it, and whatever was it that literally frightened her to death some time that Sunday evening? In the meantime, when you're thinking out the answers,' he continued, smilingly rising from his chair, 'I'll go and see what I can root out of the kitchen by way of a few, I'm afraid, rather ancient coffee-beans.'

The owl had long ceased her whoopings, and the only sound that now could be heard was the repeated plop of percolating coffee – the aroma gradually suffusing the entire ground floor of the cottage with the tang of best Jamaican *Blue Mountain*. Despite his protestations, Diana had followed her host out into the kitchen, and there, in the shadowy lamplight, had made herself useful by grinding the beans in the little yellow enamel coffee-grinder attached to one wall (a happy purchase made at a local jumble sale). Now, with the washing-up completed and the dishes put away, Blanding removed the percolator from the top of the stove and bore it into the parlour. 'Well,' he said after pouring out the coffee and passing a cup to his guest, 'we'll have to gulp this down rather quickly, I'm afraid. It's getting rather late, and unless Cinderella returns from the ball before too long, we risk not just coaches turning into pumpkins and coachmen into mice, but another visit from Squadron Leader Walker

238

and his merry men, this time demanding to know why yours truly has abducted one of His Majesty's Waaf officers.'

Diana shook her head. 'I hardly think that's likely,' she replied with an enigmatic smile. 'At least, not this particular evening.'

Blanding looked confused. 'What do you mean?'

Not immediately answering, Diana leaned back in her chair and sipped her coffee. 'Only that,' she said, eventually lowering her cup slightly to view her companion over it, 'before coming away this evening, I took the precaution of signing myself out of the Waafery for the night. Naturally,' she added, 'I had to get the Queen Bee's permission, and I'm not at all certain that she completely believed me when I said that I planned to stay with an elderly maiden aunt in Cambridge who's been feeling unwell of late. But then, of course,' she went on with a mischievous grin, 'as an ex-Girton girl, she's far too much of a lady to accuse a fellow officer of lying to her face.' Diana paused and then burst out laughing. 'Oh, come on, Alan! Don't look so absolutely horrified, for goodness sake! It could shake a girl's confidence! I can, after all, if you absolutely insist, always curl up over there on that sofa. Anyway,' she added with a teasing smile, 'if nothing else, an overnight stay on my part will do much to please your friends next door.'

In Blanding's mind, they nested as snug and closely fitting as a pair of beechnuts in their pod or twins in the womb. Foetus-like, he lay curled about her, face snuggled against the nape of her neck, inhaling the faint fragrance of her hair and listening to the even, soft rhythm of her breathing. He himself clung on the very cusp of sleep, seemingly able to float for moments outside his body at will and hover a few feet above, looking down through pitch-blackness to see both of them entwined in bed. But even then, lying there in euphoric exhaustion and utter content, there was yet some doubting part of him remembering an incident once related to him by Peter Palmer. According to the engineer, a crowd of mainly squadron aircrew and station Waafs had been taking part in one of the usual Friday night drinking sessions down at the Red Lion back in January when the winter bombing campaign was at its height. Losses had been particularly heavy of late due to the enemy's recent introduction of the new – and as yet unjammable – SN-2 airborne radar carried by the nightfighters. As a result, the drinking was even heavier than usual, and wedged among the crush round the bar as closing time approached, one of the younger of the Waafs present was overheard propositioning the much older male officer that she had been chatting with throughout the evening. Feeling protective towards someone who had only recently joined the station, and thinking the girl was either dazzled by the glamour of operational aircrew or simply wished to comfort someone facing every prospect of imminent death, one of the older Waafs present had discreetly taken her aside and pointed out that the man concerned, despite his navigator's brevet, was no longer employed in flying duties due to the mind-numbing panic attacks and bouts of debilitating airsickness he'd suffered from when flying on operations. After less than ten sorties he'd been permanently grounded, but was now merely an assistant intelligence officer, a person whose life was no more threatened than her own. Surprisingly, the girl had answered that, not only had the man concerned already told her of all the details, but it was precisely for that very reason that she felt he needed all the solace it was in her power to give.

Blanding had been strongly struck by the anecdote at the time, and lay now, wondering if a similar sort of pity had drawn Diana to his bed – either that or simply because, just as the young Frank Nelson would have seemed to Summerfield, he was someone safe, an earthbound administrative officer, a mere desk-jockey – someone so far from harm's way that there was not the slightest danger of him becoming the victim of any supposed evil eye.

'What are you thinking about?' As if telepathically linked to his thoughts, Diana's muffled voice suddenly came out of the dark, slightly startling him as he'd been certain until then that she was deeply asleep.

'Nothing at all really,' he lied, 'just conscious, I suppose, of how utterly content and smoothed-out I feel – almost as if all the creases and rumples had been ironed out of my soul.' He pressed his lips to her neck. 'It's amazing, but it really does feel as if this bed was the very centre of the entire universe, and that the war and its horrors existed on some other plane of reality as mere unreal aberrations of what you and I have here.'

Although Diana made no reply, Blanding felt her take his hand, squeeze it and then press it back against her left breast. Again the two of them lay in silence, but then, just as he was beginning to think that the woman beside him had finally fallen asleep, he began to hear the faint drone of a multi-engined aircraft approaching from the direction of the coast – some lone returning bomber or maritime reconnaissance plane, he supposed, heading homeward from some distant sortie. As the sound grew gradually louder, careful not to disturb Diana, he eased himself a little over to peer up between the open curtains above him at the night sky, conscious as so often before of lying there in warmth and silence while the crew within the roaring, vibrating, freezing-cold belly of the unlit machine passed invisibly overhead somewhere in the obscurity above. Again, as if somehow connected to his mind, Diana suddenly spoke out of the darkness at his ear. 'I ran into Tex Crawford in the mess this morning,' she murmured sleepily, 'and June Summerfield came up in conversation. He told me that, although it's always comforting for the aircrews to hear any of the station wireless Waafs welcoming the individual aircraft back at the end of an operation, it was always especially nice to hear her voice – he said, there seemed always something specially warm and reassuring about it.'

The sound of the plane faded into silence. Turning over and snuggling down against Diana's back once more, Blanding reclosed his eyes, thinking of June Summerfield and all the other young female wireless operators crouched over their sets, listening out night after night for the returning bombers' call-signs, and growing familiar with the various pilots' voices – Crawford, Kelly, Kochanowski and the rest calling up over the VHF radios for their landing instructions. And, of course, there had to be also those nights when a feeble, distant 'Darkie' message told of some lost or damaged aircraft struggling back across the North Sea with leaking fuel tanks or failing engines perhaps, and then of those desperate, often futile struggles to get a fix on a weak and often intermittent signal before plane and water finally met. The radio operators were often the last earthly contacts that many an aircrew had, and Blanding found himself visualising what it must have felt to the girls involved, returning to the Waafery in the grey light of early morning after being on duty all night, there to lie sleepless in curtain-drawn rooms, remembering those despairing final calls in their earphones – the ghostly tapping of a mayday message from the very edge of reception, and of the turning up of a wireless set to maximum volume as the fading bleeps vanished for ever into the crackling static.

Just as he was finally slipping into sleep with this image before him, Diana suddenly moved in his arms, struggling free of his embrace to wriggle over to face him in the darkness. 'You know,' she

241

said, all at once sounding amazingly fully conscious and awake, 'lying here like this, I've suddenly had a thought about those missing items.'

'What missing items?'

'Summerfield's, of course — the ones that may now after all have been hidden on top of that lavatory cistern in the administration block as Walker thought — her shoes, clothing and gas-mask satchel that the service police have not yet been able to find.'

'Not forgetting,' murmured Blanding drowsily, his eyes still closed, 'the other of that pair of pink, hand-knitted mittens that so interested you.'

'Forget the mitten for the moment,' came the instant reply. 'Tiny objects like that or her tie and stockings can easily be squirreled away and then later dumped somewhere far away from the camp. Her greatcoat, respirator bag, service cap and skirt are a completely different kettle of fish, however. The first three are bulky objects, occupying a comparatively large amount of space, while even a skirt is not something that can easily be smuggled out through the main gates in something like a coat pocket. Clearly, if it was indeed used, the top of a lavatory cistern was only a very temporary overnight place to hide such large items. To conceal such things for any real length of time, whoever put them there would have needed a much more secure place to move them to later — somewhere where they could remain almost as long as they liked without being discovered.'

'Such as?' Stirring himself, but still drowsily half-asleep, Blanding opened his eyes to see the dim outline of the other's face a few inches in front of his own. 'Surely there's nowhere like that in the camp.'

'Well, maybe there is,' answered Diana. 'Where, for example, would you conceal a tree?'

'Oh, I don't know,' yawned Blanding, his eyes again closing despite himself. 'Hide a tree, you say?' He paused, trying to force himself to think. 'Well, I suppose if I were Father Brown or some other detective character like that in a novel I'd say the answer has to be in a wood or forest.'

'Exactly so — a wood or a forest, and ideally one full of the trees and leaves all of a uniform colour and type.'

Lost, Blanding again opened his eyes and blinked at the dim profile of the head besides his own, but then suddenly he saw what Diana was getting at. 'My God,' he exclaimed, half-rising to one elbow and looking down at the shadowy shape beside him, 'I see what you

242

mean – you're obviously thinking of the main clothing store. If you somehow gain access to those, you could place the items among all the other items of uniform kept there.' He paused. 'But surely,' he went on after a moment's pause, 'it's kept tightly locked and a strict record is bound to be kept of everything that's signed in and out – and if I know anything of military administration, the quartermaster staff must have a record in triplicate of every item in their keeping.'

'Yes, of course, but only on paper – how often is an actual inventory taken? Once a year at the very most, and even then one extra greatcoat, skirt or respirator bag is hardly going to cause a fuss among scores of such items.'

'Good God!' exclaimed Blanding, now sitting fully upright and looking down at Diana's smiling face. 'But I think you may have something there.' He paused slightly. 'But,' he asked, his voice growing grave, 'if those items you mention are really hidden in the stores, you realize what that means?'

Diana nodded. 'Yes,' she answered, 'it points to the killer being in collusion with somebody who has access to stores, as well perhaps as at least one other person to help smuggle the body out through the hole in the fence. In other words, it suggests not just one or two individuals being involved in Summerfield's death, but even a whole little group or gang – and that her murder was part of quite a widespread conspiracy.'

Still half asleep and dazed with tiredness, Blanding was digesting the implications of the speaker's words when he slowly grew aware that he could clearly see the expression on the face gazing up at him from the pillow. A short while ago it had been inky-black in the room, now the walls and furniture were bathed in silvery light. The effect was eerily strange, and as if in some dream or trance, he continued to stare uncomprehendingly around him until he happened to glance up through the window directly above the bed – and there, gleaming through a chasm between monstrous black clouds, was the waxing moon, that same blessed talisman of peace that he'd gazed up at from beneath the Lancaster's wing two nights before. In the forty-eight hours intervening hours, it had thickened from a sickle crescent to an almost complete half disk; nor now was its light mistily veiled as out on the airfield, but instead shone forth in full naked brightness, illuminating the entire room and beaming down as if in ghostly benediction upon the two occupants of the bed.

CHAPTER NINETEEN

One of the window panes began faintly resonating.

The bowed figure at the desk paused in his reading. Raising his head from the Air Ministry directive he was perusing, he turned and frowned at the square of glass that, set slightly loose in its green metal frame, had now begun to vibrate more strongly. For six months and more, the sound of aircraft had been an almost unnoticed constant to the background of his life; now, after only a few days of squadron inactivity, the thunderous roar of aero-engines that was shaking the pane already seemed intrusive and alien. Blanding continued to listen as the noise reached its bellowing crescendo and then began rapidly to diminish as the machine taking off raced away down the runway. As it faded to a low, distant drone he got to his feet and, taking up his cup of mid-morning coffee, went over to the window and stared thoughtfully down the almost deserted roadway towards the main gate.

With a chilly northerly wind blowing and an unyielding blanket of cloud overhead, RAF Frampton Wissey appeared even more inhospitably bleak than the previous day. Gazing out at the dreary greyness, Blanding sipped his coffee, finding it almost impossible to believe that it was only two days since he and Diana had strolled leisurely over to the mess together through warm sunshine. Their conversation during their walk and afterwards over lunch had done much to establish the bond between them, and thinking back to that time now, light-headed from lack of sleep and lulled by the intimacies of the night, he stretched himself luxuriously before the window. As he did so, there came a brief knock at the door behind him, and he turned to confront Peter Palmer's grinning face.

'Ah, our good adjutant – safely back from the great snare of the world!' With his curly white hair and genial, pink features, RAF Frampton Wissey's station engineer seemed more than ever the epitome of health and good fellowship at that moment. 'And where,' he asked, glancing towards the pair of empty desks with a smile, 'has the delectable one disappeared? Word has it that she didn't return to the Waafery last night, and that you and she quite brazenly drove through the main gate together this morning in the fiery red chariot!'

'Diana's just slipped off to speak to Squadron Leader Walker about some little idea she's had,' answered Blanding, blushing despite himself. 'But tell me, Pete,' he hurried on, anxious to move the conversation away from the subject of his assistant, 'that aircraft just now – wasn't that one of our Mosquitoes taking off?'

'Just another of these damned Tampa calls,' answered Palmer with a shrug. 'Apart from the odd meteorological flight, nothing's happening at all – the whole damned place seems as dead as Aberdeen on a Sunday afternoon. But come on now,' he continued, breaking back into a smile, 'don't try to divert me with a lot of shop talk. Since yesterday afternoon, the station has been abuzz with the rumour that, between you both, you and the delectable one somehow managed to track down the fellow that young Poppy Summerfield was involved with, and that he turns out to be someone intimately connected with your own good self.'

A look of pain flashed over Blanding's face. 'Yes,' he said, returning to slump down into his chair, 'As a matter of fact, he was an old pupil of mine from my school-teaching days.'

'But he had nothing to do with Poppy's death, I hear?'

'That's right,' answered Blanding with a nod. 'And as you can imagine, he was absolutely shattered to discover what had happened to his girl. But how exactly she was killed, and by whom and for what reason remains at least as much a mystery as before – though, I regret to say, that the finger of suspicion increasingly seems to point towards some sort of group or gang from here on the camp being involved.'

'Group or gang on the camp, you say?' murmured Palmer, his expression darkening. 'Good God!' he breathed, 'but I only hope you're wrong.' Uncharacteristically sombre, he went over to stand hunched and silent before the window. 'I don't know if it's just the very idea of you've just said or merely this miserable damned weather,' he sighed after a few moments, 'but for some reason I suddenly have the distinct feeling of something unpleasant hanging over us all – and I don't just mean that bloody awful dark clag up there!' Continuing to peer grimly up through the glass at the louring cloud, the speaker drew out his cigarette case. 'And that reminds me,' he went on, extracting one of its contents, 'the padre happened to mention over breakfast that when he went over to visit young Ellis in Ely yesterday, he could hardly get a word out of him, the poor fellow seemed so depressed.'

'Depressed?' repeated Blanding with surprise as his visitor lit a cigarette. 'I wouldn't have said he was exactly that when I saw him a couple of days back – more just sort of nervy and on edge. Still,' he added, 'I don't suppose depression is not altogether a surprising reaction, not after what the poor chap's been through, and especially now that he's had time to take in the fact that he'll most likely be hobbling around on a stick for the rest of his life.'

There was no time for any further discussion on the young patient's state of mind as, at that moment, the telephone rang at Blanding's elbow. Picking it up, he listened a moment. 'Yes, of course, sir,' he answered. 'That will be no trouble – I'll be over straight away.' Replacing the receiver, he looked triumphantly round at the figure framed against the window. 'Well, Pete, that was none other than our own dear special investigator. Not only, it appears, is he impressed with Diana's theory that Summerfield's missing items of clothing may have been surreptitiously smuggled back into the main stores, but it seems as if I'm also suddenly back in favour. Apparently, he wants the pair of us there when the service police spring a surprise search on the main clothing store.'

'I should think so too,' smiled Palmer, 'after your little Sherlock Holmes stunt yesterday. But look,' he continued, consulting his watch, 'I'd like to tag along also if that's okay. Apart from the lads I've got working on K-Kitty, there's nothing doing around the sheds, and, truth is, at the moment I'd welcome anything to divert my mind.'

If the majority of Frampton Wissey's fitters and mechanics had little to occupy them that morning, the same was equally true of the small army of technicians and clerks employed in the various camp's armouries, storerooms and workshops. It was not wholly surprising, therefore, that when the side door to the main clothing store was unlocked and thrown open from outside, the rather elderly NCO in charge and his five underlings should have been revealed, sitting round a table just inside the entrance, engrossed in a quiet game of pontoon. Hastily stubbing out cigarettes, the players looked up in consternation as Sergeant Evans and two service police corporals burst in, followed by Squadron Leader Walker, the adjutant and his assistant together with the station engineer bringing up the rear.

It was Walker who broke the shocked silence. Pushing between the service police, he surveyed the now suddenly unnaturally pale circle of faces round the table, and then looked down at the scatter of cards and coins in front of them. 'All right, Sergeant,' he said, turning to Evans, 'take their names and put them all on a charge.'

'Very good, sir.'

Feeling distinctly uncomfortable, almost as if some visiting school inspector or governors' representative had chanced upon a collection of boys illicitly smoking in his house boiler-room or behind the bicycle sheds, yet at the same time resentful of what felt like the usurpation of his own role (also experiencing a quite unexpected and novel feeling of sympathy for the grizzled NCO storekeeper and his mainly young female staff), Blanding stood between Diana and Palmer as Walker turned to look about them.

Like the majority of camp buildings, the store was prefabricated – nothing more, indeed, than a couple of the larger type of Nissen huts placed end to end together to create a long, corrugated-iron half-tube. Apart from the wide aisle beyond the issuing counter, most of the windowless, musty-smelling interior was taken up by a maze of narrow passages, criss-crossing at right-angles between ceiling-high, crude sets of wooden shelving and labelled drawers. Clearly daunted by the labyrinthine complexity of the dimly-lit space, Walker's initial look of brisk confidence faded as he peered around. 'Well, Mrs Taylor,' he said somewhat coldly, turning back to Diana, 'as this search is by your instigation, perhaps you can suggest where we best start.'

'Well, sir,' came the confident reply, 'apart from differences in size, one pair of issue shoes is just like another, as indeed is a service cap or skirt. Therefore, unless Corporal Summerfield wrote her name and number inside, and those markings haven't since been removed or inked over, there'll be no way of knowing if any such items belonged to her. Her greatcoat, however, could well be a different matter.' Breaking off, Diana turned and, without a further word, began moving forward, scanning the gloom either side. Eventually, spotting a number of clothing racks containing Waaf greatcoats, she began weaving across to them, followed by her three fellow officers and one or two corporals. 'As Summerfield was much the same height and size as myself,' she resumed, reaching and beginning to move briskly along the first heavily loaded rack, 'we need only look through the coats which roughly fit me.' Reaching the end of the thick hedge of blue-grey serge, she moved to the next, and then, about a third of the way along this second rack, she paused and, bending, began minutely examining each of the protruding sleeves in turn. 'Summerfield was a corporal,' she explained as she moved slowly forward, 'and had held that rank for over a year. That, of course, means that her greatcoat would have had twin chevrons sewn on each arm – and though anyone depositing the coat here would certainly have first removed the stripes, there's almost bound to be some discernible marks left.' Breaking off suddenly, she stopped and, bending over the sleeve she was holding, called out, 'Can someone provide me with a light of some kind?'

'Here, ma'am,' called the police corporal, stepping forward to place a wooden-boxed flashlight in Diana's outstretched hand.

Shining its beam first on the sleeve she was holding and then over at its fellow opposite, Diana went on to check the side pockets before thrusting between the tightly packed garments to direct the torch briefly up and down the back of the coat under examination. As she did so, she gave an audible sigh of satisfaction. 'There,' she said, straightening and again taking hold of the nearer sleeve to display it to the men grouped closely about her, 'if you look carefully, you can see the slightly deeper blue here where the chevrons protected the cloth. You can also just make out the little white ends of the thread originally used to sew on the stripes, and which have not all been fully picked out and removed.' She turned triumphantly to Walker. 'Well, sir, as you can see from the width of the chevron marks, this coat definitely once belonged to a Waaf corporal of a similar height and size to Summerfield.'

'I agree,' replied the investigator with a certain asperity in his voice, 'but that hardly proves that it was the deceased's coat – large numbers of Waaf NCO's must have been stationed here over the years, and it could, you must agree, have belonged to any one of them.'

'Of course,' answered Diana, unabashed. 'Nevertheless, I believe there's a very good chance that this was indeed Summerfield's coat, especially if you notice,' she continued, removing the greatcoat from the rack and spreading it downwards over her arm as she spoke, 'these traces of dust here on the back – the result, I imagine, of having originally been placed on top of the toilet cistern with the smaller items folded inside. And anyway,' she went on, 'if nothing else, at least we now have even more reason to think that her missing clothes and personal equipment was smuggled into the stores – and that, if we're lucky and search the place from top to bottom, we're eventually going to find shoes, skirt and service hat of her size, some perhaps still with signs of her name and number inside.'

'If you're right, that means, of course, at least one person here among those staff over there was involved,' murmured Walker thoughtfully, turning to peer towards the little knot of figures standing illuminated in the shaft of daylight pouring through the open door. 'And that's partly why I wanted you here, Flight Lieutenant,' he continued, turning to Blanding as he began leading the way back towards the waiting group. 'As station adjutant, I imagine you're able to supply me with the name of everyone else who has a key or any means of access to the building.'

'Of course.'

As he answered, Blanding's mind went back to those many occasions as a schoolmaster when, after some elaborate prank, serious breakage or theft, he had done to groups of obdurate boys precisely what Walker obviously intended to do with the storeroom staff – that is, separately to cross-examine each suspect in turn, carefully comparing the various times and details given by them until one or other finally broke down and confessed. That such a simple and well-tried method of ascertaining the facts would eventually lead, not only to the names of everyone involved in June Summerfield's death, but to the discovery of how and why it had ever happened, he hadn't the slightest doubt, especially remembering Walker's skill in cross-examination. Due to Diana's inspiration, the end of the hunt was therefore in sight – and, with that realization, Blanding felt an unexpected lowering of spirits. Whatever human weakness or failure lay behind the girl's killing – jealousy, greed, petty corruption, superstition or sexual depravity – soon the truth would be wrung from those who had either participated or at least had knowledge of the crime. When that happened, then the mystery that had so dominated his thought for days, and which, in a curious way, had drawn Diana and himself together, would be exposed in all its doubtless squalid, everyday ordinariness.

'Excuse me, sir – I've an urgent message for you and Mr

Palmer.'

A familiar voice rang through the store, breaking into his thoughts. Looking up, to his surprise Blanding found himself confronting his chief clerk, who stood bareheaded in the open doorway, peering in with an agitated look on his normally gravely imperturbable face. 'The CO rang through and ordered me to find both you gentlemen,' called out the newcomer, dipping though the entrance and hurrying forward, his glance darting between Blanding and Palmer. 'He says I'm to inform you that we're on tonight.'

Blanding blinked as the speaker halted in front of him. 'I don't understand,' he faltered. 'Whatever do you mean, Mr Starling? On what for God's sake, man?'

'On ops, sir!' burst out the clerk with a wild grimace. 'The Goodwood signal has just come in from Group – Goodwood, sir!' he repeated louder as if his superior had forgotten the dreaded code word. 'Another bloody maximum effort! Every available aircraft ordered to take part!'

Whether it was the memory of the moonlight glowing down on the sleeping camp those two mornings before and then again bathing his bedroom in its silvery light the previous night and thus seeming to guarantee no imminent air operations, or simply that, after three days of stand-down, he and everyone else on the station had allowed themselves to be lulled into the comforting notion that somehow RAF Frampton Wissey had been allowed to slip temporarily out of the war whilst the investigations into Corporal Summerfield's death continued – whichever it was, Starling's news struck Blanding like a hammer blow. Staggered by the unwelcome tidings, all thought of the girl's killing and its reasons was temporary driven from his mind. As if in a trance, he glanced at his watch and noted that it was just past midday, and then, still mentally reeling, hastily excused himself and hurried out behind Palmer to arrange for the immediate sealing of the camp.

Like a huge ants' nest stirred by some invisible stick, within half an hour of the stand-by signal, the station was seething with activity. Under an increasingly bruised-looking sky, from which brief showers of sleet began whirling on a rising wind, fuel bowsers and lorries towing accumulator starter-trolleys began heading out towards the widely dispersed bombers – aircraft which, after standing deserted for days, already now had a host of tiny figures clambering them, stripping soaking covers from cockpits, turrets and tyres in preparation for the usual thirty-minute pre-operational flight test. Even more distant groups were swarming around the half-sunken bomb stores and their protecting blast walls along with a number of forklift trucks and mobile cranes. At the same time, while the clattering teleprinters were still spilling out details of individual fuel and bomb loads, the first whispers began spreading among the airfield staff that the night's operation was going to be no mere 'milk run', but another deep penetration raid, possibly as far or even further than the dreaded 'Big City' itself.

None of these disquieting rumours had yet reached Blanding, however. Having overseen the sealing of the station, he was once more cloistered in his office with Diana, both occupied in a myriad of pre-operational administrative details. Everything from late lunches for the aircrews to the provision of sandwiches, coffee flasks and emergency rations to be carried on the night's raid had to be arranged with the senior catering officer, along with the special meals for before and after the flight. There was the dreaded 'blood list' – the names of all those flying that night – to be collected from the squadron office, typed out and duplicated copies posted throughout the station and the details transmitted by teleprinter to Group HQ. Even the sardonic old ex-Chesterfield miner in charge of the station pigeon loft had to be contacted to make sure that he and his long-suffering airwoman helper were ready to issue two birdsto each aircraft that evening. In the midst of all this activity, Blanding's mind was fully occupied; he thus hardly heard the soft tap on the door, and looked up with mild surprise to see Chief Inspector Stanley entering the room.

'Excuse me, Flight Lieutenant,' said the new arrival, raising his voice above the distant roar of engines being warmed prior to the air tests, 'but could you tell me what's happening? For some reason, my telephone has gone dead, and I've no way of getting in touch with my headquarters.'

Until that moment, Blanding had utterly forgotten the elderly detective. Just as the news of the impending operation had driven all thought of June Summerfield from his mind, so the investigation into her death and everything connected to it had similarly been overtaken by the overriding demands of war. A so-called 'maximum effort' was in preparation and, everyone from the station commander to the humblest cook or officer's servant was reduced to a mere cog, turning in its allocated places within the complicated engine of activity necessary for the transportation of a certain tonnage of bombs to a stipulated target. To that end, justice for one obscure Waaf had to wait – as indeed it would have had to even if it had been the Marshal of the Royal Air Force himself who had been struck down and left sprawling half-naked outside the airfield fence. Nevertheless, during their short acquaintanceship, Blanding had developed a considerable respect, even liking, for the lugubrious, rather shabby figure before him, especially after Stanley's humane treatment of the devastated Nelson the previous day – and guessing that Walker hadn't yet bothered to tell him either of Diana's theory regarding Summerfield's missing items of clothing or the result of the initial search of the stores, he rose to his feet with an embarrassed smile.

'I'm so sorry, Chief Inspector,' he said, 'that no one has informed you of the situation. Our squadron is ordered to take part in air operations tonight. Consequently, this station is now sealed off. That means, I regret to say, that no unauthorised messages can leave the camp, and that you and your team won't be free to leave or communicate with anyone outside until tomorrow. However,' he continued, glancing round at Diana, 'I'm sure Section Officer Taylor will be only too pleased to arrange a visitor's room for you in the officers' mess, and a bed in the sergeants' mess for your assistant. As for the young woman police constable, I suggest she makes use of the temporary quarters we keep for Waafs during operations – they're a trifle Spartan, but at least they'll give her somewhere comparatively warm to sleep.'

Not immediately answering, Stanley turned to the window just as a flurry of what looked like snow came whirling past. 'This operation,' he said with a frown, 'do you really think it will take place in weather like this?'

Turning to follow his gaze, Blanding studied the threatening sky as the first Lancaster began its thunderous take-off. 'I don't know, Chief Inspector,' he replied, 'but, for what it's worth, my guess and my hope is that orders for its cancellation will arrive at any time.'

Despite Blanding's prediction, and the weather growing, if anything, even darker and more forbidding as the day passed, no stand-down was announced, however. Thus when the aircrews returned to their quarters after lunch to rest before the exertions of the night, out on the airfield the tempo of activity continued. The wind having increasingly shifted to the west, the temperature rose perceptibly, and rain replaced the earlier brief showers of sleet as various technicians began moving between the Lancasters, fitting and adjusting photographic equipment as well as the various electronic jamming and fighter detection devices known as 'goon boxes'. At the same time, aircraft fuelling having now finally been completed, a succession of tractors began emerging from the fuze-shed, each towing a train of low-slung trolleys. Loaded with incendiary canisters and massive dustbin-shaped 4000-pound 'cookies' as well as the stubby 500-pound general purpose bombs, they clattered out towards the waiting bombers, leather-jerkined armourers sitting astride one or another of their drab charges like some ghastly parody of children riding gaily-painted miniature trains along peacetime seaside esplanades.

As the long, slow, often dangerous struggle to hoist the deadly cargoes into the Lancasters' capacious bomb bays commenced, tension steadily increased throughout the camp. Incessant Tannoy messages rang out, calling for this or that specialist technician to report at a particular hangar; twice the time of main briefing was announced but then cancelled. By now, the rumours of the likely depth of the impending raid had reached even the adjutant's office, and both its occupants were affected by something of the same gut-tingling dread suffered by the majority of the aircrew. Despite their privacy and close physical proximity, neither felt able to indulge in the slightest small talk or flirtation, and the looks between them were expressive only of a mutual anxiety.

Clearly Palmer had been right all along, Blanding mused gloomily as the afternoon waned. From the amount of equipment arriving, the rapid replacement of lost or damaged aircraft and the numbers of met flights flown, Bomber HQ had obviously been planning some spectacular end to a murderous six-month bombing campaign which, although severely weakening enemy war production and drawing vast numbers of German fighters, guns and personnel from the Russian front, had failed to achieve that quick and comparatively bloodless end to the war its planners had confidently predicted. Only, he thought bitterly, his almost obsessive struggle to solve the mystery of Corporal Summerfield's death had blinded him to the inevitably of this grand finale – that perhaps, and the self-deluding fantasies of a fool in love. As the wind and rain continued to lash the windows, his eyes kept straying to the telephone at his elbow, willing it to ring with the news of the cancellation of the approaching operation.

It remained obstinately silent, however, but it was only when he had almost given up hope of it ever ringing that it suddenly sprang to life. With a mute interchange of apprehensive looks between him and Diana, he lifted the receiver to his ear. 'Right, sir,' he said a moment or two later with a studied neutrality of expression, 'I'll get that announced straight away.'

Diana anxiously studied his face as he replaced the phone. 'Well?' she asked. 'Is it on or off?'

'On,' he answered, avoiding her eyes. 'Main briefing is at 1900 hours, and all aircrew and everyone on night duty to eat an hour earlier.' Breaking off, he looked out at darkly overcast sky. 'At least, I suppose all that cloud up there will give the planes plenty of cover on their approach,' he sighed, 'and this wind should carry them to their target in no time at all.'

'Yes,' murmured his companion grimly, 'but the faster it carries them, the slower and harder will be their return.'

Ever since the first stand-by order reached the station, everything had slipped into place with practised precision and moved according to accustomed procedure. Similarly, exactly twenty minutes before the time of main briefing, having returned to the office with Diana after eating, Blanding mechanically rose from his desk, and, exchanging a strained smile with her, left the room and headed towards the Station Commander's office to conduct him and Wing Commander Birdie across to the operations block as he'd done scores of times. Both men were waiting, and, as always on these occasions, there was a sombre, almost funereal gravity about them and their escort as they left the building with hardly a word being exchanged.

The huge collection of bicycles stacked outside the operations block and the murmur of voices within showed that the crews were already gathered. After exchanging salutes with the service policeman at the entrance, the trio stepped into the briefing hall. As they did so, there was a hush of conversation and a noisy sliding back of chairs as two hundred and more uniformed figures rose to stand behind the tables at which they'd been sitting. With Chesterton leading and Blanding bringing up the rear, the new arrivals passed down the central aisle between the serried ranks to take the seats reserved for them immediately before the stage.

Hardly had they and the men behind taken their seats before

the portly form of 'Daddy' Dunnock, the station's senior intelligence officer, came forward, billiard cue in hand, to take up his customary role as master of ceremonies. Having greeted his audience and given the audience permission to smoke, he signalled towards some invisible helper in the wings and the back curtains were drawn aside to reveal the usual huge wall-map of northern Europe with the courses to be flown indicated by the usual ribbons. Flourishing his cue towards it, he beamingly announced, 'Gentlemen, your target for tonight is Nuremberg.'

From behind, there were incredulous gasps and various half-stifled cries of 'For God's sake' and 'Jeezus'. For a moment, Blanding couldn't understand the strength of the reaction – everyone on the station had known this was to be a deep penetration raid, and although Nuremberg was approximately the same distance as Berlin, its defences were nothing compared to those of the German capital. But then he realized what was so disturbing the aircrews – after joining the main stream above the North Sea, their stipulated course ran south-eastwards across Belgium as far as Charleroi, and then, swinging east, headed bar-straight for nearly three hundred miles, only turning sharply southwards when approximately eighty miles north of Nuremberg. Such a flight plan was very unusual, to say the least – ordinarily there would always be a whole series of violent course changes in an attempt to mislead the enemy as to their ultimate destination and hinder his efforts to vector fighters into the bomber stream: this time, however, the bomber force would advance across the very heart of heart of Germany as straight and boldly as Lord Cardigan's Light Brigade at Balaclava trotting in formation up the valley towards the waiting cannon.

As if unaware of the reaction to the flight plan, Dunnock began in the traditional manner by explaining the choice of target, laying stress on Nuremberg's importance as an industrial and transportation centre. Raising his voice above the muttered whispering, he announced that it contained both tank and electrical-goods factories, including the massive M.A.N. armament works and an almost equally large Siemens plant. Also, he added, its extensive railway yards were packed with munitions, and finished by underlining the huge symbolic importance of the city to the Nazi Party.

His place was then taken by the senior navigational officer, who, with the use of the same billiard cue pointer, began justifying

255

the route chosen. It was, he explained, to be a double bluff – the enemy would not believe that the bombers would continue straight for so far, and think that they would either divert north to Cologne or south to Frankfurt, or even turn north-eastwards towards Brunswick or Berlin. On the other hand, by continuing their course due east, he smilingly assured his listeners, the bombers would have the full benefit of the powerful tail-wind that would carry them right through Germany like the proverbial dose of salts. There was no answering smiles from those in front of him, however – and, glancing sideways, Blanding saw the stern look on Chesterton's face and the equally sombre expression on the aquiline features of the New Zealander at his side.

It was now the turn of the meteorological department – represented by the same civilian who had clashed with Fluff Brewer over the lunch table. With the aid of previously chalked diagrams on sliding blackboards, he indicated strato-cumulus high above Nuremberg, and assured his audience that thick cumulus and convection cloud would shroud their approach. By now, the initial stunned shock had worn off and been replaced by a sort of wild, almost exuberant fatalism – and as Dunnock once more took over the stage to assert that the Americans had carried out a fighter sweep across the area that day and had reported 'shooting down every goddamned Jerry fighter in the area', wild jeers and sardonic laughter rocked the hall. Finally, when a further blackboard was slid out to show a chalked diagram of the actual target with its aiming point at the centre above the city railway yards, and the speaker mentioned almost matter-of-factly that 'you'll notice the area is roughly in the shape of an axe', a jeering chant of 'chop, chop, chop' began at the back and rapidly rose to echo through the smoke-fugged hall.

Leaning slightly forward, Blanding again glanced past Birdie to witness Chesterton's tight-lipped scowl. He looked back round to see the hunched, twisted form of 'Fluff' Brewer dragging himself unsteadily up the stage steps to explain the evening's taxying procedures and to announce engine start-up and take-off times. Finally, watches having been synchronized and all navigators instructed to attend the senior navigational officer in the map room straight afterwards, and wireless operators to go with them to meet the signals leader, the briefing was essentially over. Before it actually finished, however, Birdie went up on stage to stress the necessity of pilots adhering strictly to their stipulated altitudes and to warn crews

256

to watch for the course change marker-flares laid by the pathfinder squadrons. Lastly, Chesterton rose to wish the flyers the best of luck, and with his final 'Happy landings' and Kochanowski's equally traditional cry from the back, the meeting was finally at an end. With the mass of aircrew stumbling to their feet behind him, Blanding rose from his chair and stood aside to allow the two senior officers to proceed him out.

Throughout the briefing, he'd been acutely aware of the strong emotion in the room. Now, however, following Chesterton and Birdie up the aisle, his attention was caught by a tiny group among the blur of faces on his left. It was the crew of A-Able, and they stood, a silent, unspeaking group on each side of their wan-faced pilot, oblivious apparently of the crush of other bodies about them, staring as if mesmerised at the huge map and the long lengths of blood-red ribbon stretched out across it.

Blanding's blood ran cold at the sight. In all the excitement to track down Summerfield's killers, and then under the sudden pressure to prepare for the coming operation, he'd utterly forgotten the young Scot. Although the lists of those flying that night had passed through his hand, he'd not studied them, although, as he now realized, it was obvious that a Goodwood call, meant Mackenzie and his crew would be going with the rest. Observing their faces, he understood – they must have been hoping for some comparatively easy flight to ease them into operations; instead, they were condemned to one of the deepest penetration raids possible, and, knowing this, they seemed to be staring at their own extinction.

Aghast, Blanding continued to observe them, remembering what he'd heard so often since joining Bomber Command: that it was often quite obvious to experienced airmen which of their number would not be returning from a particular operation. Thinking this, there amidst the bustle of those beginning now to push past him and with Chesterton and Birdie already vanishing among the converging crowd ahead, Blanding suddenly knew with dreadful certainty what thing it was that duty and decency demanded. Stunned and horrified by this terrible knowledge, he felt his mouth going dry, and with his heart beginning to pound at the thought of what lay ahead, he turned away abruptly and began pushing his way through the jostling throng towards the exit.

CHAPTER TWENTY

'Of course, my good friend, we help, but you fly with the Polskies. You remember, we already invite you and Squadron Leader Palmer? Come, you're welcome – we have plenty fun! Knock plenty heads!'

Why Blanding had chosen to confide in Kochanowski and his crew he wasn't quite sure. It was perhaps an instinctive knowledge that the survivors of the brutal overthrow of their homeland, consumed as they were by a raging determination to revenge themselves on its bloody-handed invaders, were unlikely to feel themselves constrained by any of the pettifogging rules and regulations of the British Air Ministry – either that, or simply because during his time at Frampton Wissey, Blanding had observed that of all the numerous nationalities who flew the bombers, there was a wild, reckless abandon about the Poles unequalled by even the most recalcitrant and bloody-minded Australian. Anyway, whatever the reason, catching sight of G-George's crew heading away through the dusk from the briefing, he'd hurried to catch them up, and now found himself standing at the centre of a group of rather squat, broad-faced, wide-smiling men who seemed to smell faintly of scent. 'Thank you but no,' he answered, addressing Kochanowski. 'It's very kind of you, Wing Commander, but I must go with that crew back there.' Turning, he pointed through the dusk towards where Sergeant Mackenzie and his equally doleful-looking companions were emerging from the operations block. 'It's those chaps I need to fly with.'

It was Kochanowski's navigator who spoke – a strikingly handsome, dark-haired man who had been studying mathematics at Cracow when the Germans invaded, and was the only one of G-George's crew whose spoken English, despite being liberally laced with RAF slang, approached the orthodoxies of the language. 'Forgive, Flight Lieutenant,' he said, 'but that a sprog crew – and this

258

trip to Nuremberg will not be piece of the cake. Look at the faces of those types, I bet socks they will be chop-meat before tomorrow!'

'Exactly so,' answered Blanding, glancing back at the cluster of figures on the path behind, 'and that's why I must fly with them. It was me who convinced the station commander to allow them to stay with their present skipper and continue operational flying – honour therefore demands that I should accompany them.'

At this, the Pole clicked his heels and gave a slight bow before turning to say something rapidly to his companions. Whether it was the reference to honour or something else, there was no further argument. The entire group nodded gravely and Kochanowski, placing a comforting hand on Blanding's shoulder, beamed a tooth-gleaming smile. 'Of course, Flight Lieutenant – we understand and we help. You come for kitting-up to crew room, and everything you need, we, the Polskies, find and give.'

Blanding had now just over an hour to himself. His first and strongest impulse was to go over to the mess to seek out Diana. Realizing, however, that he could not risk telling her of his plan, as she would certainly be vehemently against it, and guessing that she would be bound to sense something in his manner if he tried to disguise his intentions, he instead hurried back to the now almost deserted administration block. Going straight to his office, he locked the door behind him and, after carefully closing the blackout blinds, took his place at his desk – and there, beneath the cone of light from the anglepoise lamp and with icy fingers of horror kneading his stomach, he quickly sketched out an informal will. Having signed and sealed it, he then wrote letters to Chesterton and Diana, informing them both of the reason for his decision, and, in the case of his commanding officer, apologizing for any upset or inconvenience caused.

Leaving all three documents propped up on the desk, he went through to the back storeroom-cum-bedroom to put on an extra winter flannel vest, thinking of King Charles I doing the very same thing on the freezing cold morning of his execution. This done, he stood a moment looking about him, feeling as if, in leaving the bleak little room, with its sparse utilitarian furniture and low, iron-framed camp-bed, he was finally bidding farewell to his whole life up until that moment. Night having now fallen, he let himself out of the unlocked back entrance to the administration block and slipped through the darkness across to the now thronging crew rooms.

259

There was nothing unusual about the sight of administrative personnel pushing their way among the mass of flyers donning their flying clothes, and Blanding slipped through the crush unremarked. The general gloom at the end of the briefing had obviously lifted to judge by the prevalent atmosphere of schoolboy horseplay and banter – that resilience was, of course, one of the boons of youth. Finding the Poles already grouped round their neighbouring lockers, he squeezed in between them until he was effectively screened. He then, head low, began pulling on the articles he was handed – silk socks to protect his feet against the freezing cold, a grubby white roll-neck pullover to go under his uniform jacket, and over that an all-enveloping Sutton flying suit, to which one of G-George's gunners attached a silver whistle. Finally, having managed to cram his feet into a pair of under-sized fleece-lined boots and wearing a leather helmet with attached oxygen mask and intercom microphone flapping loosely before his face, and with the Poles grouped defensively around him, he hobbled, avoiding all eye-contact, down the short passage to the parachute section. Here, he felt, lay his greatest danger of discovery. He needn't have worried, however, for the WAAFs behind the issuing counter were the targets of such a barrage of hand-kissing gallantry and outrageous flirting from his companions that he was hardly given a second glance. A parachute and yellow lifejacket were shoved across, which he wordlessly signed for, and then, next moment, he was guided out through the further door to join the crews assembling outside.

In the faintly blue-lit darkness, the Poles stayed close, helping him buckle on his harness so tightly that he was left trussed up, quite unable to straighten. They then demonstrated how the parachute pack was secured to his chest with four clips when needed.

'You jump before, adj?' Blanding shook his head, once more reflecting that this was turning out to be rather different from, say, stowing away in the back of a lorry. 'Count ten before you pull this,' said Kochanowski. 'Jump out after your head,' said another of the Poles with a wolfish grin. 'Don't pull now, one pound fine', added a third with equal cheerfulness. Blanding nodded and smiled and nodded. Everyone seemed to be having a wonderful time.

With relief he awkwardly followed them outside. Standing on the steps of the ops building waiting for the crew buses to arrive was, he thought, managing a wry smile to himself, reminiscent of waiting for taxis in the West End when the cinemas emptied. Here, too, in the cold night air after the warm fug indoors, cigarettes were being lighted, tossed to friends, raucous laughter even floated over from one group. Having now at last both the leisure to observe the scene as well as the security afforded by the shadows, Blanding peered over the shoulders of his helpers at the mass of similarly heavily-padded figures about him, all emitting clouds of condensing breath or the dull grey of exhaled cigarette smoke. The first person he was actually able to recognize was Wing Commander Birdie – the New Zealander stood at the edge of his crew, the only one among them not smoking or speaking – a solitary, austere-looking figure, distanced by rank and responsibility from those with whom he was going to fly, someone whose voluntary presence underlined for everyone both the importance and danger of the coming operation. Blanding's eyes moved to what he vaguely recognized as the crew of K-Kitty, presumably flying one of the two replacement aircraft while repairs to their own continued. Whatever they were feeling at being sent out to face the same dangers again after having so recently just scraped home in their shot-up machine, they were an animated cluster of dark shapes, laughing and jostling among themselves, for all the world like overgrown schoolboys awaiting nothing more terrifying than the school bus. Marvelling at their seeming indifference to what lay ahead, Blanding's attention moved on until, with shock, he caught sight of Pat Kelly's crew.

In complete contrast to the other crews, who could be made out in the gloom as denser clumps in the overall herd (in their steaming bulk he was reminded of cattle in a farmyard on a winter's evening), these were a loose scatter of individuals, each keeping his face averted from the others, each silent and head-bowed as if lining a graveside but for the dull glow of their cigarettes. As he watched them, he saw no form of contact between any of them, no gestures, no quick turn of the head, only their hands mechanically bringing their cigarettes up for another drag. Then he noticed another solitary figure, not smoking and standing slightly apart from them, and as separate and remote from the rest of the crew as Wing Commander Birdie was from his. At first, Blanding couldn't identify the slim figure, but then he realized it was Pilot Officer Nightingale, the young navigator who was the replacement for the wounded Ellis. At the sight of him and his motionless comrades, Blanding felt much the same shudder of guilty shock as when, on his way out of the briefing

261

room, he'd spotted the shattered Mackenzie and his crew. He automatically glanced back at Birdie, cursing himself for not having risked the wing commander's fury to voice his doubts about Kelly's condition to fly and also for having focussed on Mackenzie's problems to the neglect of the Australian pilot.

'Here's the transport!'

The cry and the ironical responding cheer broke through his thoughts, and he turned to see a straggling line of tarpaulin-covered lorries lurching towards them out of the gloom, each vehicle swinging round smartly in turn to back up towards the two hundred and more waiting men who had now more or less fallen silent. Nevertheless there were sporadic ribald shouts, an occasional burst of laughter, scattered calls of 'good luck' between various individuals as the crowd surged forward to meet the lorries, pilots with their seat-type parachutes thrown over one shoulder, navigators carrying flat canvas chart bags as well as their rectangular parachute packs, wireless operators and other crew-members burdened with various items including, it seemed, coffee flasks – the mass of figures moving forward like some strangely subdued excursion crowd as the girl drivers, dropping lightly down from their cabs, like street vendors began crying out the call-signs of the various aircraft.

With muttered thanks to his Polish companions, and receiving in return good-luck thumps on back and shoulders, and from Kochanowski something pushed down into the cuff of his glove that he later discovered to be a tiny crucifix, Blanding moved across to join the figures scrambling up into the back of the lorry assigned to A-Able and two other crews. Putting a foot into the stirrup-like cut-out in the lowered tailboard, he heaved himself upward, assisted by hands that reached out from the blackness above to pull him aboard. Encumbered by the unfamiliar clothing and harness, he lurched cumbrously forward, grabbing at a metal support strut above his head to prevent himself cannoning into one or other of the dark shapes inside. 'Ooh, Arthur, do give over,' someone shrieked in a piercing falsetto as his hand blindly encountered unyielding masculine flesh in the darkness and the sally was greeted with sniggers of appreciation.

Now bodies pressed up against him on all sides as the last members of the three crews pushed themselves into the lorry. Tailboards slammed with a rattle of chains, and then suddenly with a jerk and shouts of encouragement from the few figures left outside the operations block, the lorry began to move off. As they rumbled out into the semi-darkness the usual singing began, spreading from truck to truck and growing in volume as they began heading around the peri track, the tone and the words every bit as mockingly ironic as the songs sung by their fathers, plodding the long straight roads toward Arras, Beaumont, Hamel and Passchendaele.

I don't want to be an airman,
I don't want to go to war,
I'd sooner hang around
Piccadilly Underground,
Living off the earnings of a. . . high-born lady.

The singing grew louder as the lorry gunned out onto the airfield, and now the glow of the amber taxi lights briefly flickered over the faces of the singers about him, and then suddenly close at his ear came the burring drawl of a well-known voice and a strong hand pulling him round by the shoulder.

'Jesus H. Christ! That *is* you, Trott Blanding! I thought so! What in the goddamn name of hell are you doing here?'

It was, of course, Tex Crawford, and the two of them shuffled and squirmed in the crush to face each other in the jolting, roaring darkness. Deep inside the layers and padding of his clothing Blanding felt a cold rillet of sweat run down his chest. Crawford bent forward again, and shouted into his ear over the singing and the whine of the differential.

'So who are you flying with?'

'Young Sergeant Mackenzie over there,' called Blanding, bellowing with assumed insouciance into the American's ear. 'Just a little jaunt with him and his chaps over the Reich. Moral support, you might say.'

'Christ, man, are you serious? – why, you're not going on some ten-cent flip over Coney Island, for Chrissakes! This raid's gonna be a bitch! Why in hell *are* you doing this, Trott?'

'I told you, Tex - to encourage them, I suppose. I'm not going to leave them in the lurch. It's my own fault, in a way. I'll tell you when we get back. Sorry, *if* we get back. I can't just sit on my arse here and watch them fly off to die.'

' Like all the others.'

'Like all the others,' murmured Blanding.

Neither spoke for a moment, each aware of a shared pool of pregnant silence amidst the uproar around them. Finally Crawford punched him lightly a couple of times on the shoulder and the man's lips pressed close to his ear. 'God, man, I can't say I ever thought that much of you – ya know, desk johnnies and all that – but I reckon there can't be much wrong with you after all. But Christ, you're one crazy sonofabitch.'

The lorry jolted to a halt and the girl's shrill shout came from the cab. 'N-Nan – and good luck to you all.'

This time the singing did not recommence. The tailboard closed with a crash and the lorry started to roll again. Crawford, standing to leave, suddenly bent and put his mouth close to Blanding's ear again, and to Blanding's amazement, barked into it like a dog or a demented coyote. Crawford cuffed him lightly and affectionately on the cheek before vaulting lightly over the tailboard to join his gathered crewmates now arrived at their dispersal. The barking left Blanding stunned and he stared after the American even as the lorry accelerated away from N-Nan, a high shadow looming over the dark figures beneath her.

He felt the lorry slowing down again and stopping, and now he waited until Mackenzie's crew had disembarked. Finally he too dropped down feet first onto the ground, and stood back in the darkness as the now empty lorry moved off with tailboard rattling and tarpaulins shivering on the flimsy tubing framework. Now the crew had seen him – this puzzling supernumerary figure padded out in flying kit – and stood staring, Mackenzie at their centre. One of the erks called out 'This is A for Able, mate, you've got off at the wrong stop.'

Blanding stepped forward – the fliers happened to be one of the many all-NCO crews and his voice cut through a chorus of jocular remarks from the ground crew with all the authority at an adjutant's disposal. Mackenzie may not have recognized him from his shape but the voice was certainly familiar.

'I have been ordered to come with you men,' he lied, 'as an observer. I'll try not to get in your way, but I'm here to monitor the resolution of you and your crew for the squadron commander.'

What they thought none said – this utterly unexpected turn of events obviously staggered them, but apparently shaken by the authoritarian tones of the speaker and intimidated by his officer status, Mackenzie merely replied rather uncertainly, 'Well, sir, if you're sure. I'll do my very best to get us there and back safely. And do the job, of course.'

'I am sure you will,' murmured Blanding. He glanced at his illuminated watch. 'Well, I think we should be getting aboard.'

'We've a while yet, sir,' said Mackenzie, not quite so deferentially. 'If you'll excuse me, I'll be getting on with the checks.'

Now, as Blanding, the only man on dispersal with no task to perform, looked round at his new companions, he saw a thing he'd not been expecting: a raw, nervous excitement and anticipation of what lay ahead. Up to this moment, through his almost middle-aged eyes, he'd seen the aircrew as doughty warriors who, despite their courage, still had to steel themselves to risk death; what he realized he had forgotten was that spirit of youth – the thing that made battle and war possible – the sheer thrill of testing oneself to the uttermost and the pride in going right up to the boundaries of death – that same spirit which had possessed mankind ever since the first spear had been plunged into the woolly mammoth or the sabre-toothed tiger – indeed, the very thing that had made him as a young man take to rock climbing and mountaineering. And now, beneath the icy-cold fear in his knotted stomach, and the strange dryness in his throat, he felt his own former excitement kindling from the fire radiating from the youths about him.

Time seemed to have slowed right down again for him and he fidgeted and wished they could just get on with it – not least due to his fear of being discovered or fetched back by Chesterton. Finally Mackenzie popped up in front of him again from the deepening darkness. 'I've just got a small question, sir. I take it, sir, that you've had physical clearance from the medicos?'

'Quite correct, flight sergeant. That is the regulation, I believe,' said Blanding. 'No one flies without an examination.'

'Well, if I have your assurance, sir,' said Mackenzie quietly. 'You see, if you've never been to those altitudes, well, it makes some folk scream in pain or even go berserk.'

'Why on earth would they do that?'

'It's the pressure of the air trapped in wee cavities within their skulls. Or teeth, even. Only happens to a few, of course. The medical chappies have ways of seeing if it's likely. Or then again, you could be airsick and choke on your vomit. Or there's nosebleeds ...'

'I see – well, let's be getting on, then.' Blanding was growing more and more nervous at standing around outside the plane, fully exposed to any passing official car. Now he could see the dim silhouette and bouncing headlight beams, narrowed into slits by

265

black-out masks, of what might have been the CO's Humber Hawk nipping across the grass to another dispersal bay. The young Scot did not move. Blanding shot him a keen glance which he was surprised to note was returned unflinchingly.

'All in good time, sir. There's no hurry. Once we've done the checks I'll need to sign the 700 form and then we'll probably still have ten minutes or so for a fag.'

'Perhaps I'll go on board now, no point standing around getting cold.'

Mackenzie shook his head, almost with a tinge of regret. Blanding flushed – in the ten minutes since his arrival at the dispersal authority had very definitely flowed steadily away from him and towards the captain of the plane; his own position as station adjutant clearly counted for very little here at the sharp end. Perhaps that was how it should be, he reflected, feeling rather like a bystander trying to badger a chess player into a rash move.

'We'll have a wee briefing first, adjutant, since you probably haven't flown before – or not for a while anyway. In our air force, as you probably know, the pilot is the senior officer, so to speak, in his own plane. Unlike the Yanks. That means even a humble sergeant pilot like me would outrank even the boss, Air Marshal Harris himself, if he were on board. In fact, you, sir, cannot even order me to turn back. Right, let's see. Um, we address each other over the intercom as skipper, nav, rear-gunner –'. He paused and looked at Blanding.

' "Passenger" ?' suggested the adjutant, almost diffidently.

'No passengers in my kite,' said Mackenzie firmly. 'We'll just say 'adj' pro tem, and drop the 'sir'. You are part of the crew.'

'My dear fellow, I quite appreciate your point, but I'm merely here to observe, nothing more. There's nothing I can do anyway –'

'If ye're looking for a job, adj, ye can drop the "window",' thrust in a ruffianly looking crew member, another Scot, if not more so, by his accent. 'I hate and abhorr that bloody stuff.'

'Now then, Tom, will you leave us alone a moment?' Mackenzie turned back to Blanding, shaking his head slowly. 'If I need you to do something, you'll please do it, or you can stay here, adjutant or no adjutant.'

'Confound you, you young pup,' said the older man with a laugh. Mackenzie waited. 'Yes, you're quite right, Mackenzie, I quite understand – um, skipper,' he added.

'You'd better meet the boys properly.'

Once Blanding had nodded at Sandy the mid-upper gunner, Pete the flight engineer, someone else whose name he didn't catch, ground crew erks were milling around their precious plane again and introductions were abandoned. Mackenzie and the flight engineer were beckoned over to the forward end of the aircraft by an authoritative-looking flight sergeant in a leather jerkin and turned-down gumboots, and all three looked up from time to time at something just below the bomb-aimer's window. The broad rear of the petrol bowser slowly trundled away, one of its ecclesiastically-shaped rear half-doors swinging negligently. Three or four erks pushed savagely at a rickety maintenance platform with a flat tyre to get it out of the way. Nobody was taking the slightest notice of Blanding.

Mackenzie strolled back looking unconcerned, nodding at his crew. Blanding had the suspicion that Mackenzie used every absence from him to examine the situation once again, perhaps from a new angle, and each time the plane's captain had clearly gained a whit more confidence from the examination. It occurred to Blanding too that perhaps Mackenzie was more nervous about him than about the impending operation, 'dicing' over Nuremberg as the RAF slang had it.

'You'll be writing a report on this, I imagine, adj, but you don't seem to have brought anything with you. Nav, you can sort the adj out with something to write on?'

'I'd be grateful for a pencil of some sort too, I appear to have forgotten mine.'

'Right-oh, I'd better explain things as we go, if I have time, so you can get it right. Right,' said Mackenzie and shot a glance at his wristwatch. 'Now's the time to board. Adj, you go on fourth, after Nav there. He'll show you your station.' Turning, he addressed the crew in a louder voice: 'All in line now and a-one, and a-two, and a-three –'

From its faintly harassed, dogged, cold-skinned sort of expression, the pilot's face had suddenly creased into a broad boyish grin, instantly echoed by the rest of the crew, and the seven of them got into a rough line. Without ceremony, an invisible hand reached out and tugged Blanding into his place, and then, with a 'one-two-by the left' they broke into

'Hey, ho; hey, ho, it's off to work we go
With bombs and flares and a cookie to share

267

Hey, ho; hey, ho, it's off to work we go ...'
shuffling in line back past grinning erks towards the door in the rear part of the aircraft fuselage where the short ladder waited for them to mount. Blanding, fourth in the column, reflecting with a rueful grin that if they were the Seven Dwarfs, that made him Snow White, was taken aback when they all shuffled past the ladder and dark waiting doorway and deployed into a shallow semi-circle facing the rear wheel half-hidden beneath the fuselage and tail. Blanding wondered what was the matter with the wheel, it looked all right to him but at the same time he could hear laughter and wind-torn shouts from the ground crew. 'It's an old bomber crew tradition this, adj,' said his neighbour, the navigator, he thought. Erks stood by, grinning in the shadows. Flashes of light at the neighbouring dispersal, and the cough of a more distant Merlin starting up.

'Good job we don't carry ladies on board, they couldn't do this,' chortled a shortish lad next to him whom Blanding imagined must be the bomb-aimer.

'Crew unbutton,' commanded the gallant captain, and his crew fumbled amidst their bulky flying gear to extract the equipment needed to wet the rubber of the tail wheel.

'Come on, adj,' said Mackenzie, leaning forward to peer along the line, 'you must have something to shoot with. You'll be as nervous as we are, unless there's something wrong with you, and it's a hell of a sight easier to go now rather than wait till we're aloft.'

'Sorry, Mackenzie,' said Blanding wishing like never before that he had not come and privily wondering at the pilot's utter transformation from the callow, nervous, eager-to-please airman he had seen that time up before the board. Even the rest of the crew now seemed men rather than youths.

Blanding began taking off his outer gloves nevertheless.

Seven streams bounced off the wheel. Blanding's body responded automatically but he realized he had now idea how to actually get through all his bulky clothing.

'I'll be damned if I can –'

'Look, adj, we'll all turn round, but it's for good luck, you have to do it.'

Suddenly a green light hurled itself into the night sky, illuminating the curves of the Lancaster and everyone's faces with witchlight. Blanding knew that this was the final go-ahead.

'Ah, fuck it,' said the rear-gunner, 'I was hoping for a scrub.

Just my wee joke, adjutant. Ay'm as keen as mustard reahlly old boy.'

Blanding ignored the schoolboy cheek and turned to negotiate the ladder. He felt as if two utterly different impulses were contending inside him – one like a cold, heavy weight in the pit of the stomach, the other a weakness of the knees which threatened to make the step up onto the first rung impossible but which was still nevertheless not able to defeat the trembling anticipation which made him drag himself up and through the dark hole in the bomber's side.

Scrambling into the narrow, dimly-lit tunnel which was the Lancaster's fuselage, he made out the dull glint of bullets in ammunition trackways running down the wall facing him. Pausing to catch his breath, he wrinkled his nose in instinctive reaction to the rank smell of the bomber: an oily dankness combined with whatever chemicals were used in the Elsan, an unenclosed cylindrical toilet situated immediately to his left and just forward of the still open rear turret doors. There were yet other strong odours (the smell of damp metal, oil, perhaps a residual acrid wisp of vomit, perhaps paraffin and some others that he couldn't for the moment identify).

He felt a shove from the wireless operator behind, and almost plunged down the single step into the aircraft and then he was stumbling slightly uphill along the metal floor of the fuselage. It was much narrower inside than he could have imagined. His shoulders almost brushed the metal walls, how on earth two men in bulky flying gear could ever pass...

'Keep your head down, adj' came the warning voice from behind, and then, ducking low, Blanding tackled the climb over the main spar that obstructed the way up into the bomber's cockpit area, wondering as he struggled ungainly over it how he would ever manage to get back to the rear hatch in a burning, perhaps a spinning aircraft. From aircrew conversations he had overheard with a horrified entrapped fascination in the mess he knew that in a diving plane you could be pressed immoveably to the plane's walls or ceiling by the strong irresistible fingers of gravity and never make it to the escape hatch. In his mind whirled images of flies struggling in the thick, chemical glue of flypaper and of people stuck high on the spinning cylindrical walls of a ride at the funfair as the floor dropped away from beneath their feet. Blanding shrugged off these thoughts and pushed on in his nightmarishly bulky flying suit which seemed to catch at every unseen obstacle in the gloom. Again a trickle of sweat slid down his chest like an icy string of diamonds.

269

Once over the main spar, he pressed himself to one side to allow the wireless operator to get to his 'office' behind the bulkhead. Up forward, the pilot and the flight engineer were dark shapes against the perspex windows of the wide canopy. Strangely the night sky seen through the cagelike framework of the canopy was bright, pearly, and coldly indifferent. On the crew room steps he had heard two navigators behind him gloomily exchanging remarks about moon transits and moonsets and forty percent moons. The sun had long gone down now, twilight had faded away and somewhere, hung high somewhere in the blackness, a crescent moon would be watching their crawling progress over dark lands and silvered wrinkled seas.

Now the navigator was in occupancy of his long stool and busy pulling charts out of his bag onto the desk top in front of him, a pool of light making the paper almost dazzle Blanding's sight. The bomb-aimer, he supposed, had gone down to his station in the chin of the bomber, and would probably come back for the take-off. Blanding knew that it was now forbidden by RAF regulations for anyone to remain in the nose during landing or take-off. Feeling once more somewhat *de trop*, he backed up slowly until he was sitting on the front part of the main spar, where there appeared to be a long seat with a backrest.

Blanding could almost taste a menacing silence, as if there were a hostile landscape around him which was as yet invisible to his eyes but which very shortly would be revealed to him. He had a strange feeling around his throat which he had not felt since he had been a toddler on the brink of sobs and tears; now it felt to him as if he were grieving intensely and with unbearable pain for someone very close to him. His rib-cage too had become rigid and unresponsive, so much so that he deliberately inhaled and exhaled with force to prove he was still alive. Against the menacing, invisible silence he heard scraps of sound flutter and flash: voices of the ground crew from outside, Mackenzie shouting something out of his open window, and creaks and groans from the aircraft as it shifted slightly. Blanding's body was almost tuning into the silence and he forced himself to pay more attention to his surroundings to distract himself in an effort to avoid communing with that dreadful silence.

Conscious of simply pottering around and of not having a job to do, he lowered the pipe-cot that was secured on hinges to the fuselage – after all, he could not stand up for the entire flight. Then he realized he would need to find somewhere to plug in his oxygen line

270

and the intercom. It was hard in the gloom to see if there were any likely sockets on outlets near where he was standing. Standing up from his stooped search he sensed the flight engineer had turned round and was looking back at him. Feeling once more somewhat foolish, Blanding gestured towards one ear-piece of his flying helmet and then shook the dangling mouthpiece to indicate he was at a loss.

It was the bomb-aimer, coming up from his position in the nose, who read the adjutant's semaphore and wordlessly, but with a smile, plugged in the intercom, with a fat triple-padded finger showing Blanding the send button, the supply socket for his oxygen mask and intercom, and as he pushed it in he heard a strangely high-pitched voice in his ear.

'Adj, I'm going to be starting my final checks now. I'll be telling everyone when it's time to go onto oxygen, and someone will show you what to do – one thing it's vital to remember is to keep squeezing the oxygen tube, it's going to be so ruddy cold up there that the moisture in your breath will condense and freeze and gradually cut off the oxygen. You won't notice this, you'll fall asleep and bye and bye you'll have crossed that bourne from which no traveller returns.'

' Good God,' exclaimed Blanding involuntarily.

'Just give the tube a squeeze from time to time and you'll be fine. Right, I'll be getting on with the checks.'

A new voice was heard – Blanding detected a Mancunian accent – and the long litany commenced.

'Ground flight switch ... on flight ... altimeters ... set to zero ... pressures and temperatures? All OK ... Bomb doors? ... Closed...'

The checks continued, with Blanding listening attentively although most of it was sheer gibberish to him. A shadowy figure eased past him, going aft and the ladder was pulled in and the door closed – Blanding understood that much at least. The man grinned and gave him the thumbs-up as he passed on his return journey.

'Ignition on – start Number 3'

There was a long grinding cranking, a coughing and spluttering and then the first of the Merlins started with a sudden and enormous loudness which seemed to physically rock the plane on its wheels, settling rapidly down into a steady all-shaking thunder, the sheer volume of sound yet growing as one after the other the three remaining engines burst into life. Blanding gloomily asked himself how he would be able to stand the racket for eight hours: it was the malignant opposite of silence, and instead of isolating him with his thoughts in a form of deafness, the noise probably would not even allow him to think but instead place him at the mercy of all those feelings engendered by his fears and imaginations. Nor did he have any job or useful function to distract him. With a feeling of utter depression now flooding him, Blanding sat heavily down on the pipe cot, and slumped so the back of his head rested against the vibrating fuselage wall, closed his eyes, tried not to weep, and waited for all the world like a prisoner in his condemned cell.

CHAPTER TWENTY-ONE

On its dark dispersal pan, amidst the jumble of maintenance scaffolds now night-shrouded, a few ground crew keeping an eye on things, someone standing ready with bats for signalling, the plane vibrated, like an enormous eager monster awaiting the word of command from a hidden master. Mackenzie released the brakes with a squeal as they were waved out onto the narrow ribbon of the taxiway along which other bombers were slowly and ponderously moving until each in turn arrived at the end of the takeoff runway. A-Able had only trundled forward a few yards along the peri track when they stopped. Mackenzie swore softly.

'Maybe someone's gone off the taxiway,' he said. 'It's always suspected to be deliberate, you know, but I can tell you it's bloody difficult to steer the plane – you have to do it with the engines, there's a lot of inertia from the weight, and if you don't get it right, the plane keeps bloody well turning when you want it to stop and one of your wheels drops off the concrete into the mud. And that's it, you've bogged down. Naturally, of course, you did it on purpose.'

Mackenzie fell silent, and Blanding wondered if he was imagining the build-up of tension. God knew this next part could be almost as bad as when they were over the target – on several occasions he had seen with his own eyes a heavily laden Lancaster somehow not get off properly and explode in flames a few fields away, or there was that time when two successive planes collided only a few hundred feet up, exploding instantaneously in a fireball that scorched the leaves off the trees hundreds of yards away. Not to mention landing, when some poor devil who had nursed his plane back from Berlin ran out of fuel just a sprint away from safety and made yet another blackened crater in the Cambridgeshire countryside.

'Skipper, the engines are beginning to heat up a bit with this hanging around.'

273

Blanding waited for a reply but none came. There had been a hint of something in the flight engineer's nasal, almost wheedling tone that he did not care for overmuch. Too many years winkling out slackers at school, he thought. His thoughts were interrupted when presently, with a roar of throttle, the plane started rolling again, with the bomb-aimer peering down through his perspex bubble and calling out the distance of the great rubber wheels from the edge of the peri track at Mackenzie's request.

'Good God, who's that crazy idiot?'

Ahead, they saw the slitted headlights of a vehicle apparently driving straight at them but weaving from side to side as it approached them on the peri track. The driver started flashing his headlights. For a moment, Blanding wondered if it might be Chesterton himself come out to stop him.

'There's a hold-up ahead,' came the flat-sounding, commercial traveller's voice of the bomb aimer. 'Looks like two kites have collided.'

'Ruddy imbeciles,' said Mackenzie, in tones of supreme tetchiness, for all the world like a motorist delayed for a few minutes at a level crossing. The aircraft lurched as it braked again, and Blanding thought the pilot must have throttled back as the enormous noise of the engines subsided somewhat.

'Lofty, I mean bomb-aimer, flash that damn lorry with your Aldis.'

As they came closer, Mackenzie slid open the window at his elbow and peered out into the gloom. Ahead of them, two bombers had fused together on the peri track like a couple of prehistoric monsters clumsily mating.

'Why don't they just call you on the radio?'

'Radio silence, adj. Gives the game away to the Jerries if you use the radio – except in an utter emergency, right at the end when you're back over England –'

'Damn,' said Mackenzie, interrupting his explanations, 'they're flashing us to go round. Last thing I want, adj, is to bog down in the bloody grass again. Still, this bit of the drome's a bit drier, I suppose. It's the hump in it. Bloody nuisance. All this build-up and it won't even count towards our tour if they scrub us. Maybe you can see now this is what everyone says is the worst time, not when you're actually off and on the job.'

Blanding nodded in whole-hearted silent agreement.

'Engines still heating up, skip.'

Mackenzie boosted one of the port engines and the great plane slowly, with a squeal of released brakes, started to wheel round and off the peri track.

'Flash them behind, rear-gunner.'

'Aye, aye, skipper.'

After some uncomfortable jolting and revving up of one of the engines on the other side, A-Able regained the hard surface.

'We're swinging in to the end of the runway now, adj.'

Finally they felt a buffeting from the four props of the plane in front of them as it revved to full power, swung surprisingly smartly round the corner onto the runway and started moving off. Us next, thought Blanding watching its navigation lights, and listening to the engineer fussing.

'Port outer in the red, skip.'

Anticipating the start, Mackenzie ordered full throttle, holding the brakes. There was the slightest movement of the deck beneath Blanding's feet as the tail seemed to start rising slightly. Blanding could make out the silhouettes of people in the illuminated doorway of the chequered control caravan and another, dimmer and less distinct gaggle of them beside the runway, standing and waving. Maybe Diana was among them. Paradoxically he felt sorry for them, standing in the cold wind and the noise. At least it wasn't raining. A double green flash came from the control caravan and 'we're off,' said Mackenzie, almost with relish.

There was sudden grim silence on the intercom as the plane hurtled down the runway. Blanding could not see anything, having resumed his seat on the cot, but he could feel the huge wheels trundling heavily over the concrete, then bumping and banging and skipping. It seemed to continue for ever and all the time he was very aware of a knot of snakes writhing in his stomach and his molars grinding involuntarily. Then he sensed the plane was no longer vibrating in the same way, and for a moment there was an near-imperceptible feeling of lightness, his stomach surged and amidst the earsplitting noise he felt bile ascending. Then came an unexpected heavy bump, he experienced a moment of panic, heard a curse from Mackenzie, and once more the plane seemed to float. Abruptly the floor tilted as the nose rose.

'Christ, come on girl.'

'Skipper, the port –'

'Shut up, man, I'm not going to shut it down now am I ye damn fool! It's okay, we're off. We're unstuck. Come on, girl, climb, climb.'

'Thought we were goners there, skip, the way those trees –'

'All right, bomb aimer. Keep off the intercom everyone now, unless it's really important. You all right, adj?'

Surprised, he tried to reply to Mackenzie in measured tones but his voice cracked like an adolescent's. He cleared his throat, realized he hadn't pressed the intercom button, did so and gravely assured the pilot that he was fine.

'We're going to have to climb slowly, we're not getting full power out of the engines.'

'Port's easing back out of the red now, skipper,' said the flight engineer. 'Must have been all that stooging around on the peri track.'

As they spoke in the strange overpitched voices created by the intercom electronics, Blanding had the impression that he could hear the roar and hiss of great ocean waves crashing as surf onto a vast beach. No one was now speaking and the sea sound continued. It seemed to have the same rhythm as his breathing.

'Whoever's still switched on, switch off,' said Mackenzie suddenly, 'it's bloody irritating.'

Blushing unseen in the darkness, Blanding switched off his throat microphone which had faithfully been transmitting his breathing to the crew. Well, at least we've got through the take-off, he thought, but even he, a complete landlubber as he was now forced to admit, could tell that the climbing for height was a continuing relentless struggle. From time to time he glanced forward and saw minor movements of the flight engineer's head and shoulders as his unseen arm made some adjustment to the controls.

'Think port outer's on fire, skip. There was a flash of something –'

Was that the bomb-aimer? The voices all sounded the same.

'Feathering.'

'Fire extinguisher.'

'Seems okay now, skip. No more flames anyway.'

'Still got three engines - '

'All right, flap over. No more chatting.'

After some minutes, during which time Blanding strained his ears listening for any change in the rhythm of the engines, Mackenzie clicked back on again.

'Not the best start, adj. Means we'll not get to our height so easily. If at all. And we'll be slower. Keep an eye on the other engines, flight engineer.'

'We're at 9000 feet, switch on oxygen.'

Darkness and one continuous vibrating roar, the muffled shape of the pilot against the banks of low-glowing instruments, the bulky shape of the engineer beside him on his right, an occasional popping in the ears. He wondered what would happen if his nosebleed started again. Even Blanding knew that although the many other bombers in the vicinity were still showing navigation lights, they all shared the unspoken fear of collision as the huge machine clawed its way blindly upwards through the wisps of cloud Even through the intercom, Blanding could hear the strain in the young pilot's voice. This was what he had volunteered for – indeed, what he'd almost pleaded to return to – to bear the responsibility for this aircraft and every soul in her, and here he was rushing blindly upwards in darkness with invisible aircraft ahead and behind, a small fleck amongst the three streams of aircraft converging on the assembly point halfway across the North Sea to Holland, knowing every minute as they climbed that the second most dangerous enemy to the night bomber was the risk of collision – a hardly glimpsed shape suddenly through the cloud ahead and then an almost instant annihilation. The anxiety was almost palpable, and Blanding found himself swallowing hard and willing his stretched nerves to somehow calm themselves.

'Right, skipper, according to my calculations, we should just about be clearing the coast now – another fourteen minutes on this heading and we should have reached the assembly point.'

'Right-oh – thank you, navigator. We're still nowhere near high enough, lads.'

The plane suddenly shuddered and shook as if crashing into something solid, and there was a sharp exclamation from someone and the captain's voice, now having recovered some of its matter-of-fact air, explained: 'Just hit turbulence from a plane ahead of us.'

'Could be a Jerry, skipper, unless there's someone else flying low like us.'

Blanding tightened his double-gloved hands and drank hard at the oxygen that had been coming into his mask ever since they climbed past the nine-thousand feet mark, and wondered about

Diana – if she had gone searching for him, if she now knew where he was. He regretted causing her pain. Once more someone she cared about – possibly not as deeply as the others – might fail to return and once again she would have a long vigil to endure before knowing either way. He closed his eyes a moment and willed himself to contact her. Prayer had never felt so useless.

'Bomb-aimer to navigator, I can see Aldeburgh below.'

'Thanks, Lofty. Okay, skipper, steer 137 now, we should cross the Belgian coast in about twenty minutes.'

'Thank you, navigator. Well, adj, we're still climbing obviously, but at least we haven't collided with anyone. That bloody moon is helping us at the moment at least. Unfortunately we're not going to be able to keep up with the main bomber stream. But we'll follow our course as best we can. If we lose another engine we'll have to jettison our bombs in the sea and turn back, but with three engines I'm going on. We'll show 'em what a sprog crew can do.'

'Crossing the Belgian coast in about five minutes, skipper,' piped a voice in his ear-phones which Blanding assumed would be the navigator. Mackenzie spoke and Blanding knew that once more a lot of what he would say would be for his benefit.

'This is where we might get the first flak. Those bloody flak ships.'

Blanding came and stood behind the flight engineer and peered out down into the differing pitches of darkness, looking for the loom of the coastline where they would actually cross into enemy territory – enemy-occupied, anyway. He saw some pallid flashes obliquely ahead and thought that must be the flak. The flight engineer had seen them as well and jabbed a well-padded finger for the pilot's benefit. Mackenzie did not appear to be impressed – once again Blanding was struck by the difference between the nervous boy standing outside the station commander's office like a wrong-doer waiting for the attentions of the headmaster, and the relaxed authority of the man commanding the aircraft. He had to remind himself this was not a seasoned veteran completing his tour, but a near-sprog, on his fourth or fifth op, and his first as far as Germany was concerned. Blanding's one comfort was that he had been right to give Mackenzie the benefit of the doubt although when the chop came he would not expect to be thanked for it.

'That's not flak, those are bombs. Ours.'

The navigator put in his threepennyworth: 'It's a well-known way of gaining extra height, adj. Some of the duff kites really do need to do it.'

'Probably that plane whose turbulence we hit.'

The headphones hissed and Blanding felt some comment was awaited.

'I don't understand. You'll have to spell it out for me.'

Mackenzie replied.

'Some of our boys are well-known for dropping their cookies in the sea on the quiet – who's going to report them? There goes another.'

'That's monstrous, that's a waste of public funds.'

'Maybe, but there's a lot to be said for it,' said Mackenzie. 'Lighter plane, more miles to the gallon, higher speed, higher altitude. Bit less to blow up, too.'

'I wonder those scoundrels don't simply drop everything and run for home.'

'I wonder if you get so quite so aerated, adj, about private lives being wasted?' He recognized the navigator's voice.

'Of course that's not what I meant, I'm not a monster, but you mean it's common knowledge this kind of thing goes on?'

'Of course it is,' said Mackenzie. 'We may be sprogs but even we know which crews regularly drop early. Common knowledge.' ('That's right, skipper.')

'D'you report this?'

'Of course not.'

'Wait till we've landed back home again, adj, ('Cross fingers,' from an unknown voice) and then let's see if you feel the same way about things.'

Blanding thought this might be a good time to resume his place at the rest bed, reflecting as he sat down how inappropriately named it was. Could one imagine a crew member, the rear-gunner for example, saying 'I feel a wee bit sleepy, Skip, I think I'll nip along to the old rest bed for forty winks.' No, it was obviously provided for a wounded man, somewhere where he could perhaps be treated, or patched up, until everyone got home. Or quietly die.

It was dark where he was: he could see a thin slit of light at the navigator's black-out curtain, and further forward the pale greenhoused night sky of the cockpit, but here where he was perched even his own gloves resting on his knees were virtually invisible to him. Mackenzie's voice cut in on his headphones.

'Don't know if you can see those flickers from back there, adj, but there's a wee bit of flak from time to time. Only isolated batteries so far, but there's some nastier stuff not far ahead, so be prepared.'

Blanding realized, almost with a jolt that his two earlier emotions – bluntly put, fear and excitement – had dwindled away to be replaced by a mixture of tiredness, boredom, discomfort and impatience for the whole thing to be over. He yearned for his bed, its lumpy mattress, itchy blankets, thin sheets, hard pillow. What's more, he was missing his habitual mug of cocoa, courtesy of Sgt Tomkins, before turning in. Good God, he thought, I'm turning into an old man, I'm more put out by the discomfort than the danger. Inside the unlighted, jolting, jouncing and creaking airframe, the coldness and the vast continual noise, he was reminded of an endless night-time journey in the back of a open lorry crossing the Anatolian plateau years before when he was a student come to Turkey in his summer vacation to track down the ruined cities of classical Greece. And here he was now, helping to make ruined cities. But perhaps they were modern legionaries, representatives of the civilized values of Greece and Rome, once again dealing with the benighted barbarians in their dark forests on the other side of the Rhine.

The bomber laboured onwards and eastwards; from time to time terse words were heard, almost distantly, in his headphones as the crew did their jobs. The bomb-aimer passed landmarks on to the navigator; the navigator gave headings to the pilot; the engineer reported fuel levels; the mid-upper reported a plane on fire and going down.

Blanding found he was starting, despite everything, to nod off. That was unacceptable – although he had no duties to perform, he couldn't sleep while others risked their lives. He deliberately turned his inward attention to the recent terrible events on the station. Who on earth had killed Corporal Summerfield? What had been so terrible about her death? There was no sign of the wounds you might expect from a savage no-holds-barred assault. Rape would probably have been terrifying enough, but it did not seem that that had happened. Perhaps she had seen something horrific to produce that expression of stark terror on her features. Blanding snorted, mentally recalling the lurid cover of a Wheatley novel someone had left in the mess. The characters had been involved in fighting Nazi Germany on the astral plane, and Poppy's expression would be what a reader might have expected to find on someone who had died of fright, after coming face to face with the devil. Blanding cast around and recalled Holmes' famous advice: "Consider the facts, Watson." All very well but in this case nothing seemed to be what it was. The barking man who turned out to be not a raving homicidal lunatic but Tex Crawford, who Blanding knew instinctively was a kind man – he couldn't be the one, surely? What about one of the Poles? They sometimes turned his stomach with the bloodthirsty things they said, but to butcher a mere girl? Or perhaps the perpetrators were a gang of erks. That was an interesting possibility no one had yet considered (although Detective Chief Inspector Stanley was a sly old dog). Perhaps if a search were to be made of the scruffy huts which most groundcrews erected near their hardstandings? Botched together from scrounged material and often decorated with cheerful slogans and 'their' kite's score, typically housing beat-up old armchairs and paraffin stoves for tea-making, allowing groundcrews to wait up, often playing cards, until their lads returned, they were a very necessary evil from the official point of view. Utterly unsanctioned as they were by authority but nevertheless providing a place of relative warmth for the mechanics who had to do all but the most drastic maintenance at all hours out on the bare concrete, exposed to the howling wind and weather, Blanding did what all station adjutants did – he looked the other way. He was well aware that Waaf girlfriends sometimes went out to the planes on their dispersals when a loved one was flying – what if Corporal Summerfield had arranged a secret love nest for a day or two and something had gone wrong. Perhaps the killers were groundcrew. Maybe someone in aircrew had come to an arrangement with his erks to borrow their hut, and had met Poppy there. The paraffin smell and the oil might have come from the hut. Blanding thought he would mention it to the detective in the morning. It seemed a promising line of approach, much more so than pursuing a well-educated, harmless chap like Francis Nelson as a suspect. And yet nobody really knew what went on inside another person, the seemingly nicest people were sometimes revealed to be the most vicious.

Blanding was making an effort to gather together once more what he knew – for some reason, thinking was more laborious for him – when there was a sound like thrown gravel hitting the plane, as if off a shovel, and then, after a pause, some heftier thumps while the plane jinked and bounced. There was a sudden clang close to Blanding's right ear and simultaneously he noted the navigator's curtain twitched and a yellow hole appeared in it. Christ, thought Blanding, we're being hit. Up front he could see the flight engineer's silhouette moving.

'Christ, Pete,' it was Mackenzie's voice, 'something just knocked my bloody arm away.'

'This ruddy flak. I think we've got some damage in the instruments over my side, Skip.'

'We can't get any higher? We need another few thou quick. This is going to get worse after Liège – '

'There's nothing left, Skipper, not on just the three engines.'

'Skipper, nav here, we're past Liège I think, about half an hour before we turn south-east.'

'Look, there's some more kites burning down there.'

'There's goes somebody, port beam. Came from above us.'

'Christ, all we need are the night-fighters.'

'All right, chaps, let's settle down. Keep your eyes skinned, gunners.'

After a while, Mackenzie came back on the intercom.

'We'll be over Germany now then, nav?'

'Aye, skipper, can't be far from the Rhine. Lofty'll sing out as soon as he sees a big river. That shouldn't be too diffic –'

'Right, we've got no choice or we'll be catsmeat before we even get to the target. Bomb-aimer, drop the cookie as soon as you're ready. I hope you're noting this all down, adj, on your wee piece of paper.'

After a while Blanding felt the bomber give a sudden lurch like a dinghy breasting an unusually high wave, and he did not need the bomb-aimer's announcement to know what had happened.

'Cookie away, skipper. I've reset things so we can dump the rest in one go.'

'Good work, bomb-aimer. Right, that's four tons gone so we should get some speed and height now, maybe catch up with the stream.'

'There she goes,' came a shout from rear-gunner. 'Pity the poor bastards who caught that lot.'

'Och, it's probably just a few cows.'

'Jerry cows.'

'Poor buggers, anyway.'

'Pipe down now, crew. Keep your minds on the job.'

Only a few minutes passed and it appeared that Mackenzie

282

was satisfied with their new rate of climb. The flight engineer reported the damage to the instrument panel and as far as Blanding could gather it appeared to be fairly minimal, only the back-up bomb release controls having been damaged. Another ten minutes of intercom silence passed and then the engineer cut in to say he had a pleasant surprise, he hoped. Someone gave a knowing chuckle over the intercom. Puzzled, Blanding waited.

'Sorry, crew, didn't mean to keep you in the dark' said Mackenzie sounding very breezy. 'Pete's got the duff engine restarted and so we're going upstairs as fast as we can just in case it packs up again. We should be able to keep that height.'

Shortly afterwards came the now familiar but still terrible sound of shrapnel rattling against the fuselage, a harder clunk from forward and then a flow of cold air began streaming aft – it was obvious some of the glazing had been shattered. Blanding peered forward but could not make anything out, then for a moment they were like cats on the road in frozen surprise dazzled by the headlights of a car racing towards them. A searchlight beam flicked across the plane, the cockpit lit up like daylight – Blanding was startled to see colour again, the ox-blood brown of a flying jacket, a yellow oxygen bottle, even some pink of Mackenzie's profile as he looked over at his engineer, then blackness poured over them again. By and by the searchlight returned, lingeringly – this time it allowed Blanding to clearly see the engineer crouching and apparently looking down the steps to the bomb-aimer's compartment. Mackenzie threw the plane to port and once more gloom was restored.

'God, that wasn't too difficult for once, we've lost it. Intercom check, call in everyone.'

Only Lofty, the bomb-aimer appeared to be in trouble and cursed savagely until called to order by Mackenzie.

'Sorry, Skip. I can't see a friggin' thing. That flak's knocked a hole in the perspex, but I've got something in my eye, a lump in my eye, ah, Christ, I can feel it when I move – there's blood coming from somewhere.'

'Look, Lofty, get up here to the rest bed. Adj, see if you can patch him up.'

Presently the small figure in his bulky flying gear appeared, and slumped down on the bunk, flapping the dangling oxygen tube in a kind of desultory comic manner. Blanding was in a quandary, he couldn't unplug himself. And how could he see what to do? The bomb-aimer lay back and started wiping at his face with the back of his gloves. Blanding pulled them away, visualizing quite clearly diamond-like shards of perspex being pushed further into the man's eyeball. Someone clapped him on the shoulder, the plane lurched again, a voice shouted into his ear.

'Plug him into where you are, adj, and yourself into the walk bottle here.' This latter was a fat, yellow cylinder close at hand. The flight engineer played a torch briefly on the bomb-aimer's face. Apart from the dreadful smears of red blood, he looks drunk, thought Blanding. Such a silly smile. The bomb aimer tried again feebly to wipe his eyes.

'Maybe you'd better wrap this gauze around him, adj. He's no use to us, now, poor booger. I mean, he can't see, can he? Maybe he's got his blighty wound.'

'He's acting strangely, though, don't you think, for a superficial wound? Is it shock?'

All Blanding could make out was vague movements in the darkness as the flight engineer appeared to be fiddling with something. The torch flashed for an instant and a padded finger jabbed urgently towards the oxygen hose. Blanding gestured to show he failed to understand. Then the engineer's voice came through his headphones.

'His hose has been holed, adj. There's a ruddy great tear down here. Hopeless. It must've happened when we got hit. He's not been getting his oxygen. Christ, what are we going to do? There isn't a spare.'

'I've got it – '

'Never mind that, adj,' came Mackenzie's voice. 'See if you can wrap the hose somehow. You're going to have to leave him until we've done our run. Then you can share your mask with him. It's touch and go, but there's no choice, lads. If we fly lower, we're obviously going to get shot down more easily. If we do lose Lofty, he'll not be in much pain when he goes, that's for sure.'

'Just for a wee cut on the face? Is that wha' he has?'

'Tom, you'll let me know when you have a better plan maybe?'

'Sorry, Skip, but it seems awfu' hard on him.'

Mackenzie did not reply.

In the darkness Blanding fumblingly tugged at Lofty's helmet and goggles but could not shift them until he had taken his own gloves off, placing them carefully down on the deck between his feet so that he would be able to find them again in the darkness. Now he felt sticky blood on his fast-freezing hands, and wound a roll of gauze round and round the wounded man's head. There was nothing to cut it with so he kept going until it was all used up. He secured the bandage by putting the bomb-aimer's goggles back on, down over this eyes. The other roll of gauze he wrapped around the oxygen hose, and then as an afterthought wiped blood off the bomb-aimers's face and forehead and smeared it over the gauze. Maybe that would help a little to seal the gauze when it congealed. The man now appeared to have passed out. Blanding took his slumped weight and eased him down onto the cot, then lifted his feet in the bulky flying boots up so that he lay flat. With every movement he made some part of his body came into contact with part of the plane – he felt as if he were some nightmare, steadily growing like Alice inside a tiny house, or maybe the other way round. As he worked his gloves on again Blanding feverishly tried to remember all the first aid courses he had attended. Had anyone said "Always elevate a head wound" or was it the feet? God knows, he thought wearily.

'Crew, skipper here. We're going on although Lofty's in trouble. We're pretty sure we can see the show's already started up ahead, so there's not far to go. Adj, you'd better get down into the nose.'

For a moment Blanding thought Mackenzie was thinking of his comfort, knowing that the cot was now occupied by a wounded member of the crew and Blanding had no alternative but to stand. He was soon disabused of that idea.

The gloomy outline of the flight engineer stood and flipped the seat up (it made Blanding think of someone in a cinema letting a late arrival pass after the film had started) to allow access. Blanding hesitated, and looking Mackenzie's way he was surprised to be given a kind of slow, almost rhythmic thumbs-up. He found he took comfort from this fatherly gesture from someone who was nevertheless really no more than a boy. The plane bucked a little and the adjutant almost tumbled down the two or three steps down into the nose. It was surprisingly roomy – indeed it felt almost like stepping outside – and afforded a forward and downward view of darkness blotched and smeared with fires, constellations of distant flashes and steadily burning lights far ahead.

Blanding slid into the prone position on a fat oblong cushion on which he could see dark smears which had to be blood. His eyes were drawn with fearful fascination to the light show outside although he knew his first priority was to find the outlets and plug in his oxygen hose and his intercom. Searchlights toppled around the night sky like vast pillars of light somehow mounted on swivels. Occasionally they crossed and he almost expected to see them shatter against each other in clouds of smoke and sparks. In this part of the bomber the roaring of the engines was not quite so loud – indeed there was something calming in the aquarium-like feel of the bomb-aimer's 'office'. The patter of flak shrapnel did not now make his bowels contract – seeing what was outside, he recognized, was making things a little easier. For the first time that evening he felt relatively at ease. He could smell the cordite in the night air.

'One of ours I think on our starboard beam about 200 foot higher.'

'Got him. Yeah, that's a Lanc all right.'

'That's about ten burning on the ground I've seen from back here in the last five minutes.'

'It's sheer slaughter –'

'Quiet now, laddies,' came Mackenzie's calm, crisp voice. 'Bomb-aimer – that's you from now on, adj – we may have to jettison the rest of our eggs. But we'll do our damndest to drop 'em somewhere near the target. If we do jettison, you'll need to look back through that wee window behind you there afterwards to make sure there are no hang-ups –'

'Hang-ups?'

'Bombs left in the kite. Engineer, you'd better go down and brief the adj, tell him what to do, there's not long to go now.'

In that confined space, the engineer came as close as he could, gave him a rather sickly smile and then started bellowing into his ears beneath the lifted earphones and occasionally jabbing with a gloved hand towards the instruments.

'Well now, adj, see that panel with the row of switches on your right? ...'

It appeared that they couldn't drop the bombs from the cockpit as the bomb release controls up there had been damaged by the flak. The front turret was probably unserviceable as well. That meant that dropping the rest of their bombs and incendiaries had to be done using the jettison bars in the nose, and that meant Blanding had to do it. Blanding was told not to worry too much about the bomb sight but just to drop on command. Finally the engineer seemed satisfied that Blanding knew what to do and left him in peace. He lay there gazing through the bubble at the soft blackness of the night — the great mass of distant flashes and the steadier less intense lights among them had in the meantime come much closer. Paradoxically the land below them now looked utterly black, with very occasional pin pricks of light. Then they passed majestically over what appeared to be a large rural bonfire, almost a cheery sight. A few minutes later, another one. Gradually Blanding realized that the flames came from downed bombers burning on the ground, these were the bonfires that the rear-gunner was counting, each one a grim pyre to seven dead. As the minutes went by he saw more, off to the left and to the right: the dead planes were performing a last service of guiding their comrades to their target or, was it, of escorting them to their deaths.

Blanding lay there, his chin resting on his arms crossed in front of him, seeing in his imagination the shades of warriors, still bewildered by their sudden ejection from this world, gathering on the far bank of the Styx, waiting for more of their comrades who they knew would soon be joining them.

The sky was still too light for the flyer's comfort but not as harshly moonlit as before. Ahead the distant conflagrations, swinging this way and that across the useless bombsight as Mackenzie made the plane weave. Very, very slowly it seemed, burning Nuremberg moved inexorably towards him. Occasionally the plane bounced and jigged like a boat crossing a wake. Now he had time for his night thoughts. Like a tumbling leaf his mind's eye skittered down thousands of feet of cold air to where there were forests and fields, hills and meadows, sleeping rabbits and roosting buzzards, lanes and bridleways, ploughland and orchards, farm worker's cottages with curtains drawn to stop light escaping, children abed, wide-eyed in the gloom of bedrooms, listening to the terror flyers droning past overhead like giant invisible bumblebees in the dark. In the cities the picture would not be so cosy perhaps: grizzling overtired children in dank basements amid the tense silence of adults. And it would be his finger on the button that would bring death to these women and children.

CHAPTER TWENTY-TWO

'I'm worried about the engines, skip. That port outer keeps desynching.'

'Deal with it later, Pete, no time now, we're there.'

Suddenly they were there too, hanging above an awesome brightness of teeming and rolling fire, constantly changing, bubbling and boiling. It was a moth's eye view into the coals of a vast fire, a fire spitting out streams of red and yellow sparks, a fire which pumped out billowing clouds of acrid smoke (Blanding could even smell it). Like avenging angels they flew above a map of a city in hell, printed in blackness and flame, and it was hard to think of there being living creatures like themselves down there. Searchlight beams thrashed in slow dreamlike motion about the sky like the canes of blind men, occasionally catching a tiny silver plane, whereupon others would swing across with malign intelligence to pin the intruder so the flak could get him. There were horrifying mid-air explosions too. Blanding felt utterly exposed.

'Okay, adj, when your bombsight – I mean the whole sight – covers the markers – those green flares down there – count a slow twenty and press the tit. Just say 'ready' first and then 'bombs gone' check for hang-ups and that's it. We'll no bother about the photo in the circumstances.'

Blanding heard a couple of ironic cheers.

Events moved very quickly. More flak pattering, a dark shape passed very close below them and with horror Blanding realized it was another Lancaster. Pulling his eyes away from its flame-defined silhouette he realized with a shock he couldn't see the markers now, then he saw them away to one side, moving away from the plane's heading.

'Um, adjutant here. We're going off-line, I think, skipper. To the right.'

288

'Okay, bomb-aimer' – Blanding noticed the slight emphasis – 'guide me back, just say "left", "right" or "steady".'

Blanding did as he was told, guiding Mackenzie until the core of the inferno slid behind the outline of the bombsight. He began slowly counting to himself and with a tremble in his voice said 'Bomb-aimer to pilot, ready', pressed the tit and said 'Bombs gone.'

For a moment he felt himself pushed into the cushion as the aircraft jumped in response to the weight shed.

'Let's get out of here. Adj, you'd better get back here and look after Lofty.'

'Something on our tail, skipper! Corkscrew left! Left!'

Mackenzie threw the plane into a sudden dive, almost standing it on a wingtip and Blanding, who had, preparatory to leaving the nose, unplugged his air and intercom, was in the midst of turning on the cushion on his hands and knees when he was thrown up towards the turret, and held there and then dropped, not feeling the agonizing impact of angular metal against his skull until after it had actually happened. The next corkscrew came without any warning at all for Blanding as he now had no intercom. Something took him by the scruff of the neck and shoved his face up hard against the bomb-bay window before releasing him just as suddenly. He lay panting where he was until things quietened down. Another surge of panic: how long had he been without oxygen? Was it already too late? Blanding almost shot up the steps to the cockpit, thrust his way to his old position by the bunk and plugged in. At that point he remembered he was supposed to check for hang-ups.

'– think we've lost him, skipper.'

'Right-oh, home and glory.'

Blanding found Lofty lying unattended on the deck in front of the main spar. His oxygen mask had come off. With a sinking feeling, Blanding realized he had no choice but to swap oxygen masks with someone who might already be dead. Passing a mouthpiece back and forth would be ridiculously impracticable. First he heaved the unconscious bomb-aimer, heavy enough despite his bantam build, back onto the rest bed. Switching the mouthpieces was not as difficult as he had feared but chill fear returned as he clapped the other man's bloody leather cup over his own nose and mouth. He couldn't feel or taste anything different in the air although he was now plugged into the walk bottle. He knew about the old trick of holding the mask in front of one eye to feel the oxygen blowing against the eyeball. It was all too much effort. Gently he held the torn section of the hose inside his gloved hands, cupped them together almost as if in prayer. If it did not work he would slowly and imperceptibly become intoxicated and pass out and die. There was no alternative as far as he could tell. At least he had performed the duties expected of him and a younger man might live.

'Adj to skipper. Just to say I've fixed up Lofty's oxygen. He's passed out, I'm afraid, but I think he's still breathing. Um, I need the Elsan –'

'Good show, adjutant. Yes, go ahead. You might as well stay back there for the moment. Good show.'

For some reason Blanding was experiencing a strong urge to vomit, but he dreaded making a mess of the plane, not to mention the fact that he would never hear the end of it. Clambering yet again over the main spar, it occurred to him that he probably had more elbow room in his own little Morris two-seater. It wouldn't be too long before he could be seeing it again, now they were on the homeward leg. No, he had forgotten – he wasn't going home. Feeling his way aft in the darkness, he nearly smacked his head into the dangling boots of the mid-upper gunner, and had to chuckle. There was no problem finding the Elsan – quite simply, it stank. He must have issued quite a few memos about the need to clean them out between flights, but nobody wanted anything to do with latrine duties. Indeed, groundcrew got quite shirty if anyone did use it, and it was customary for aircrew to pay them a hefty tip to clean up if anyone did have an accident aboard. Relations became strained for a while. Arrived at the Elsan, Blanding gripped its rim with stiff arms, opened his throat and prepared to vomit, but nothing came except an enormous belch. He giggled, imagining the glances exchanged between the men aboard, and realizing the noise of the engines had masked his eructation, he giggled again. They really weren't too bad, these raids – it was the first one which was obviously the hardest, and now they were going home. God, he felt sleepy. The engines sounded as if they were in the next room and inside the engine noise he could hear the voices of his mother and father talking quietly so as not to wake him as he slept in the back of the car coming back in the late summer evening from Weston.

His ears were split open again by the engine noise, somebody was gripping his shoulder and shaking him, bellowing in his ear so close he could feel the man's warm breath. It still dark. Fear had slipped back into his accustomed place. He was pulled upright, made to lean against the thin walls of the Lanc. There was a fumbling at the front of his flying jacket and harness, and then, clarity in his ears.

'You okay, adj?'

'Oh, God, my head's splitting.'

'Press the button to speak.'

'Is he okay, Peter?'

'Blanding here. Yes, I'm okay, skipper, I must have dozed off.'

'Dozed off be damned. Your oxygen line's ripped, just like Lofty's. If that had happened on the way out, well – '

'Where are we?'

'Just crossed the coast, adj. We lost that bloody engine again ten minutes ago but there's not far to go. Still could be night-fighters around, mind.'

'Lofty?'

'Breathing just fine,' said the engineer. 'But still unconscious.'

'You'd better come up to behind the main spar, adj, ready for landing. It might be difficult, we haven't got an airspeed indicator. Some fluke bit of flak must have knocked away the pitot head.'

A few ribald remarks were added over the intercom.

'Rear-gunner here. Don't worry, adj, I know the sound the slipstream makes over my turret so I can give the skipper a good idea when he's on the button – '

'All right, quiet now chaps. Gunners keep your eyes peeled.'

Blanding stood, head throbbing, behind the main spar, looking ahead and the sky seemed to be lightening. It had to be a little after five o'clock. A shout of triumph and the airfield flares of Frampton Wissey were sighted.

'All right, everyone strap in tightly, just in case. You, too, engineer. Hold on tight, adj, we're going round. All right.'

'Permission to pancake, skip. They say we're the first back.'

'Not there yet,' growled someone.

'Over to you, rear-gunner, sing out, we're going in.'

The bomber dropped so that Blanding's stomach seemed to bob on its moorings. All the rear-gunner needed to call out was 'hold that', 'fine', 'lovely' and then finally the wheels bumped down hard, and Mackenzie applied the brakes.

Outside everything was still dark. A few points of light and a closer scatter of tiny yellow spangles – those damned leaks is the blackout blinds he was always trying to stamp out – which indicated the control tower and other station buildings or vehicles all moving relative to each other at different speeds as their plane moved. The lights suddenly wheeled away as the bomber swung at the end of the runway onto the perimeter track. Blanding, standing behind the flight engineer, with a splitting headache and a dry throat, turned his head to look through the windows on the other side and caught sight of headlights moving fast, then a shaft of light from the nose of another plane coming in – a downward-shining Aldis light where some poor bomb-aimer lay estimating and calling off the height for the pilot. A-Able was now trundling along parallel to the runway but in the other direction so they could all see the plane coming in to land. Blanding heard the now familiar voice of the flight engineer in his headphones 'He's down – oh no' and they saw a massive stream of orange sparks as if from a metal grinder. He was reminded of a puck hurtling across ice, and all the time hissing out jets of sparks. He could almost hear the screaming of metal being ground against the concrete. The dark shape of the stricken bomber seemed to lurch to one side as the port wheel collapsed. It swung with stomach-turning abruptness and lurched into the mud. The gloom was lifting rapidly now and Blanding could make out what he knew would be crash tenders and the blood wagon racing across the grass. He'd seen that often enough before, but from the tower.

'He'll be okay,' said Mackenzie in a curiously dead tone as if all tension had suddenly released. 'Adj, I'll stop very briefly on the track so you can nip out. You can't be seen from the tower for a few yards – it's the bulge in the field. You can drop down from the door at the back – leave your kit on the plane. We'll get it back for you. But make it nippy, we need to get Lofty to the sawbones.'

Blanding was dumbstruck for a moment or two. Mackenzie had obviously concluded that his passenger *had* made an unauthorized flight, probably coming to that inescapable conclusion as he had time to ruminate on the long haul home. Blanding wondered whether the young pilot wanted to protect him, or himself. Blanding was about to decline, since Chesterton would, he was sure, know by now where he was, when something – a feeling more than anything – made him change his mind. After letting Mackenzie know his decision, he went aft and struggled frantically out of his harness. He thought he might as well leave the rest of it on and hand it back in himself. He'd have to do that himself, he couldn't hide the stuff in his office and hope to sneak it back some time. Nothing could be hidden now, he knew he would have to come clean. Court-martial probably, then maybe stripped of his rank and posted as a humble aircraftman latrine-cleaner to Lincolnshire or worse.

The plane stopped, vibrating with the engines turning slowly. As he began clambering over the main spar, the flight engineer came over and shouted in his ear that he should leave the door open but not use the ladder. 'Just let yourself down easy-like.' With a friendly grin the engineer held out a hand for Blanding's oxygen mask.

'Lofty's breathing fine now, adj. We'll get that eye of his sorted out ... See you at interrogation?'

After wrestling ineffectually with the fuselage door, Blanding finally got it open and dropped down to the ground, landing a little awkwardly. It was a longer drop than he expected. His ears were ringing and he felt cold damp air on his face. In a crouching, shambling run he cleared the taxiway and looked back, got himself abeam of the pilot's window and waved. There was a roar of engines, some mechanical banging noises from the wheels and the monster moved slowly away. Blanding could clearly see the stationary prop of the engine closest to him. He gave another wave to the invisible occupant of the rear turret. Half-turning to walk on, Blandling nearly tumbled over what looked like an enormous watering can, almost invisible in the murk. He almost retched at the sickly emanations of paraffin from the flarepath marker.

In the pearly light between dawn and daybreak, Blanding suddenly realized he knew where he was. The change of angle in the peri fence, maybe, or the configuration of the lights now coming on in various parts of the station, and the disappearance of the tower lights masked as they were here by the crown of the airfield. He knew exactly where he was, and that he was back there again after precisely six days. Mackenzie had, in fact, dropped him close to that part of the fence where the dead girl had been found.

'Good God,' Blanding cried out aloud, giving himself a hefty cuff on the brow. 'Good God, it's so obvious. Of course, that's how she got here. They dropped her out of a plane.'

An implication seemed to be thrusting its head out of his mental mists and he fell silent. Whose plane? he wondered, but that wasn't it – the deeper implication was that the murderer looked likely to be one of Chesterton's beloved aircrew, or even an entire planeload. He knew which plane, too, but swerved instinctively away from the thought before a name was formulated. Blanding's elation switched abruptly to deep depression, and slowly, in his clumsy undersized flying boots and the elephantine bulk of his flying suit, he started the long trudge back across the airfield to the tower. Another returning Lanc was coming in and prudently he walked away again from the runway and waited. There was a huge jolt as it pancaked and roared past him.

By the time Blanding reached the ops room in the main building, the sun had risen above the flat horizon and A-Able's crew had already finished interrogation, and had gone to breakfast and then presumably bed. Another crew was now sitting round the table, munching biscuits and sipping rum-laced coffee while one of their number answered questions from the WAAF section officer conducting the interrogation. Blanding entered the hut to startled looks from the WAAFs and station officers. Ignoring them, Blanding walked slowly over to the ops board, and saw that his plane had been first back and two more had since landed.

As he spun on his heel to look back into the room he did not fail to notice how all eyes flicked away from his like minnows in a stream. Even the crew at the interrogation table had been gazing at him with mild curiosity. Back by the door he had entered by, he saw a familiar face, at its familiar station behind the coffee trolley.

'Thank you, padre,' said Blanding almost roughly as he took the proffered mug, hot and heavy with refreshing coffee. The chaplain raised his eyebrows and offered the nose of the rum bottle. Blanding grunted and nodded his head almost with a jerk. For some obscure reason, he felt ashamed of his desire for the slug of spirit. Thankfully, the padre was not going to pry.

'We appear to have taken some pretty severe knocks out there tonight – you'll have seen some of it?'

'Yes. I saw enough of it to last me a long time, padre. But I don't think it has sunk in even yet.'

The chaplain did not reply but Blanding caught sight of a depth of compassion in those eyes to which he could not help himself responding except by quickly closing his own doors to the outside. It was an awkward moment.

There was a sudden scraping of chairs on the scuffed floor littered with discarded paper and a confused din which reminded

Blanding more than anything of boys leaving a classroom at the end of a period. He felt an irrational flicker of irritation at the way they simply lurched to their feet, leaving their drained coffee cups and empty fag packets on the table rather than take them over to the hatch. Oh, what did it matter, was his immediate thought as he passed an automatic hand over his scalp to smooth his hair. The WAAF interrogator caught his eye and raised her plucked eyebrows in an invitation for him to bring his coffee over. It was soon clear there was no social component.

'Flight Lieutenant Blanding, sir, I wonder if you'd help me to clear up a few points regarding A-Able's mission?'

'Pleased to do anything to help,' murmured Blanding, taking a welcome seat and slumping back as he had seen so many men do who had just returned from their bout of 'dicing over the Reich.' He took a warming sip of his coffee and waited.

'This is rather difficult, adjutant,' said the WAAF officer after a while, blushing slightly and seeming to appeal to him with her eyes.

'For the record then – and I am sure this is known to the C.O. – I flew as a passenger with A-Able, and at all times came under the command of the pilot, Flt. Sgt. Mackenzie. How can I help?'

The WAAF seemed to relax slightly and gave him a hint of a grateful smile.

'Flt. Sgt. Mackenzie claims – and I should add this is backed up by his crew – that shortly after take-off he lost one engine and was subsequently forced to jettison his cookie.'

'That's correct – as far as I can judge as a mere penguin. Sgt Mackenzie explained over the intercom that we would not be able to keep up with the stream or even reach our height if we didn't. And I may add that I question the use of the word 'jettison'. We made sure we dropped it over enemy territory, that is, onto Germany, so 'jettison' is not really the correct word, is it? I take it that Sgt Mackenzie's action is already under scrutiny?'

'I can't really answer that now, sir. Perhaps if you asked me later, in your office ...'

'With my adjutant's hat on, I imagine?'

The WAAF smiled very faintly.

'What happened after that, sir? Did everything go smoothly after that? From the mechanical point of view, I mean.'

'Hard for me to say, but somehow the 'duff' engine started up again, so we actually managed to catch up with the stream.'

'But you landed on three engines.'

'Yes, it packed up again just after we started back over the channel, but I'm afraid I missed some of the last portion of our little excursion.'

Blanding found himself growing irritated when he realized the implication of the questions, and recognized too that the curtness of his replies was typical of returning aircrew until the rum had loosened them up. He stood up, and looking down at her, noticing the neat ring of plaited hair around her lowered head as she wrote on her pad, he said:

'Look, I would stake my life on the engine problem being genuine. I have come to hold a very high opinion of Sgt Mackenzie – and all of his crew. And now, if you'll excuse me, I need to find Group Captain Chesterton.'

The WAAF officer glanced up.

'You've just missed him, sir. He had just left to go to the tower – with Section Officer Taylor – when you came in –'

'Ah, good –'

'– but he did tell me most particularly to tell you, sir, that if I saw you you were to go to bed immediately as you would be worse than useless today if you didn't.' Blanding raised his eyebrows. 'He also would like you to come to his office at 10 ack emma.'

'Oh, I'm sure there's no need for that, Assistant Section Officer. I'll just cut along and –'

'No, sir.' She spoke most firmly and Blanding began to redden, aware that their interchange was being heard by a number of other people. 'I was further to tell you that that is an order and one he would like you – I'm sorry, sir, he told me to use these exact words – one he would like you to obey, for once.'

'Hmmph,' said Blanding.

'I'll have someone bring you a cup of tea at nine.'

'Damned nonsense,' he muttered and humphed again.

It was strange but no other returning aircrews had come in since his own arrival. A glance at the board told him that the squadron still had ten kites up and that now they were all starting to be overdue – that was why the atmosphere was so bleak, so tense. Egocentrically he had assumed his misdemeanour and the accompanying embarrassment was the cause of it. His little jaunt was a bagatelle in comparison with what was unfolding this night. All those planes he had seen burning on the ground or exploding in the

296

air, some of them had to be their own comrades, men from this very station. Blanding flushed and, although he could see for himself on the board, nevertheless asked the interrogating officer in a somewhat humbler tone:

'Have we had any losses, Mary?'

'We're expecting a few, sir. Um, the crew which just left told me they witnessed D-Dog – that's Kelly's boys – coned and shot down over Nuremberg. They were right alongside D-Dog and saw her take a direct hit from flak and explode immediately. No one could have got out. The SP's are already collecting their stuff but the Old Man won't let us wipe them off the board – '

There was a commotion at the door and the next crew, looking a little like a band of boisterous teddy bears in the bulky flying kit, tumbled into the room and the chaplain and coffee trolley was immediately lost to sight amongst them. Damn, thought Blanding, that's put the cap on it. With D-Dog gone, there will be no way of sorting out poor Poppy's death.

'Mary?'

'Please, adjutant. Please go, you'll get me into trouble. I must attend to this crew now.'

'No, no, don't concern yourself, I'm going – but it is absolutely imperative you get a message to the C.O. to hold Inspector Stanley here until I can see him, absolutely essential. Got that?'

She nodded gravely. Blanding in turn gave a curt nod, and threaded his way through the seven now rather more subdued airmen coming over to the table, cigarettes and pipes all smoking away. As they realized who had gone by in flying kit, he heard whistles or oaths of surprise, saw jaws drop and eyes stare at him. Halfway to the door he stopped, reflected that he could hardly be in worse trouble, and said 'Bugger orders' loudly to no one in particular. Still clutching his mug of coffee, he looked back reflectively into the room, intending to slip off his flying gear and take up his normal seat at the central desk. It must have been fully light outside and yet he still hesitated and finally decided against ordering the blackout curtains drawn, remembering Chesterton's outburst all that time ago. Daylight could be merciless: it somehow revealed the staleness of the air, the way everything human ultimately descended into squalor: overflowing ashtrays, empty cups ringed with coffee stains, scraps of paper littering the floor, sheer clutter and squalor. In that gloomy room, full of tired drawn faces, there was none of the brisk efficiency, liveliness, chaffing between the men and the women which was such a part of a normal ops night. No, the only word to use was 'funereal' and Blanding realized his further presence would be another form of self-indulgence. Better he got his head down so he could be some use later.

CHAPTER TWENTY-THREE

Despite being dog-tired, Blanding had no expectation of sleeping. His ears were still ringing, he still had a headache and his throat was sore as if he had been talking without stopping for hours. He sat down heavily on the narrow cot in his office storeroom tucked away in a largely dark and deserted building. With an effort he pulled off his shoes and sagged back against the wall, anticipating an hour or two of insomnia, his brain spinning, chewing the mystery of Poppy's death over and over, or pondering what he could usefully·say to Inspector Stanley now that Kelly and his crew had been lost, or being wracked with guilt at not being able to share what was happening in the ops room, or simply worrying about what Chesterton had in mind for him at what would certainly be a decidedly sticky interview. He could not rule out the possibility of a court martial; indeed, he thought he might count on it. The fact that he had gone with Mackenzie during his off-duty hours might well save him from a charge of desertion, but on reflection he was not even sure about that. He slept nevertheless.

Before he awoke he had heard a door close and when he awoke he knew someone had closed his door. His battered old alarm clock which resembled an engine-room gauge from a nineteenth century paddle steamer and which had so often been knocked to the floor by the sleeper's outflung arm informed him it was nine o'clock. The dark surface of a cup of RAF tea was still quivering. Blanding grunted, found that the headache was still with him. Barely had his lips touched the thick porcelain before the thought came that by the end of the day he might well be on his way to join the ranks of General Duties aircraftmen swilling out latrines or washing dishes in the cookhouse.

Now he heard muffled footsteps on the other side of the thin panel door separating his storeroom-cum-bedroom from his office. There was the low rumble of two male voices conversing, then the familiar sound of the glass vibrating in the outer door as it banged shut, presumably as someone left. Blanding swung his legs over the side of his cot, thrust his feet into the shoes waiting for him, combed his hair with his fingers until he could get to the washroom. His ears were still ringing from the noise of the Lanc, and there was the faint shrill tweedling noise in his ears too of extreme weariness.

Opening his door, after tidying his cot, he was relieved to find it was only the padre in his office. Although the latter had probably not had any sleep at all he still looked his fresh and lively self. An envelope had been placed in the middle of his desk. That could wait a few minutes he thought.

'Quite a butcher's bill last night, Blanding,' said the padre. 'News has been getting around that we may have lost as many as one hundred of our aircraft – no, be damned to that way of putting it – maybe seven hundred men – *seven hundred*, I say, Blanding – did not return at all. We personally appear to have lost six entire crews –'

Blanding muttered 'shocking, shocking' and 'if you'll excuse me a moment' and nipped smartly along the corridor to the officers' toilets to attend to a call of nature and splash some water over his face. As he stared at his gaunt face in the mirror, and noticed the unservicelike stubble on his chin, he could hear from down the corridor the voices of the WAAFs as they counted the mae wests, parachutes and other equipment recently handed back in by the returning crews – but this morning there was no cheeriness in their voices, no laughter, no need for him to send a clerk out to remind them they were not helping out at a vicarage jumble sale.

My God, he thought, six crews he said, six crews. Forty-two men. It was almost inconceivable. He could not recall them ever losing more than two kites on a single mission, most times it was just one. Obviously he had himself witnessed a few hours perhaps even more men dying but that did not seem to relate in any way at all to this terrible impingement on the daily life of the station. So many deaths in one go could not simply be shrugged aside with the usual RAF fatalism.

After another glance at the mirror with a feeling of something approaching self-disgust he pushed open the swing door into the corridor to see Diana coming out of his office. She caught sight of him and compressed her lips, approaching him at first unsmilingly and then with what to him was certainly a forced, professional brightness.

'Good morning, sir, I hope you have managed to snatch a couple of hours sleep.'

Blanding's heart sank.

'Diana, I –'

'Do you mind if I push on, sir, I'm late? I have to be over in the Technical Section in five minutes.'

He nodded. If that's the way you want it, he thought.

'Carry on, Mrs Taylor.'

Any other observations he might have had, in a private or an official capacity, would have of necessity been addressed to her departing back, so he kept silent, set his jaw and headed grimly back to his office to start tackling the unpleasant tasks this day would surely offer him. Damned women, he thought. It struck him, if he was not mistaken, that she had been wearing her service cap and carrying her gasmask case slung over one shoulder – surely not items required for talking to oily engineers in the cold draughtinesses of the maintenance hangars. Theirs, like most operational RAF stations, did not stand a great deal on ceremony, and quite a few of even the regular pre-war officers hardly wore their hats from one end of the day to the other.

Entering his office he nearly collided with a figure coming out. It was his chief clerk, Starling, who almost flinched when he caught sight of the expression on his superior's face.

'Any idea where Section Officer Taylor's headed, Starling? I'm not sure I heard right what she said.'

'Can't say, sir,' said the man, looking uncomfortable, 'but the CO's car has been pulled up outside for a while with the engine running.'

Blanding crossed to the window and there indeed was Chesterton's Humber in its drab wartime colours, and there was Diana slipping into the passenger seat. Blanding nearly strained his eyes but all he could make out of the driver was a peaked hat. With a jerk the vehicle pulled away, and Diana's pale profile framed in the car window traversed the metal frame of the window of his office and disappeared.

Blanding found the padre had come to stand beside him at the window and he now had no time to speculate why the CO should be driving her to the Technical Section, if indeed she had been telling the truth. Maybe he would find her present in Chesterton's office to

301

observe his downfall. Women, he thought despondently. One moment you were as close as two peas in a pod, the next they wanted to kill you. Roll on the end of the war and a return to good old Dulwich and what he did best. With some alarm he realized that this distant, yearned-for goal had somehow lost much of its previous appeal.

There was a dull double-thump at the door, and the padre went to let in two station policemen. Each man, shaved and immaculate of course, was bearing three large cardboard boxes balanced precariously on top of each other, and they had been compelled to knock with a well-polished toecap. Like sinister versions of Father Christmas they delivered their gifts, dropping the boxes onto Blanding's desk beside which the padre stood, now looking dismal. The SP's about-turned smartly, gave Blanding a parade-ground gaze, saluted (he thought he'd never seen so much saluting in such a short time since initial training) and left. Blanding caught sight of the names roughly chalked on the boxes, and knew the SP's would soon be back with more. They had lost five, possibly six aircraft, he knew, and they could have as many as forty boxes to go through. This duty which he shared with the clergyman reminded him of his years at Dulwich (would he ever return?) – the beat-up armchairs in his study, a small coal fire, a glass of sherry, and a quiet chat with the school chaplain about one of their youngsters who was in trouble. The SP's returned with more of their unpleasant cargo. This delivery of cardboard boxes was itself, he recognized, another hideous parody: of the school porters carrying in the boys' tuckboxes which had arrived by lorry from the railway station at the beginning of term.

'Let's make a start, then, padre,' said Blanding with a grimace. 'The sooner this justified prying is over the better.' He made a pretence of glancing briefly at a typed list. 'We'll do D-Dog and C-Charlie first.'

He thought he would have to assign some officers from stood-down crews to give a hand later. Each pair of officers officially constituted a 'committee of adjustment', a most Dickensian phrase for an unfortunate necessity. However, the fortunes of war meant that there was little risk of these officers uncovering embarrassing facts about erstwhile comrades only to find them subequently return, safe and well, to their colleagues in the mess. If those missing did return, the chances were that the officers on the committee of adjustment themselves had already departed, either for the next world or for a prisoner-of-war camp. Furthermore, most of those missing, he knew,

302

would be from the inexperienced, or 'sprog' crews, and these men would not have had a great deal of time to form relationships with aircrew who had been at Frampton Wissey for a while. Indeed, they could even be almost entirely unknown, having gone down on their first operational flight.

'Yes, it's a nasty task,' said the padre. 'If you'll permit?' He carried the first box, chalked P/O M Sherston, over to the better light at the window shelf where they habitually examined the contents of the boxes, weeding out matter which could be a security risk or even embarrass wives, sweethearts or parents (Blanding reflected ruefully on the amount of printed paper devoted to scantily clad popsies which he had torn up and deposited in his RAF wastepaper bin).

'Poor devil,' said the padre, pointing to the name on the box. 'Only the other day I was listening to Mark Sherston telling a most amusing anecdote in the mess – his father was in the church, you know, a rural dean, I believe. That laugh of his will be sorely missed.'

As he spoke both his and the adjutant's practised fingers dipped into the box and emerged with wads of letters. Blanding's heart sank. They would all have to be read, or at least skimmed through, before being sent with the rest of Sherston's belongings to RAF Colnebrooke.

'Lots of ladyfriends, he seems to have had – ' said Blanding, conscious of saying this solely to cover his embarrassment at reading private letters.

'I believe he had an inordinately large number of sisters.'

'Surely not this many.'

'Perhaps not,' agreed the padre reluctantly.

Blanding examined a couple of snapshots: one of a boy standing proudly beside a glider fuselage in what looked like a farmyard, and another of the same smiling face, but now become a young man, at the tiller of a small sailing craft, with another man grinning somewhat sheepishly at the camera and apparently tugging on a rope going over her side. Closer inspection showed that they were both, although inboard, plastered in mud up to their thighs. Then there was a battered address-book, filled with names apparently from all over the country – names of people who might not find out for months that he was gone, might even have died themselves in the meantime. None of his sisters would yet be weeping, none of this man's many friends could yet be aware that he was dead and his company could no longer be enjoyed again by anyone. His pipes would never be lit, his little open-seater would be disposed of, his well-thumbed volumes of Coleridge, Milton and Chaucer given away, the Nelson medallion from over his cot perhaps ending up in a junk shop. Once again Blanding reflected how much he hated this task: the life revealed was still fresh, the ink hardly dried on just-written letters. He wished he had the gift of flippancy or at least a thicker skin to get through it.

'Look, padre, we'll leave poor Sherston's stuff for the moment, there's much too much of it for today. Maybe we can do one more before I have to go and see the station commander. I'm going to have all these boxes put under armed guard. See to that, will you, sergeant,' he said to one of the SP's bringing in the next batch of boxes. 'There's going to be no room in here for anything else.'

'The next one's Pat Kelly,' said the padre, fetching the next box, which turned out to be much lighter, almost empty, to Blanding's disappointment. One photograph, that was all, of what were almost certainly his parents: a rangy, weatherbeaten couple standing on a wooden porch, with the vanes of an artesian well in the background. Blanding could almost smell the odour of hot, dried-out grass. It was like a view into another world, one stripped down to essentials.

'Although Kelly was Australian, I'd been seeing quite a lot of the poor chap in church quite recently. I mean, not many of the Australians here go to church,' he added, mistaking the meaning of Blanding's stare. 'Or anyone else, for that matter,' he added for honesty's sake after a while.

'Did you speak to him?'

'Well, we don't have confession here, of course, but no, Pat just said he wanted to sit in the quiet and think. I sensed he had a lot on his mind.'

'Well, we will just have a quick look at Kelly's stuff – it may have a connection with the death of Corporal Summerfield. Good God, if it isn't one person dying, it's someone else!'

The padre ignored Blanding's outburst, gently placing a cautionary hand on the adjutant's sleeve.

'Aren't the police and Special Investigation looking into that, adjutant? Don't you think we ought to leave this box alone?'

'Have no fear, padre, of me doing anything else illegal, but Kelly is not one of Detective Chief Inspector Stanley's suspects – at least, not to my knowledge. But we may nevertheless find something of interest, which I would of course tell him about immediately.'

The padre smiled bleakly but made no further protest. Kelly's possessions were meagre: disintegrating letters from home, some blurred snapshots of D-Dog with grinning aircrew and ground staff democratically mingled – snapshots illegally taken, almost certainly with Bomber Command film stock chopped up and sold by the bods in the photo lab and subsequently developed by them as well since cameras were officially forbidden anywhere but inside the billet huts – and finally and surprisingly a Bible. Blanding let the last letter fall. Reading the clumsily expressed but warm and comforting love of a wife for her husband separated from her by thousands of miles and possibly years – and now, too, unknown to her, by the grave – Blanding felt a surge of disgust at his own selfish pity for himself. No one would write like that for him, he had little confidence that his affair with Diana was anything more than a mutual urge for creature warmth and closeness engendered by the war. How many months, weeks or days even could it have lasted? It already seemed a thing of the past. Staring at the as yet unopened letter on the desk he found himself doubting whether love was even possible under these conditions. With an effort he forced his mind back to the matter in hand. He did not now think he would find anything in the boxes of the other members of D-Dog's crew either. If Kelly had been having an affair with the dead WAAF, surely there would have been something – a photo of the two of them, or of just Poppy, smiling sunnily into the camera, eyes squinted closed against the light. Perhaps, thought Blanding gloomily, the Australian had taken her photo with him. But once more his intuition insisted that there was nothing sinister about P.O. Pat Kelly. He wondered whether he felt that out of loyalty to his own version of events. It was still a theory, even if eminently plausible, and would remain so until they had evidence or a confession, and the latter was now, it seemed, impossible.

Blanding straightened up, his back aching, and pushed his fingers through his hair. He thought he had never felt so seedy.

'Tell me, padre, what do you make of all this talk about chop girls, jinxes and so forth?'

The padre pulled at his nose while he thought, and from time to time plucked at his mouth.

'Correct me if I'm wrong, adjutant, but there cannot have been many other situations in the history of warfare where a man is taken from warmth, safety, and relative comfort and plunged suddenly and *repeatedly* into and out of mortal danger, experiencing incredible nervous stress, perhaps even moments of utter hopeless terror. And that on an almost daily basis. These chaps know too that if they sat down and looked at things in a manner which their youth really forbids, they would realize that they too cannot be exempted from the almost mathematical certainty which condemns them to die long before the end of their tour. It might seem to them to be a Satanic form of roulette where the chips are mens' lives, and most of the numbers on the wheel are zeroes. (You are, I take it, familiar with roulette, Flight Lieutenant?) Perhaps I'm being overdramatic but you must appreciate the random impersonal element in whether they 'get the chop' or not.

'Now, gambling too has its share of superstitions – kissing your chips, getting an attractive woman to place them, having a lucky number, always taking the same seat at the table, and so on, and so forth. In gambling the individual may appeal to Lady Luck, gamblers are said to know when they have luck on their side, but whatever the case both flyers and gamblers are convinced there has to be some way of outwitting these diabolical mathematics. It is obvious to all that the poor devils who get the chop are not being judged by their conduct, death is meted out irrespective of whether you are a bit of a bad hat or a good man, like young Sherston, for example. Prayer, faith, and so on they feel will not help.'

'But the chop girls?' said Blanding, feeling the padre had wandered off the subject and hoping he was not being given a serving of warmed-up old sermon.

'Ah yes, the 'chop girls'. Here, too, one might say there is something almost atavistic – there are, of course, characters in Greek mythology who entice men to their deaths (we are all familiar with the Sirens). In Nordic myth, I believe there are maidens who actually bring about the deaths of heroes. In Celtic mythology, we have Vivian who persuaded Merlin to allow himself to be killed, and then, more in my field, there was Delilah who teased Samson's secret out of him and nearly brought about his destruction.

'But it is not simply something as hackneyed as the battle of the sexes,' continued the padre. 'There is something much deeper, I feel. Did you ever read Malinowski? Stuff of that sort. It was quite fashionable in my time at Jesus. All to do with mana and tabu. Somehow, mere proximity, emotional or otherwise, to one of these unfortunate creatures causes a transfer of some immanent power, a kind of negative mana – '

'I see,' murmured Blanding, unregarded.

' – which soon brings about the death of the recipient. One is reminded of the utter ill luck a menstruating woman can bring if even her shadow falls on a warrior's weapons. Christ himself sensed when a woman had touched his robes. No, somehow our airmen are digging down to a very primitive level in our souls – professionally, of course, I wish they would turn their faces upward to the light, but there it is. I'm sorry, Blanding, I don't appear to have explained anything, but merely maundered, or meandered.'

'Not at all, padre,' said Blanding with sincerity. 'It was most interesting. You don't, of course, feel the need to look for anything supernatural?'

'My cloth – my faith, I should say – forbids it, but I do feel that under great pressure the human mind may reveal powers which are otherwise scarcely suspected. In many cases, it is evident that some of our boys have a kind of precognition when some crews will not come back, and sometimes foresee their own deaths. That is something that most men will suppress immediately – just like the fact that most of their bombs will fall on women, children and innocent babies. That's something they will have to come to terms with later in life, if they survive.'

'I am sure of it,' said Blanding morosely, thinking of his own part played that night.

'All the same I do believe that 'chop girls' exist,' said the padre and Blanding gaped at him.

'I firmly believe there are women of a very intuitive and compassionate nature who sense that a particular individual is doomed, will soon die, and something makes them extend a kind of protective love over the damned man – condemned, I should say – who, of course, dies, notwithstanding this aegis over him. The sad thing is now that this faculty of empathy, instead of being a consequence of the situation, is seen by others as a cause of it, as a kind of witch's skill in pointing the bone.'

'Hmm, but I can't really see that, not of Poppy, Corporal Summerfield, that is.'

'No, no, of course not. Not everyone called a jinx girl is one. Perhaps very few. Once again, I fear I have not been helpful.'

'Not at all,' said Blanding for the second time. 'These are really very murky waters indeed, and any illumination will help.'

307

The appearance of the immaculate Warrant Officer Dawson in the office both startled Blanding and made him feel utterly squalid, unshaven as he was and still wearing the same small-clothes as he had worn that night. He hated to think of their sweat-sodden, bloodstained condition.

'Something wrong, sir?' said Dawson after a salute with which he rarely favoured Blanding: in his view, regular RAF should not need to salute hostilities-only types who were really nothing more than blue-clad civilians – but he was kind enough to make a solitary exception of those wearing the brevet. That redeemed nearly everything.

'Yes, there is as it happens. I'm to see the CO in, damn it, five minutes and I've had no time to change.'

Dawson then did another rare thing: he smiled.

'Oh, I wouldn't worry about that, Mr Blanding, sir. Not in the circumstances, sir. A little thing like airmanlike appearance –'

'Mmm,' said Blanding, cocking a suspicious eye at this man who was behaving so out of character. 'You're not trying to be funny at my expense, are you, Dawson?'

Dawson looked genuinely shocked for a moment.

'Good Lord, no, sir. But you did get the CO's letter? I brought it in first thing.'

Blanding looked over at the sinister little white rectangle at the center of his RAF standard-issue desk. After a moment or two he fluttered his fingers in its general direction.

'Sir?'

'If you'd be so good as to read it out, Mr Dawson.'

'Open it, sir?'

'Gifted as you are, Mr Dawson, I don't believe even you have x-ray vision.'

Good God, thought Blanding, I sound just like a sarcastic old dominie lording it over his Latin class. Conscious that Dawson had been speaking for a while in a manner reminiscent of a police constable reading out from his notebook in court, Blanding forced himself to listen.

'– and so I reluctantly approve your request to go on tonight's raid –'

'Good God,' exploded Blanding. 'I've got to go on another damned raid? Is that to be the CO's way of punishing me? I don't think I could stand another night without any sleep.'

The warrant officer chuckled indulgently before realizing the adjutant was being serious.

'I think you'll find, sir, that this refers to yesterday's little effort (look at the date) for which I must say, sir, I –'

'Yes, yes, of course, that must be it,' said Blanding with relief. Releasing Dawson to his duties (and receiving another salute), he wondered if a clerk, fresh on duty that morning and still sleepy, had simply typed the wrong date. As he buttoned up and belted his tunic and clapped his hat on his head preparatory to leaving his office, it occurred to him that the letter was a deliberate tactical move on Chesterton's part. The only mystery was whom was the Old Man protecting, himself or his adjutant?

CHAPTER TWENTY-FOUR

Outside, now a cool fresh morning, there was the usual bustle. Groups of men cycled past with that habitual deliberately slow weaving progress and their backsides hanging almost mockingly over the back of the saddle which had once so irritated him. A civilian delivery lorry pulled away from the cookhouse, and a patient but unusually subdued queue of servicemen and -women snaked away from the camp's sole telephone kiosk, back in service again now that the station had been stood down.

As he passed an airman coming his way on the path, the latter had saluted and Blanding only just managed to acknowledge it. Surely Chesterton had not instituted a new spit-and-polish regime in the few hours that his adjutant had been away gallivanting over Germany? Now two veteran ground crew flight sergeants, eating irons in their fists, were approaching and Blanding closed with them almost warily. It was like a scene from a training film: both sets of eyes affixed firmly to his, the smartly outwhipped hands, he could almost hear them counting off the regulation three seconds before dropping their hands. As far as he could tell there was no glint of insubordination or, worse, humour in their eyes. Blanding walked on, slightly pink in the cheeks but puzzling. Applying what he had learnt in all his years as a schoolmaster he wondered if he were now to be subjected to a period of baiting, perhaps all of his memoranda being executed to the letter?

Arrival at the admin building soon disabused him of that possibility. There was the usual untidy heap of bicycles by the steps, which he now found he regarded with indifference and wondered how he ever gave a damn. Now that he was probably about five minutes away from being relieved of his duties, that kind of thing seemed very insignificant. He passed through the mess anteroom, full as usual of shadowy figures sunk deep in armchairs but today the room was silent. No dance music from the wireless, no buzz of conversation, no bursts of laughter, no explosions of wrath as an absorbed reader suddenly found some joker had set light to his newspaper. Obviously the losses of the previous night could not be simply shrugged aside as previously. A couple of men standing by the windows flicked up their hands in greeting as he crossed the room from one door to the other.

Blanding could not put his finger on what was going on. Everyone seemed to be acting strangely that morning. As was habitual with him and just about any other officer he checked his pigeon hole and the notice board as he passed. A cartoon had been pinned up on the board, penned by the anonymous station satirist who had long been his uncaught prey. A Chad was peeping over a wall which bore the scrawled legend 'Wot no flight authorization??' and Blanding knew it had to refer to him. His usual response to these cartoons was to tear them down, crumple them up and toss them into the nearest wastepaper basket. This time he left the work of art in place.

In the station commander's enormous outer office which also housed the WAAF typing pool he was greeted with a barrage of 'Good morning, sir's and still flushing and now sure that he was the target of an all-station rag, he knocked on Chesterton's door, entering immediately upon hearing the customary bark.

The old bulldog behind the desk however seemed to have aged appallingly overnight. No-one over forty looks at his best after a night without sleep but Chesterton's leathery features were an unhealthy grey and the pouches beneath his eyes ominously dark. And the eyes – they gazed at him almost with sadness and he knew that his escapade ranked very low indeed on the list of what was troubling his commanding officer. Chesterton remained seated and almost wearily waved him to pull up a chair. Blanding turned to find a smiling WAAF corporal had performed this duty for him. 'That'll be all, corporal,' said Chesterton with his familiar growl.

'What the devil's got into everyone this morning, Blanding? Anyone would think you had issued weekend leave tickets to the whole damned station.'

Blanding gave an embarrassed cough.

'Oh, no, sir, I am sure it is meant to be satirical –'

Chesterton suddenly put his two hands together as if praying and brought them up to rub hard at his nose, his eyes closed. Blanding sat silently. The hands dropped, the eyes opened, and Blanding saw in them the extent of the man's anguish. Maybe this was something the aircrews simply did not have time for: he himself had hardly thought about the losses yet.

'Six planes we lost, Alan. Forty-two fine young men. Forty-two lives snuffed out in one fell swoop. Poor bloody sprogs mostly, but we lost some old hands like Kelly and then Mark Sherston. He almost made it: Q-Queenie picked him up coming back on two engines, and then had to watch him go down into the drink. It could have been even worse: we have had reports of two of ours landing at Woodbridge but another one tried to land at the Yank field up the road and crashed on approach. Everyone was killed.'

'I'm sorry, sir,' said Blanding, 'that I was not at my post to at least share the burden.'

'Yes, you're right, Alan, we have to deal with that little jaunt of yours, though God knows it seems trivial enough now. I can tell you, though, Flight Lieutenant, that last night you were within an ace of a court martial, and one I would have had no hesitation in initiating.'

'I gathered that, sir, from the IO last night.'

'However, in the light of what my enquiries have revealed, I may say that if you had been regular aircrew, I would now be signing a recommendation for a DFC for you.' Chesterton noticed his adjutant's look of puzzlement. 'Not for your strange sense of honour – not that's the wrong word – your, dammit, for feeling you had to put your own life at risk because you were sending Mackenzie possibly to his death. Look, Alan, how do you feel that reflects on me? I simply can't allow myself the luxury of nipping off on every kite – you take my point?'

'Yes, sir. I'm sorry, I hadn't thought of it that way.'

Chesterton grimaced impatiently.

'Well, be that as it may, the decoration would have been well-earned. Your prompt action saved the life of that young man and put your own at risk, as you will have known very well. I take my hat off to you, Blanding, as a very gallant officer.'

'So they cancel out, then, sir?'

'Yes.'

'And the letter –'

'– you may regard as your acquittal.'

'Thank you, sir. But I still don't know how word has got round so fast. Young Mackenzie must have seen through my cock and bull story fairly early on. Of course, this misplaced respect – if that really is what it is – is ludicrous. I won't say I felt the station had contempt for me before, but I know I was fairly unpopular with a lot of people, especially aircrew. I have long been aware, too, that one of my nicknames is Quelch –'

'Ah, yes, the reference is to Billy Bunter's housemaster, I believe,' said Chesterton with an amused grunt.

'– but, sir, they certainly believed a desk wallah like me could not know anything about what it is like going on an op. I suppose I do now, I've been on one. And I went of my own free will. But the point I'm making is at the time when I went I was still blissfully ignorant. So how on earth do I deserve any of this respect as you put it? Perhaps if I went on a second op now, knowing what it is really like...'

'No, please, Alan,' said his commanding officer, looking alarmed, 'Please put that right out of your mind.'

'Of course, it isn't an entirely serious proposal, sir, but I do detest feeling an utter fraud, and another op would be one way of meriting something of this utterly undeserved reputation.'

Characteristically Chesterton abruptly stood up from his desk and went to gaze out of the window at the now quiet airfield. 'You are very much mistaken in your basic assumption,' said the older man, drawing wetly on his pipe. 'These signs of respect are not, I would opine, in tribute to your guts (not that the quality of these organs is in doubt) but to your sense of honour.'

Blanding blushed. 'Not the sort of thing one likes talking about.'

'Quite so,' said Chesterton from the window, and the pipe bubbled hookah-like. 'But possession of a compelling sense of honour – or fair play, if you like – is something our aircrews in particular value highly. An old fighter like me telling them what to do is one thing but – and I mean this in general terms, Alan – being buggered around by bustling, penpushing busybodies, some of whom even cause deaths due to bureaucratic mismanagement, that is what gets their goat. And mine,' he added after a moment of silence, during which Blanding writhed on his chair, wishing he had not raised the subject and wondering if that was how Chesterton too felt about him.

'About your letter, sir.'

'Ah, yes,' said Chesterton, turning. 'Clever of you to anticipate its contents, particularly as we are now stood down and ops look as if they will be off the menu for a while yet. I'll expect a full report, though from what I gather you said at interrogation we were both right to back Mackenzie, although I really should not have put you on the spot. My own conscience is far from clear. I should have stood up to Birdie, to be frank, and followed my hunch. Still, all's well that ends well. The only blot on the horizon is that blasted murder, civilian police and Special Investigations creeping all over the place. At least I can let Stanley go home now.'

'Ah yes, I must catch him before he goes. May I use your phone, sir? To tell the main gate to stop him leaving.'

The old warrior's eyebrows lifted slightly.

'I'm now pretty certain, sir, that we won't have to worry any more about harbouring some deranged maniac in this squadron.'

'If the matter weren't so serious, adjutant, I would now enquire whether that means you are planning to leave us. But I'll do as you ask.'

'I'd better talk to Stanley first, sir, but I may well have some news later about the affair.'

'Some good news about that poor girl would be very welcome, but even more so would be the sight of the hemp around the scoundrel's neck who did for her. All right, Alan, on your way.'

'Thank you, sir.'

'Oh, and Alan – don't cut Squadron Leader Wilkins out of this. Between you and me, he could be a nasty piece of work. Writes reports and so on...'

Blanding nodded, saluted smartly and left the CO's office to once more run the gauntlet of almost affectionate glances from WAAFs and administrative staff alike. It almost made his old schoolmaster's heart melt.

CHAPTER TWENTY-FIVE

Blanding reentered the admin block after a brisk walk along the familiar concrete paths, taking his usual care not to tread on the rather weary, mud-smeared turf or to cut corners. Once inside the building he paused a moment before a familiar door and knocked. A gruff cough was the response from within and he entered. As usual the bare, shabby room was redolent of stale smoke and as usual a clutter of tea cups loitered uncleaned on top of a filing cabinet alongside an old pipe tobacco tin overflowing with fag ends and ash. Chief Inspector Stanley was half-sitting on a table by the window, his sallow face not reacting at all to Blanding's entrance. For a moment Blanding was reminded of an old Chinaman from a film he had seen with his Dulwich boys before the war. Inscrutable as the detective may have looked, the adjutant knew very well the reason for his coldness. Evidently on the point of departing when Blanding's message reached him, Stanley had already put on his shabby gaberdine raincoat over his old brown suit. His trilby lay on the desk and his creased old briefcase slumped beside it, containing, Blanding hazarded, no more than pyjamas and shaving kit.

'I'll need to be getting home, adjutant. The wife will be worried – eeh, I'm not as young as I was.'

Blanding nodded but said nothing.

'By the way, Mr Blanding, allow me to express my sympathy at the grievous losses I understand your boys suffered last night.' His eyes twinkled briefly. 'I have to say I was made up to hear of the gallant part you yourself played. It takes a lot to warm the heart of a policeman, as you can imagine. Now, perhaps you can tell me why you are not allowing me to go home and change my shirt?'

Blanding recognized a similar shifting of power to the time he had stood with Mackenzie on the dispersal but this time the tide was flowing his way.

315

'May I suggest, Inspector, that we breakfast together? I believe have some information which may make you less eager to leave the station.'

Stanley shook his head wearily in the manner of one much imposed upon.

'Can you tell me why it is, adjutant, that everyone wants to play Sherlock ruddy Holmes? People don't insist on showing their plumber a nice little bit of brazed pipe they think might solve the airlock problem.'

'We all have our crosses to bear, inspector,' said Blanding, rather enjoying expressing that particular sentiment. 'But I'm sure I can nevertheless help to relieve at least some of your gloom.'

Stanley nodded fatalistically, took his raincoat off with a sigh, and together they strolled over to the mess where breakfast could still be had. Blanding was pleased to note that the salute-the-adjutant epidemic had abated somewhat but he could not fail to notice the gloomy faces he saw everywhere. In the dining hall the atmosphere was very subdued. Men and women ate silently, without pleasure and with bowed heads. A line of stewards watched with concerned faces from near the serving hatches. One of them detached himself and minced over to Blanding and his guest. Blanding had had occasion to reprimand him before and this time the youngster's inappropriate if well-meant chirpy 'What's it to be, then, gents?' in imitation of an ABC waitress failed to amuse, drawing such poisonous glares from the adjutant and the detective that the poor boy almost wilted. Sgt. Tomkins, observing this as a good mess sergeant should, glided over, dismissing the steward with a vague motion of the fingertips and minor aeration of his moustache. Tomkins took the orders and departed.

Neither man was in a hurry to get down to brass tacks just yet. Blanding needed his coffee, such as it would be, and the good detective knew that an uninterrupted conversation would be easier after they had eaten and drunk. The cowed waitress-imitator returned and placed one heavy RAF plate in front of Stanley first as was proper for a guest of the mess. There was the usual vile powdered egg, some canned tomatoes and a dash of baked beans. The solitary sausage did not look very appetizing either. The steward, giving Blanding a significant look, removed the aluminium cover from the other plate and set Blanding's breakfast down before him. Blanding flushed scarlet to see two real, fried eggs on his plate.

'What's the meaning of this?' he cried. 'Is someone trying to make me look a fool?'

'Aircrew's perk, sir. We all know you were over Nuremberg with the boys last night – Sgt Tomkins approved the eggs personally.'

Blanding's features contorted and some new inner Blanding whispered to him, 'Steady, old chap. Don't get so worked up over a trifle.'

The boy looked frightened, having aroused real anger instead of pleased acknowledgment. Blanding became aware of Stanley's fingers on his sleeve, and saw the older man close his eyes briefly and shake his head.

'Sorry, um, Wilkins, is it? Haven't caught much sleep I'm afraid. Didn't mean to bite your head off. But no matter if I were Guy Gibson himself, a guest of the mess must never take second place. Please give my thanks to Sgt Tomkins for the thought anyway.'

The boy departed, somewhat mollified.

'I hardly get time these days for breakfast anyway, adjutant,' said Stanley with a smile, firmly resisting the plate with the genuine fried eggs which the other was trying to slide over to him. 'So this, even the powdered eggs, is a bit of a treat.'

'You're very kind, inspector.'

The two men looked at each other. Stanley inclined his head and raised his eyebrows to indicate he was waiting.

'Well, inspector, as you know I flew with the squadron last night, but what you may not know is that I did not come in with the rest of the crew but walked back over the airfield from the far side, from very close to where Corporal Summerfield's body was found. I don't know why I didn't stay with the crew but I think it was because I unconsciously realized I needed time to think.'

'Go on.'

'You remember all of those strange parallels with Poppy – the copy of Boethius, the brass-rubbings and so on? Well, that was all clarified when Section Officer Taylor and I discovered that her mystery boyfriend was an old pupil of mine, Francis Nelson –'

'Yes, Mrs Taylor has acquainted me with the details.'

'But it struck me suddenly that the parallels had not finished there. To cut a long story short, Corporal Summerfield and I both flew as unauthorized passengers on an operational flight, but in this case, she died on her flight.'

The detective leant forward, his fingertips braced against the edge of the table.

'What made me realize this was when Mackenzie let me nip out at a point on the perimeter track which was hidden from sight to anyone in the control tower. I almost fell out of the plane and when I was on the tarmac it suddenly came to me that her body was found only a few yards away. She was carried there by a couple of the crew. That's why she was half-naked – they had to get her flying kit back to stores.'

'Her mittens showed she knew she was going on a plane that night,' said Stanley, nodding.

'I hadn't thought of that, inspector, but yes, of course, you're right. The oil was from the plane, and I bet the paraffin came from one of the gooseneck flares that had gone out. I nearly fell over one myself.'

'And having been subjected to low temperatures on the plane was what made it seem she had died late the previous night.'

'Yes, she could have died as recently as two or three hours before the CO found her,' said Blanding, pleased at his explanation being taken seriously.

'The intense cold up there could explain the expression frozen onto her face, which rigor mortis merely made permanent. Hm.'

Stanley fell silent, withdrawing behind his eyes to ponder. Blanding found he was sitting right on the edge of his seat in his eagerness to convince the detective, and now deliberately sat back trying to regain a little more dignity. Finally, Stanley nodded his head.

'All right, adjutant. I'll buy it.' Blanding nodded with a smile. 'But we still don't know who cracked her head with that massive blow, nor which plane she was on. Or why on earth she was flying. Surely not for kicks? Perhaps she wanted to fly once before resigning. Perhaps a tribute to one of her dead lovers.'

'Yes, that's a point,' said Blanding reflectively. 'But I think I know who agreed to take her, maybe even suggested it. Which crews were wild or bolshie enough to buck authority and take her? It has to be either the Poles or the Aussies. For various reasons, I think the latter, and this points the finger right at Pat Kelly and his crew. That is what they have been so down in the dumps about. Somehow she died on the flight.'

'Right, well, we'd better get them in for a little chat,' said Stanley. 'And your squadron leader chum as well, while we're at it.'

'That's just it, inspector,' said Blanding unhappily. 'Kelly's plane has been reliably reported as having been shot down last night, exploded with a full bomb load over Nuremberg.'

'Wonderful.'

'Well, at least that lets Frank off the hook.'

'And yourself, Mr Blanding. No, I'll be fair – I've long taken you off the list of suspects. I wonder if we'll ever find out for certain why she went, and why Kelly, if it really was him, allowed her to go, or even invited her. Perhaps she was not entirely true to your old pupil?'

'It certainly could look that way, inspector,' replied Blanding, frowning. 'But I had a look at some of Kelly's effects this morning.' He saw the detective's face frown and darken. 'It's regulations, inspector, when aircrew do not return. And besides, I had been given no indication that Kelly was among your suspects.'

'I see, adjutant, you have already thought that aspect out. For the moment we'll pass over your interfering with a murder investigation, if you'll enlighten me as to your findings.'

Blanding apologized somewhat shamefacedly and told the grim-faced policeman about what he had found, or rather not found, in the cardboard box the station police had brought to him.

'So you see, I don't really believe Kelly was having an affair with Corporal Summerfield. I think he was friendly with her, yes, and doing her a favour. It's all got to do with this blasted chop girl nonsense.'

'Maybe that's why Kelly took her – to prove it was nonsense.'

There was a silence as each thought of the obvious rejoinder.

'I can't imagine Kelly as the type to believe in that silly superstitious twaddle,' said Blanding, trying to be helpful. 'But then again I did not know him very well.'

'And he's dead.'

'Look, inspector, it's not just a hunch but I'm bloody sure that three-quarters of this station by now know the real story, and when it's all over there are a lot of people who are going to be on a charge. But I've had experience before about RAF inquiries: nobody's seen anything, nobody knows anything, nobody says anything. And the court of inquiry disbands without coming to any conclusions.'

'You may accept that kind of thing in the RAF, adjutant, but I can assure you that the Cambridgeshire Constabulary are not got to let this die a death. So to speak. Even if we have to interrogate every man and woman on this station five times over.'

Blanding knew this was for form's sake.

'So we what do we have? A good, almost watertight hypothesis, but hardly a shred of concrete evidence. No confessions. We can't arrest anyone. We don't have a leg to stand on.'

Blanding smiled unhappily at the older man, and then suddenly smacked his forehead in exasperation.

'We do, inspector, we do. Damn fool that I am, I'd forgotten. There's Ellis, their navigator. He was on that flight, got shot up and is in Ely Hospital. I went there with Diana, ah, Section Officer Taylor, the other day. He'll know.'

'Very good. But pray tell me why he should be different from anyone else on this station? Why will he spill the beans and no one else?'

'That's surely rather obvious, inspector. He's racked with guilt about it. He needs to get it off his chest.'

Stanley appeared to come to a quick decision and rising pushed his chair back with a prolonged loud scraping noise, attracting pained looks from the people at the tables around them.

'I'd better get over there straight away,' said Stanley. 'That is, if I'm permitted to leave now.'

'Of course, sir,' said Blanding. 'The station has been open for hours now. But look, what about if you let Diana and me go over there. He doesn't yet know his friends have all been killed and I can use the emotion that will arouse to... even if we can't get him to come clean straightaway, we can easily persuade him we already know so much that we'll get something from the WAAFs on the parachute counter or clothing store, or from the mess sergeant. Anyway, he can't run away with his leg in the state it is.'

Stanley pulled pensively at his lower lip and nodded. 'All right,' he said. 'It's probably irregular but I see no great harm in it. He'll more likely speak to you than to a policeman. But I'm coming over – in fact, the three of us will go in my car. But I need results quick, if you don't get anywhere, I'm coming in. Don't be too hasty, adjutant, in assuming you've got your bird. Many a time I've seen the perfect solution overturned at the last moment.'

CHAPTER TWENTY-SIX

'For God's sake, Alan,' both the use of his Christian name and her low-pitched voice told him that this was to be private. 'Why on earth didn't you tell me? Have you any idea what I've been through since I read your letter? I didn't think you stood a chance with that bunch of sprogs, especially at your age. It's going to happen again, I thought, I find another man I –'

'Another man you – ?'

'I'm not going to give you the satisfaction – but you bloody well might have told me.'

Blanding smiled, having overcome his initial irritation: 'Diana, I may be regarded by some people around here as an overgrown schoolboy who has been reading too much Boy's Own Paper – perhaps with some justice it has to be said – but can you really see me running to you to ask if I could go?'

Her eyes blazed but he did not fail to notice a telltale twitch at the corner of her mouth.

'We'll talk about it later, Diana, but now, I fancy, is the time when I put my rather precarious adjutant's hat back on and you become Section Officer Taylor again. God knows we have enough work to do after these terrible losses. We lost six last night – did you know?'

She nodded.

'I was up in the tower with Group Captain Chesterton until the last moment. I don't know exactly who bought it, apart from Kelly's lot. But the Old Man was hopping mad with you.'

'Yes. I was on the headmaster's carpet earlier but he's been very decent indeed and fixed it. Off his own bat, no reprimand, not even a reproof.'

Her eyes roundened. 'Sweet old bugger. He must think a lot of you. You thought you were for the high jump too.'

'Yes, but the main thing is I'm alive, Diana, I was very lucky indeed.' He glanced at his watch. 'Look, I've arranged for us to meet Inspector Stanley in the car park in ten minutes. I don't wish to sound pompous but this is official business. We have to take another drive over to the hospital Ely again, Diana. With Stanley. I'm sorry to have to put you through it once more but there's a poor tortured navigator there who'll need to be told about deaths of his crew and there's something else we'll need to let him get off his chest. On a private note now, perhaps we could go for a quiet drink later. I owe you an apology.'

The inspector's car was already there waiting for them with the engine running and Stanley at the wheel. Blanding opened a rear door for Diana and saw her settled before taking the passenger seat alongside the inspector who had observed this gallantry with another of his faint, somewhat sardonic smiles. Stanley waved a hand at the white-belted sentries who swung open the main gate for them and headed out onto the country lane which eventually joined up with the Ely road. He drove sedately, as befits a representative of the forces of law and order, and in silence. Blanding also kept quiet, thinking that the detective probably had a lot on his mind and a road journey was an ideal opportunity for him to ponder theories, hypotheses and possibilities, or whatever detectives did in the privacy of their own skulls. He did not feel the circumstances permitted him to engage in idle chit-chat with his assistant in the back, let alone anything of a personal or too familiar nature. Diana, whose eyes he could see in the rearview mirror, appeared quite content to gaze at the passing countryside. Before long Blanding lapsed into a brown study, recognizing gloomily that his former confidence was seeping away with every mile – he would probably get nothing out of Ellis at all. Maybe the inspector was cynically aware that an amateur would make no difference whatsoever and until actual evidence was found linking the dead girl with this plane, nothing short of a full written confession would help. Then Blanding found himself thinking painfully about poor Nelson. The youngster had taken it very hard, and according to the old farmer had hardly emerged from his quarters.

'Eh, what's that?' he cried, jerked from his reverie.

'I said, tell me about your old pupil, adjutant, if you will. It'll pass the time.'

Blanding was happy to reach back to the pre-war days at

322

Dulwich when a new boy, Nelson, joined his history set and expressed as keen an interest as his own in the early middle ages in Europe. Blanding talked on, evoking a world which, he now realized, was vanishing, its already archaic habits and customs perhaps to be fossilized in school stories of the Bunter variety. Warming to his task, he told the policeman about cubicles and studies, fags, beatings, school colours, reminiscing freely and somehow with a new sense of detachment. He even permitted himself a few criticisms of a system which he would once have defended to the hilt. Once more, he was faced with the fact that when the war was won – and that he hardly doubted – he would find himself on Queer Street, along with all the other fresh unemployed who had no wish to return to cosy, dreary, safe existences. He smiled inwardly to think that just one operational flight had made all this difference.

Upon their arrival at the hospital, there was a brief discussion of tactics and it was decided that Diana was to go in first and break the sad news to Ellis about the loss of the rest of the crew. Blanding would follow after ten minutes had elapsed. Diana gave a nod and a somewhat sickly smile of agreement.

The back door of the old police car clicked to and the two men watched Diana's trim figure walking smartly up the path towards the hospital entrance. Few women looked good in RAF uniform with the low-heeled heavy shoes but Stanley's gaze seemed to betoken his appreciation, something which Blanding, strangely enough, found he did not mind. It was not a purely masculine moment – he knew very well that the inspector was also quite aware of the terrible task she now had of breaking the news of the deaths of his closest comrades to a young man weakened mentally and physically by his own injuries and doing this with the ulterior purpose of breaking down his resistance to admitting their rôle in the death of another friend.

'She's a brave gal,' said the inspector quietly, shifting in his seat behind the wheel to lean with one shoulder against the door. With a gesture familiar to Blanding he fumbled in his pocket and took out his tin of tobacco and the rolling machine. Feeling Blanding's eyes on him he looked over and smiled in what the other recognized as a very private way – not one of the inspector's repertoire of official expressions.

'Well, adjutant,' he said, passing his tongue deftly along the gum of the cigarette paper, 'I don't think Squadron Leader Walker is going to be very pleased about this.' Seeing Blanding's expression, he frowned. 'Have I said something funny?'

'No, no, not at all, inspector. Excuse me, I was just thinking how twenty-four hours on a bomber station have almost got you speaking like a real Brylcreme boy. "Adjutant", forsooth! What happened to the good old police standby "sir"?'

The inspector smiled ruefully but remained silent.

'Yes,' said Blanding, returning his eyes to the almost greenhouse-like façade of the hospital, 'Well, as a matter of fact I don't really care tuppence what that puffed-up smarmy little pipsqueak thinks. I might have been worried about it yesterday, but... Dammit, I don't have to clear my every action with him anyway. I'm simply here with Section Officer Taylor to lend a feminine helping hand – hers, I mean – to visit one of my wounded airmen and break some unwelcome news.'

'In my car?'

'You very kindly, for reasons of your own with which you did not acquaint me, offered us a lift, perhaps to save petrol for the war effort.'

'So I did. But Squadron Leader –'

'– him,' said Blanding in a for him almost unique use of that particular expletive.

'You're pretty sure you're going to get the gen then?'

Blanding raised an eyebrow in mock reproof. 'Be difficult to fail, I would have thought. That poor little devil in there has got no cards left to play. Poor Nelson, too. That's another. I'll have to go over and offer what comfort I may, once we've finished here. I wonder how far Boethius can help him now.'

'Right,' he said, glancing at his watch and reflecting that Detective Inspector Stanley must have been perhaps the only policeman in East Anglia to appreciate that classical reference. 'I'd better get in there, Diana will have done her stuff. One of us will come out to fetch you once things are that far. God willing, of course.'

'You're still very confident.'

'That's because I'm batting on his side now. Ellis will see that, want to get it off his chest.'

'Mm, we'll see. By the way, adjutant, and off the record, I happen to know that your precious Squadron Leader is over on a what will turn out to be a social visit to the Chief Constable. He wants to look at our files on all the perverts in the area since the end of the last war. Fat chance,' snorted the inspector and tossed his fag-end out of the window.

On the highly polished linoleum Blanding found it impossible to make a quiet entrance into the small ward with eight beds in it, seven of them empty and with drum-taut blankets and sheets. In the corner he saw Diana, seated, turn abruptly at the fusillade of sound his heels made and give him a private wink to indicate, he supposed, progress. Intimacy of any sort between them had now, he took it, disappeared like the sun behind the clouds. The pyjama'd figure half-sitting up in the bed did not move.

Blanding approached the patient from the other side of the bed and greeted him by name, trying not to sound too bluff or hearty. To his surprise he thought he heard a muttered comment about 'another bloody penguin' in allusion to his wingless status. For a moment Blanding was bewildered, not knowing what tack to take.

Diana interposed sharply. 'Mr Ellis, for your information Flight Lieutenant Blanding flew on the op last night, over Nuremberg. He did so of his own free will, knowing full well, as adjutant, it would be one of the diciest ops there could be. During the op, his plane was severely damaged by flak, the bomb-aimer blinded, and he himself had to –'

'Yes, yes, thank you Diana,' murmured Blanding, flushing. Ellis looked shocked, and abruptly shook his head as if clearing it of muzziness.

'I reckon we must have got you all wrong, sir.'

'No, I don't think so, Ellis. You all had my number, you were quite right. But since last night I really can understand what is meant by a baptism of fire. I don't believe I am the same man as before – in fact, in the last day or two I've been given a good shake by the scruff of the neck by both Mars and Venus.' Blanding gave an instinctive shy glance towards Diana who reddened.

'Right-oh,' said Ellis, his pinched face suddenly lighting up with a grin. But his grin soon faded and his expression resumed the utterly crushed look that Blanding had seen when he walked in. The adjutant hardened his heart and spoke.

'But what I have really come here to do is to talk to you about *your* last op.' Blanding gazed mildly at the face on the pillow and gently added: 'Ellis, I know what the burden is that you're still carrying and what your friends also had to carry, and went to their

325

deaths still oppressed by, even perhaps in the few minutes they had, believing they were to die because of it.'

From the way the boy strove to meet his eyes he now knew he was right and it was just a matter of time.

Silence fell. He waited. Diana's eyes met his for a moment.

'Strewth, sir, you're certainly piling it on –'

'Ellis, listen. We know very well that Poppy Summerfield was aboard D-Dog that night. She was alive when she boarded and by dawn she was dead. Suspicion has been thrown on her fiancé, even on me, and it is now very much on you and your crewmates – and there, I have no doubt, it will rest. At the very least you will be charged with taking an unauthorized passenger on an official flight.' Blanding felt Diana's eyes on him and looked up to see her mouthing 'hypocrite' with her lips, her eyes smiling. 'It will more likely mean a court martial and you getting thrown out with a dishonorable discharge and an enormous stain on your character. And that would be the best outcome for you, believe me. At worst, Detective Chief Inspector Stanley, who is waiting outside, will come in here and arrest you as an accessory to manslaughter or even murder. And that means your neck, as I am sure you are very well aware.'

Ellis stared appalled from the pillow. Blanding suddenly felt as if he were mercilessly kicking a man who was down and was sickened with himself. And yet he saw the beginnings of defiance in the boy's eyes. With a sinking feeling Blanding knew that Ellis was on the point of deciding, in the obstreperous Australian manner, to keep obstinately silent and damn the consequences.

After a somewhat reproachful look at her superior officer, Diana leaned forward, placing her hand on Ellis's and spoke gently: 'Ellis, what the adjutant is trying to say is get it off your chest, make a statement, and at this end we can probably fix no charges – you were under skipper's orders, after all – Mr Blanding's recently had some useful experience in this regard.'

Ellis shakes head violently, almost irritably. 'No, no, I don't need bribing, I'll talk. I don't give a damn about prison or anything else, but it's all changed now that there's none of us left to stick together – that's what Pat said we should do, and I can't live knowing what I do.'

Blanding in fairness said: 'You realize you'll be talking in presence of a witness?'

'All the better.'

There was a long silence during which Blanding and Diana exchanged worried glances but after closing his eyes for a moment and taking a deep breathing the airman continued.

'Poppy and Pat got pretty close, mainly because he saw her as his guardian angel, when we had a dodgy landing it was Poppy on the wireless who saw us through. And she trusted Pat, knew he was married, a serious type, not a lineshooter. We knew, too, she had a new bloke, and it was serious. She wouldn't tell us who he was, even said we wouldn't approve – first we thought he must have been a darkie or something – you know, one of those black Yanks from up the road – or a brown job, but a lot of blokes were pretty keen on her. They were always hanging around, and when – well, she'd been serious about a couple of pilots before, both got the chop over Hamburg as it happened – and then when some more of these moonstruck jokers bought it as well, then the rumours really started. Pat said it sickened him – I dunno, the rest of us thought there might be something in it – not her fault, you understand. Anyway, he's the skipper, so one day he tells us she's coming with us on an op. All hush-hush, nobody would know, and since she was on leave next day, everyone would assume she'd already gone so we'd sneak her out through the wire next day. It's actually not that difficult ...'

'I know,' said Blanding wryly. 'But tell me, Ellis, did she ask or did Kelly offer?'

'I don't see what difference that makes,' said Ellis, with a touch of belligerence. 'She's dead, ain't she?'

'All the same, I should like to know.'

'Well, I wasn't there, you understand, but I would be pretty sure she came to him and put it to him. There's not many blokes in the squadron would do it, it's two fingers up to authority in a way.'

'Our Polish friends?'

'Yeah, the Polskies'd do it all right, but I don't think they'd keep it under their hats afterwards.'

'I'm sure you're entirely in the right of it,' said Blanding equably.

The navigator fell silent again, and Blanding and Diana exchanged glances as his face worked. Finally Ellis almost burst out:

'Poppy just died, she just died – we'd dropped our ruddy eggs and were well on the way home, could almost smell the coffee. I'd say we were over Belgium then and there was a bit of flak and a few searchlights, not much really. We were probably a bit off-course –

327

anyway she was standing behind Pat and probably not plugged into the intercom when we had a nightfighter behind us and Stan – he was the rear-gunner – screamed out and Pat corkscrewed immediately, my oath he nearly tore the fucking wings off – anyway Poppy must have slid under the flight engineer's seat into the nose – the bomb-aimer thought she'd fainted but we couldn't get her up to the rest bed for a while because we had the attack to deal with and Pat was rolling all over the sky, I nearly threw up myself – then when finally we got her to the rest bed, we couldn't find a pulse – it was the flight engineer who tried to revive her, massaged her heart but it was no good, she was dead all right. Not a scratch on her kit.

'We all knew – everyone was jabbering over the intercom - and Pat told us pretty sharpish to all shut up until he had time to think. We crossed the Dutch coast. Somebody said we should drop her into the drink, no-one would be any the wiser. Well, nobody liked that idea. Although two of them – I won't say who – had started to take her flying kit off ready. Pat was bloody dark about that when I told him. I covered her with the flying jacket but she was already stone cold – it's the altitude, and we had some holes in the kite so some freezing air was whistling through. Wasn't so bad for me in my office.

'Then just after we crossed the pommy coast we got bounced again by another bloody nightfighter – that's when I got my packet. One of those bastards who hang around waiting to pick our blokes off as they're coming in to land. Maybe none of us was concentrating, Poppy's death had hit us all for six. We finally landed, no time to think. Pat says we should still go along with our original plan, so we stopped on the peri-track at that part that's out of view of the tower because of the way the 'field bulges. Even that was a balls-up. It was taking ages to get the back door open – I think it had got damaged in one of the attacks – and Pat was telling them to get a move on. If we hung around much longer they'd get suspicious in the tower, I suppose. The bomb-aimer dropped down first and I think it was the flight engineer who was passing her down – they had to get the rest of her flying kit off as well – and I dunno who, but someone fumbled and she smacked her head hard on the concrete. God, just to think of that almost makes me vomit. They got her through the fence somehow, not after they all went arse over tit over one of those bloody flare cans. The last bit they told me later, because I suddenly passed out about then from loss of blood –'

'Ah, so that was the paraffin on her,' said Blanding. 'Then they had to get the kit back and dispose of the rest of her clothes, which you'd hidden behind the cistern in the toilet for her to collect later.'

'If you bloody well know everything Mr Sherlock bloody Holmes,' snarled the navigator, rising from his pillow, 'why the hell are you asking me?'

'Calm yourself, Ellis, calm yourself. I assure you this isn't an intellectual game for me. We were all distressed by the events, and I know you and the other members of your crew are basically decent types, but we have to clear this up for the sake of the poor girl herself, her parents, her fiancé, for all of us, even for the squadron. The police have to be convinced. You've all been clots but it's a great relief that we do not appear to have a pervert killing at will on the station.'

'Yer,' said Ellis, slumping back on the pillow. After a while he opened his eyes and gave a mirthless laugh.

'The funny thing is that none of this need have happened if Pat would have just believed the rest of us that Poppy was a chop girl. She was,' he added with finality.

'Nonsense, man.'

'My oath she was, poor kid. Not her fault, but look how many of us – '

Blanding held his hand up. 'Ellis, have you any idea how many planes failed to return last night?'

'Apart from my mates, no, sir, I don't.'

'Bomber Command lost nearly one hundred aircraft, that's perhaps 700 men. Think about that. Now how many bloody chop girls does that mean? Of course it's a lot of ruddy nonsense.'

'And you flew last night, sir? You didn't say any prayers or anything, even when it got hairy?'

Blanding leant forward on his chair. 'Look, Ellis, chop girls is just an instance of that pagan superstition which is really everyone's last refuge. All those little good luck symbols, teddy bears, and so on. Harmless on the whole, but in the end it cost that poor girl her life. If we maybe could in all simplicity believe that we are always in the hand of God who for reasons best known to Himself disposes of us or lets us return ...'

Ellis rolled his eyes and seemed to writhe in his bed. 'Pretty bloody hard to believe that over Hamburg or Happy Valley.'

'Terrible, yes, but I've seen it myself now, I had no idea. That...um, *incomprehensible* combination of terror and beauty... even that somehow has to be part of God or his plan too. You're a bit of a poet yourself, Ellis, I'll wager. You know what I'm talking about. But it made me think of Rilke, a *German* poet as it happens, who said that even an angel – if you got too close – could be a being who was utterly terrifying and inhuman – you know, like a fire in the hearth, pleasant and comforting at a distance but put your hand in and ...'

From where she stood behind him, Diana spoke and in that place her unexpected words in their enemy's language sounded as if they emerged from a world which was different in its very essence: *'Wer wenn ich schrie hörte mich aus den Engeln Ordnungen?* Who, were I to cry out, would hear me from amongst the orders of angels?'

Nobody said anything for a while until the white-faced man in the bed broke the silence.

'So, putting it another way, it would be our fault, not God's. I can see that.' Blanding and Diana exchanged glances. It was time for the inspector. 'I suppose it's not too different from us doing terrible things in the name of good – not that I would compare us with God, but the principle's the same as what you're getting at. Yes, I can see that.'

It was still brightly sunny when Blanding and Diana emerged from the ward building and stood for a while on the front steps beneath the porch. Nurses in starched linen passed in and out of the swing doors. Blanding thought of bees at the entrance of a hive and in an image, perhaps somewhat sentimental, of angels flitting into and out of the portals of heaven. He became aware of Diana looking at him with a fond half-smile.

A flash of sunlight reflecting off the window of an opening car door drew his attention and he saw that Stanley had got out of his car. Blanding raised an arm as a signal to which the familiar figure of the detective in his shabby old suit responded in kind.

'You can go in now, Inspector,' he said with a smile when Stanley reached them.

'You know, Diana,' Blanding murmured when they were alone again, 'I can't stop myself thinking about poor Nelson. A mystery may have been solved but poor Francis is left to cope on his own with his dreadful loss –'

'And poor Ellis,' added Diana.

'Yes, of course, but he'll being going home soon, as soon as his leg has mended. Home to his people, whereas Francis is quite alone, no parents, no fiancée ...'

'Don't be so gloomy, Alan. I expect she's watching over him. Well, why not? Anyway, you can still keep in touch. I expect he'll move away from a place that now must hold so many sad memories for him.'

'As you did. Damn, here comes Stanley already. Ellis must have changed his mind. I was sure he was ready.'

Once they were all in their usual places in the battered old police car, Stanley explained to them that he had only needed to take the briefest statement, witnessed by a nursing sister who disapproved of all these visitors, and when Ellis was stronger he could take a typewriter over and the navigator could make his full considered statement.

Blanding suddenly felt as if an immense load had floated off his shoulders, that he found himself a rather different person that a week previously when he had been roused from his narrow bed to drive out to the perimeter to find a young woman lying cold and lifeless in the wet grass. With something like pleasure he looked forward to resuming his duties at Frampton Wissey.

'You know, inspector, the one thing that puzzles me is the look of terror on her face. I thought that kind of thing was a figment of the lurid imaginations of penny dreadfuls.'

An amused laugh came from Diana behind him.

'You're so old-fashioned sometimes, Alan.'

Stanley half-smiled.

'As a matter of fact, Flight Lieutenant, the post-mortem concluded that her expression was artificial, that the face muscles had probably been held in that expression until rigor mortis froze them, but then, of course, we had no idea of how she died ...'

'Ah, yes,' said Blanding. 'I wouldn't mind guessing that it was when she slid into the bomb-aimer's compartment. Possibly her face was pressed against something and the cold air from holes in the perspex there simply accelerated the rigor mortis.'

'Hmm, sounds very likely,' said Stanley, starting the car and pulling away. 'I'll put your interesting hypothesis to them when I get back to the station, but perhaps you wouldn't mind filling me in on the details you got from Flying Officer Ellis?'

As Blanding recounted what he could remember of Ellis's account to the inspector he felt something touch the nape of his neck. He fidgeted away from whatever it was but then realized that it was

Diana, that her warm hand was softly caressing him, unseen as she thought, by Stanley but unaware that the rear-view mirror had betrayed her to the policeman's watchful brown eyes.

EDITOR'S AFTERWORD

Michael Anthony died suddenly in May 2004, leaving amongst his papers and on his computer about three-quarters of the mystery story he had to my knowledge been working on for five years or so. Progress had been slow during his last two years on account of a massive heart attack which had initially wiped out even his desire to write, but in time he had begun to pick up speed again. Unfortunately he left no notes whatsoever regarding the further development of the novel or its dénouement. What he had written was, however, in a fairly finished form and only required some minor revisions and the attentions of the copy editor. On the other hand, the last two chapters were a jumble of mis-spelt words, incomprehensible sentences and logical omissions, obviously representing his first drafts of these sections, still smoking from the forge. There was also a page or two which was a kind of rough chalking-out of his final scene: I suspect it represented more a point for him to aim at, a possible landfall, rather than how he really expected the final pages to turn out. To sum up, his manuscript took the reader to the point where all the elements of the mystery had been assembled but the climactic scenes of the book were as yet unwritten, as too the solution.

During the late 1990s Michael used to drive up from Greenwich from time to time to visit me in my Bedfordshire cottage of which, I later learned, Flt Lt Blanding had also once been a tenant. In some respects, no, in virtually every respect, Michael was an Edwardian literary man, and most of our conversations revolved around books. He had been thinking about a follow-up to his Colonel Harrison books, ecclesiastical mysteries set in Canterbury Cathedral, but one day he started quizzing me about what I knew about female figures in mythology who brought bad luck and even death. A year or so later he turned up on a visit with a hundred pages or so of the present novel, for me to read and comment on, while he read and commented on the hundred pages of something I was writing. At this point I did know one key to the mystery, which was the dip in the ground which hid part of the perimeter track from the sight of the control tower. I was very much taken with my own idea of giving the book the title *Dead Ground*: I can see now that if Michael Anthony had been a Geoffrey Household or a Mickey Spillane he might well have adopted my suggestion.

Michael was a man of many friends, all of whom loved him dearly, and I know he discussed the book with a fair number of them, but I don't believe anyone of them had been vouchsafed the solution to his book. I do not claim any special ingenuity in solving the mystery, although I am confident enough to believe I have found the correct solution. The underlying logic of the story, the basic soundness of what he had written, is what revealed the solution to me, and confirmed it, as it would for any writer undertaking the task of completing this book.

As to my motivation, I simply found it was a pity that so much good work on his part was apparently wasted, that so many people would not enjoy another production from his hand. My reasons for wanting to finish the book had nothing to do with Michael as a friend or individual. For me it was like seeing a beautiful house building, to the point where completion was not far off, and then there was the choice of either watching it decay and collapse or going in there and finishing the job. Nor was that task irksome or tedious.

I now live near Hay-on-Wye, a town of second-hand bookshops on the border between Brecon and Herefordshire, and thanks to its proximity have over the last couple of years accumulated around twelve feet of books about Bomber Command during the Second World War. I have also acquired RAF training films, documentaries dealing with the bombers and their work, and even a contemporary colour record of an actual bombing operation in a Lancaster. I never imagined I would find the material of such absorbing, not to say humbling, interest, and this new involvement even took me to Lincolnshire to ride in the bomb aimer's compartment of a fully working and restored Lancaster. To my surprise, the safety officer of the gliding club two fields away from my house turned out to be a retired senior RAF officer whose father – also top brass – had worked on a daily basis with Air Marshal Arthur Harris at Bomber Command headquarters; another local man had been a waist gunner in an RAF Liberator. As I worked, not sure whether Michael would approve of what I was doing, coincidences began to abound. One occurred when

I was in a Hay bookshop and idly flicked open a battered paperback to chance immediately upon the original and almost unknown poem from which he took his title.

Gradually I came to feel that Michael would approve of what I was doing and I had a sense that he was on my side. By the time I had finished, I was no longer entirely sure where I had started and Michael had finished. His characters had become so real to me that I could even imagine I had created them myself. In fact, they will not die at this point either: I have already made a great deal of plotting notes for a follow-up in which Flt Lt Blanding also takes a central rôle. But there remains one small mystery which I have not been able to solve: why was Blanding given 'Trott' as a nickname?

Whether or not I have been successful in my endeavour is up to the reader to judge. Some threads could well have been taken further and tidied up (I feel that Michael would have given Francis Nelson more lines than I gave him, that Boethius may have figured more in the concluding chapters). Michael wrote a fairly dense prose – sometimes too dense in my view, as we frequently discussed. He defended himself with teeth, claws and obstinacy, but might well phone the next day to gracefully concede a point. My natural style is probably more open, perhaps faster but I do not say in any whit better. I have tried to write in a style approaching his, but again the reader is the one to assess how well or how badly.

If it is of interest, Chapter Twenty is where my work really began. I already had an earlier version of the first fourteen chapters in typescript, and then his good friend and literary executor Robin Buss provided me with the latest text up to Chapter Twenty, but this version strangely omitted the Prologue. Later I found it in the earlier typed version, and reinstated it, realizing it was essential for the story.

For support and encouragement I owe many thanks to Michael's sisters, especially Jane (the short one), to Frances Gibb, Robin Buss, Louis Buss and, of course, to Michael himself. Thanks are very probably also due to the late Rev. R. J. Pope, who completed a full tour of 30 operations in Lancasters with XV Squadron, 3 Group, RAF Bomber Command and with whom Michael frequently corresponded on matters of technical interest.

R. T.
New Year, 2006

335

WHEN HE IS FLYING

When I was young I thought that if Death came
He would come suddenly, and with a swift hand kill,
Taking all feeling;
Want, laughter and fear;
Leaving a cold and soulless shell on earth
While the small winged soul
Flew on,
At peace.
I used to think those things when I was young,
But now I know.
I know
Death stands beside me, never very far,
An unseen shadow, just beyond my view
And if I hear an engine throb and fade
Or see a neat formation pass
Or a lone fighter soar, hover and dart,
He takes another step more near
And lays his cold unhurried hand on my heart

Olivia Fitzroy

(in *More Poems of the Second World War*,
ed. Selwyn, London 1989, p 183-4)

Printed in the United Kingdom
by Lightning Source UK Ltd.
113435UKS00001BA/1